Praise for
THE OMICRON SIX

"*The Omicron Six* is part Stephen King (think *The Institute* with a little *Stand By Me* tossed into the mix) and part *Hunger Games*. Wright has written an engaging story with characters you can't help but root for and want to learn more about. If you're looking for a great escapist read, look no further than the *The Omicron Six.*"

—Jonathan Smith, former producer for NPR's *The Diane Rehm Show*, present executive public radio producer and avid reader

"Endearing characters and intriguing story that keeps you reading. It makes you wonder if this could be happening today."

—Randi Beers, author of *Teal Haven*

"Write another one. Now, please."

—Thomas Eissenberg, professor of psychology, Virginia Commonwealth University

"*The Omicron Six* balances the tension and nuance of the best science-based fiction with layers of narrative that shine a light on family, relationships, destiny, and the wrenching realities of child abuse and neglect. By drawing characters that are believable and worthy of empathy, then carrying them through a narrative both subtle and powerful, Endy Wright has created something of immediate interest and lasting merit. This book has legs."

—Greg Fields, author of *Arc of the Comet*, 2017 Kindle Book of the Year Nominee in Literary Fiction

"Lawyers like Endy Wright and I see human tragedy in its raw form. Mr. Wright has taken one such tragedy and turned it into a remarkable story of survival and triumph. By shining a light on the brutality and tragedy that formed one of his main characters, he avoids cliché and easy plot devices. Instead, Mr. Wright manages to create three-dimensional characters in a complicated world. With the resilient optimism of youth and complementary superpowers discovered along the way, Wright's characters manage to endure long enough to discover their origins, their powers, and a cast of others to team up with . . . or defeat.

"*The Omicron 6* has enough science to challenge an adult reader and lots of humor, too. It's a gripping story that left me eager for the next volume.

"I don't remember stories this honest when I was a young adult. By writing *The Omicron 6*, Endy Wright has shown a level of respect toward his audience that distinguishes literature from mere stories."

—Barry S. Edwards, PhD in English literature, lawyer in Minneapolis

"*The Omicron Six* by Endy Wright is a quite different kind of sci-fi book. On the surface, it's primarily a book about two (barely) high-school-age boys who have superpowers. Still, unlike other 'superhero' stories, the two main characters (Cooper and Coupe) are characterized just as much by their weaknesses as by their powers. Cooper has incredible physical strength. Still, he is somewhat of an outcast amongst his peers as he keeps to himself and rarely talks. Coupe is quite verbose—sometimes crudely so—is highly cerebral, clever, and also physically fast. Yet Coupe is also an outcast—he comes to his New England small-town community with a reputation as a thief. Coupe is also bullied, both at home and at school.

"Cooper and Coupe manage to find each other (through a mutual bully confrontation) and find that they are even stronger as bonded friends. The first part of the book explores the bond that strengthens these two boys, while the second half reveals the sci-fi conspiracy (though one with good intentions) that explains their superpowers. There is plenty of dialogue, so the story moves briskly and rarely gets bogged down. It is also surprising to discover how much more there is to Cooper and Coupe than there seems to be early on. Parents should be advised that the story does delve into some gritty realities (some harsh language and passages detailing terrible abuse); thus the story would be geared more to high-school-age students. Still, a story that should appeal to readers who understand what it feels like to be an outcast, and how strong friendship and family ties can become a 'superpower' in themselves."

—Todd Cook, author of *The Bleeding Door, Madame,* and *Uncovered: The Lost Coins of Early America*

"*The Omicron Six* is an exhilarating adventure that would leave any reader satisfied and longing for the next installment. This story really hits its stride and grasps the reader with its poignant portrayal of the value of true friendship, and the power contained therein. The resiliency of these brilliantly crafted characters to confront and overcome the demons of their past (and present) could serve as both solace and an example to anyone challenged by their own experiences of abuse.

"Adolescence is hard enough, but compounded by abuse and neglect it can be hell. These 'brothers' can show a young reader that there can be light in the darkness, and the light can come from within."

—Daniel Turcotte, crisis counselor, youth worker, and assistant educational director

"Two close friends discover they share surprising abilities and an unexpected connection in this YA SF thriller.

"Wright's series opener offers dynamic protagonists and supporting characters and fast-paced suspense. Cooper and Coupe are effective and likable heroes whose friendship and quest to figure out how they differ from their peers anchor the story. Some of the novel's strongest moments focus on the boys' connection and the positive effect it has on them, particularly Coupe, who finds a stable and supportive home with Cooper and his parents. The well-rounded supporting cast is led by Stein and three members of the Omicron Six, Cotovatre, Corwin, and Chase. The briskly paced narrative moves from bucolic Vermont to the woods of Maine as Cooper and Coupe discover more about the role the mysterious Stein plays in their lives.

"A promising start to a new series bolstered by engaging characters and an intriguing premise."

—Kirkus Reviews

"*Omicron Six* by Endy Wright is a very readable book.

"In the beginning, two young men become friends. One is strong physically, immeasurably so, and silent. The other is wiry, quick-witted, and brilliant but crippled both physically and emotionally. The development of their friendship, their growing reliance on each other to fill in the gaps of their personalities, their joy and delight as they overcome their seemingly insurmountable deficiencies, and their just genuine friendship are a delight to read. This part of the book concerns friendship as it used to be known. The inclusion of a functional, loving family as a framework for healing is also a refreshing change. Part two introduces an increasingly complex set of characters. There is a doctor, the creator of the genetic wunderkinds, and the question becomes whether he is a Victor Frankenstein or not. That question kind of hangs in the air throughout the book. The genetic results of his tamperings are so good, the only antagonist powerful enough to challenge them is one of their own gone rogue.

"The dialogue used in the book, extensively, is good; it is how the characters are developed. You spend a lot of time reading the characters' speech. Not all reactions are given to you from the outside. The action is a little slow in the first half, but it is needed to build up a sympathetic view of the two main characters.

"The book also builds the heroes by increasing the difficulty of the adversaries the heroes have to face and defeat. From bullies to abusive adults, and from uncaring caregivers to uncaring institutions, Coupe and Cooper triumph by acting together and helping each other. This is a positive story about the importance of friendship and loyalty. Only late in the book are the powers of the other four genetically altered beings really introduced.

"The plotline is a little pat. The use of religious bigots is a bit too convenient—no one cares what happens to them because they are religious bigots—and a little overdone. The ultimate antagonist is unpredictable, which is a plus.

"I enjoyed the book. It is obviously going to be the first part of a series. It will be interesting to see how the author creates bigger obstacles for his people to overcome."

—Ralph Peterson, San Francisco Book Review

"*The Omicron Six* tells of a friendship between disparate children who each have their own special-needs issues—and special superpowers. Cooper is supported by loving adults, while Coupe has been abused and is on survival mode. Both have cultivated strengths and independence apart from outside influences, but more importantly, both begin to acknowledge the presence and strength of the other as a possible ally in a noisy, confusing world.

"*The Omicron Six* provides the initial lure of being a superhero story, but actually, it's much more. Endy Wright probes the emotions and motivations of his young heroes and considers the world which continually challenges them in many ways. This approach imparts psychological depth and a component of self-discovery that goes beyond the revelation of superpowers to probe the evolution of close connections that begin with shared adversity.

"Coupe is a quick healer, a generous person, a trickster, and the victim of sexual assault. As his relationship with Cooper begins to unlock both their barriers to let in a few adults who want to help them both, their connection gives rise to another superpower.

"Those who choose *The Omicron Six* for its promise of superhero action may initially feel disappointed because the story is about a different kind of hero—not a caped flyer who saves the world, nor even a Harry Potter who comes into his own powers.

"Both kids are in the process of realizing their abilities to interact with the world and save themselves while making a (for them) rare connection with another person. This is the heart of a story that revolves around hidden secrets, special abilities and disabilities, and a healing process that could destroy everything.

"It's a superhero story on steroids, holding different forms of action, bad and good guys, and encounters that defy the usual image of a superhero as being a relative loner who doesn't let anyone in on his secrets.

"An evil man is jailed after getting away with abuse with the help of well-meaning adults such as the police chief. As the boys become freshmen in high school and continue their long journey towards adulthood, missing pieces begin to come together. Their discoveries continue to push the boundaries of good and evil and normalcy and abnormality, drawing teen to adult readers into a series of close encounters with extraordinary circumstances.

"As the lure of a 'safe place' away from well-meaning community and parents draws Coupe and Cooper from relative safety into a different kind of danger, the two must hone new abilities to survive.

"Multifaceted, peppered with social issues and fantastic scenarios, and representing a gem far beyond the usual superhero clichés, *The Omicron Six* cultivates a blend of social inspection, superpower evolution, and psychological draw to keep all ages thoroughly engrossed in an unexpected saga that involves the creation of something that may ultimately destroy them all."

—Diane Donovan, senior reviewer, Midwest Book Reviews

The Omicron Six

By Endy Wright

Published by

◄ köehlerbooks™

3705 Shore Drive
Virginia Beach, VA 23455
800–435–4811
www.koehlerbooks.com

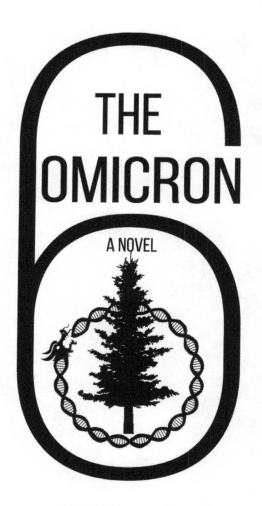

THE OMICRON

A NOVEL

ENDY WRIGHT

VIRGINIA BEACH
CAPE CHARLES

ONE

CHAPTER 1

Cooper was nonverbal. That was how the school classified him. It was clear he was a bright kid. He could answer questions with a nod and follow simple directions, even complex ones when asked. He simply did not speak.

Teachers worked with him, smiling to show their encouragement. In short, they liked Cooper, even though he was nonverbal. Underneath his mop of thick brown hair, he peered out upon the world with two large, bright-blue eyes. But from first grade through eighth he had not spoken. Not one word. And the more teachers tried to get him to talk, the more he appeared to withdraw.

Then there was Coupe, whom everyone just called Single. He tried to make it to school as much as he could. Often he was absent.

His clothes were old, but usually clean. Sometimes when he came to school, he had bruises. In the beginning, when he was young, he would try to look at his teachers like Cooper did, because Cooper always got their sympathy, their smiles.

But Coupe was not special. He was just poor. He lived in a small apartment downtown, located over a bar where his mother worked. The teachers did not tousle his hair or admire his eyes. There was no way to compete with that, so Coupe preferred not to be noticed and did his best to hide in the back of the classroom.

Coupe and Cooper had both started at the school at the same time. Then Coupe had left. He had remained in the school until the end of fourth grade when he and his mom moved away. He had been gone for three years, moving around New England, mostly with his mother, sometimes in care. They were now back in Riding, Vermont, and Coupe recognized a few faces. Cooper was one of them. He had grown. He looked strong, like the farm boy he was. Coupe, on the other hand, was thin and spindly. He always looked like he needed a good meal because, generally, he did. He was not as tall as Cooper, and he walked with a limp because of an injury to his foot a few years back.

Coupe noticed that Cooper had changed in other ways too. It started in the last quarter of eighth grade. The two boys shared the same class each afternoon, the last class of the day. As usual, Coupe sat in the back with his head down. Cooper was over by the window. Coupe had begun to notice Cooper in an odd sort of way. When it was quiet in the classroom he sometimes felt that Cooper was watching him, but not with his eyes. He could sense Cooper's presence inside his head. At first Coupe dismissed it as some sort of weird daydreaming.

The sense he got from Cooper didn't feel intrusive. It was benign and inquisitive—innocent—like he was just looking around. He liked to sense Cooper exploring, for want of a better word. He was, at least, getting someone's attention.

One day he decided to try something. Coupe was sitting at his desk doing his schoolwork when he felt Cooper, like he was wandering over to see what he was doing. Only he did it with his mind, not his feet. When Coupe felt Cooper's presence he closed his eyes and tried to direct a thought back at him. *Is that you, Cooper?*

Cooper, who had been staring out the window, spun around. Coupe smiled and gave him a wink. *Don't worry, buddy. I won't rat you out.* He sensed a moment of relief, and then Cooper's presence was gone as he turned back to the window and refused to turn around again.

Coupe wanted to meet with Cooper at the end of class, but Cooper was ushered out to meet his mother, who then gave him a ride home, and the other students leaving blocked his path. Coupe walked home, as he did most days. Coupe did not always go home. Sometimes it was better not to.

Coupe knew his teachers did not like him overly much. He was not really sure why. He tried not to bother them. He was attentive to their instruction, perhaps more so than any student they had ever had. And he was never disruptive—rather, just a quiet kid in the back of the classroom with his nose down. Perhaps his only fault was missing school a lot. Even so, he was a solid B. Coupe liked being a B student. No letters home complaining about grades and no extra attention and awards that the A students always got. No extra attention at school meant no extra attention at home.

Coupe also had some habits that struck his teachers as odd and off putting. When he spoke with others, he could not keep his eyes on theirs. His gaze darted from their eyes to their lips, to the sweat above their lips, to little movements hidden in their eyebrows and the corners of their mouths and a host of other actions that informed him of their intent. He had an uncanny ability to judge whether someone was lying, whether someone was going to do what they said they were going to do, whether they were going to try to hurt him. That's why he scanned their faces. He also sniffed a lot, which annoyed his teachers more than anything else he did. But his nose told him a lot about others, too.

Although well liked, Cooper's school days were not pleasant either, especially when things were boisterous and loud. Not only could he hear the raucousness, he could feel it inside his head. And while he could put his hands over his ears to quiet the noise, he could not block the chaos or noise from his mind.

Cooper hated recess. Usually, he would find a spot at the edge of the playing field and look deeply into the woods. If any other kids tried to approach him, he would not even acknowledge them, but instead stare into the solitude of the trees. It made him unpopular with other students, who thought Cooper antisocial. The teachers looked out for him as best they could, given his special needs. But their supervision was sometimes lacking.

···················

One day, Kevin Hannigan was bored. He was looking for someone to torment. He decided Cooper Callister would be the subject of his special treatment during recess. Kevin did not like that the teachers gave Cooper special attention. He did not like that Cooper did not talk. The boy's inability to talk made him an inviting target for bullies like Kevin. On this day, the children on the playing field were especially loud. Perhaps it was the weather—it was an unseasonably hot day; perhaps it was just enthusiasm that the end of the school year was getting near, but it was hot and loud. Cooper was overwhelmed, and Kevin Hannigan noticed.

Cooper had moved to sit alone along a stone wall that ran between the edge of the playing field and a deep pine forest that comprised a majority of the town of Riding. It was obvious Cooper was in distress. He looked hard into the woods.

A girl on the playground shrieked as she was playfully chased by a boy. Hers was followed by a chorus of other playful shrieks. Cooper covered his ears and looked at the ground as if in pain, then got up and moved deeper into the trees. Kevin noticed him leave.

He waited a moment, looked around for any teachers, then slipped into the woods after him.

As Cooper walked deeper into the woods, the sounds and screams of the other students faded. Cooper began to relax. He lifted his head and looked up into the trees. A pleasant light seeped through a great green canopy of leaves. He liked it under the trees. He found a small grove of hemlock with a large rock in their midst. He liked the smell of the hemlock and breathed it in deeply as he sat on the rock. It was quiet. The harsh noise of the playing field was replaced with the breeze passing through the needles overhead. The air was cool and inviting. He rested his eyes.

Kevin watched Cooper from a distance. An easy target for some fun because who would he tell? Kevin smiled. As he got closer, he saw that Cooper appeared to be asleep, an even better opportunity to frighten him. He took slow, careful footsteps to creep in closer.

Even though Cooper's eyes were closed, he sensed someone approaching from his right. Cooper opened his eyes and looked over to see Kevin creeping toward him. *Kevin Hannigan.* Cooper knew who he was, knew what he did to other kids. Cooper had always avoided the mean-spirited bully.

Kevin was a big kid for eighth grade. Bigger than Cooper. Bigger than everyone. But his size made it difficult for him to sneak up on someone. Cooper could hear every footfall. He heard his breathing. Kevin looked up to see Cooper staring back at him. A brief look of disappointment spread across his face as he realized he would not be able to scare Cooper while he was napping. But Kevin's mind quickly settled on the other half of his plan. He smiled and walked toward him, putting on his best smile. Cooper recognized it for what it was.

"Hey, Cooper, how are you doing?" Kevin asked, waving. "You've come a long way into the woods. Do your handlers know you're so far out?"

Cooper said nothing as usual. He just stared at Kevin, not moving. Kevin continued to approach.

"Teachers really seem to like you."

Cooper just stared back at him impassively. Kevin began to circle. But as he got back in front of him, Kevin's smiled dropped.

"I know the teachers like you, the lunch ladies like you. Hell, even the principal likes you. But guess what, Cooper? I don't like you. And none of them are here to help you now." Kevin grabbed hold of Cooper's shirt and pulled it up under his chin. "So, do you know what's going to happen now?"

Cooper stared back at Kevin with neither fear nor apprehension, annoying Kevin, and he shook Cooper's shirt so hard that it ripped. Cooper looked down at his torn shirt and then back at Kevin, but still did nothing.

"Hey, I ripped your shirt, retard. What are you going to about it? If anyone ripped my shirt, I would punch them in the face." He paused for a moment, then said, "Like this!"

Kevin's fist flew out and struck Cooper in the mouth. Cooper did not respond. He hardly moved at all. Cooper's reaction was not what Kevin had expected. He was used to kids falling down and crying, pleading with him to leave them alone. Not Cooper. The muted reaction unnerved Kevin, so he punched Cooper again, this time harder. No response. He punched him harder. Not only was there was no response, there was no blood. Cooper's big blue eyes gazed back at him impassively and innocently.

Kevin pushed Cooper up against a tree and hit him in the stomach almost as hard as he could. Again, Cooper didn't flinch, and Kevin felt his fist throb with pain. It was as if he had punched the tree instead. He punched Cooper's nose. Whack! Kevin knew he got him good because his hand and his wrist were aching. He looked down at it, opening and closing his fingers to ease his pain. His dad would be proud when he told him about it. Then he looked back at Cooper to see what sort of damage he had done. Cooper was just standing with his back against the tree, staring at him. There was no blood, not even a red mark.

Kevin pushed Cooper's head hard against the tree, preparing to hit him again. He had to. What would people say if they learned that Cooper shrugged off his attack unharmed? Kevin grabbed hold of his chin—like his father had shown him—so he could get a good solid shot. Cooper just stood there staring back, now with a furrowed brow.

It was as his fist was traveling with all his strength to meet with Cooper's face that Kevin felt his knee being kicked out from under him. The punch never landed. Instead, Kevin fell to the ground holding his knee. When he looked around, Cooper was still standing against the tree. He had not moved, except now he was looking down at him. That's when he felt the small shoe kick him in the ribs.

"Why don't you go pick on someone your own size? If you can find someone, that is."

It was Coupe Daschelete. Coupe had been on Kevin's ass-kicking list for a long time. Trouble was the kid was too quick and too slippery and usually got away, even with that limp of his.

"I'm going to kick your ass, Single," he said, getting up.

He went after Coupe and tried to grab him, but Coupe swiftly ducked under his grasp. Kevin swung wildly back at Coupe, but Coupe was already a pace away and smiling at Kevin.

"I'm gonna wear you out just by letting you chase me, Kevin. You're big but *slow*."

Kevin got increasingly annoyed as Coupe seemed to always be just out of reach. Again, he lunged toward him, but Coupe quickly spun to his right and ended up standing behind him. Kevin threw a blind mule kick toward Coupe. Coupe saw it coming and leaped over it. Kevin turned and advanced again. Coupe let him get within striking distance, still smiling as he closed. Kevin thought he had him now and threw a quick punch to Coupe's head. Coupe slipped the punch, again. The small kid was simply too fast.

"I can do this all day, Kevin, how about you? Why don't we just call it a draw and leave each other alone?"

"Not a fucking chance," growled Kevin. He came after him again, and Coupe spun away from Kevin's grasp. This time, however, his lame foot struck a root from one of the hemlock trees, and he tumbled to the ground. Kevin pounced, grabbing hold of his hair. Coupe struggled, but Kevin's grasp was secure. It was not long before Kevin pinned him.

"Okay, runt, where do you want it?" Kevin asked, raising his fist.

Coupe, who had been struggling, stopped long enough to smile up at Kevin and say, "How about New York City?" and started laughing.

Coupe continued to laugh as Kevin's fist came down and struck him in the eye and then the mouth. Coupe swallowed the pain, determined not to give him any satisfaction. He laughed as the fist came down a third time. But unlike with Cooper, blood began to run freely from Coupe's mouth and nose. The next shot knocked out a tooth. Kevin was just too big for him.

He could feel Kevin firmly pinning his head to the ground. He could feel his large body on top of his, preventing him from getting up. He was in for a good beating from this much larger kid, and he resigned himself to the fact he would likely be beaten unconscious.

And then Kevin was gone.

He did not get up and walk away. He simply was not on top of him anymore. It was not as if Coupe did not know where Kevin had gone, either, because he could see him. Presently, he was flying through the air toward a large maple tree about thirty feet away. Coupe watched as Kevin hit the ground with a satisfying thud and a high-pitched grunt of pain. He fell awkwardly, but he wasted no time in getting back up and looking back in fear. He turned and ran back toward the school.

Coupe stood and watched the bully retreat until his footsteps were no longer audible. He turned to see Cooper staring at him with a look of concern, most likely caused by the blood dribbling out of Coupe's face. Then he felt it. Coupe's head began to swim and his knees buckled. He fell back down toward the ground. But before

Coupe struck the cool earth, an arm caught him around his waist. Coupe offered a bloody smile.

"Thanks, man. You can put me down. I think I got it now."

Cooper put him down on the rock where he had recently been sitting with eyes closed.

"You did that, right?" continued Coupe. "You pulled him off me and then threw him through the air for what? Maybe thirty feet?"

Cooper nodded slowly.

"That's pretty good. I wish you could teach me how to do that. It could improve my face situation a little bit."

Coupe studied Cooper's face. There appeared to be no mark on it all. He felt the cut above his own eye and the blood still trickling from his nose. On the ground he spotted his tooth. Cooper steadied him as he got off the rock and went over to pick it up. Coupe looked at the tooth and put it in his pocket. Then he turned back to Cooper.

"How is it I look like this and you haven't even got a mark? I mean, I saw him landing shots; that's why I ran in. I thought he was going to wreck you, and I thought maybe together we could scare him off. But look at you. It's like he missed each time . . . which he didn't. And then, *voom*! You chucked him like a sack of spuds all the way over there."

Coupe looked at Cooper, knowing he would not get a response. But he patted Cooper on the shoulder as if he had answered and said, "It's okay, bud, I understand. Thanks again, Cooper. They call me Single, by the way, should you ever decide to use it."

Then came the shocker.

"That's not your real name."

Coupe's eyes widened in surprise. *Holy shit. The mute kid can actually talk!* he thought.

"What?" he replied.

"Your real name is *Cooper*, just like mine. I remember that's what they called you back in first grade when we started school together. Then you left. But now you are back."

Not only could he talk, he had been paying attention to what was going on for a long time.

"Yeah. Kinda, sorta. My real name is *Coupe*. C-O-U-P-E. It sounds like yours, just spelled different."

"So why don't you use that name?"

"Because no one would use it. They call me Single no matter what I want. Do you know why everyone calls me Single?"

"Yes," Cooper replied. He had a surprisingly soft voice for such a strong kid. "Mrs. Greene started it in first grade. She used to call you Single Shirt because you wore the same shirt to school every day. Everyone in the class laughed at you and started to call you Single. They still do. Why do you let them?"

"Cooper, buddy, it's not like I have a choice. There's no point showing anybody it hurts, so I just wear it like a badge or a medal."

"I'll just call you Coupe."

"Well, that might get a little confusing, but okay, thanks." Coupe thought for a moment and then added, "Hey! Does that mean you're gonna keep talking to me?"

Cooper smiled. "Maybe, but not in school. I don't talk in school." He momentarily looked pained. "I can't talk in school. With all the other people around, all those other voices . . ." Cooper trailed off. "I can't handle it. I have to shut down to stop all the noise and stuff from making me go deaf. But I am working on it. My folks want me to work on it, so it's good I'm talking to you."

"Yeah, that's good. I know what you mean about the voices getting in your head and stuff. It used to happen to me with . . . other stuff. But I learned to just concentrate on one thing you can find in the moment, and it helps it all pass.

"I'm thinking that you have some pretty unique talents beyond chucking bullies. I mean, I can feel you in my head sometimes. That is you, right? And don't worry, I won't tell on you. I just wanted to make sure I'm not going crazy."

Cooper stared at him for a moment. "You're not going crazy.

It started happening earlier this year. I've always felt other people in my head. It only just started that I could reach out and sense them. You're the first person that realized what I was doing. I'm sorry if you thought I was spying. I wasn't. To me, it's just like looking around, only different." He paused. Coupe sensed the conversation was uncomfortable for him, like he was not sure he should be telling anyone about what he could do. "We better get back."

"You don't need to apologize. I'm just happy I'm not going crazy. When you first did it I didn't know what was happening. Then I answered back, and I saw you react. I figured out what was going on. So, nobody else has *talked* back to you?"

"No, you're the only one who seems to know I'm there. Even my parents can't sense me. We better get back," said Cooper.

"Yeah, you said that before. You go, Cooper. They'll be missing you if you don't."

Cooper turned and began to walk back toward the school, but Coupe did not follow. Instead he turned and headed the other way.

"Hey! Where are you going?" asked Cooper when he saw he was alone.

"You go, man," replied Coupe. "They'll be missing you."

"And you?"

"Not so much."

"But where are you going?" asked Cooper as Coupe retreated into the woods.

All he got in response was a cryptic, "This way!" as Coupe shouted over his shoulder and disappeared into the undergrowth.

CHAPTER 2

Coupe turned around to make sure that he was not being followed. Once he knew he was by himself, he threw himself back on the ground and groaned in pain. Kevin had busted him up pretty good, but he wasn't willing to let anyone know that. His head was swimming and his jaw hurt from where the tooth had been knocked loose. *What a friggin' goon*, he thought, as he felt for the gap in his teeth with his tongue. A goon who knew how to punch. The best thing for him now was to get down to the river and get some cool water on his face. He stood but stumbled as he did so.

It was an all too familiar feeling. He would throw up once, fall asleep for a while, and then wake up with a headache that would last for a few hours. But he also knew he healed quickly.

Once steadied, Coupe tottered through the brush down to the river. He was probably concussed. It did not make his walk any easier. It was hot for the time of year, and every step jarred his head with pain. Once out of the brush he found a thin but familiar trail. He knew he was not too far now, maybe a half mile or less. But every step dragged. Time seemed to slow, even though he knew it had not. Each footstep made his head pound. He wanted the cool water of the river.

Finally, he saw the sandy ledge where the forest stopped and the river started. Over the years the river had eaten into the forest, and now the trees hung precariously on its edge. One tree had half of its roots exposed, which was good for Coupe because he used them to climb down the embankment to the water about thirty feet below.

Coupe reached the edge. As he did, the sun hit him fully, and he winced at the light in his eyes. He looked down at the water only to see the sun bouncing off it. It made his head spin. He stepped back to avoid falling down the steep embankment. The last thing he needed was to pass out, bounce down the embankment, and land facedown in the water. If that happened, he would be found three days later floating down the Connecticut River.

But as he thought about it, his knees finally gave up. He fell forward, and his extended hands hit nothing but air. The last thing he saw was the sand of the embankment coming toward him. At that moment he lost consciousness.

He awoke to the feel of water on his face, but he was not in the river. The water was being wiped on his face by a piece of cloth. Coupe opened his eyes in panic, and he tried to get up and run. But strong hands gently pushed him back down onto the sand. His eyes came into focus, and he saw Cooper kneeling and leaning over him. He had stuck his sleeve in the river and was wiping Coupe's forehead with it.

"What happened?" Coupe asked.

"You started to fall."

"But how—"

"I followed you, and then caught you as you started to fall."

Coupe had been sure Cooper had turned back. He had not heard a thing as he walked. Coupe had extraordinary hearing, and he had a good sense when he was being followed. He could hear other people in the woods a mile away. His focus had gone to shit.

"How did you stop me from falling?"

Cooper just shrugged, and Coupe did not push it. He had seen this kid throw a fat tub of lard against a tree thirty feet away. He should be happy he was being kind to him. He sat up and looked around to get his bearings. Then he threw up.

Once done, he looked at Cooper, who had jumped out of the way. "Should have warned you that was coming, sorry."

"What do you mean?"

"When I get walloped in the head, sometimes I puke and then sleep a bit. Then I'm better."

"How often do you get hit in the head?"

"More than just today," replied Coupe, moving to the water. He washed out his mouth and then splashed more water on his face. It was cool and brought relief to his head. He dunked his head in and then turned back to Cooper. He was on his knees, just looking at him.

There was something about him, other than his freaky strength. There was something else. Perhaps there were a bunch of something elses. He decided to trust Cooper, perhaps more than he had trusted any other kid. Perhaps more than anyone else, period. Cooper had earned his trust.

"I got a camp down around the bend over there," said Coupe. "You wanna come see it?"

Cooper nodded. Coupe tried to stand and stumbled a bit. Cooper reached out and steadied him.

"I'm okay, but thanks," said Coupe, separating himself. One thing Coupe did have was good manners. "It's just my foot," he said, shaking his right foot that was bent inward at an awkward angle. "C'mon, it's not too far." He started walking and then turned back to

Cooper. "Promise me you won't tell anyone where my camp is; will you do that?" Cooper nodded. That was enough for Coupe.

Coupe led Cooper along the shore of the river. They walked slowly, Cooper following Coupe, watching his steps, until they came to a stretch that was quieter and wider. On the inside of the bend was a sandy beach. On the outside, a flat piece of land before the embankment started up again. On this stretch was Coupe's camp.

From this distance it looked like nothing more than a collection of blowdowns and driftwood. As they got closer, it began to look more organized. The timber supported a brown tarp. It was an improvised tent. Underneath that tarp, Coupe had built a floor of deadfalls. As they got even closer, Cooper could see that two live trees also supported a hammock hanging in the center of the tent. Beside the hammock were stacks of books. As Cooper entered the tent, he saw they were all from the school's library. Cooper began looking at them.

"The librarian lets me take them out," said Coupe, somewhat defensively.

"I didn't think you stole them."

Coupe's tent was bigger than Cooper had expected. He could easily stand up in it, and it had some depth where Coupe had stored other things, like a towel, and a couple of jars of peanut butter. It looked comfortable. The hammock, which also looked to be made of an old canvas tarp, hung in the center of the tent, and the books were within easy reach. Some of them were on shelves fashioned from stumps and other odd pieces of wood from the forest.

"You like to read?"

"I love to read," replied Coupe, smiling broadly.

"Why?" Cooper asked.

"Because it's a way to go places! Places I will never get to see, whether they are real or made up. Reading the books takes me there." He paused and closed his eyes and said, "I love books."

Cooper picked up one of the books, *The Swiss Family Robinson*.

Coupe smiled. "Dude," he said, putting his hands in the air and pointing all around him. "This *is* Swiss Family Robinson . . . Want some peanut butter?"

Cooper looked at all the books. "Did the Swiss Family Robinson have all these books?"

Coupe laughed. "You know, Cooper, to most of the world you only just started talking. I think it's a little too soon for you to become a wiseass."

Cooper giggled.

"I don't have much, but I do have some peanut butter, and considering you somehow saved me from falling down that big old embankment and somehow got Hannigan off of me after I, of course, got him off of you, the least I can do is show you a little hospitality and offer you some peanut butter. I mean, it's the good stuff."

He held it up to prove the truth of his words.

"Do you have any bread?"

"No, I do not have bread. I do not have crackers. I do not have any jelly or marshmallow stuff other than"—he held up a shiny round object—"a spoon. So, do you want some?"

Cooper smiled. "Sure. I'll have some peanut butter."

"I've only got one spoon. I'll let you go first."

"Have you used it before?"

"Ayuh."

"So what's the difference?"

Coupe smiled again, so wide Cooper could see the gap where his tooth had been. "You know, you're a lot smarter than I thought you were."

The two boys sat together in Coupe's camp and ate some peanut butter. Afterward, Coupe fell asleep, but Cooper did not leave. He picked up *The Swiss Family Robinson* and read it while Coupe slept.

....

Back at their school, their disappearance had not gone unnoticed. That is to say that Cooper's disappearance had not gone unnoticed.

At the end of recess, students were asked if anyone had seen Cooper. No one responded. It was Mrs. Bellisle who noticed Kevin Hannigan nursing some new bruises and asked what had happened. He replied with a tale of how Coupe and Cooper had tricked him and beaten him up. This story got no traction whatsoever from the teachers and vice principal, who had gathered around to hear his distorted confession. The school staff were well aware of Kevin's fighting and bullying.

Kevin then changed his story to say that Coupe alone had jumped him. None of the assembled adults believed the slight-framed Coupe could have inflicted any damage on the bulky Hannigan, who changed his story again, insisting he was double-teamed and that Cooper had thrown him like a piece of firewood. They dismissed Kevin as a liar but remained concerned about Cooper, who never missed school. The next call was to Cooper's parents.

·················

Back down by the river Coupe awoke with a start. He was in his hammock but did not remember getting there. As he looked around, he saw Cooper sitting on the floor looking back at him, a book in his lap. Coupe swung his legs over the edge of his hammock and stood. He was a little unsteady but feeling better.

"I'm okay," he said to Cooper.

"I know," he replied.

Coupe studied Cooper's face. Coupe was a kid who had learned how to read people at an early age and had gotten really good at it. He had survived so far because of it. Cooper seemed to be able to do it too, but in a different way. Coupe had initially written him off as *special*. Perhaps autistic, perhaps something else. But he was something different.

"All the noise from the other kids bothers you. You feel it, I know," Coupe said. "But you can learn how to deal with it. You can make it so it just washes over you instead of drowning you. That's how you feel, right? Like you're drowning in all the noise?"

Cooper stared at him for a long time. Again neither boy said a thing. To Coupe, it was clear that Cooper was making a big decision. He had already spoken to him, for the first time in his life. He knew Cooper was going to trust him. Deep down it made him feel good.

"Yes," he said, simply.

Coupe smiled back at Cooper. "Well, you are no longer alone. I'll help you if I can. If you will let me."

Cooper found Coupe's smile infectious. The poor kid had a big black eye. He had a slow trickle of dried blood coming out of his left nostril. He had lost a tooth and his lip was split, but he was standing there and smiling at him. Cooper smiled back.

"Does that hurt?" he asked.

"What, my face? Sure it does, but I don't care. Pain is just another badge, buddy. They think they hurt me? No way. Every time I get hit, it is just another chance for me to show how much I don't give a shit that they can hurt me. If I don't give it any value, they don't get anything from it. Besides, I heal really quick."

"What about the tooth?"

"It just adds to my winning smile!" Coupe smiled broadly and pointed to the new gap in his teeth.

Coupe looked again at Cooper's face. Cooper's clear blue eyes stared back at him. He was more than a few inches taller than Coupe, so he looked up to him. Coupe searched Cooper's face, then sniffed.

"You do that a lot. Why?" Cooper asked.

"I'm sorry. I can't help it," Coupe replied.

"I've noticed. What do you smell?"

"Everything. Well, more than most, I guess." Coupe studied his face again, then said, "For instance, in your case, if you had taken the same beating I took, you would smell different. Then each day as you began to heal, you would start to return to normal. But if you got an infection or something, the smell would be entirely different."

"Where did you learn—"

"Like I said, I like to read."

It was clear that Coupe had not learned that from any book. And Cooper sensed as much, but he did not push.

Coupe looked closely at Cooper's face again. It was clear and unblemished. "I watched that turd pound your face just as hard as mine," he said. "Why is it I look like this and you look like that? Seriously, why?"

Coupe watched Cooper's smile retreat. In turn, Coupe took a step or two back as well. He studied Cooper's expression and knew he had pushed too hard. Quickly he added, "Forget it. I don't need to know your secrets. Just, thanks."

They stood facing each other, each taking the measure of the person who stood before them. Coupe maybe sniffed a little, but tried not to. Eventually Cooper spoke.

"I'm not supposed to talk about it. I'm not even supposed to show I can do it, but I guess I did. It just doesn't affect me the way it does you." Cooper looked back up the river. "We should get back."

Coupe sensed the tension in Cooper and tried to put him at ease.

"Don't worry about it, buddy. I won't say anything. And if Hannigan says anything, I'll just say you pushed him off of me after he beat me up for my lunch money." Coupe started laughing.

"What's so funny about that?"

"Like I would have lunch money!" With that Coupe fell over laughing and did not stop until Cooper lifted him back up to his feet.

"Seriously, you will not say anything?" asked Cooper.

"Trust me, one thing I am good at is keeping secrets." The happiness that had been on his face was briefly gone, replaced by a darkness. Then he looked again at Cooper. "I've been back at this school for the entire school year. Why is it now that you feel okay talking to me? You obviously know who I am. You know I got some weird habits." He sniffed to make his point. "You remember me from before I left. Why now?"

"Like I said, with all the kids, it's too much for me. If you were to come up to me tomorrow, I probably wouldn't talk to you. Please don't be mad if I don't. It's just that I don't think I could."

"Okay, I understand. So why now?"

"I don't know. Something set you apart. You hear me when everyone else doesn't." Cooper tapped the side of his head.

Coupe looked back at him for a long time.

"Yeah, I get it. I don't know what it is either. Kinda weird. But there is something different when I look at you."

· · · · · · · · · · · · · · · · ·

Back at the school, Cooper's parents had arrived. The vice principal had also remembered to call Coupe's mom, but there had been no answer. Cooper's mom, Evelyn Callister, was obviously distraught, asking many questions and not waiting for the answers. Cooper's dad, Everett Callister, was stoic, listening for a while, and then he simply pushed his cap back on his head where it covered his salt-and-pepper hair. He went out into the parking lot and opened up the back of his pickup. Cooper's dog, Roscoe, had been patiently waiting and jumped out as the tailgate was lowered. He was part border collie and full of energy. As he danced around Everett's feet, Everett looked toward the woods where the boys had last been seen.

"Let's go find them, Roscoe," he said. He headed toward the woods, Roscoe with him.

Through the window, the vice principal watched as Everett and the dog entered the woods, impressed with his calm demeanor.

· · · · · · · · · · · · · · · · ·

It was late afternoon, but the sun had not yet set. The two boys were quietly reading books when Coupe's head shot up.

"What is it?" asked Cooper.

He sniffed the air and turned his head to the side. "I hear something."

"What is it?"

"An animal coming this way, and someone walking with it. We should get outta here."

"Why?"

"Dunno," said Coupe, standing. "In case it's something bad."

"What makes you think it's something bad?"

"I didn't say I thought it was something bad. It's just that if it *is*, well, it's better not to be anywhere near it. Trust me."

Coupe was putting some of the books in a plastic bag when he suddenly looked up toward the embankment he had nearly fallen over earlier in the afternoon. "Whatever it is, it's here."

The boys stepped out of the tent. A few seconds later a dog came charging over the edge of the embankment and ran down to its steep bottom with ease.

"Roscoe!" shouted Cooper. In a matter of seconds the dog was at his feet, circling and jumping at him, his tail wagging.

Coupe smiled broadly. "You know this dog?"

"He's mine."

"I love dogs," said Coupe.

Hearing Coupe speak, Roscoe immediately turned his attentions to Coupe. Coupe wasted no time in dropping to his knees and rubbing the dog's ears. For a moment they both sniffed each other's faces. Cooper thought it was both odd and predictable at the same time. Once it was done, Roscoe backed up for a moment, stared at Coupe and began dancing around Coupe as well.

"I love dogs," repeated Coupe as he tried to catch hold of Roscoe and pet him.

"I think he loves you, too."

Roscoe's antics were perhaps why Coupe never heard Cooper's father descend the embankment and walk over to the boys.

"Boys. Are you okay?" Everett Callister asked as he came up to them.

In that moment Coupe looked around quickly for an escape. He was angry with himself because he had allowed someone to sneak up on him so easily. Now it was too late to run. But Cooper just smiled.

"Dad! This is my friend Coupe," said Cooper.

Everett was momentarily taken aback. He obviously knew his son could speak because he spoke at home. But he was also aware that he had yet to speak at school—that he found it profoundly difficult to even look at the other students, let alone speak with them. Yet with this boy he obviously had.

Everett turned his grey-eyed gaze upon Coupe, the apparent wonder boy of speech inducement. He immediately saw the bruises upon his face. He also saw the worn clothing he was wearing and shoes that looked too small for his feet. Coupe was holding a plastic bag full of books. He saw that the boy now seemed to be sniffing at him. He also noted that the boy was staring at him intently and appeared to be actively assessing him, but then quickly averted his gaze. His initial assessment was that this young man was both intelligent and a little bit off.

"You boys have been missed back at school. You've got a lot of people worried."

"Sorry, Dad," replied Cooper. "It's just that Kevin Hannigan started picking on me, but then Coupe here came over and tried to make him stop, and well, Kevin didn't stop. Coupe got hurt and I was worried for him when he decided to come down to the river. But everyone is okay now."

It was the most that Cooper had said to him all week. Everett looked at them both silently. He walked up to Coupe and got a closer look at his face.

"How are you feeling, Coupe?" he asked.

Coupe would not make eye contact with Cooper's father. He stood rigidly, almost at attention, and said, "Fine, sir. I heal quick, sir. Sorry I led your boy down into the woods. It was my fault, so please don't hold it against him. It was all me. Sorry, sir."

Everett looked at Coupe for a second time, sizing him up again. "I don't hold it against either one of you. Sounds like a rough afternoon and you handled it. I expect I would have done the same when I was a kid. So no one is in trouble; no one is getting any blame. Let's just get you both home before the night sets in."

Coupe spoke up quickly. "I'm all set getting myself home from here. I know my way through these woods pretty good. So, thank you, and let me just say Cooper is a real good kid, sir. I would be glad to call him my friend." As he finished he started to walk past Everett, but the man put his hand on the boy's shoulder and stopped him.

"Hang on a second, Coupe. We'll give you a ride home after we all go back to the school and let them know you are both okay."

"Both?" replied Coupe.

"What?"

He paused, then said, "Nothin'."

It was the look on Cooper's face that made him stop protesting. The three of them walked back out of the woods with Roscoe running circles around them. Cooper noticed that Coupe was more silent than he had been. He could not read him. Coupe had shut him out.

Back at the school neither of them spoke. Everett explained generally where he had found them. He did not mention anything about Coupe's camp. He also told the vice principal that he was willing to give Coupe a ride home. The vice principal was relieved. Even though he was concerned about the obvious beating Coupe had taken, when questioned Coupe would say nothing. He just stood there looking at his feet with an occasional look up to see what was going on. They did not even bother to ask Cooper, not expecting any response.

It was dark before Roscoe was put in the back of the truck and the two boys were buckled in behind Everett and Evelyn.

"Where do you live?" asked Everett.

Coupe hesitated before answering. "Do you know the Gypsy Rose bar?"

Everett had heard of it, though he had never been into it. "I do," he responded.

"My mom has an apartment above it," replied Coupe quietly.

Cooper and his family lived outside of town. They had a small farm of mixed crops and mixed livestock. They also had a larger set of acres devoted to timber. A good portion of their income came from the timber they processed into firewood each year. They came into town to shop or to sometimes socialize, but they never went to the Gypsy Rose. It had a reputation and not a good one.

Everett looked into the rearview mirror at Coupe, but his head was down and Everett could see nothing as it was now getting dark outside. He put his eyes back on the road, realizing it was not his job to choose where the boy lived, just to get him back there safely.

They drove into town and pulled up in front of the Gypsy Rose. It was early evening and there was a line of trucks, cars and motorcycles in front of it. Loud music played inside, and outside a few of the rough-looking patrons stood around smoking cigarettes.

"Oh, Everett, are you sure?" asked Evelyn.

"He said he lives above the bar, not in it," replied Everett.

But it was a rough-looking place. Everett had misgivings too, but he knew his obligation was to get Coupe back to his mother safely. It was what he would want someone to do for his son, after all.

Everett parked the truck. As he got out, he heard the loud voices of the people inside. Along the side of the building was a long staircase that worked its way up to the second floor.

"I live up those stairs," offered Coupe. "I can take it from here. Thank you for the ride, sir," he added, opening the door and trying to bolt. But Everett stopped him with his voice.

"Wait," he said. "I want to take you to your mom and explain what happened. I expect she is going to have some questions about your new bruises."

"Probably not," replied Coupe. "I'll take it from here."

"Want me to come, Coupe?" offered Cooper.

Coupe wheeled quickly. "No!"

Evelyn was staring at Cooper with open amazement. It was the first time she had ever heard him speak with anyone other than her or Everett.

Everett came around the side of the truck and opened the door for Coupe. "C'mon, Coupe. I'll walk you up and do all the explaining. Everything will be fine."

Coupe stepped out of the truck and for a moment looked for a possible route of escape. He heard Roscoe whine behind him, sensing his anxiety. But Coupe now knew his only path was up the rickety wooden steps on the side of the bar. He felt Everett's hand on his shoulder and momentarily winced until he understood it was not meant to be hurtful. He looked up into Everett's eyes for the first time since he had seen him. They were clear grey and devoid of deception. He looked at the corners of his mouth and his eyebrows. He briefly sniffed. He knew Everett did not mean him any ill will. He simply did not know any better.

"What's your mom's name?" asked Everett.

"Mary Daschelete," replied Coupe. "But she won't be home." He hesitated, then added, "She's probably at work."

"So who is going to be home for you?"

"Her boyfriend, Mark."

"C'mon. Everything will be fine."

Coupe shot a last look at Cooper and then let his friend's father lead him up the scaffold of stairs. They reached the top of the stairs, and Everett knocked on the thin wooden panels. After a moment he heard movement, and then the door was opened.

"What do you want?" asked a disheveled man with three-day stubble and a head topped with messy black hair. Then he saw Coupe and he grinned. "Where did you find him?" he asked, grabbing hold of Coupe and pulling him into the house.

"Over by the school. I thought his mom would be worried, so I brought him home. She can call the school tomorrow. Coupe got into it with a bully, but the school is aware of what happened, and I expect they'll take care of it."

"Yeah, I'll have her call the school tomorrow. Thanks for bringing him back." The man slammed the door shut.

Everett would have preferred to speak directly to Coupe's mom instead of her unkempt and rude boyfriend. But if Mom was okay with this guy, who was Everett to interfere? He walked slowly back down the stairs to the truck and got inside.

"Did you explain what happened to his mother?" asked Evelyn.

"She wasn't there, just her boyfriend. I told him she could call the school tomorrow to get the full story." He turned to Cooper. "Cooper, did Coupe ever say anything about his mom's boyfriend to you?"

"No. But I get a sense he doesn't like him. I get a sense he's afraid of him."

Everett knew well enough to trust Cooper's senses. He would make sure that Cooper checked on him at school in the morning, just to ensure that everything was okay. He started the truck and began the drive home. Changing subjects, he looked over at Evelyn.

"Did Cooper tell you he spoke today?"

Evelyn's eyes opened wide with surprise.

"No, he didn't tell me he spoke at school," she replied. "I am so proud of you, Cooper. I knew it would happen eventually."

Cooper looked back at her with his steady deep gaze. "I didn't speak in school," he replied. "You know I can't. It's too loud there. But after that thing with Kevin Hannigan, I started talking with Coupe in the woods. It seemed sorta natural, like talking with you. He's a nice kid."

Evelyn pursed her lips. "Is this the boy they call Single, the one that took the money from the church back in third grade?"

"Yes, but don't call him that. It's mean." He explained why. "And I don't think he took the money from the church either."

Evelyn was not so sure of that. She knew that the police had been called to investigate. She'd heard he was found with the money. If not for Father Hatem stepping in, he might have been prosecuted. But still she knew well enough to trust Cooper's senses.

"I thought he left the town after the church money thing?" she asked.

"He did. He only moved back into town last year. He said he remembered me. He said . . ." Cooper paused.

"Go on, honey. He said what?"

"He said he can feel me in his head when I am close by. I believe him."

Evelyn was surprised. Cooper certainly had some gifts, one of which was his ability to sense people in a way she could not describe, but she had never heard of anyone who was aware of him doing it.

"You should invite him over for dinner some night," she offered.

"Okay, but you better make sure we have peanut butter."

"Why is that?"

"I think that's all he eats."

Everett looked through the rearview mirror at his son.

"This fight with the Hannigan boy. He hit you?"

"Yes."

"Did he hit you as hard as he hit Coupe?"

"Harder probably."

"What did you do?"

"I just stood there, until Coupe tackled him. Then he started hitting Coupe. He was hitting him hard, Dad. He knocked out one of his teeth. I know I'm not supposed to do it, but I had to do something, so I pulled him off."

"And then flung him thirty feet into a tree?"

Cooper looked down at his feet. "Yes," he said quietly.

"You've got to be smarter than that. People will start asking questions."

"I know, but he was really hurting Coupe."

"Then just push him off like a normal kid would. Or when he was hitting, you fall down and act like it was hurting you. Now the Hannigan kid is going to tell people what happened."

"I don't think people will believe him," replied Cooper.

Everett knew the Hannigan family. Kevin's dad was a boozing bully. He had seen him working at the lumberyard, swaggering around, loud and abusive. He avoided him. It was no wonder his boy was a bully at school. But Cooper was probably right. Kevin would likely not go telling his dad that he could not punch out Cooper Callister or that Cooper had thrown him thirty feet like it was nothing, especially after his words had been dismissed so quickly at the school. But it might be different if Coupe started talking about it. As he often did, Cooper started answering before his father asked the question.

"Coupe won't say anything about it. He told me he wouldn't. I believe him."

"You've been saying that a lot, that you believe him. Why?"

"Because I do. I got a sense."

Cooper's parents had known for a long time that their son was different from other boys his age. He had always been especially quiet, but when he did speak, it was as if he had been listening all the time, even if no one had been speaking out loud. As he grew, his dramatic increase in strength was at first amusing and impressive, but as it continued, it became alarming. Everett was afraid that if Cooper's doctors found out, they would conduct all sorts of tests on him, study him, scrutinize him.

Everett knew that Cooper was a sensitive boy. He was concerned that kind of scrutiny was exactly what he did *not* need, so he and Evelyn had always worked to conceal his special abilities. They cautioned Cooper to do the same. But they need not have bothered. Cooper had figured out the same thing himself. He had always been careful about revealing what he could do.

"Yeah, Cooper, why don't you invite Coupe over for dinner tomorrow," Everett asked.

"Okay."

The rest of the trip home was in silence, which was not unusual for the Callister family. Well, silent for Everett and Evelyn. Cooper sat in the back seat sensing them. They were concerned for him. They were concerned about Coupe and what he might say. But his mother was also very happy. He could read that loud and strong. She had been waiting for the day that he finally broke through his protective shell when he was at school. She loved him deeply and he sensed that in her. It made him feel happy and safe. *So why didn't Coupe feel the same way about his mom?*

Everett pulled the family truck down the long gravel drive that wound through the woods to their home. When they finally reached its end, Cooper jumped out and whistled.

"C'mon, Roscoe! Let's go!"

The dog jumped over the side of the truck and bounded over to Cooper, who ran up onto the porch in front of the house and opened the front door. His parents followed, closing the door on the night air.

CHAPTER 3

The following morning Evelyn wrote a note for Cooper to give to Coupe, inviting him to dinner. He could come home with Cooper after school, and she would drive him home afterward.

At the end of the day she went to pick up the two boys. Only Cooper came out.

"He wasn't in school today," said Cooper.

"Really? Maybe he was hurt more than we thought."

"Maybe. But he misses a lot of school, Mom. I don't think he's ever made a full week."

It was Wednesday, so Evelyn told Cooper to just hold onto the note and he could give it to Coupe tomorrow.

When they got home Everett was waiting. When Evelyn told him that Coupe was a no-show, a look of concern crossed his face. Evelyn shared that he often missed school, but Everett thought back to the place the boy lived and his mother's boyfriend, Mark. It didn't seem like a healthy environment for a teen boy. But he reminded himself again that other folks didn't live the same way, nor raise their children the same way as he and Evelyn.

The following day Cooper was standing outside the school waiting for his mother, alone.

When Cooper was all alone again on Friday, Evelyn asked Cooper if Coupe usually missed three days in a row.

Cooper looked at her. "No," he said and looked down at the now dog-eared note he was holding in his hand.

Everett's concerns grew when he learned Coupe was once again absent. He turned to his son to gain insights Cooper might have.

"Cooper, do you get any sense with what is going on with Coupe?"

"No," replied Cooper. "He's too far away for me to do that." He then added, "But if you were to drive into town, close to his apartment, I might be able to."

"Okay, go get in the truck."

As they finally pulled into town and got closer to the Gypsy Rose, Cooper leaned forward in his seat. He saw a line of cars parked outside the bar already. He got a sense of the people inside there, and it made it difficult to know whether Coupe was nearby. They were about to leave and check the river when Cooper said, "Wait, Dad. He's up there."

"And?"

"He's not good."

Everett pulled the truck over near the bottom of the stairs and got out. "Stay here," he said to Cooper.

"No," Cooper replied, getting out of the truck.

"Cooper! Wait!"

Everett had to hurry to catch up to him. He grabbed Cooper by the arm, but Cooper simply pulled through his grasp as if his father were a child. Cooper had never disobeyed him like this before.

They quickly climbed up the stairs. Everett worked his way in front of Cooper and knocked on the door. The same grungy man answered.

"Hi," Everett said. "I've come to look in on Coupe."

"Fifty bucks," replied the man flatly.

Everett was confused. "What? Listen I—"

"You wanna see the kid, it's fifty bucks." The man then recognized Everett. "Wait, you're the guy that dropped him off the other night, right?"

"Yeah, I wanted to make sure he was okay. He got beat up pretty bad. Listen, what was all that about fif—"

"He's not here; he took off."

The man tried to push the door closed, but Everett's powerful hand was still on it.

"Look, I told you he's not here. Now get your fucking hand off my fucking door before I kick your fucking ass!"

"He's here," said Cooper quietly. "He needs help."

The man grabbed hold of Everett's jacket and tried to push him back away from the door. Everett stumbled back into his son, who didn't budge. Cooper reached from behind his father and with one arm shoved the man, who went flying across the room, bounced over a table and struck the wall beyond it. Everett and Cooper walked into the small, untidy living room and kitchen combination. The sink was full of dishes, and trash overflowed from a container near the sink. There were empty beer bottles and liquor bottles everywhere. It smelled of old sweat and looked dirty and used.

Cooper looked around and locked on to a short hallway and a closed door near its end. "He's down there," he said and started walking toward it.

Mark stood. When he saw Cooper start down the hall, he grabbed a set of keys off the kitchen counter and bolted out the door. Everett stared at him for a moment but then followed Cooper.

Everett caught up to Cooper as he reached the door. Cooper

opened it. As he did, Everett gasped and pulled Cooper's head into his chest so that he could not see.

The poorly lit bedroom had nothing but a bed and a dresser. There in the center of the bed, covered by nothing more than a sheet, lay Coupe. His eyes were closed. He was not moving; he could not move. His arms had been tied securely to the corners of the bed.

Everett tried to push Cooper back out of the room. "Wait outside, buddy. I'll get him."

"No," replied Cooper, defying him for second time.

"Then help me get him untied."

Everett started untying one of the ropes that held Coupe's hands, and Cooper quickly snapped the other. Coupe roused, startled, but Cooper put his hands on his shoulders and steadied him.

Cooper and Everett could still see the bruises from Kevin Hannigan's fists three days ago, but they were well faded, and the cut in his lip and over his eye had almost completely healed. But he had new bruises on his face, and there was blood on the sheet where his head had been resting, and crusted blood in his hair. He also had dark abrasions and bruises where the ropes had been holding him down.

"He wants water," Cooper said. "He's very thirsty. There's some in the dresser." Everett went over to the dresser to get it. "Second drawer," Cooper said.

Everett opened the second drawer and found half a bottle of water inside. Coupe drank all of it before coughing up some of it.

"Don't worry, Coupe. We'll get you some more once we get you out of here and to a doctor," said Everett.

Coupe began shaking his head and tried to speak, but still his voice had not returned.

"He doesn't want to go to the doctor," said Cooper.

"He's got to see a doctor, Cooper. He might be hurt . . . he is hurt," reasoned Everett.

"Dad, he doesn't want to go to a doctor—I think for the same reason you don't like for me to go to the doctor."

Cooper's strange affinity for this down-on-his-luck street kid was starting to make more sense as Everett looked at them both. They obviously had some sort of link that he did not fully understand.

"Okay, for now. We'll get him home and see how he is doing then."

Coupe was naked under the sheet. Everett found clothes on the floor near the foot of the bed. His shirt had been nearly ripped in half, and he did not want to put the underclothes back on him. But his pants were still in one piece, so they helped him into those. Cooper took off his own hoodie, and they put that on him as well. They could not find his shoes anywhere. It did not matter much, as it appeared Coupe was unable to walk. As he tried to stand, Cooper just stepped in and scooped him up. He started walking toward the door before Everett stopped him.

"Are you going to walk down all those stairs with him in your arms, in front of anyone who might be watching or waiting?"

Cooper thought about it for a moment and then handed Coupe over to his father. He secretly hoped that Mark was waiting somewhere outside for them. He sensed his dad was thinking the same thing too. But when they got outside, he was nowhere to be seen. They loaded Coupe into the truck and drove away.

·················

Cooper held Coupe in the back seat. Everett shuddered to think what had happened to the boy over the past three days. Everett decided he would notify the chief of police about Mark.

Everett parked in front of the farm, and Evelyn came out to greet them. Cooper stepped out of the back of the truck holding Coupe in his arms and walked him into the house.

"Everett? What happened?" she asked.

"Let's get him settled. I'll explain then."

They followed Cooper inside. He laid his friend upon the couch in the living room. Coupe woke up and looked at him.

"Where am I?" he asked.

"You're at my home. You're safe here," replied Cooper.

Evelyn gasped. She was still not used to hearing him speak in front of others.

Roscoe whined as he came up and started licking Coupe's face. Coupe smiled and reached out to pet the dog.

"Could I have some more water? I haven't had much to drink since I last saw you."

Evelyn ran from the room and returned with a full glass of water.

"Who knew that water could taste so good?" he said, chugging the entire glass.

"I'll get you some more. When was the last time you had anything to eat?"

Coupe looked up at her. "When Cooper and me were down at my camp reading books we ate some peanut butter."

Tears welled up in Evelyn's eyes. "I'll fix you something," she said and quickly fled back into the kitchen.

"Cooper, why don't you go upstairs and get your buddy some of your clothes. I suppose they will be a little big, but I think he'll feel a lot more comfortable."

"Sure, Dad," said Cooper, and he disappeared upstairs.

Coupe's face was drawn, and his skin seemed to be almost paper thin. His eyes darted up to look at Everett's again, and Everett suddenly realized that he was making the poor boy feel uncomfortable. He quickly looked away. He then grabbed a chair and pulled it over to the couch where Coupe was sitting.

"Coupe. I want to say I'm sorry," said Everett. "I'm sorry I took you to that place and left you there. I should have followed my instincts and waited for your mother. I should have brought you back home to us. If I knew what would happen to you, I never would have left you there."

Coupe looked up at a him intently. He studied his face, moving his eyes all around it. Then he sniffed. "You didn't know any better, sir."

"So, now do you want to tell me where your mother is?" he asked.

Coupe turned his head away. Everett thought he was going to cry, but he didn't.

"I haven't seen my mother in over a month," he said quietly. "She and Mark had an argument over money or something. Last time I saw her she was walking out and telling Mark that he could try looking after me for a while to see if he liked doing it."

Cooper returned with a pile of clothes and placed them on the couch next to his friend.

"How have you been living since she left?" Everett asked.

"I've been spending most of my time down at my camp. I would sneak back to the apartment for food and stuff when I thought the coast was clear or if it got too cold, but mostly I tried to stay away from Mark. He hadn't seen me in over a week when you took me back. He was pissed. He said I cost him money."

Coupe looked at the stack of clothes Cooper had brought down. He picked them up and held them to his face. He inhaled their cleanliness. He rubbed the soft fabrics against his skin. "I don't suppose there is anywhere I can clean up before putting these on?"

"There's a shower upstairs," replied Cooper. "I'll show you."

He went to pick Coupe up again, but Coupe stopped him. "Easy, big guy," he said. "The water has really helped. I think I can walk to it. Just show me the way."

"C'mon."

Cooper picked up the pile of clothes and led Coupe upstairs to the shower. Coupe's steps were tentative. His limp seemed more pronounced. But Cooper patiently waited. He pointed the way up the stairs and then followed closely after Coupe, making sure he didn't stumble or fall. Coupe made it up the stairs without issue, and soon Everett heard the water running and the boys talking.

Once Cooper had the water running, he showed Coupe where the towels were kept and helped him into the shower. He then stepped back out into the hallway but insisted that Coupe leave the door open a little just in case he should need help. Coupe did not protest. He just smiled and gave Cooper a thumbs-up.

"Whoa!" Coupe shouted moments after Cooper had left the bathroom.

"What's wrong?" asked Cooper.

"Nothin'. It's just that the water is warm. Is it always this warm?"

"Sure," replied Cooper.

"This is great!" Coupe shouted back, his voice obviously returning. "How long do I have?"

"Take as long as you want."

"This is great!"

Everett had gone into the kitchen to help his wife. He told her as gently as he could what they had found, but it was still too shocking, and she had to bury her head in Everett's shoulder for a few moments. When she had calmed down, he left to go make a phone call. He then came back to help her finish making dinner.

She had decided on chicken noodle soup and grilled cheese sandwiches, but she made a few peanut butter ones too, just in case Cooper had been right about Coupe's monotonous diet. The food was complete and being set out upon the table when Evelyn and Everett heard the boys coming down the stairs. They were surprised to hear them laughing, as if nothing bad had happened.

"You feeling any better, Coupe?" asked Everett.

Coupe brightened a little and nodded. "Yes, sir, very much," he said. "I forgot how good warm water can feel. I've been washing down by the river for a while now, and the apartment don't get hot water."

"He said he drank half the water!" offered Cooper, still smiling.

"I was really thirsty."

"Are you hungry?" asked Evelyn. "I made some soup and grilled cheese, but Cooper said you prefer peanut butter, so I made some sandwiches with that too."

"Peanut butter is usually all I can get, but I'll try the other stuff too," he replied, sniffing the food on the table.

Evelyn poured each of them a bowl of soup with a grilled cheese sandwich on the side. Coupe tasted the soup tentatively. His face showed Evelyn that he obviously liked it.

"This is really good, ma'am," he offered. He then sniffed the sandwich a few times and took a bite. He smiled. "This is good too!"

Coupe had eaten half of the sandwich in small soup-soaked bites and half of his soup when he suddenly stopped. Evelyn looked at him with concern.

"What's the matter, Coupe? You can't be full already? There is more soup and more sandwiches after that if you want."

"No ma'am," he replied. "It's just that I haven't eaten for a long time. Usually when that happens I have to pace myself when I get food again or it can, you know, come back up."

"What do you mean *usually when that happens*? How often do you go without food for three days?"

"Enough that I've learned how to eat once I get some decent food!" With that, he smiled at Evelyn and gave her a wink. *Charming, resilient and evasive,* she thought.

"You take as long as you like, Coupe," Everett said.

"Thank you, sir," he replied

Coupe sat quietly and watched as they ate. There was little talk around the table, but it did not feel uncomfortable. Everett and Evelyn were used to Cooper's silence. After a while, when Coupe felt his stomach was handling the food, he dipped the sandwich in the soup and took another small bite. He sat there chewing, staring into the soup bowl and slowly stirring it with his spoon. Then he looked up at the other three people sitting around the table.

"Thank you," he said. The three stopped eating and looked at him. "Thank you for the food and the clothes, but especially thank you for coming to look for me and getting me out of there. I wasn't expecting any help. I didn't think anyone would even think to look for me. But you did. That really means a lot. I really can't put into words how that feels, to go from not having a hope left in the world, helpless and alone. And then to be sitting here with all of you, eating nice food with nice-smelling clothes and to not be scared about what is going to happen next. I don't think I can put into words just what that feels like, but it sure feels good. I know that much."

They were all silent for a moment, and then Everett said, "I wish I had known, Coupe. I never would have left you there. Why didn't you tell me what was happening, Coupe? I would have helped you."

"Maybe. Maybe you would have helped, but I'm guessing if I had told you my mom was gone and that Mark was, well . . . you would have just called the police. That never works out well either, especially down where I live." He dipped his sandwich in the soup and took another bite.

"I have called the police, Coupe. What happened has to be reported so that it can stop."

Coupe grimaced in disgust, tossed the sandwich down, and pushed away from the table.

"Are you upset about that, Coupe?" Everett asked.

"No, sir. You just don't know any better."

"You don't have to," Cooper said.

Coupe looked at him and they stared at each other for a few moments. It was obvious to Everett and Evelyn that even though nothing was being said, the two boys were communicating.

"What's going on?" asked Everett.

"He wants to go back down to the river before the police come. He knows they will put him in a group home or youth detention, and he doesn't want to go to either."

Everett looked at Coupe. "Is that right?"

"Yes, sir. Look, I have been through this before. Foster homes are a roll of the dice, and youth detention . . . there's no fucking way I'm going back there."

"Let's see what the police say when they get here," said Everett.

"You can talk to them, but I won't," replied Coupe. "In fact, I would prefer to be gone before they get here."

"Coupe, they are coming here to help you."

"No, they aren't. I know the cops in this town. They never helped me before, and they will not help now. In fact, I'm going to go now." Coupe began to stand up.

"You're not going anywhere, Coupe. Stay here and—" Everett started to say.

"And what? Stay here and stare silently at the cops? No, I gotta go. Again, thanks for the food and stuff."

Coupe started walking out of the kitchen. Everett stepped in front of him and put his hands on his shoulders. Coupe pulled away and glared up at him.

"Get out of my way!"

"You can't just leave now."

"And you're gonna stop me? You gonna tie me to a bed too?"

Everett was pained by his words and took a step away from the boy. "No. I would never do that. I'm trying to help you."

"You think you're trying to help, but you are not. You just don't know any better."

Coupe started for the door again. He was stopped by a hand on his shoulder, but this time it was Cooper's. It was just resting on his shoulder, but it stopped Coupe in his tracks. The two boys stood for several moments, silently communicating until Coupe relaxed and Cooper smiled.

"He's going to stay . . . for a while, at least," Cooper said.

Everett turned to look at Coupe again. "Is that true, Coupe?"

"Yes, sir."

"And you'll talk to the cops?"

"I'll listen to them at least. They're coming now. I can hear them on the driveway."

Everett raised his eyebrows. "Okay, I will go wait for them. You stay here with Cooper and Evelyn."

He shot a look at Cooper, and Cooper just nodded. He knew

after looking at Cooper that Cooper was going to make sure his new friend did not bolt as soon as Everett left the room.

Everett stepped outside onto the porch. As he closed the door, he could make out headlights coming down the drive, followed by the sound of tires crunching on the gravel. He shook his head in disbelief, wondering what other special senses Coupe might have.

Chief Altus Dale eased his large frame out of the car. The two men had known each for a long time, having grown up together in the same small town.

"Everett, what's up?" said Chief Dale, extending his hand.

"Alt, you didn't have to come out personally," he replied, shaking the extended hand.

"I heard the call come in. I heard the tone of your voice and some of what you said. I figured I should come out personally. This is the Daschelete kid, right?'

"Yeah, Coupe. He said you knew him."

"Minor stuff from when he lived here before. He stole some money from the church, but we sorted that out without any charges. Some other minor stuff too. Shoplifting, petty theft. Then he and his mother left. I did not see him or his mother for what? Three, four years? Until she came back to town around last summer? Then I started seeing a lot of her and her new boyfriend, Mark Skinner, for a bunch of different stuff. And we end up at the Gypsy Rose more times than we should have to. I think I saw the kid a couple of times when we were out there. He has obviously grown some, but I knew it was him.

"Once I found him dumpster diving. I tried to catch him, but he's a slippery little fella. Surprisingly fast for a kid who can't run because of that limp. He scurried away. I looked for him but never found him. And it's not like I wanted to hook him up for stealing food out of a dumpster. I wanted to help him."

"I told him that too, but I have to warn you, he is very wary of cops. He was about to bolt until Cooper talked him out of it."

"Cooper talked?"

"Yeah, he did. Well, at least here at home, but it's a step forward, right?"

Chief clapped him on the arm. "Absolutely. Good for him. Let's see what we can do for Single."

"Good, but don't call him that," replied Everett. He explained why. "We call him Coupe."

"I never knew. Another reason for him not to like me. Strange he never told me it bothered him or to call him Coupe instead."

"It doesn't. He wouldn't."

Everett explained what had happened over the past three days, starting with the encounter in the woods with the Hannigan boy and ending with them bringing him back to their home, cleaning him up, and feeding him. Everett could see the chief was pained to hear it all. When Everett had finished speaking, the chief thought for a moment.

"So, he's had a shower?" asked the chief.

"Yeah. He's wearing some of Cooper's clothes now and he's had a good meal."

"Let's see if he'll talk to me."

CHAPTER 4

The two men entered the house and found Cooper and Coupe sitting at the kitchen table. Coupe was showing Cooper a card trick. They were smiling and giggling as Coupe manipulated the cards.

"Boys, how are you doing?" said Chief Dale.

Cooper nodded and smiled.

Coupe was more neutral. "We're both fine, sir."

Chief Dale sat down at the table and Everett joined them.

"So, what's the game you're playing?" the chief asked.

"It's not a game. It's a trick. Watch."

Coupe took the deck of cards that was sitting close to his chest and pulled two aces and a queen from the top. He laid them faceup on the table, the queen between the two aces.

"This trick is called spot the lady. I am going to turn the cards over and move them around. All you have to do is point to the card that you think is the queen. Think you can do that, Chief?"

"Okay, I'll give it a try," he replied.

Coupe turned the cards over and began to move them around the table. He started slowly but picked up speed; though, not enough to fool the chief. Once done, he pointed to the card on the right. Coupe turned it over. It was the queen.

"Pretty good, Chief. Care to put some money on the next round?"

The chief smiled. "Gambling is illegal."

"I know," replied Coupe without looking up. "It was a test. You passed. Still, things are going to get more difficult."

Coupe showed them the cards again, turned them over, and shuffled them along the table as he did before.

"Which one is it now, Chief?"

Chief Dale pointed to the obvious queen. He had seen that the corner was slightly folded, so it made it easy to spot. But when Coupe turned it over it was an ace.

"What the—?"

"I can see this is getting difficult for you, Chief, so let's say I dump one of the aces and add two queens." Coupe grabbed the deck and found two more queens. He put them on the table and removed one of the aces. Now the chief had three queens and one ace to pick from. The chief smiled. Even if the kid was slick, the odds were in his favor.

"Okay, Sin— ahh, Coupe, let's see what you got."

Coupe smiled and said, "You can call me that. I don't care. Everyone else does."

Then Coupe picked up the cards, two in each hand, held between his thumb and first two fingers. The chief saw the ace was in his left hand in the front.

"You ready, Chief?"

"Go."

Coupe's hands now moved very quickly. He put the cards down, then shuffled them around so quickly the chief could hardly keep his eyes on the ace but was pretty sure he had. When Coupe's hands finally stopped, the chief quickly pointed at the card farthest right. He was surprised how into the little game he had become.

"You sure, Chief? You sure you want to pick that card?"

"That's the one," he said.

With a flash of his hand Coupe turned over the card. Out of the four cards on the table, the Chief had picked the ace.

"Son of a bit—" The chief caught himself quickly. "How did you do that?"

Coupe flashed him a smile and winked. The chief could see a gap near the back of his teeth where the Hannigan boy had knocked one out.

"I feel sorry for you, Chief, so I am going to make it really easy for you." Coupe picked up the deck. He found the last queen and also pulled out a joker. "Here's the deal. There are four queens, one ace and one joker." Coupe held the cards up in his fingers, three on each side. Once again the ace was in the lowest position in his left hand. The joker was the lowest card in his right hand. The queens were stacked behind them.

"See them all, Chief?"

"Ayuh," he said, smiling back at Coupe. There was no way he could lose now.

"So, here's the deal," said Coupe. "All you have to do is pick one of the four queens and avoid the ace, okay?"

"Sure. What's the joker for?"

"The joker's for you, Chief. I am pretty sure that you are going to pick it, and if you do, the joke is on you, and you have to pay a penalty."

"What?"

"If you pick the joker out of these six cards, you have to pay me a penalty of twenty bucks." Coupe saw the chief begin to protest, but quickly cut him off. "No, it's not gambling, it's a penalty. Just like the tickets you write. If you can't pick one of the four queens out of six cards with an extra safety card and the one card you do pick is the joker, I get to write you a joker ticket for twenty bucks, payable on demand."

Chief Dale quickly started to work out the odds of picking one card out of six in his head. Coupe did it for him. He was good with numbers.

"You have a 16.66 percent chance of hitting the joker, Chief. That means you have an 83.33 percent chance of winning. You'll never get those odds down at any casino, so what do you say? Care to chance a twenty-dollar penalty?"

Chief Dale smiled at the boy. He was charming in a peculiar way. He appeared as if he had all but forgotten the trauma from which he had been relieved only a few hours ago. Coupe didn't seem to be fazed at all. The chief could see the boy studying his face intently, and then Coupe said, "I'm a quick healer. So, are you in or what?"

Chief Dale smiled. "You don't have to pay me anything if I win?"

"Nope. Risk is all yours."

Chief Dale stared at him for a moment. "How about this. I pick the joker, I pay you twenty bucks. I pick any other card—including the ace—you agree to have an honest talk with me and answer my questions."

Coupe looked at the chief closely. He looked at his eyes, and his mouth, and the way his eyebrows moved ever so slightly. He even looked at the side of his neck, seeing a steady, slow pulse. Then he looked at Everett and Cooper, who were waiting with obvious interest. Then he sniffed. He turned his attention back to Chief Dale and smiled again.

"Okay, Chief, you have a deal."

Coupe held up the six cards again so the chief could see where they were. Then he went to work.

There was no way that Chief Dale's eyes could keep up with the speed of Coupe's hands. He was stunned watching just how fast he could move. They moved so quickly they were almost a blur. When he finally dropped the final card on the table, he began to manipulate them, up and down, side to side. Chief Dale knew he had lost sight of the joker, the one card he did not want to pick. He would instead rely upon the favorable odds to win. Suddenly Coupe's hands came to rest, and the six cards were laid out in front of him.

"Okay, Chief, pick a queen."

He chose as he did the last time, the last card on the right.

"Well, that was predictable," said Coupe. "Why don't we start on the left?" he said, turning over the card farthest left. It was a queen. "One down, three to go." The chief gave Coupe a quick smile, knowing the odds were still in his favor, but wondering if they ever were. Coupe turned over the next two cards quickly. Two more queens. Coupe was now grinning. He looked directly at the chief and turned over the next card. Another queen. "Uh-oh, not looking good, Chief. But the ace is your safety card. If you picked that ace, you win a free chat with me! You've got a fifty-fifty chance now."

Coupe began to turn the next card and then stopped. "I'll tell you what, Chief. I'm a generous person and I like to give people chances, sort of make up for their mistakes, you know what I mean? So, if you want to, I am going to let you switch your choice. You picked the card farthest right, but if you want, you can change to the card I have my hand on right now. What do you want to do, Chief?"

Chief Dale looked at Coupe. He realized for certain now that Coupe had been playing him. Coupe obviously knew which card was which, but he was willing to let him switch cards. Chief Dale saw that the boy was again studying his face, his eyes darting up and down. He sniffed a little, eyes glinting.

"Have I got you a little rattled, Chief? It's just a trick. Go on, pick a card, either one."

Chief Dale figured Coupe must be trying to get him off his choice. That had to mean he had picked correctly. "I'm not gonna bite," he said. "I'll stick with my pick."

Coupe smiled widely. "Chief Dale! Everyone knows you always go with your first instinct! Good for you! But maybe not today . . ."

Coupe grabbed the card Chief Dale had picked and flipped it over. It was the joker.

"Son of a bitch."

Behind him he heard Evelyn clear her throat.

"Sorry, Evelyn," he said. "I was sure he was trying to get me off that last card."

The chief then saw Coupe had fixed him with a stare. He was not smiling now. Coupe grabbed the one remaining card and turned it over. It was also a joker. He flung it down in front of the chief.

"Joke's on you, Chief Dale."

Coupe slowly pushed away from the table, got up and walked out of the kitchen. Cooper looked at the chief and then at Coupe. He followed Coupe out of the room.

"Son of a bitch!"

This time Evelyn remained quiet. She was staring at the cards with wonder. Chief Dale looked over at Evelyn and Everett. "Did I just get played by a fourteen-year-old?" Everett scratched his head and looked away, but Evelyn smiled at him.

"You're not done yet, Altus. He sat here and talked to you already. Now you owe him twenty dollars. Go pay your debt and see if he will still talk."

Chief Dale got up and fished twenty dollars out of his wallet and went after the boys. He found them in the living room. Coupe was sitting in a chair, Cooper on the couch. It looked like they were waiting for him. Chief Dale sat next to Cooper and looked over at Coupe.

"Hey, Cooper, can you give me and Coupe a minute to talk alone? I want to talk to him about stuff that maybe a kid shouldn't hear." Cooper did not move.

"I'm a kid too, Chief. Can I leave?" replied Coupe.

Coupe tried to leave, but Chief Dale motioned him back down. "Relax, Coupe. I'm here to help you. I really am."

Coupe remained standing but did not walk out. "Help me? Cooper's already done more to help than you ever have. His dad too," he added.

"Coupe, I just want to help sort this out."

"Like the way you did with the church money, Chief?"

Everett was listening in the hallway with Evelyn. He came into the room and stood just inside the doorway. Evelyn stood next to him, still in the darkness of the hallway.

"I did help you with that, Coupe. You didn't have to go to court. You didn't have to stand in front of a judge or get a juvenile record. It was good for you."

"Good for me?" Coupe shook his head and turned to look through the window at the night outside.

"Coupe, you had to give the money back and wash some cars. That wasn't so bad, right?"

"Yeah, wash the church vans. That's all it was. I also got labeled the kid who stole the church money. I heard it every time I walked by teachers at school, people on the sidewalk in town. I got kicked out of stores."

"Coupe, you got kicked out of stores because you stole from them."

Coupe laughed again. "Yeah, I'll cop to that. Some of it anyway. I took stuff from some of them, but not all of them." He turned and looked at Chief Dale. "Do you know what it was like as a nine-year-old to have a store manager grab you by the ear and physically throw you through a door for everyone to see? I do." He paused and looked down toward his feet. "I took stuff from some of them, but not all of them." He looked back through the window. "And I only took stuff when I was really hungry. I mean, I would try not to do it."

Coupe breathed on the window to fog it up and then put his fingerprint on it. He pushed at the window with it, feeling its strength.

"The third day without food was usually my breaking point. That's when I would start looking. And I didn't take stuff right away,

Chief. First I would go scavenge, look for stuff behind restaurants and stores. But if there was nothing to be had, well yeah, I would go and swipe stuff."

"Coupe, why didn't you come see me? I could have helped."

"Help the kid who stole the church money? How would you help? Send me back over to the church for a free meal?"

"Coupe, if you had asked me or Father Hatem, we would have helped you. We would not have let a young kid go hungry."

"Yeah, good old Father Hatem. He helped me out a lot. He's a real good friend. Hell, he came to see me just yesterday."

"Coupe, what are you talking about?" asked Chief Dale.

Coupe turned on him. "You lost, remember? Where's my twenty bucks?"

Chief Dale handed it to him. Coupe took it, looked at both sides of the bill and then stuffed it in his pocket. "You lost. I'm done talking."

Chief Dale did not want to give up on Coupe, but he had to hear what happened from him. Without it, there was nothing he could do. He would have to turn him over to social services. Right now, he was an orphan, a ward of the state.

Chief Dale hadn't noticed that Cooper was now staring at him intently. Cooper looked at Coupe and then said softly, "Tell him."

Chief Dale's head snapped up to look at Cooper. It was the first time he had ever heard him speak. Cooper was staring intently at Coupe, who returned it with the same intensity. The chief felt like he was watching a battle of wills. Eventually Coupe slumped and turned back to the window.

"Okay, Chief, I'll tell you everything you want to know. Hell, I'll tell you more than you want to know. But on one condition. No foster homes, no youth detention, and no social services."

Chief Dale frowned. "Coupe, I can't have you wandering the streets. I've got to make sure you're safe."

Again, Coupe laughed. It was uncomfortable and not born of joy.

"Sorry, Chief, you got me there. But those are my terms. Agree, or I am going through this window here, and good luck finding me after that." Everett took a step forward and Coupe put his hand up. "That's close enough, sir." He fished the twenty dollars out of his pocket and placed it on the windowsill. "I'll leave this here to help cover the cost of the window."

Chief Dale did not want to lie to the boy. But Coupe was demanding he exclude the only options he had to help.

"What's it gonna be, Chief?"

Coupe put his hand on the window and pushed on it again to gauge its strength. He had been thrown through a window before— never voluntarily, but he was pretty sure he could do it. Everett took another step into the room, and Coupe stopped him with a single glare.

Chief Dale was considering his chances of grabbing the boy before anything else happened, but he had just seen how quick Coupe could be. Coupe started searching his face as if he knew what he was thinking. Coupe turned back to the window and closed his eyes. He pulled back his hand to smash the glass.

It never fell.

Cooper jumped up, showing some surprising speed of his own, and grabbed hold of him.

"He can stay here," Cooper said quietly.

Coupe couldn't move. Cooper was not using his most gentle grip, but Coupe was not struggling.

Chief Dale looked over at Everett and Evelyn. They nodded in unison.

"Sure he can," said Everett.

Chief Dale scratched his head. "Well, I suppose I could work something out temporarily and then put a word in with social services to have you approved on an expedited basis as an acceptable foster home." He looked back at Coupe. "But if I do, you need to tell me what has been going on."

Coupe looked at Cooper for a moment and then nodded. Cooper let him go.

"Okay, Chief, I'll tell you. But I'm gonna start with the church money thing because I never done that and it still pisses me off."

"Okay, start with the church money. I'm listening."

"I never took that money. Father Hatem gave it to me. It was back when I was nine. He found me looking for food behind the supermarket. Father Hatem seemed like a pleasant guy. He asked what I was doing. I saw his collar so I trusted him. I told him I was looking for food. He invited me back to the church for a meal.

"He took me back and cooked up some great noodle dish," Coupe continued. "He gave me a couple of glasses of wine, too. I was nine years old. I hadn't eaten in three days. With my belly full of food and wine it wasn't long before I fell asleep. I only woke up when I found Father Hatem rooting around in my pants. I screamed and pushed him away. He told me to calm down and gave me a wad of cash out of his wallet to keep my mouth shut. It was a lot of dough, so who was I to say no? I was always going hungry, so I took the money and left.

"I was about halfway home when you picked me up, Chief, with all that money in my pocket. Remember that, Chief? Remember how you told me Father Hatem had called you to report he had seen me running away from the church and there was money missing? Remember all the questions you asked me?

"Do you remember asking me where a kid *like me* got so much money? Do you remember ignoring me when I said Father Hatem gave it to me for food? You remember that? I do. And you had to know I was a kid living from meal to meal. But what did you do? You took me back to Father Hatem. You gave him back the money and asked if there was anything he could do to help me.

"I remember the grin he gave me when he said he was willing to keep an eye on me if I was willing to do some community service. 'Sure, that would be great,' you said. 'How about ten hours,' you said. 'Seems a bit light,' he said. 'After all, it is church money.' 'How about

twenty?' you said. 'Sounds good,' he said. My fate was sealed before
I ever got to stand in front of a judge and say what happened to me.

"Chief, I did my twenty hours . . . and more. In fact, the only thing
that stopped me from doing any more time with Father Hatem was
the fact that my mother lost her job and we ended up moving down
to Worcester. That move was a blessing for me. At least for a while.
But it got me away from Hatem."

Coupe turned and walked over to stand in front of Chief Dale.
He was diminutive compared to the chief but seemed to have grown
in size as he spoke. "Do you really want to know what that dirty old
priest did to me?'

Chief Dale looked at him.

"C'mon, Chief. You have to ask. I'm not gonna tell you unless
you beg for it."

Chief Dale screwed up his face. "Coupe, please. We want to help."

"Yeah, that sounds so good but ends so badly."

"Coupe," he said, "either you tell me what you want to tell me, or
you and me leave together and let social services sort it out."

Coupe's eyes flared, and he took a step forward. "Okay, Chief.
You got it. You sent me to that church for twenty hours of unofficial,
off-the-books community service. I'd say I spent four hours washing
the church vans and the other sixteen with Father Hatem, his hand in
my pants, or worse." Coupe was now glaring at Chief Dale. "He liked
to take me into the church. He told me he was God's messenger and I
had to do what he said. He made me stare at the pulpit while he was
at it. He is one creepy customer." Coupe turned back to the window.

"But you believed him. Didn't even listen to me. And I got
molested until my mom lost her job and we moved down to
Worcester." Coupe looked up at the ceiling, as if he was about to cry.
But he didn't—he just looked back out the window.

"Coupe, you said you saw him again yesterday. What did you
mean by that?" asked the chief.

"Mark was selling me to him for fifty bucks a pop. He showed up. He covered his face and quickly put something over my face, but it was him."

"Coupe, how did you know it was him if he covered his face?"

"He's got this weird-shaped scar on the right side of his belly, like a *J*. I saw it before. Plus he smells the same. He covered my eyes, not my nose."

"Coupe, if I were to bring charges against Father Hatem, would you testify?"

"No. Of course not."

"Why not?"

"Cause I took a nice hot shower as soon as I got here. I could not wait to get the stink off me. It would be my word against his, and I am the dirtbag kid that stole money from the church. How's that gonna play out before the judge? Nope, nothin' I can say that will stop him."

Chief Dale looked down at his feet. He felt real shame. He would have never suspected Father Hatem. Coupe glared intently at him.

"Holy shit. You've sent other kids over to him."

Chief Dale looked miserable. "Coupe, I didn't know."

"Chief, I'm only fourteen, but I've got this theory about people that seems to be pretty accurate so far. There are three types of people in the world, Chief. There are good people, there are bad people, and then there are people who simply just don't know any better. Only one of those groups is good. Guess where you are?"

Chief Dale said nothing.

"Listen, I'm damaged goods when it comes to testifying against Father Hatem," continued Coupe. "You made sure of that. I'm the kid that stole the church money. I've got a motive to lie about him. But if there are other kids you sent over there, well, you may want to talk to them. Or just stop by there unannounced once the church vans have been cleaned. Just walk in and have a look-see. You'll probably find him at work right there in front of that pulpit."

Everyone was silent. No one wanted to move. Eventually, Chief Dale stood and looked over at Everett and Evelyn. "I'll be leaving him with you, if that's okay. I'll work with social services on the paperwork."

"That's fine with us," said Everett.

Chief Dale turned to look at Coupe. "I'm sorry."

"Me too, Chief, but that doesn't make it hurt any less. Good, bad, and I didn't know any better. Only one of them is good."

Coupe turned his back on him to look out the window. Everett showed Chief Dale out of the house.

CHAPTER 5

After saying goodnight to Chief Dale, Everett came back into the living room. Coupe was still staring out the window.

"Listen, I want to thank you all for being so good to me tonight, but you do not want to take me on. I am a mess and more of a pain than you could ever manage. You will have a much happier existence without me in here messing things up."

"Why don't you give us a shot, Coupe?" said Everett.

"I am trying to do you a favor. Just let me go back down to the river. We can pretend I'm staying here."

"No! You promised me!" protested Cooper.

Everett could not remember any promise being spoken between them, but that was no longer surprising to him.

"You know you did. Admit it, now!" said Cooper forcefully.

"Okay, okay, I did, but, Cooper, you need to know . . ." He trailed off.

"Need to know what?"

Coupe seemed conflicted. Before, he was able to speak about his horrible abuse with apparent ease, but now he was struggling. Eventually he turned and addressed his comments to Cooper.

"Cooper, you need to understand. This happy-go-lucky demeanor of mine? Well, at night, it slips." Coupe sighed. "Listen, if you want to get a good night's sleep, you do not want me within half a mile of you. Sleep is tough for me. I get bad dreams. I wake up a lot. And I don't wake up quietly. Mark didn't make it any better by beating the snot out of me every time I woke up and started making noise. And I make a lot of noise." Coupe hung his head, embarrassed and obviously ashamed.

"It's okay. We'll get used to it," offered Cooper. Coupe laughed.

"Maybe. Maybe for one night, but who can get used to a kid waking up like that three or four times a night? Trust me, you will all be sleepless and hating me by next Friday. Just let me go back down to the river. I can come back up here for showers and meals. Ma'am," he added, "your grilled cheese sandwiches are awesome!"

"You're not going anywhere, Coupe, if that was your promise to Cooper," Everett said. "And now Chief Dale expects you to be here, or we will be called to answer why not. As for what happens at night, let's see. We'll put an extra bed in Cooper's room for you."

"Well, that's another problem. I don't do beds. Beds don't hold an especially positive place in my mind, and that goes back before Mark. I can't sleep on a bed. They scare me. I'm comfortable on the floor."

"Either way, we want to make you comfortable," offered Evelyn.

Coupe rolled his eyes but then relented. "Okay, but don't say I didn't warn you."

Evelyn found some blankets and put them on the floor in Cooper's room with a pillow. She worried how Coupe would impact Cooper. And what if her son got tired of having him around? How would he be able to voice that?

What she didn't know was how much about themselves the boys had revealed to each other, and how committed they already were to one another.

························

The Callisters were farm folk, so ten was a late night for them. As that hour arrived, it was time to turn in. Cooper made sure that Coupe was comfortable and then got into bed. He leaned over to look at Coupe lying on the floor next to him. He had his hands behind his head and was staring at the ceiling.

"Good night, Cooper."

"Good night, Coupe."

He rolled over to sleep. After about ten minutes, he rolled over again to look at Coupe. He worried his friend would bolt in the night, and he could not get a good sense of him. Coupe could shut him out. But he was still there, still staring at the ceiling. Cooper then fell asleep.

About an hour later Cooper started to have a bad dream. He thrashed back and forth, breathing heavily. He was locked in it and could not wake up. He was seeing horrible things, experiencing terrible, terrifying things. Then Cooper realized it was not his nightmare, but Coupe's.

Cooper woke with a start to see Coupe thrashing, just as he had been. Coupe was screaming, shouting unintelligible words, but he could not wake up. Cooper reached down and shook him. Coupe awoke gasping. He looked up and could see the fear in Cooper's face.

"Don't say I didn't warn you," said Coupe quietly, regaining his composure. He studied Cooper's face and then realized Cooper had sensed his nightmare. "You were in there, weren't you?" he asked. "Cooper, you gotta keep out of my head at night. It's not a good place."

"I don't know if I can."

"Well, you've got to." He rolled over, putting his back to Cooper. "Go back to sleep."

Cooper found it hard to do so. Coupe's nightmares were

frightening. He did not want to experience them again, and it took him some time to settle down enough to fall back to sleep.

Cooper awoke again about an hour later, but not because of any bad dream. He rolled over to check on Coupe. He was gone. So were the blankets and pillows. But Cooper could still sense Coupe and knew he had not gone far. He quickly put on his shoes and went outside. He was wondering where to look when the screaming started again. It was coming from the barn. Soon it stopped and the night was quiet again. Cooper went back in the house. He came back out about a minute later, this time with his pillow and blanket. He made his way over to the barn and climbed the stairs into the hayloft. He could make out Coupe's outline on top of the hay bales in the dim light. He climbed up next to his friend and put his pillow down next to his. Coupe woke up.

"Who's there?" said Coupe, jumping.

"It's just me. Go back to sleep."

"Cooper, you don't want to be near me when I'm sleeping. I don't want you to have to go through my dreams."

"I'll keep out of them."

"But what if you can't?"

"Let's find out. Now go to sleep."

He put his head down next to Coupe's and pulled his blanket over him. He could sense Coupe looking at him; he could sense he was trying to make up his mind. Silently, Cooper reached out and urged Coupe to sleep. Almost immediately, Coupe did so. As Cooper fell asleep he told himself not to enter Coupe's dreams.

Two hours later it happened again. Coupe thrashed about. This time, however, Cooper had not been in his dream. Cooper stretched his arm over on top of Coupe to quiet him and hold him down. He then reached into Coupe's mind and urged him to sleep, told him to sleep, that he was safe and could sleep the night through without worrying about those things that came to him. Coupe's thrashing began to subside, and he returned to a peaceful sleep. It happened once more that night, and Cooper did the same thing.

CHAPTER 6

The following morning, the boys did not wake up until Everett came up and woke them. Cooper had left a note on the table.

"So, how was the campout?" asked Everett.

Coupe stretched and sat up. "I slept good. Well, better than usual." He looked over at Cooper. "Thanks, Coop."

Down in the kitchen Evelyn had breakfast ready for them. Coupe ate well. Evelyn noticed that the bruises that had seemed so pronounced yesterday appeared to be quickly healing, very quickly in fact. His cuts were gone. Coupe had said he was a quick healer, but the speed was remarkable.

As they ate, Everett raised the issue of Coupe's mid-night move out. "Coupe, we said you were welcome in our home. Why did you go out to the barn?"

"I didn't want my shouting and such to wake you all. I felt bad for

Cooper having to put up with it. I figured moving up into the hayloft I could keep my word to you and also not disturb Cooper."

"Well, give us a shot," responded Everett. "But if you do go out to the barn, let us know."

"Sure, I understand, sir."

"You don't have to call me *sir*. You can call me Everett. *Sir* seems too formal."

"I'd prefer it."

"Okay, *sir* it is then," Everett said.

"Anyway, I'm hoping I can sleep inside tonight without so many problems. Looks like Cooper has another special talent along with super strength."

"What are you talking about?" asked Everett. Evelyn stopped to listen.

"He helped me sleep!" Coupe smiled broadly. "Like I said last night, I don't sleep too good. But Cooper somehow just got inside my head and helped me." He turned and looked at his friend. "Cooper, I said thank you before, but I don't think you understand what nights have been like for me, for as long as I can remember. I don't sleep. I mean, I nap between nightmares, but then I'm just waiting for the next one to happen and waking up again.

"Last night was the same as always. I *know* I scared you. That's why I moved to the barn. And then you came out there and I . . . I'm not sure what you did, but I slept with the first sense of comfort I have had since, well, since I can remember. Thanks, buddy."

Cooper looked up from his breakfast and just smiled, then went back to eating. Coupe did not need much more than that. He got a sense of what he was thinking. Everything was okay.

Everett noted that Coupe had mentioned Cooper's strength and wanted to address the subject.

"Coupe, you mentioned Cooper's, umm, super strength." Everett searched for the right words. "Coupe, for a very long time that is something—"

Coupe cut him off. "Oh, don't worry, sir. I won't tell anyone about it. They could pull out my fingernails and I still wouldn't say anything." Coupe actually looked at his fingernails when he spoke, which made Everett's skin prickle.

"I told you he wouldn't say anything," said Cooper between mouthfuls.

"Yeah, don't worry about me, sir. I'm good at keeping secrets. Cooper's my new buddy now! I won't say nothing. Hell, I'll keep watch for others who may be saying something and tell you. I will look after him just like he has looked after me, sir. Trust me, Team Callister is now one member stronger."

Everett smiled. He liked this kid. He did not need Cooper to tell him that he believed in him. As he though that, Cooper laughed quietly.

"What?" asked Coupe, looking around.

"Nothing, Coupe. Welcome to the family," Everett said. "Though, I have to say that Cooper may not be the only one sitting at this table with extraordinary abilities."

"I knew it. You can play the harmonica underwater, right, sir?"

Everett laughed. The kid was quick and funny. "I think you know what I mean, six-card lady. Eat up. Once you're done we should drive over to White River Junction and get you some clothes of your own."

"Really?"

"Of course."

Coupe looked like he was about to have a moment, but then quickly recovered. "Thanks," he said. "I mean, I didn't want to say anything, but the underpants Cooper gave me had some embarrassing stains and I didn't want you to think they were from me."

Cooper laughed so hard he had to spit out his food.

"Boys," said Evelyn in mock disgust.

CHAPTER 7

White River Junction was a good thirty minutes down the road. When they got to town and started filling up a cart with clothes for Coupe, Everett and Evelyn could see it was overwhelming for him. As a kid who had to survive on government peanut butter on good days and stolen peanut butter on not so good ones, he was not used to people doing things for him. Everett and Evelyn got his sizes and told him and Cooper to go play in the arcade up in the front of the store.

They played a few games, but Cooper quickly found the noise and the people too much. They ended up sitting on the bench up front usually reserved for bored or henpecked husbands. They sat quietly for a long time before either spoke, but it was a comfortable quiet.

"Cooper, I know what you did last night—at least I think I know.

You gotta know that I haven't slept that good since forever. I can sort of remember waking up as I usually do with my dreams, but then I felt as if you were there in my mind, beside me. It's like you were telling me that everything was okay, chasing everyone away. You were telling me you would keep them away and I shouldn't worry or be scared, telling me I could go back to sleep. And I did. Is that what you did?"

Cooper was quiet for a while. "I think so."

"How do you do it?"

"I don't know. I just kinda think on it and then it happens."

"When you did that, could you see what I was dreaming?"

"Only the first time. After that I kept out." Cooper paused. "I sensed Father Hatem. He's a bad man. And I sensed other stuff that really scared me. After that I kept out."

Coupe sat up straight and turned to look at Cooper. "Promise me you will always do that? Promise me? Don't go into my dreams." He paused, then added, "It's not that I have anything to hide. Hell, you know more about me now than any rational person would ever want to know. But it's no good for you in there, Coop. Promise me?"

Cooper thought back to the brief glimpse he had gotten last night. There was no way he wanted to experience any more of what Coupe had gone through every night since he was a young kid. Cooper looked back at Coupe and banged his fist on Coupe's thigh a couple of times.

Coupe looked relieved. "Thanks, Cooper."

They sat in silence again. Then Cooper asked, "Why don't you want to tell people what Father Hatem did to you?"

"Because no one would believe me. They can't get inside my dreams like you can, Cooper. Besides, he'll be dead soon anyway."

"What do you mean?"

"He's got cancer. I could smell it in his lungs when he came to see me."

They fell silent again as Cooper considered Coupe's words.

"Hey, Cooper."

"Yeah?"

"You know how you helped me sleep?"

"Yeah."

"Do you think you could do that with anybody?"

"Dunno. Why?"

"See that asshole right there?" Coupe pointed to a man standing nearby berating his girlfriend, who had just stormed off crying. "See if he is ready for a nap."

"Okay."

Cooper stared at the man for a moment. It did not take too long. Soon the man started yawning. He looked around. The bench next to Cooper and Coupe was open. The man walked over to it, yawning again. He sat down. He looked over at the boys and nodded. Coupe nodded back at him, smiling, and watched as the man closed his eyes and abruptly fell asleep.

He was still snoring loudly when Everett and Evelyn finished checking out and found them. They could not understand why the two boys were giggling.

The next stop was the shoe store. Coupe needed some sneakers and a set of work boots. Coupe kept saying he was fine with Cooper's old shoes, that they fit fine and that they should not waste any more money on him. Evelyn explained it was not a waste and that he was getting shoes whether he wanted them or not. It was not until they were in the shoe store and he was trying on shoes that she realized why he was so reluctant.

Coupe removed his shoes, exposing the deformity to his right foot. It was much worse than he let on. At the ankle his foot turned inward. It was clear he walked on the edge of his foot instead of the sole. Coupe saw Evelyn staring, and she looked embarrassed.

"It's all good, ma'am. It don't hurt and I'm still here. What's done is good and gone. I may walk a little funny but who gives a shit. Oops, sorry, ma'am."

It was clear Coupe was trying to contain his colorful language, but it was also clear that Evelyn would have to start accepting more of it. They found Coupe a pair of high-top sneakers that provided him with pretty good support for his right foot and a pair of work boots that did the same. Coupe insisted on wearing the work boots home. On the ride back, he sat looking at them with appreciation.

"I really got to thank you again for these boots," he said as he sat in the back musing. "And the sneakers too."

"You're welcome . . . for the third time," replied Everett. He looked into his rearview mirror. Coupe was staring at his feet. It was obvious he was moving his feet back and forth, enjoying the feel of his new footwear. Everett wondered, though, if there was more that could be done.

"Coupe, when did you"—he searched for the right way to put his question—"injure your foot?"

"Third week of fifth grade."

"What happened?"

"I broke it."

Everett left it alone after receiving a cautionary glance from Cooper.

"Coupe, a doctor might be able to fix that for you. Just because it was broken doesn't mean it can't be fixed."

"Thank you, sir. I'll think on that, sir."

Everett knew he was being dismissed by Coupe's response, but at least he had planted the seed.

·················

Back at home Evelyn and Everett sat on the front porch and watched the two boys as they played in the yard. First it was with the dog, then with a football, and finally they sat with Everett and Evelyn on the porch talking and laughing. The Callisters had always considered their family complete with just the three of them. But with the addition of Coupe, Cooper was showing an entirely new part of himself.

Usually they sat quietly with conversation between Everett and Evelyn and an occasional word from Cooper. But now he was more verbal. He was more outgoing. He was more willing to do things. It was easy to ascribe it all to Coupe pulling him out of his shell, but there was more to it than that.

Cooper had never had friends. Since starting school, not once had a schoolmate come over to play. Why would they? He was nonverbal, and as a result ostracized. Coupe had changed all that. He had come to Cooper's defense, even though he hardly needed defending. But Coupe could not have known that at the time. And it was as if their friendship was one that had been waiting to happen since they first met back in first grade.

Everett and Evelyn reveled in it, though a voice in the back of Evelyn's mind still made her cautious given Coupe's history. But for so long they had seen their son as a loner. He needed a friend like any child, but they knew his special qualities would likely preclude that. Then along came Coupe. On the surface certainly not the first choice as friend material. But under the surface, Coupe was showing he was made of noble metal. As the afternoon turned into evening, Everett and Evelyn found themselves sitting on the porch watching the boys with a sense of wonder and joy they did not think they could experience.

As they sat down to dinner that evening, they discussed plans for the following day.

"Normally we would go to church," said Everett. "But I'm thinking we may not be going there much anymore."

Coupe smiled. "You can go if you want. Just leave me behind."

"No, Coupe. We do things as a family. We're not going."

Coupe looked at him and smiled. "Thanks for that."

"Is there anything you want to do?"

"As a matter of fact, there is."

That was how the Callister clan ended up agreeing to take a hike down to the river behind the school. But not before Coupe spent his first real night in the Callister household. As it came time for bed, the boys went into Cooper's bedroom. Coupe was clearly getting nervous. He did not want to upset his new family.

Cooper came back into his bedroom after brushing his teeth and looked at Coupe. His gaze spoke volumes. "You're sleeping here tonight."

Coupe was noticeably upset. "I dunno, Cooper. What if it doesn't work like last night? What if I upset your parents? You know what I'm like. What if I keep *you* awake? I dunno. Cooper, I'm scared." It was the first time Cooper had seen him that way.

"Just lie down," was all Cooper said.

When Coupe did so, Cooper pushed his fist into Coupe's chest. Coupe took a deep breath as if hitting cold water and then exhaled and relaxed. He immediately fell asleep. Several times during the night Coupe appeared to be waking in a panic, but Cooper's fist was then solidly planted in Coupe's chest each time, and he immediately calmed. He awoke in the morning surprised he had been able to spend the entire night inside the house, and ready for the family hike.

CHAPTER 8

Before going to sleep, Coupe had explained why he needed to take one last trip down to his river camp. He had library books there and wanted to make sure they were returned. Given all that had happened to him over the past week, Everett and Evelyn were impressed with how responsible Coupe was, and she was curious to see how the boy had been living.

For Coupe, the trek to the campsite was an opportunity to see just how his new work boots would support his ankle. He was pleased, but still walking with a noticeable limp.

When they got to his camp Coupe invited them all into his tent. Like Cooper before them, Evelyn were surprised by how large—and neat—it was inside. She had expected that Coupe would be messy given his turbulent surroundings and threadbare clothing.

The books were stacked neatly by his hammock. She noted that they were even in alphabetical order. He had a towel hanging neatly on a line and several jars of peanut butter on a little makeshift shelf he had built out of branches.

"How long have you been living down here, Coupe?" asked Evelyn.

"Since Mark came to town? Pretty much every night I could. Mom started dating him the tail end of last year. Before that, not so much. It would depend on how much Mom was drinking or drugging, or who she was seeing, how sick of me she was. In the winter I didn't have much of a choice. It was too cold here, so I had to go home."

Coupe quickly packed everything up into a backpack they had brought for him. Evelyn noted he even packed his towel and the peanut butter. He would never be hungry again if she had anything to do with it. The last thing he packed was a blue marble. It had been on the shelf next to the books. Coupe quickly looked at it before putting it into his pocket. He did not tell them, but it was the main reason he wanted to come to the camp.

Once home, Cooper found Coupe sitting out on the porch. He sat next to him.

"School tomorrow," said Cooper.

"Yeah?"

"You know that while we're at school I probably will not talk to you."

"I kinda figured," responded Coupe. "So, same as usual?" he asked, smiling.

"No," replied Cooper. "I just can't talk at school. But you and me, we're not usual."

Coupe punched Cooper in the arm. He was surprised again by how solid his friend was. "I get it, Cooper. Hell, we can probably talk at school without even talking. You know what I mean."

"I do."

Coupe punched him again and then reached into his pocket. He pulled out the marble he had retrieved from his camp and gave it to Cooper.

"Here."

"Thanks," said Cooper, looking at it. It was a deep blue.

Coupe could sense the question in Cooper's mind and answered it before it was asked.

"Yeah, I know it's just a marble. I don't got much, but I want you to have it, and there's a good reason." Coupe paused, collecting his thoughts. "I know they call me the kid that stole the church money. I never did take that money. But I did swipe that from Father Hatem, though I don't think he ever noticed. So I guess I am a thief, but as far as I was concerned, that marble was a little bit of payback.

"I want you to have it tomorrow in school to see if it helps. It helped me. I held it in my hand when Father Hatem was . . . doing stuff. The more he hurt me, the more I stared at it. I would look deep down into it, closer and closer, deeper and deeper, until all I could see was blue. And then I would see the different hues of blues, shooting out like lines from the center. Then I would look down even deeper into those lines until all I could see was tiny spots of different shades of blue. All different shapes, all different sizes. And I would hide myself in there among all the little dots of blue that made up all the long, long lines of blue until it was safe to come back out.

"It was a tough lesson to learn, but it was a good one because now I know there is somewhere I can go where no one can get me, no one can hurt me. I know it don't make much sense, but I go inside that marble, in my head at least. Sounds stupid, but it works for me. And I was thinking maybe it can work for you in school when you get overwhelmed by all the people all around you, all pressing down, getting in your head."

Cooper looked at the little marble thoughtfully and then back up at Coupe. "I don't know if I can do that."

"There's no harm in trying, Cooper. Go on; try it now."

Cooper stared at the marble. He looked at it closely. It was a pretty shade of blue. He could see sparkles of other blues hidden in its center, but as much as he tried, he could not see what Coupe was describing. After few minutes he handed the marble back to Coupe.

"Sorry, it doesn't work for me. I wish it did."

Coupe took the marble back, looking down at the little marble in his hand and rolling it between his fingers. He stared at it intently for a few moments.

"I have an idea. I'm going to stare at it, and I want you to do whatever it is that you do when you get inside my head. Then tell me what you sense."

Cooper smiled. "Okay."

Coupe looked down at the marble in his hand. He stared at it intently. It was not long before he found himself zooming down into the details of the marble. Soon after, he felt the benign presence of Cooper in his head. He did not let it distract him. Instead, he once again found himself surrounded by blue, studying the lines of blue pigment, made of varied dots of blue in varied hues of blue. It was a peaceful place, a safe place. He remained there for a minute or two before looking away to see what Cooper had experienced.

Cooper was staring back at him with a look of wonder on his face.

"Coupe, what you did, I don't think other people can do that."

"Could you see it?" asked Coupe, excited.

"No, not see it in the sense that I was looking through your eyes. But I could sense what you were sensing. I could sense blue, spots of blues, waves of blue. But even more, I sensed calm and quiet. Wherever you were it was peaceful. I liked it. Maybe you can teach me how to do that because I think that might help me when I'm in school—or any place that gets to be too much."

"Hell, I may not have much, Cooper—a marble, a few jars of peanut butter, and until this weekend one set of clothes—but you are welcome to it. But not the peanut butter. I've got to draw the line somewhere."

Cooper laughed. This time he punched Coupe in the arm, gently, but it still hurt.

CHAPTER 9

When they arrived at school together the following morning the only person who noticed was Kevin Hannigan. And he made himself scarce in a hurry. They went to their respective classes for the day and did not see each other again until recess. Cooper went to his usual spot by the stone wall, but this time he was not alone. Coupe sat with him. They did not talk. They just sat there. Cooper stared into the woods and Coupe stared at the playing field. He saw Kevin staring back and gave him a friendly wave followed by a one-fingered salute. Kevin's face screwed up in anger, but he just looked away. He wanted nothing to do with Cooper after his last experience.

The last class of the day finally arrived. It was the only one which

Cooper and Coupe shared. As he entered, Coupe immediately felt Cooper's presence in his head. Cooper had been waiting for him but continued to just stare out of the window. They sat in class in their usual seats on opposite sides of the classroom. Coupe felt Cooper's anxiety rising as all the other students poured into the classroom before class started. He felt bad for him. He really had not realized just how much the noise bothered him. Cooper was silent despite his teacher's attempts to get him to talk. Word had gotten out that he had spoken to the kid who had stolen the church money. But Cooper did not respond verbally to anything he was asked.

....

When they got home they found Everett on the porch talking to Chief Dale. True to his word, Chief Dale had gotten Coupe's placement at the Callister home a semipermanent status. There would be further paperwork and a home visit, but for the time being, Coupe was officially part of the family.

Chief Dale also told him that he had stopped all community service with the church, though there were no kids actively assigned there. Not that it made much difference. He had learned that Father Hatem would be retiring effective immediately. Father Hatem had revealed he had terminal lung cancer.

"I'd love to hear his last confession," was all Coupe said in response. Cooper stared at him with sympathy for some time.

Coupe was pleased he was now legally part of Clan Callister.

"So, now when I screw up you get to kick my ass, right, sir?"

"Coupe, so long as you are here, no one is going to kick your ass. We never hit Cooper and we will not hit you. We might tell you what to do. And, yeah, we might hand out punishment when we have to. But you need to understand, from this day going forward no one ought to hit you, and if they do, they will answer to Evelyn and me."

Coupe was quiet for a moment, more moved than he wanted to reveal. "What if I would prefer a beating instead of whatever punishment you and your wife come up with?"

Everett laughed. "It doesn't work that way, Coupe. I mean, why would I hit you when I can get you to stack firewood instead? See what I mean?"

"But a beating is so much easier."

"Sorry, no more beatings."

"Damn."

"I'll help with the firewood," added Cooper.

"It's good to hear you speak, Cooper," added Chief Dale.

Cooper looked at him and just nodded.

"Well, I'll leave you folks now." He turned to go but then turned back to look at Coupe. "Coupe, I have thought a lot about what you said to me—you know, good, bad and doesn't know any better. I hope I am making some amends now."

Coupe smiled. "Chief, this falls into the *good* column. Thank you. Chief, one more thing."

"Yeah?"

"Where's he now?"

"He's still staying at the rectory at the church."

"What if he were to come out here?"

"I think Everett would welcome the opportunity."

Everett rested a reassuring hand on his shoulder. "Don't worry, Coupe. You're safe from Hatem now."

Cooper and Coupe sat on the porch steps watching Chief Dale leave. Everett sat behind them in a wooden rocker. Coupe started giggling.

"Okay, what's so funny?" Everett asked.

"I was just thinking of you trying to spank Cooper. I mean, how would that work? Wouldn't you have to hit him with the truck or something?"

Cooper and his dad laughed. "No, Coupe, I would never do that. I expect I would use the bucket on the tractor."

CHAPTER 10

As the end of the school year drew closer, classroom work became less of a focus as the students became more hyper with the approach of summer break. In years past, Coupe would have shared that frenzied enthusiasm. But not this year. Now he was acutely aware of its impact on Cooper. He could feel him withdrawing. He looked at him and saw him with his head down on the desk, staring desperately out the window, wishing he could be free.

One day their teacher gave them busy work and then disappeared out the door. The class quickly became loud and unruly. Cooper was outright suffering. Coupe wanted to help, so he pulled his marble out of his pocket and started to look deeply into it. Soon he was deep within the blue of his marble. He felt Cooper's presence by his side.

He could sense that Cooper was relaxing, that the tumultuous noise was being pushed back out of his head.

Cooper, on the other hand, had lifted his head off his desk to look over at Coupe. He saw Coupe staring into his hand. He felt bathed in a cool blue light that took his mind out of the chaotic classroom and allowed him to relax. It was like being taken out of the hot sun and placed into cool water.

Cooper was feeling enormous relief until Kevin Hannigan walked past Coupe and smacked the marble out of his hand. Coupe immediately came back into the classroom with a snap to hear Cooper screaming in pain, near fury in his eyes. Everyone else in the classroom was now staring at Cooper. The boy who had never spoken had made a sound, a loud and frightening sound, screaming as if he had been struck. Coupe quickly looked around the floor for the marble.

Cooper stared right at Kevin, stood up, and started walking slowly toward him. The classroom was silent, sensing confrontation. Coupe's first thought was to get up and stand in front of Cooper, but then he realized how futile it would be to attempt to stop Cooper physically. Instead, he closed his eyes and tried to communicate with Cooper's mind. But Cooper's anger overpowered him, driving everything else out. Cooper approached Kevin, who kept backing up until his back was squarely against the wall.

In desperation, Coupe stopped fighting against the anger and just let it wash into him. It was like water flowing into a submerging car. Once he had let it fill him, he was able to reach into Cooper's mind, just like opening the car's door underwater. As Cooper readied to thrash the boy in front of him, Coupe filled Cooper's mind with just one word: *NO!*

Cooper stopped. Coupe felt Cooper's anger being replaced by something else. Soon Coupe recognized what it was. *Pity.* Pity for Kevin Hannigan. Cooper felt sorry for the bully and remorse for his own response to his actions.

Cooper turned aside and bent to pick up Coupe's marble. Other than being a bit dirty, it was no worse off. He handed it back to Coupe.

"Thanks," he said.

The problem for Coupe was that in taking Cooper's anger, he still felt it, along with his own. Coupe felt that anger, and little to no pity. Kevin had been picking on Coupe for years, and his resentment of the bully ran deep. But now Coupe was not so inclined to run and hide. He was no longer alone.

Coupe put the marble in his pocket and climbed up on his desk. Kevin, who had been watching Cooper retreat with great relief, now looked over at Coupe, wondering what the crippled little twerp was up to. He did not have to wait long. Coupe launched himself from the top of his desk and onto Kevin, knocking him to the ground. Kevin tried to grab hold of him and throw him off, but Coupe was too fast. Coupe started raining down fists with incredible speed. Though he could not hit with the same ferocity with which Kevin had beaten him, he was winning on points. The assault only stopped when Cooper dragged Coupe off of him. Once he felt Cooper's iron-like grip on him, he stopped. Cooper put him back down near his desk and shook his head at him. Coupe nodded back. He looked over at Kevin, who had now propped himself up against the wall. Blood trickled from his nose. Coupe smiled as Kevin wiped the blood away.

"Welcome to the club, Hannigan," he sneered. "You just remember, from now on, whatever you do to me, you're getting it back."

It was then that the teacher came back into the room. She saw Kevin sitting on the floor staring at Coupe. It did not take her long to figure out what had happened. A flurry of voices told her. Coupe and Kevin were taken out of the classroom and sent down to the vice principal's office. Coupe had earned himself a three-day holiday.

CHAPTER 11

Everett picked him up. He had been in town at the hardware store when he got a call from Evelyn about what happened, so he went over to the school to get him. The vice principal was not unsympathetic, but he could not have kids fighting in the classroom. The police would not be called, but both boys had been sternly warned that the next time they would be.

Everett and Coupe walked out of the school together. Coupe had been allowed to stop by the library and get some books to read during his suspension. He carried out ten.

"You've only been suspended for three days, Coupe. Don't you think one or two books would be enough?"

"No, sir. I read a lot, and pretty quick too. I'm going to have three days on my hands, so this will keep me occupied."

"And you don't think I have anything planned to keep you busy?"

"I'm gonna be stacking firewood, aren't I?"

"Ayuh."

Everett looked at the titles. A couple were fiction. He saw Charles Dickens' name on one spine. But he also had a good number of science books and even one on philosophy. They all appeared to be geared toward kids, but Everett was not surprised given it was the school library.

"Do you have a library card for the public library here in town?" Everett asked.

"No, sir. I'm, uh, not welcome in there."

"Why not? I would think they'd love a bookworm like you."

"I think they did, to start. But they caught me trying to sleep in there a couple of times, and the last time I was told I could not come back." Coupe looked up at Everett a little defensively. "I wasn't stealing anything if that's what you were thinking. It's just it was wintertime and it was cold. I couldn't go down to the river then and I . . . well, I didn't want to go home either."

"I didn't think you were stealing." He paused. "Coupe, I wish I had known of you back then. We would have helped."

"I know you would have. Well, I know that now." Now it was Coupe's turn to think. "In a way it turned out to be a good thing that my mother dumped me when she did."

"I expect that's a tough thing to deal with either way, Coupe, but yeah, that's a good way to look at it, I suppose. We're happy to have you."

"Thanks."

"No more fighting though, okay? You come to me or Evelyn. You don't want to have the police involved."

"Yes, sir."

They pulled into the public library parking lot.

"C'mon, Coupe, let's see if we can get your reading privileges back."

Coupe brightened. "You think so?"

"No harm in trying," he replied as he parked.

As they approached the circulation desk a woman looked up sternly at Coupe. Before she could speak, Everett started to plead Coupe's case.

"Hi, I'm Everett Callister. I think you know this young man. I wanted to see if I could get him his library card back. You see, he's living with us now. I'm his foster dad. He told me why he was not allowed back in here. I think you should know his circumstances were pretty rough back then. But he's with us now. He's a good kid and he loves reading. Is there any way he could start borrowing books again?"

The librarian looked at Everett as if sizing him up. "Did he tell you we found him sleeping in the back of the nonfiction section, and on more than one occasion?"

"He did. It was pretty cold out. Did he tell you he had nowhere else to go?"

The librarian's face softened. "He did not." She thought for a moment. "I suppose if he is always supervised by you while he's here, he can start coming back in—on a probationary basis to start with."

"Excellent."

They left the library with a brand-new card and five more books. Coupe was positively beaming. Everett had insisted he get one on the basics of small engine repairs. He hoped Coupe might be able to help him with some farm projects.

When they arrived home Coupe placed the books inside and then immediately went to the wood pile. He was told that he would be stacking wood until Cooper got home, which would not be too long. Evelyn was getting ready to go fetch him. Roscoe came running out of the house to keep Coupe company. The dog had taken a strong liking to the new boy, and it looked like it was mutual as Coupe reached down and quickly rubbed Roscoe's ears. *Dogs always know,* thought Everett.

"No chance of a beating instead?" Coupe asked as he started stacking.

"I'm afraid not," replied Everett.

Inside the house Evelyn was not so calm once Everett had explained.

"Did we make a mistake?" she asked. "Do you think he will be a bad influence on Cooper?"

Everett just shook his head. "No, we did not make a mistake. He has already shown he is a good influence on Cooper, and the kid was just standing up for himself."

"But the school said they would call the police next time."

"Then let them! That poor kid has been picked on all his life by other kids—and adults. Today he stood up for himself. I'm thinking today is a pretty good day for him, and we are going to back him."

"That's not what I meant," replied Evelyn, somewhat mollified. "I just worry; you know I do. What if Cooper starts getting into fights?"

"You and I both know that is not going to happen. You would be better off worrying about Coupe overhearing you because that kid has ears like a deer."

As if called, Coupe came into the kitchen where they were talking.

"I'm sorry, ma'am. I would never try to get Cooper in trouble. I promise to always look out for him and I will never try to be a bad influence on him. You may not think my promise is worth much. But it is." He turned and walked back outside.

Evelyn felt terrible. "What do I do?" she asked.

"Don't worry, I'll talk with him. But you have to understand, I think he is a special kid too. Not like Cooper is with his strength and how he seems to know what's in our heads. But in other ways I haven't figured out yet. He can sure as hell hear real well. He can spot a lie a mile away. He's got real quick hands like we saw with those cards. And I am beginning to suspect he is more than just book smart. I'm thinking that if they were to test him, he would surprise everybody. Spend some one-on-one time with him, Evelyn. Talk with him. That should put your concerns to rest."

"Everett, why? First Cooper and then Coupe. Here with us. Why?"

"I don't know, but I'm going to put it down to luck for now. We are lucky to have two exceptional kids with us, and we need to be the best role models we can because, well, they are going to be special. One way or another, good or bad, they are going to be special, and we can have a lot to do with just how that works out."

Evelyn hugged her husband.

"I'll go talk to him," he said as he kissed her forehead.

Outside Coupe was stacking wood at a pretty good pace. Roscoe cocked his head to the side, looking back and forth between Coupe and Everett.

"Relax, Coupe," he said. "You're in the wood-stacking business for the long game. Take your time."

Coupe looked pained when he turned to Everett. "I'm sorry, sir," he said. "I didn't mean to upset your wife. I don't mean to be a bad influence. At least, I'm not trying to be a bad influence. But I understand if she is worried. If you want me to go, I understand."

Everett sat on a splitting stump near the wood pile. "Coupe, relax. No one is asking you to leave. No one wants you to leave. And for all legal purposes, hell, you can't leave! We're your family now, so you're stuck with us. Even when we piss you off. Even when you piss us off. That's normal in families. It doesn't mean you are owed a beating. It doesn't mean you have to leave. When things like this happen we stop and *talk* about it."

"But your wife, she seems pretty upset at me. I heard her—"

"Yeah, you *heard* her." Everett gave him a wry smile. "That's some pretty good hearing you've got there, Coupe. Maybe we should have a chat about that someday because you seem to have some special talents yourself, just like Cooper. But with hearing like that, you had better understand pretty quick that not everything you hear is meant for you to hear. Evelyn doesn't want you to leave. She just needs to understand you better.

"Listen, until a few weeks ago, it was just the three of us. That was good, but maybe it wasn't . . . complete. Cooper is a great kid, but he has always been guarded. You know he did not talk at school, but he didn't talk that much around here either. And then you came along and suddenly it's like he's a normal kid, like you two have been friends all of your lives. School is not a huge emotional ordeal for him each and every day. You are good for him, Coupe! Of that I have no doubt.

"But neither one of you is *normal*, and you know what I mean. Maybe that's why it's best that you are both out here, because you seem well suited for each other and perhaps balance each other, almost like you were supposed to."

"But the fight. And your wife?"

"You're stacking wood for that fight. But just between you and me, that peckerhead got just what he deserved. I don't think women understand that aspect of being a guy like they should. And given the way the law looks at it these days, I strongly advise you to not do it again. But a little voice in my head also tells me that you are probably not going to have problems with Kevin Hannigan anymore."

Coupe stared at his feet for a few moments and then said, "Thank you, sir."

"We talk things out here, okay, Coupe? We don't assume that someone has to leave or that they are somehow all bad for one mistake. We all make mistakes. Evelyn just made a mistake. We talk about it. Trust me. You'll see it works."

Everett walked over to the boy. He grabbed hold of him and pulled him into a hug. For a moment Coupe was startled, almost afraid, and Everett felt him tense up. But then he relaxed and his arms slowly snaked around Everett's back. "Now keep stacking wood."

· · · · · · · · · · · · · · · · · ·

When Cooper got home he immediately went out to the woodpile and started helping Coupe. They did not stop until dinnertime.

Everett started to think that he could pull in some extra money this year with that kind of help. He might need to cut more timber if Coupe kept getting into fights.

After dinner they went up to their room. Coupe lay on the floor and Cooper on his bed. Coupe thought about what had happened in school that day. Cooper knew that Coupe was thinking about what happened in school that day.

"You know you didn't have to do that," Coupe said.

"I don't know why I did," replied Cooper. "It scared me. I don't remember feeling angry like that ever before."

Coupe was silent for a while. "Was it because of me you got angry? I mean, I don't want to be a bad influence on you."

"You're not. I got angry because it was such a shock to my mind. It was like I was in a warm bath and someone threw a bucket of cold water on me when he knocked the marble out of your hand. It seems so stupid saying it, but that's what it felt like." Cooper leaned over the side of the bed and looked at Coupe. "It helps, what you do. You know that, right?"

Coupe nodded.

"It wasn't what he did. It was the shock is all."

Coupe looked up at his powerful friend. "You do know that if you had hit him, you might have killed him, right?"

"I know, but I didn't. And that wasn't the normal me."

"Cooper, I felt your anger."

"I know. I have never felt that before. But now I know what it feels like and I know how to deal with it."

"I know." Coupe wondered if Cooper would have been able to deal with it if Coupe had not been there, but then he remembered the strong sense of pity he sensed when the anger had passed.

"Cooper, once your anger passed, you really felt bad for Kevin, didn't you? Even though he is a class-A douchebag."

"I did."

"Why? I mean, he has treated me like shit ever since I first met him. I don't feel any sympathy for him at all, but it was almost shining out of you. Why?"

Cooper was quiet for quite a while. Then he said, "Coupe, I have known for a long time that I am not normal, not like other kids. My strength isn't normal. My sensing isn't normal. When I see kids like Kevin Hannigan . . . I don't know." He turned over and looked at Coupe again. "Let me ask you this. If some four-year-old kid was getting in your face and being a pain, would you beat them up?"

"No, of course not," replied Coupe. "But Kevin is not . . . Oh, I see what you mean."

Coupe had a deeper appreciation for his friend. It also made him feel smaller and inadequate. Cooper had already come to realize that his strength set him apart. It set him apart in a way that meant he had to view his classmates not as equals but as children in need of protection, even when they were having temper tantrums, like the Kevin Hannigans of the world. Striking out would be like an adult striking a baby. Coupe realized there was much more depth to Cooper Callister than he initially surmised.

"Cooper, buddy, you are one righteous dude."

Coupe slept the night through without waking, Cooper's fist planted firmly in the center of his chest each time he began to stir.

CHAPTER 12

In the morning Cooper went to school and Coupe began his first day of suspension. When Evelyn returned from taking Cooper to school, Coupe was in the living room reading but quickly retreated upstairs when he heard his foster mother. Evelyn suspected it was because of what he had overheard the day before. She felt badly about it now and knew it was up to her to make him feel welcome and accepted. She went upstairs and knocked on the bedroom door.

"Yes?"

Coupe was sitting on a blanket next to Cooper's bed with a book open in his lap. "C'mon, young man," she said. "It's chore time. Grab your shoes."

"Yes, ma'am," he replied, scurrying to get his shoes on.

She was waiting for him downstairs with keys in her hand.

"Where are we going?"

"Into town. I've got my own chores and I could use your help."

She saw him searching her face. "Yes, ma'am."

Once in the car Evelyn could sense Coupe's discomfort. "Coupe, I want to apologize to you about what I said yesterday. I've got a lot to learn about you, and I should learn not to rush to judgment. I want you to be comfortable in your new home, okay?"

"Yes, thank you, ma'am. But you should know, the more you learn about me, the more you're gonna find out I come with a, um, history. I don't mean to saddle you with that, and I'm not gonna do anything in the future, especially if it means getting Cooper in trouble. I'm sorry about what happened yesterday."

"Coupe, I want you to know I don't think you are a bad influence or going to be a bad influence. It's just new to me, and you are going to have to be patient with me, just as I am going to have to be more patient with you."

Coupe searched her face again. Then, as if on cue, he sniffed. But his face brightened, and Evelyn felt that she had somehow passed his test.

They finished their journey into town in much more comfortable silence. But Coupe became much more fidgety when Evelyn pulled the car into the supermarket parking lot.

"C'mon, Coupe. Let's get some groceries," she said, starting to get out of the truck. Coupe didn't move.

"What's wrong?"

"Um, yeah. You know how yesterday you learned how I got kicked out of the library? I'm not allowed in the grocery store, either. All part of that history I come with."

"Did you try to sleep in there too?"

"No. If I go in there, they're gonna kick me out and tell you I took stuff. And they would be right. I did take stuff. Maybe I should wait here in the truck."

"Nonsense. What did you take?"

"Mostly peanut butter. And a few pieces of beef jerky."

"Okay, let's go deal with it. C'mon."

Evelyn took Coupe into the grocery store and up to the manager's kiosk. The manager on duty was heavy-set with thick glasses. Coupe recognized him immediately. He had preferred to take stuff when he was working because he was too blind to see him and too fat to catch him. But eventually he had caught him, and was mean when he did it, too, grabbing him by the hair on the back of his head and hauling him around for everyone to see. Then he threw him out by his ear.

"Good morning, Mrs. Callister."

"Good morning, Dwight. How are you?"

"Fine." Dwight saw Coupe standing just behind her. "Hey, kid! You know you're not allowed in here. Beat it before I call the cops!"

"He came in with me, Dwight. I'm his new foster mom."

"What? You sure you want to do that, Mrs. Callister? I mean, the kid's a thief. He stole stuff out of here plenty of times." He leaned forward to whisper, but Coupe heard every word. "You know, he even stole money from the church. He'll probably thieve you blind."

"No, he won't, Dwight. He's a good kid, and I've come to pay for what he took so he can help me with my shopping. Is that okay with you?"

Dwight did not look too pleased. He gave Coupe a distrusting stare.

"Are you going to be with him whenever he comes in?"

"Either me or Everett, if that is okay with you."

"Sure, sure. I guess."

"Thank you. So, how much stuff did he steal?"

Dwight rubbed his neck and thought. "I don't really know. I suppose that he's the only one who really knows. And I'm not sure I would believe him."

"Coupe, tell Dwight what you took."

Coupe looked directly at the man. "Before you chucked me out of here by my ear when I was nine, I took fifteen jars of peanut butter and three pieces of beef jerky. That September I took three regular-sized jars. In October I took two of the large ones you had on sale on the end displays on aisle four. In November I took three more regular-sized jars. In January I took four more jars, and February I got three more. I took all of the beef jerky the day before you caught me on March 4. I also took a couple of plastic spoons off the salad bar, but those were free."

"Free for *paying* customers," snipped Dwight.

"So, how much would that all cost, Dwight?"

It was Coupe who answered. "The medium sized jars were $2.69 each, and the large ones on sale were $3.09. The beef jerky was $1.79 apiece, but you gotta add 6 percent sales tax to them, I think. So all totaled up it's $46.84, not including the spoons."

Evelyn handed Dwight two twenties and a ten. "Dwight, here's fifty dollars. Keep what's left for the spoons."

Dwight was beginning to feel a little awkward about the whole situation. "Nah, he can have the spoons. And the kid seems to have a pretty good memory. I think I remember that sale. We'll go with his numbers." He took the money from Evelyn. "Let me get you your change."

They left the store forty minutes later with a cartful of groceries. The groceries included peanut butter, both chunky and smooth. Coupe was crookedly walking on air as he pushed the cart. "Thank you, ma'am," he said as they loaded the groceries. "You went to bat for me and I won't forget it. With you and your husband, well, Cooper really lucked out."

Evelyn smiled. "Hopefully your luck has changed too, now."

"Sure feels like it."

Coupe spent the rest of his suspension either reading or working with Everett until Cooper got home. Then he would spend the rest of the day with his friend. On the morning of the second day he read the book on small engines that Everett had suggested. Everett returned home that afternoon to find two of his chainsaws laid out in pieces on the porch. He said a brief prayer for them as he walked by. Coupe looked up only to nod before returning his attention to them. Everett supposed he needed a new one anyway. They had been running kind of rough. But when he came back out about an hour later, they had both been put back together. Coupe was waiting expectantly.

"You got any oil and gas for them?"

"Ayuh."

"Then let's fire these babies up!"

Everett took them to the barn with Coupe following him excitedly. He added the gas and oil and pulled the cord on the first one. It roared as if new. He turned it off and did the same for the second one. That one took two pulls, but it sounded healthier than it had in years once it was purring. Coupe was grinning.

"You don't clean them enough!" he chided. "The carburetors were all gunked up and the spark plugs really ought to be replaced. But I cleaned them with some sandpaper and regapped them for you. I also tightened the pull starts on both of them so they will be easier to start. If you've got a file, I'll sharpen the chains."

Everett smiled at his newly minted mechanic. "Impressive, Coupe. Very impressive."

On the last day of his suspension they found an old basketball hoop in the still-good shed at the transfer station. They brought it home, painted it, and attached it to an old piece of plywood. Then they hung it on the barn above the door. By the time Cooper came home, they had been to the store and gotten a ball and net. Cooper and Coupe spent that afternoon shooting hoops.

Everett and Evelyn sat on the porch watching them play. They were both surprisingly good. Coupe was deceptively fast. But for his bum leg he would be unstoppable dribbling in. He also seemed to have a dead eye when it came to outside shots. Despite his surprising skills, Cooper had the edge, mostly because of his size advantage. Everett's jaw swung wide open when he watched his fourteen-year-old, five-foot-ten son dunk on a regulation rim with more than apparent ease. One time he had to wait until he came back down to put the ball through.

·················

School ended a few weeks later. Coupe's teachers had paid a little more attention to him once they knew his new living arrangements were long term. They noticed his new clothes. Cooper seemed to be more responsive to them as well. He did not speak, but he started to look at them when they spoke, and he was no longer alone at recess. Coupe was always with him. They sat together without speaking, and the teachers had started to notice Cooper smiling now and then.

What they did not know was that each day, Coupe was with Cooper not only during recess but now all throughout the day, just not physically. The link between the two had grown considerably stronger. If they noticed Cooper was more receptive, it was because of Coupe trying to help him, and shield him when necessary. If he could not look at his marble, he could think about it. Doing that seemed to have a positive effect on Cooper just as if he had been looking at it. Cooper had been there for Coupe when he most needed him. Coupe was returning the favor as best as he could.

CHAPTER 13

The boys were glad when summer vacation finally started. Everett and Evelyn also found themselves looking forward to it more than any school vacation in the past.

One sunny Saturday Everett was sitting on the porch going through the mail. Evelyn had gone into town to do some shopping. Two boys meant twice the amount of food. They were yet again playing basketball. Everett marveled at Coupe's ability to hit any shot from nearly anywhere, sometimes without even looking, sometimes with only one hand, sometimes from thirty or forty feet away. But he still had a hard time getting many of them past Cooper, who would routinely jump up and block them or steal them, sometimes jumping five or six or eight feet to get them. It had now become routine, but at the same time Everett was left with a feeling that what he was seeing was simply unbelievable.

The boys' report cards had come in the mail, along with the standardized tests they had both taken during the school year. He looked at Cooper's grades first. He was a solid student, getting mostly As with a few Bs. The teachers were generous in their comments about his effort and progress. His test results showed the same.

Then he looked at Coupe's grades. Coupe had gotten a B-minus in every class for every single quarter. There were no effusive comments praising Coupe, only "many missed assignments" noted repeatedly. Everett looked at his standardized test scores. In every category he had scored 80 percentile.

I know he is a lot smarter than that, thought Everett. But before he came to live with the Callisters he had missed many days of school, had no secure place to live, and spent a good deal of his time simply trying to find something to eat.

Everett decided to look at Coupe's actual tests. They had also come in the packet of records from the school. The tests were divided into eight subjects with one hundred questions for each. As Everett looked at them his eyebrows went up. Coupe had scored 80 out of 100 on each test all right. It was the way he had done it that left Everett wondering. Coupe had answered the first eighty questions in each category with a perfect score. Then left the last twenty blank. *But why?* Everett had no doubt Coupe had gotten just the score that he wanted to get.

"Car coming!" Coupe shouted.

Everett could hear nothing coming. Still, he had learned to rely on Coupe's hearing just as much as Cooper's senses. Sure enough, about a minute later Everett heard a car coming down their long driveway. It was Chief Dale.

Everett came down from the porch to greet him. "Chief, good to see you," he said, holding out his hand. The boys had stopped their game when the chief arrived. They waved and then went back to playing though not in the same manner as before.

"Looks like Single's fitting in real well out here," said Chief Dale.

"He is. And his name is Coupe," replied Everett.

"Yeah, it is. Sorry about that. How's school going for him now?"

Everett gave him a brief rundown of Coupe's progress, though he chose not to mention the fight.

"Do you mind if I speak with him, Everett?"

"What about?"

"It's about Father Hatem. He's been arrested. I want to talk to Coupe about it. Do you mind if I call him over?"

"Okay. You don't have to call him over. He's standing right behind you."

Chief Dale turned to see that Coupe had come over, like he heard his name. Cooper had come too.

"What's up, Chief?" said Coupe. "Come for another card trick?"

"No, Coupe, I know better now. How are you doing? Are you liking it out here?"

"Yeah, I like it a lot. They're good to me . . . and no shortage of peanut butter, either, so I'm eating well. I heard you mention Father Hatem?"

"Ayuh. I was talking with your foster dad here. Father Hatem has been arrested. We had the mom of another boy, younger than you, who came in to report that Father Hatem had been . . . touching him. When I talked to the boy about it, he reported a J-shaped scar, just like the one you did. After he was arrested we brought him to the station. I made him strip down, and sure enough, there was that scar. I took a photo." Chief Dale opened a folder he was holding and showed a photo to Coupe.

"Yep, that's his," said Coupe, glancing briefly at the photograph. "I thought he was dying of cancer?"

"Well, he's not dead yet, and if there is justice to be handed out, we will keep on trying. Coupe, I know you did not want to testify when it was just you, but now, well, there is another boy involved. Your testimony would corroborate his. Would you consider it?"

"Hold on there a minute, Altus. You're putting Coupe on the spot here," said Everett.

"It's okay, sir," replied Coupe. And then, "I don't expect he will live long enough to go to trial, Chief, but if he does, I will testify, so long as I get to say what happened about the church money."

"You're a brave kid, Coupe."

"One more thing, Chief. Where is he now?"

"He's over in the county jail, in Milan."

"Are you going to see him again?"

"Ayuh, I expect so. Why?"

"Give him this message from me." Coupe lifted both hands and gave the Chief a double bird to take back to Father Hatem. "Promise me you'll do it. I'm not trying to just be rude. He'll know exactly what it means. Give him that message from me when you tell him I am going to testify against him. Then look at his face. Do you promise, Chief?"

"Suppose you tell me why."

Coupe put the ball on the porch and then sat down next to it, turning to look up at the Chief.

"You sure you want to know, Chief? I mean, I'll warn you now, stories of my childhood are not exactly full of warm, welcoming hugs."

The chief nodded. "I'll hear what you have to say, Coupe. I've been doing this job for a long time now."

"Okay, Chief. You asked. I'll deliver.

Coupe paused a moment. He closed his eyes, gathering his thoughts.

"You ever see that poster where there is a mouse sitting on the ground, and out of the sky there is an eagle screaming down on him with its talons opened wide ready to grab him and rip him apart? And the mouse, knowing he is completely fucked over with no place to go, just looks up at the eagle and flips him the bird? Ever see that?"

"I don't know if I have, but you painted a pretty good picture of it for me."

"I saw it once on a poster in a store when I was a little kid. It had the definition of *defiance* written on it. I liked it as soon as I saw it. I mean, I fell in *love* with that poster. That mouse was my superhero, man. Sure, my superhero had only a few seconds to live, but he was going out with style. He was going out on his own terms. The eagle may have won, but the mouse had the last word."

Coupe paused and looked off into nothing.

"I fucking loved that mouse," he said. "Like I told you before, Chief, he liked to take me into the church, set me up in front of that big pulpit when he was at it. You ever see the pulpit in the church, Chief?" Roscoe came up from behind Cooper to curl in front of Coupe's legs.

Chief Dale thought about it a moment. He was not a regular churchgoer, but he remembered it. It was in the shape of a big brass eagle. He had a moment of realization.

"Yeah, big brass eagle. I remember it."

"Well, one time Papa Hatem finished and started telling me how that pulpit is where the word of God comes through him, like it was something holy and sacred, like *he* was something holy and sacred, and he rubs his sleeve on it to shine it a bit. Then he looks down at me. I'm flipping it the bird!" Coupe started laughing. "That really riled him. Man did he get pissed! So he hit me, 'cause that's what adults did to me, until I got here of course." He looked over at Everett and gave him a quick nod. "After he finished hitting me, I flipped it the bird again. So he hit me again. I flipped, he hit, I flipped, he hit. You get the idea.

"I mean, this was a battle I could win! I think I was only ten back then, but I had him up against a wall. I was finally beating up an adult. I loved it! He could've hit me all night long and I would still keep on flippin' the bird to that bird! So long as I was able, it was getting the double one-finger salute.

"What really got him is when I started laughing too! I mean, by then I was bleeding and I must have had blood all over my face, sitting in a pile on the ground by his feet, but it was with both birds in full salute!" Coupe made the gesture again, just for good effect, and started laughing too. It was not a healthy laugh. "At that point he could've killed me. I didn't care. I think he finally realized that. He told me to go to the bathroom and clean myself up. Then he drove me home."

The chief looked dismayed and shook his head in disgust.

"Hey, I warned you, Chief! You asked, I told. Like I said, my life is not exactly stories from the heartland. So, Chief, are you gonna deliver my message?"

Chief looked at Coupe, wondering what else the poor kid had been through, but also amazed at just how well he seemed to be dealing with it. "Yeah, Coupe, I'll deliver your message."

"You promise?"

"I promise."

"Thanks, Chief!"

"I've got another question for you."

"About what?" he asked.

"Yeah, about what, Altus?" asked Everett.

"Probably nothing, but I've got to rule Coupe out. I'm just doing my job, Everett. And if Coupe has nothing to hide, he's got nothing to hide."

"I've got nothing to hide, Chief. I haven't stolen anything since the Callisters took me in."

"We've been with him. I can vouch for that," said Everett.

"You don't have to, Dad. He hasn't done anything," added Cooper.

"That's not what I'm saying. Everybody just relax. I just want to rule Coupe out."

"Rule him out of what, Altus?" Everett pressed.

"Coupe, you lived here for a while and then you moved away. When you moved away with your mom, where did you go to?"

"Wait, Coupe, you don't have to answer that!" said Everett, moving in front of him as if to protect him from the question.

"No, sir, I'll tell him. I'll tell him where I lived, and I'll tell him that I sometimes stole food there too. If that's what it's all about, so be it. Time for me to face the music."

"No, Coupe, you keep quiet," replied Everett.

"It's a little late for that now, sir. I mean, I just made the confession." Then he turned to Chief Dale. "Chief, when I left after fourth grade my mom and me went down to Worcester. We were there for a while, then we went up to Manchester, and just before coming here we spent a good amount of time in Brattleboro."

"Did you ever live in Ohio?"

"No, Chief. I've never been out of New England so far as I know."

"How about New York, back around the first week of May?"

Coupe gave the chief a look of contempt.

"Like I said, Chief, I've never been out of New England, and so far as I know New York is not part of New England. And if you think back real hard and check your calendar, I was a little tied up back around the first week of May, Chief, so whatever it is you need to rule me out of, it couldn't have been me."

"I know, Coupe. I figured as much but I had to ask. See . . ." Chief Dale handed a surveillance photo to Coupe. Everett came over to look at it as well.

The photo was grainy and obviously from a surveillance camera. It showed the image of a young boy, say twelve or thirteen, approaching a girl about the same age.

"That photo was taken in Ohio about two years ago. The FBI released it to law enforcement to help them with a missing persons case. A girl of about twelve was last seen with this boy. She hasn't been seen since."

Coupe looked at the photo. There was an obvious similarity between him and the boy in the photo. The same age, the same build at that age, the same hair and face. But it was not him. He had never been to Ohio, if that was where the photo was taken.

"It's not me, Chief. Though I see the similarity."

The chief pulled out a second photograph, much more recent and much clearer. It was a photograph of Coupe, or could have been.

"This one was taken back in the first week of May, just outside of New York City. It was taken from a surveillance camera near where an eighteen-year-old boy disappeared from a college campus."

Coupe looked at it in shock. It was like looking at a blurry photograph of himself. He felt Everett's hand on his shoulder pulling him into his side. He felt Cooper in his head and then by his side.

"It's not me, Chief," Coupe insisted. "You know it can't be. *You know* where I was at that time!"

"I know, Coupe. But you see why I had to ask?"

"I can. But it ain't me. It couldn't be me."

"I understand, Coupe. I do. So help me rule you out. Let me take your fingerprints. I'll run them against the comps, and you'll be out of it."

Coupe stared at him with cold anger building in him.

"Really?" he said. "You come out here to ask me to testify against Father Hatem. You're my best friend talking about that. You're willing to put me on the stand under oath to prove what he did to me and the other little kid *you* let him abuse, but you won't believe me when I tell you that person in that photo is not me, *even when* you know exactly where I was and what a big part of your case against Father Hatem that would be? Really?"

Everett stepped in front of Coupe. "Altus, I think you had better go."

"I'm just doing my job, Everett."

"Wait!" said Coupe. "The first photograph, when was it taken?"

"August fourteen, two years ago," replied the chief, looking at the back of the photograph,

"Then if that is accurate, I've got some homework for you, Chief. August fourteen two years ago I was in supervised care down near Worcester, Massachusetts. My mom had disappeared and the cops had picked me up stealing food. You know what *supervised care* is to adults, Chief?"

"Ayuh, I do. Where did they hold you?"

"YDC, Cranemore. Great place if you ever get a chance to visit, Chief. They lock you in to make sure nobody from the outside can hurt you. Trouble is, they don't really care who they lock you in with.

"That's where I learned all my fancy card tricks! I also learned that the biggest kid always gets a cut, whether he helped or not. And if you don't give the cut, you get cut. So much for being safe. I went to kiddie prison for having a shit stain for a mother. You should be able to verify that pretty quick, Chief. I'm not the boy in your pictures."

Roscoe stood up in front of Coupe and quietly growled at the chief.

"I think you better go," said Everett. He was angry now, though it was usually not in his nature. "And call next time if you want to come out for a friendly visit."

Chief Dale looked at the three of them and stepped off the porch.

"You guys have a good afternoon. I was just doing what I needed to do, and I believe what Coupe has told me."

"Sure you do, Altus," replied Everett. "You just have a good afternoon somewhere else."

Once the chief drove off, Coupe sat down on the edge of the porch. He was shaken by what he had seen.

"It wasn't me," he said with pleading eyes to Everett and Cooper. Roscoe came up and licked his face.

"We know it wasn't," said Everett. "We know where you were when that picture was taken in May."

Cooper simply said, "I know it wasn't you."

"That photo . . . it looked just like me."

"But it wasn't you, okay? Some people just look alike," said Everett. "And if anyone says it is, we can prove it was not, so do not let him get in your head."

"Why did he want my fingerprints?"

"I don't know, but he's not going to get them. From now on Chief

Dale gets to speak with me and no one else, okay? Whatever he wants, you just walk away and I will deal with him."

Everett noticed Coupe visibly relax. "Thank you, sir," he said.

Cooper put his arm around him and then took him back toward the barn. Soon they were back to playing ball, but it looked like Cooper was letting him score a few more.

CHAPTER 14

When Evelyn got home Everett told her what happened. She erupted.

"I will never trust that man again. First he asks Coupe to testify, and then he is accusing him of crimes in Ohio and New York?"

"Well, he said it was to rule him out."

"You know what that meant, Everett!"

"Ayuh, I know. But we know where Coupe was in May. And I would be very surprised to find him kidnapping young girls in Ohio when he was twelve if he was being held in Massachusetts."

"How is he?"

"I think it shook him," replied Everett, looking out to where the boys were still playing ball. Whenever he could, Roscoe would run in to try to steal it. "I think we need to do something for him, a little treat maybe."

"What are you thinking?"

"He sure seems attached to Roscoe. Jeff Bronson's dog had a litter of pups a couple of months back. I know he was trying to get rid of them. I think he only had the runt left; though, I hear it is a smart little fella. Sorta makes sense in a way. Suppose I take a ride over there and see if he'll give it to me for Coupe? He would be responsible for it, and that would help take his mind off Chief Dale's questions and the whole Father Hatem ordeal."

Evelyn smiled. "I think that's a great idea. Go over to see him now."

Everett grabbed his keys and put on his cap, then left.

"Where did Dad go?" asked Cooper when the boys came in to take a break.

"Just to run some errands," she replied, smiling. "I'm going to make some cookies!" She disappeared into the kitchen, concentrating on cookies and nothing but cookies.

Evelyn had time to make the cookies and let them cool before Everett returned home. The boys were sitting at the kitchen table enjoying them with a glass of milk when Everett came into the kitchen holding something inside his shirt. Both boys looked at him with obvious interest.

"What have you got there, Everett?" his wife asked.

Everett reached into his shirt and put a fluffy white puppy on the floor. Roscoe was upon it immediately, sniffing with interest, his tail wagging wildly. The boys were not far behind, diving onto the floor to look at the new addition to the family.

"Awesome!" said Coupe, reaching out to pet it. It turned and walked into his lap. Cooper reached in and started scratching its ears, and it turned to look at him as well.

It was an adorable fluffy white pup, maybe eight, ten weeks old. If it was a runt, the rest of the litter must have been huge. Its paws were massively wide compared to the rest of its sizeable frame. As it looked up at Coupe, he noted its most remarkable feature. One of the dog's eyes was brown and the other one was blue. Jeff Bronson's dog was a Pyrenees mix. Jeff Bronson told Everett he was pretty sure the dad was a husky that lived nearby. The blue eye sure was strong evidence of that.

"Cool, look at its eyes! They're different! What's its name?" asked Coupe.

"It is a she," replied Everett. "And as for the name, well, we thought that we would leave that up to you, Coupe."

"Why me?"

"Because she's yours."

Everett and Evelyn were expecting Coupe to whoop with delight, throw his hands around the pup, hug it and, once settled, say thank you. Instead, Coupe looked panicked. Cooper felt his friend's distress. Coupe quickly pushed the puppy away, handing it to Cooper, and stood up, backing toward the door that led out of the kitchen.

"No, no, no, no!" he said with obvious agitation.

"Coupe, what's wrong?" asked Evelyn.

"You are not giving me a dog. I will *not* take that dog! That is *not* my dog! *I do not want a fucking dog!*"

Everett came forward, alarmed by Coupe's reaction. "Coupe, what's going on here?"

"Nothing!" replied Coupe, holding his head, squeezing it tight with his eyes screwed up and shut. He bent over, as if in pain, then stood up again. He was trying to regain his composure but failing. "I need to go outside for a while."

Coupe pushed open the kitchen door and burst through the screen. Everett watched as he hobbled around the corner of the house as fast as his twisted foot would take him.

"What was that?" asked Everett.

"You really hit a nerve. He was really upset, like scared upset," said Cooper. "I don't think I've sensed anything like that from him before, at least while he is awake."

"Should we go after him?" asked Evelyn.

"No. He hasn't gone far. I can still sense him. I'll let you know if he tries to take off. But he has to have some time to deal with what's going on in his head."

The family returned their attention to the new puppy. Evelyn got her a bowl of water and she happily lapped it up. The puppy was beautiful, a big fluffy ball of white with a broad chestnut patch like a saddle on her back. The eyes were near hypnotizing. For such a young pup she seemed to have an old soul as her eyes were constantly assessing and absorbing whatever and whomever she was looking at. She also kept looking at the door. Everett was not sure if she was waiting for Coupe's return or simply wanted to explore. But when they eventually heard his telltale footsteps coming back toward the house, the little pup seemed to brighten with anticipation.

Cooper was sitting on the floor with the puppy in his arms and Everett and Evelyn were sitting at the table when Coupe came back in.

He quickly looked down once he had entered the room.

"I'm sorry for doing that," he said. "I'm sorry for those words, ma'am. I guess I owe you an explanation."

"You don't owe us anything, Coupe," replied Everett, "but, as you would expect, we are curious. We thought bringing the pup home would be a nice surprise for you and get your mind off of . . . other things."

"Yeah, I see that and I thank you, I really do. But, look," he added, "I'm damaged goods; you all know that. You just don't know how I got to be so damaged."

"Coupe, you are not damaged to us," said Evelyn.

"It's nice of you to say that, ma'am, but I really am." Coupe paused to collect his thoughts. "Since I'm gonna be living here—hopefully for a long time—maybe even until I get out of school, I think I should explain. But, again, it's not a pretty story, what I'm about to tell you. If you don't want to hear it, just say so and I will understand."

No one said a word. They just looked at him expectantly. Coupe took a deep breath and looked up at the ceiling.

"When I was in fourth grade, the year I left here, my mom started dating this guy. Keith was his name. I don't remember his last name." That was a lie. Coupe remembered it very well. "He seemed okay at first, always pulled me onto his lap and talked to me when he visited with my mom. I liked that he paid attention to me, and not in a creepy way, like Father Hatem.

"Then one day he brought a present. He had gotten two little puppies for me. They were mine, he said, if I took good care of them. My mom wasn't pleased, but he was bringing money in with him, so she didn't object. They were mutts of some sort, probably collie and shepherd and lab and who knows what else. I called them Wig and Wam, because even then I had learned to build a fort away from home." Coupe looked down at the puppy in Cooper's arms. "They were great. And for two weeks I would rush home to take care of them, take them out and feed them. I'd spend the rest of the afternoon playing with them.

"Then one day I came home and Keith was there. Mom had already gone to work. He was holding the puppies. I went to take them from him, but he would only give me one. He kept Wig. I sat down and started to play with Wam. Then he told me to look at him. When I did, I watched . . . I watched him kill Wig."

Evelyn gasped, and Everett put his arm around her shoulder. On the floor Cooper put a protective arm around the new puppy as he looked inside Coupe's mind and experienced this painful memory with him.

"Keith said if I didn't do what he wanted me to do, he would kill Wam too. You can expect what he wanted, and you would be right to guess I did it. After Keith was done, he left. I took Wig out back to where my fort was behind our apartment and I buried him. I remember I sat on the ground when I was done and I cried for a real long time, holding onto Wam.

"Keith visited a lot, sometimes when my mother was there, other times when she was not. I would hide Wam whenever I could. I had Wam for maybe a month longer.

"One night Keith and my mom got into a big fight. They were both drunk and being really nasty to each other. It was clear to me their relationship was coming to an end, which would be great for me. I just had to steer clear of this last fight. I figured it was best to retreat to the fort until they were done. I grabbed Wam and made a run for it. But Keith saw me and threw a chair at me. It knocked me over and I dropped Wam. Keith saw Wam struggling to get back to me. Keith kicked him across the floor. He let out a yelp and then didn't move anymore. For once, my mom stood up for me and started screaming at him and hitting him. I did not waste the opportunity. I ran, grabbed Wam, then shot out the door.

"I tried to get Wam to breathe again. But he was gone too. So I dug another hole next to Wig and buried him too. That was the last time I ever cried, because I decided I was not going to let anyone hurt me that way again. No one and no thing was ever going to get that close to me that it could cause that much hurt if it was taken away. I did a pretty good job too, until today." Coupe looked at Everett and Evelyn.

"Ma'am, sir, what you did was a real nice thing. I know you didn't know what happened the last time I got a dog. And I also know that you would never do those things to me. I just can't get around ever owning a dog again given how badly it ended for me last time. My mind just won't let that happen to me again. I hope you understand."

Coupe now looked down at the puppy in Cooper's arms.

"But I really like the puppy and I want her to stay. If you would just oblige me with a strange request. How about you give the puppy to Cooper and I will help *him* take care of her, feed her and that sort of stuff? And also play with her and stuff like that. Is that okay?"

Everett's eyes began to water up. "Sure, Coupe, that's fine," he said.

"Thank you, sir."

Cooper opened his arms, and the puppy bounded out of them toward Coupe's feet. Coupe knelt and scooped the puppy up into his arms and held it to his face. The young puppy looked deeply into his eyes for a moment and then started licking him. Everyone in the room could see the deep appreciation that Coupe had for the little ball of fur. Cooper felt it and smiled.

"If you don't mind," said Coupe, "I'm going to do something that I haven't done since fourth grade."

With that Coupe sat down, lowered his head into the puppy's fur, and began to cry—silently at first, but then deep mournful sobs. Evelyn and Everett watched as Coupe's head bounced up and down. Cooper came over and sat next to his friend, each one sensing the other. Coupe never stopped petting the little dog in his lap and she never left. She seemed content to sit there with Coupe leaning over her, sobbing, her eyes searching out his as if to see what troubled him.

Eventually Coupe settled down and looked up with red eyes.

"Sorry for all this fuss," he said, "but I think it has been good for me."

"I think it has been, Coupe," said Everett. "You know that no one here would ever purposefully hurt that dog. But if you want Cooper to have her, and like you said, you can help care for her and play with her—*if* that's how we work this out, we're just fine with that."

He turned to his son.

"Cooper," Everett said, "I got you a new dog."

"Thanks, Dad," said Cooper as if on cue.

"What are you going to name her?" asked Everett.

"I was hoping Coupe could help me with that," he replied.

Next to him Coupe laughed a little and wiped another tear. He put an arm around his friend. He seemed to be regaining his composure and cocksure attitude.

"Naming a dog is not an easy decision, Cooper, and certainly not one to be rushed," he said, leaning back, talking as if he wanted to be sure everyone in the room could hear. "It takes time. We have to see what sort of a name would suit her, and for that we have to see just what kind of a dog she will be. So for now I suggest we just call her *Dog*."

"Makes sense to me," said Evelyn. "Now, why don't you take her outside and show her around the place."

"Good idea!" said Coupe enthusiastically, scooping up the little puppy and heading for the door. "C'mon, Cooper, I'll show you what to do with her!"

Once they were outside Evelyn buried her head in Everett's shoulder. "My God, Everett, my God!" she said. "Is the world really such a horrible place?"

Everett hugged her tight.

"Not all of it, Evelyn, not all of it. Right here is pretty good, I'd say. But there are some pretty scary pockets of hate and viciousness out there. We've just been lucky enough to steer clear of them. Coupe, well, Coupe wasn't so lucky. But his luck is changing with us, Evelyn. We'll make sure of that."

CHAPTER 15

Evelyn made a special dinner of roast chicken, mashed potatoes and corn. She knew it was Coupe's favorite—after peanut butter, that is. When they ate, Dog was sitting at his feet. Evelyn pretended not to notice when Coupe's hand disappeared underneath the table with a morsel of chicken. She had to pretend not to notice probably ten times. Everett looked at her and smiled each time. He knew she did not approve of feeding Roscoe from the table. Cooper, sensing what was going on, began to slip Roscoe pieces of chicken too. By the end of the meal all the chicken was gone and everyone in the room was full, both dogs and humans.

As Cooper and Coupe turned in for bed that night, Dog was on the floor with Coupe. Roscoe joined Cooper up on his bed in his usual spot.

"I will have to get up at least two, maybe three times to let Dog out tonight. It's part of her house-training. So, you have to let me wake up, okay?"

"Sure, I understand, Coupe," replied Cooper. He was quiet for a moment, watching Coupe on the floor, still playing with Dog.

"Coupe, the first night you were here . . ."

Coupe looked up. "Yeah?"

"You remember you woke all scared, you asked me if I had been in your head, and then you asked me not to go in there while you were sleeping?"

"Yeah?"

"I kept my promise. I didn't go in your head. But that first night before you asked me—I saw what you were dreaming. Part of it was about Keith and what he did. It scared me an awful lot. I was glad I didn't go back in your head. And then I thought that's what you relive every night, and I wondered how you could do it."

Coupe put the puppy down and looked at his friend. "Yeah, he's a regular customer in my dreams. Him and a few others. But you've helped me with that, Cooper. You've helped me a whole lot!"

"But before you met me, what did you do?"

"It was rough," Coupe said. "But today, today was something special for me. I feel like I have crossed a bridge or something. Up until today that was a drawbridge and I wasn't getting over. But now I am over it, and I hope I can raise it behind me too. So, let's see how I sleep tonight, and remember, I have to get up to let Dog out, so don't stop me!"

"I won't, Coupe."

Coupe got up, turned off the light, and returned to his place on the floor. Dog, sensing it was sleep time, stretched out next to him, putting her big puppy paws up against Coupe's side. Soon all four were asleep.

Coupe awoke twice in the night. He quietly got up, scooped up Dog, and took her outside so she could pee. He waited patiently for her to sniff for just the right spot, and perhaps follow a scent or two. Coupe could understand that. Once done, he scooped her up again and went back to bed.

Coupe slept again until he started having a nightmare. Cooper did not want him to wake up that way, so he willed his friend back to sleep and then took Dog out. When Dog returned, she curled up on the floor next the Coupe.

Cooper smiled. *My dog?* he thought. He climbed back into bed and fell asleep.

CHAPTER 16

Summer vacation seemed to fly by, both for the boys and for Everett and Evelyn. The puppy drew them closer together as a family. Everett was especially grateful for the extra help around the farm, especially when the summer crops started to come in. Without Cooper and Coupe's help, he likely would have had to hire someone. Cooper's strength was put to good use; it was like having ten men helping. During haying season, Everett would marvel at the young man. He was only fourteen, but he could stand in a hay field and toss sixty-pound bales up onto the hay truck well above his head. To him it was easy, and he seemed to enjoy it. He would work in the field shirtless and bronzed, exercising his broad shoulders with each toss. The dogs would run about, and often Cooper would laugh. Cooper had not laughed much before Coupe had arrived, but now he did.

While Coupe could not match Cooper's strength, he was just as essential around the farm. He kept all of the machinery purring. He could detect problems before they turned into something big that would stop them from working. Sometimes he could do it just by listening to an engine or a belt. When Coupe warned Everett about something, Everett would stop to check. Sure enough, he was always right.

He was no lightweight during the haying season either. Coupe would be on top of the hay truck while Everett drove, dodging those bales and stacking them together nice and tight so that they could build a tall pile to take back to the barn. On one occasion Everett had to tell them to stop and pull them down. The stack was ridiculously high and would topple on the drive back. Everett was not even sure the pile would fit under the power lines at the edge of the field leading to the road. But Coupe had assured him it was packed in a special interlocking pattern he had thought of that would hold them nice and tight. He also told him he had measured, mentally at least, and was certain they could get under the power lines. Everett was not convinced, but the worst that could happen would be them toppling over and having to be restacked, maybe a few bales lost, so he agreed to try. He was surprised yet again when Coupe was right. The bales stayed together and cleared the power lines with about two inches to spare.

Coupe had Everett rolling in laughter one hot sunny July day as they loaded and stacked the last bales of hay. Cooper was standing next to the truck after tossing the last bale up to Coupe. He had his shirt off again, and his strong bronzed frame was admirable. Everett doubted any other fourteen-year-old kids looked as muscular as Cooper. But then Cooper was special that way.

As if on cue Coupe jumped down from the top of the stack and pulled his shirt off. Coupe's tan stopped near the tops of his arms, the rest of him being fish-belly white. He stood next to Cooper and started flexing and grunting as if he were in some sort of muscle-man competition. Coupe was strong and wiry, but scrawny by comparison.

Finally, he sat down and said, "Admit defeat!"

"You win, Coupe, you win," is all Cooper said, smiling.

Once the haying was done, the corn had to come in, and Evelyn usually joined to help with that. Roscoe and Bryn would ride in the tractor with her, keeping them safe from the machinery. Bryn had earned her name perhaps two weeks after she arrived. Coupe had suggested it to Cooper, who readily agreed. Coupe said it meant vigilant, and with her blue watch eye, she always seemed to be alert to what was going on around her. It also did not hurt that her chestnut patch gave her a certain brindled look too. She grew quickly during the summer and soon was the same size as Roscoe. It was clear, though, that he was in charge.

Everett also noticed that Evelyn and Coupe grew closer over the summer. He was pleased. However, he suspected Coupe had a difficult time relating to a mother figure, given his had up and abandoned him.

Evelyn was trying to show Coupe what a good mother would do for her son. She asked after him, made sure he was well, made sure he had good food and clean clothes. She got after him if he was slow with his chores, but she always did it with a smile. She wanted to hug him, but she had not. Coupe rarely liked being touched, except of course if it was Cooper, and that was because they had a special way of relating to each other. Everett could get away with hugging him, but only every once in a while. The boy could still be aloof. Evelyn sensed there was still some distance she needed to close before he would be ready to let her hug him. She began to worry less and less about him being a bad influence on Cooper, but she still kept her eyes on them nonetheless.

Everett hoped one day Coupe would let her give him a hug, perhaps call her *mom* instead of *ma'am*. And him *dad* instead of *sir*. But Coupe had been steadfast in those labels and avoided talking on the subject.

CHAPTER 17

Coupe made one request of Everett during the summer. He asked him to drive him over to the county jail so he could see where Father Hatem was being held. Everett realized that Coupe needed to see that the evil man was behind bars and could no longer hurt him.

"I want to come too," said Cooper.

One afternoon after the work was done, Cooper, Coupe and Everett piled into the truck and took a drive over to the county jail. They stopped about ten yards from its gates. Coupe simply asked that they pull over to the side of the road. He had been sitting in the front seat. Cooper was in the back. Coupe rolled down his window to look at the jail.

It was a grim-looking place. Though it was surrounded by

cornfields and looked out upon the quiet summer countryside of Vermont's farmlands, Coupe could see the jailhouse was not a place of pleasure or a refuge for peaceful contemplation for those housed inside its walls. Its imposing brick face spoke to its solid nature, and the two high fences surrounding it ensured those inside stayed inside. On top of those fences were rolls of razor wire. The long vertical windows looking out on the world were perhaps ten inches wide. He saw light poles everywhere to illuminate the building and its grounds during the night, lest anyone try to escape. Slowly Coupe nodded in satisfaction.

"I'm okay. We can go now."

Everett started to leave and then stopped when he heard Cooper from the back seat.

"Not yet."

Surprised by the command, Everett turned around to see that Cooper had lowered his window too. He glowered at the building. Cooper was having a private moment that Coupe could not sense.

"We can go now," Cooper finally said.

CHAPTER 18

All too soon, fall was closing in, and the boys would be going back to school. But not just any school; this year they would both be freshmen at the high school. A new school with new faces. Cooper was nervous. Coupe was not. Given what he had experienced so far in his life, a new school was low on his list of worries. But he felt Cooper's anxiety like heat radiating off a woodstove.

One evening, a few days before school was to start, Evelyn found the boys having an earnest discussion in their room. Cooper was on the bed and Coupe sat on the floor with his blankets and pillows, as usual. She could see Coupe was trying to convince Cooper of something. It was odd because while some of the conversation was being spoken, it was obvious parts of it were not. She had seen the boys communicate this way before, but still it intrigued her.

"What's going on, boys?" she asked.

"I've been talking to Cooper about starting high school. He's worried about the new school and all the new people. It will be bigger than the middle school, so that's a lot more voices. But I was telling him we have all the same classes as freshmen, so I'll be with him all day. And maybe this year is the year Cooper can see if he can talk while at school. I think he can do it, and I'll help him, but only if he wants me to."

"Well, Cooper, what do you think?" Evelyn asked.

"I dunno," he said, slowly. "I would like to do it, but I'm not sure I can."

"If you can, that would be great. If not, well, when you're ready, it will happen," replied Evelyn.

"That's what I've been saying to him!" said Coupe. "He can at least start off by trying to talk to me. Then see if he can talk to a teacher, then maybe another kid later."

"Then what happens if I can talk to some people but not to others? They'll think I'm being rude."

"They'll think you're being Cooper," replied Coupe. "Everyone knows you don't talk at school, so if it starts out slowly, I think they'll figure out why. And if they think you are rude, who cares? If you want to, you can write out a little card that says *Sorry! Can't talk right now.*"

Cooper laughed. "Okay," he said. "We'll see what happens in school."

Evelyn smiled and thought how wonderful it would be if it happened. Once again Cooper looked at her and smiled. He was reading her thoughts again.

"I know you want me to do it, Mom. I will if I can," he said

"And if you don't, everything will be fine just the same," she said.

· · · · · · · · · · · · · · · · · · ·

The first day of high school was hectic. The freshmen gathered for a large assembly. Cooper had to leave. The noise and chaos in the auditorium was sensory overload. Coupe found him in the bathroom.

"I got the handouts, so I know where we're going," he said. "I'll come get you when it's over."

Cooper nodded. Coupe left and went back to the assembly. Cooper leaned up against the sink and looked at himself in the mirror. He was not happy with what he saw. He had wanted to start off this new school year by controlling what got into his head. He knew he was getting better at it. He also knew that Coupe was a big part of that, but he wanted to be able to do it himself too. He wanted to talk. He wanted to be seen as normal by all the other kids.

The door opened, and three upperclassmen entered talking and joking. Cooper decided to leave and find someplace else to hide out until the assembly was over. As he tried to leave, the boy in the lead stepped in front of him. Cooper could sense he was not overly mean, but he was looking to have some fun.

"Look what we got here, guys—a lost frosh! Where you goin', kid? You need some directions back to your class?"

Cooper said nothing. He just tried to maneuver around them. But they lined up tight and would not let him pass, grinning mischievously.

"Are you ignoring me? You should know it's not allowed to come into the bathrooms during class unless you have a pass. Do you got a pass?"

Cooper looked away and tried to walk around the senior, but the kid pushed him backward, or rather, Cooper let the kid push him backward. He did not want his first day of high school to be about all the other students learning that some freakishly strong kid knocked over three upperclassmen in the bathroom. The kid pushed him again.

"Answer me, frosh."

Cooper stared at him, silently. The kid pushed him again.

"What? You think I'm not worth talking to?"

The kid pushed him up against the wall and held him there. He gave Cooper a shove with both of his fists. Just then, the senior fell to the ground. Coupe, sensing his friend's distress, had stormed into the bathroom, shoved the other two upper-classmen aside, and kicked the backs of the knees of the boy threatening Cooper.

"You think you're some sort of tough guy?" asked Coupe.

"Grab him!" the kid shouted to his buddies. The two other kids grabbed hold of Coupe and tossed him against the opposite wall and held him there.

"Looks like you need some special freshman initiation. First, you don't go around hitting upperclassmen, because we hit back!" The kid snapped out a punch and hit Coupe squarely in the mouth, which filled with blood.

"How's my fist taste, frosh?"

Coupe spat a mouth full of blood onto the floor, then said, "Just like your ma's tit! What have you been doing with that hand?"

One of the other kids laughed, but it earned Coupe another shot to the face. The kid grabbed Coupe's chin to hit him again when a loud voice commanded from behind him.

"Leave him alone!" shouted Cooper, now standing directly behind the kid who had been hitting Coupe. He said it again, quieter and slower. "Leave him alone."

The kid wheeled on him. "Oh, so now you're gonna talk?" He grabbed Cooper's shirt and went to push Cooper back into the wall, but this time Cooper did not move. He did not even budge. The kid was surprised. It was like he had pushed into the wall itself rather than the kid standing in front of him.

Cooper did not want to fight him; he was not going to fight him, or anyone else. He simply wanted them to stop and go away. And he tried to make them leave in a different way. Cooper concentrated on the other boy and then sent a mental spike into his head: *GO AWAY!* The boy looked momentarily confused, but then let go of Cooper's shirt and turned to his friends.

"C'mon, let's get out of here. We can use the bathroom upstairs." He turned to Coupe. "You're on my list, punk!"

Coupe fell to the ground when he was released. "Yeah, yeah, I'm on your list. Say hi to your mother for me!"

That comment earned him a kick as the boy quickly turned around to put his laces across Coupe's face, but Coupe saw it coming and the kid mostly missed. Then they were gone.

Cooper went over to the sink and grabbed some paper towels. He wet them and walked them over to Coupe, who was still sitting on the floor, his face bloodied. But he was smiling as Cooper came over to him.

"You did it!" he said, taking the paper towels from Cooper.

"What?"

"You don't even realize it, do you? You just spoke in school, Cooper! You did it! When push came to shove, literally, you did it. You spoke to someone other than me or your parents. Congratulations, buddy! This is a big day! We should get you a cake or something. Do you wanna skip? Go cake shopping?"

It was only now dawning on Cooper that he had spoken. He started to smile as he picked his buddy up off the floor.

"You need to get cleaned up. There's blood all over your shirt."

"That will rinse out with some cold water, and it will be fine once it dries."

Coupe took off his shirt and started to spot wash where his blood had stained it. It was obvious he had done it before. Soon he had the stains out and he put his shirt back on.

"So, care to tell me how you got that guy to turn around and leave so quickly? You didn't throw him across the floor like you did with Kevin Hannigan."

"I just told him in my mind he should go, and he did."

"*The force is strong in this one!*" said Coupe. "Seriously, that is impressive. If you are getting to that level of doing stuff, wow. I mean, it's one thing to put people to sleep, but to get them to do what you want. Use that wisely, my friend, and absolutely do not abuse it."

"What? How could I abuse it? Oh, no, I wouldn't do anything like that, Coupe. You know me."

"Yeah, I know. But wow, that's a lot of power. Hey, do me a favor. Try to make me do something, right now. I want to see if it would work on me."

"Like what?"

"I dunno. Pick something, and I don't want to know what it is."

Cooper thought for a moment and then said, "Okay." He stared at Coupe.

Coupe concentrated and said, "Oh wow, that's weird. It's not like when we usually sense each other at all. It's like I have an overwhelming urge to . . . tie my shoes! It's like needing to scratch an itch real bad! Is that you, Cooper?"

Cooper smiled. "Yeah."

"Wow, that is like nothing you have ever done before. Now do it just as hard as you did it to Mama Tit Boy. I wanna see what he got."

Cooper's smile disappeared. "No."

"C'mon, Cooper, this is friggin' science! *Do it*!"

Cooper thought for a moment and then looked hard at Coupe. Coupe's eyes opened wide. He seemed to be struggling for a few seconds and then dropped down to one knee and began to tie one of his shoes, even though it was not untied. Cooper quickly stopped.

"No, Coupe, stop! It was just me!" He grabbed hold of Coupe and pulled him back up to his feet. Coupe shook his head as if to clear it. He then looked up at Cooper, whose big blue eyes were staring at him with nothing but concern. Coupe put his hands on his shoulders and stared back.

"Cooper, use that wisely, do you hear me? What you can do there can make you a hero or it can make you a hound. Do you understand? You could do so much to help other people with that or you could be another Keith. Your choice, and you will need to make that choice each and every time you decide to do that. Do you hear me?"

Before Cooper could answer, Coupe's hand swung out with alarming speed and slapped Cooper in the face. "I will never do that again, but I wanted to make sure you heard me. Did you?"

Cooper's hand came up to his cheek where Coupe's hand had landed. It had not hurt him, but it came as a shock. "Yeah, Coupe, I heard you. You didn't have to hit me to make me hear you. I would never do it for . . . for bad."

"And that's why I hit you. Every time you ever think of using it, I want you to think back to you and me, here, today, in a stinky boys' bathroom. And I want you to remember that I hit my best friend in the world, and the only reason I hit the best friend I ever had, hell, the only friend I have ever had—screw it, the kid I consider to be my brother. The only reason I hit you is I want you to think back to this day and this warning each and every time you do that."

"I understand, Coupe. But you didn't have to hit me."

"I think I did. So, are we good, or are you going to crush me up against the wall and then make me tie myself to a toilet?"

"No, Coupe, we are good, and I would never do those things to you. And, Coupe, I think of you like a brother too. We're connected. I don't understand why, but we are."

"You and me against the world, bro. Fist bump it out, but not too hard."

Coupe held up his fist and Cooper hit it lightly.

CHAPTER 19

With Coupe's presence inside his head, Cooper said "hello" to each of his teachers that he met and "thank you" when they handed him class schedules and assignments. The students that had grown up with Cooper and heard him speak for the first time were shocked. Several of his female classmates thought his voice was "just dreamy." Cooper sensed the positive energy, which seemed to calm him even more. He also felt assured that Coupe was there with the cool blue light.

When they got in the truck that afternoon with Evelyn, they were both all smiles, albeit in Coupe's case a bit battered.

"Cooper spoke in school today!" Coupe shouted from the back seat as she drove away.

Evelyn immediately hit the brakes and pulled over. "No?" is all she could say.

"Yes!" came Coupe's playful response from behind her. She looked over at Cooper, who was in the passenger seat, smiling bashfully into his lap, slowly nodding.

"So, tell me what happened?" she asked.

"I was hiding in the bathroom when three boys came in and started being mean to me. Coupe came in to get them off of me and they started punching him and I told them to leave him alone. So they did."

Evelyn knew there had to be *much* more to this story, but at this point she had to congratulate her son.

"Cooper, that is great! It's one small step, and each time you take it, it will get easier and easier."

"It did!" shouted Coupe. "Tell her, Cooper! Tell your mom!"

"What happened?"

"I said 'hello' and 'thank you' to my teachers."

Evelyn started clapping. "Cooper, that is wonderful! I am so proud of you. Your first day of high school has been a first day of many firsts!" She leaned over and gave him a hug. In the back seat, Coupe leaned away.

At home the story was repeated for Everett. He was just as happy to hear his son had experienced such a successful day in school, but he had many questions.

Later that night he caught Coupe out on the porch reading. Lately Everett had noticed Coupe reading books on ancient philosophy. Everett had never had any interest in such subjects, while Coupe seemed to be eating it up; but then, he absorbed everything he read. Right now Everett was impressed to see he was reading a book by Aristotle. Bryn was curled up at his feet. Each day she seemed to get bigger. As he came out, he felt her eyes upon him, though her head did not move. He sat down in his rocker next to Coupe.

"So, Coupe, this fight, what's the whole story?"

Coupe put his book down and looked up at Everett. "The freshman assembly was too much for Cooper. He bolted and I went after him. I found him in the bathroom and told him to hang tight. I would get all the scheduling stuff for both of us. I wasn't back there more than a minute when I felt Cooper starting to lose it. I mean, his stress just spiked, so I ran back up there to find three guys picking on him. One of them had him up against the wall. Cooper did nothing that gave himself away. He let them push him around. But he was stressed, and I did not know how much longer he would be able to keep it together. The guy picking on him was your typical douchebag bully, so I tried to take him out at the knees. But he had friends, so I got thrown up against another wall and then the festivities began."

"Meaning they started to beat you up?"

"Yeah, same shit—different day. I'm happy to take one for the team, and I told, or communicated, with Cooper to head on out. But he didn't. Instead he spoke. He spoke for me. He stood up for me and he told them to leave me alone. And they did."

Coupe left out the part about Cooper's apparent ability to control the actions of others. It was obvious that Everett noted something was missing, but he was not going to push for it.

"You know what I take away from that story, Coupe?"

"What, sir?"

"That you would do anything to help Cooper, and you did, taking another beating to help him."

Coupe smiled and looked away. "He would do the same for me, sir."

"You and I both know he could not if he wanted to keep his special talents quiet."

"He can do other things to help me."

Everett leaned forward. He was pretty sure that was the missing part of the story. "What? What other things can he do?"

"He looked out for me, sir. Just as much as I look out for him. It's mutual, sir."

Everett tried to get a good look at his face, but Coupe would not look up at him.

"I'm not getting the whole truth from you, Coupe. Normally I would be annoyed by that. I am not going to push, but I do hope one day you will trust me enough to tell me everything that's going on."

"Yes, sir," said Coupe. "I will leave it at that for right now, other than to say I will always have Cooper's back."

Everett felt a moment of frustration. "Coupe, is there some reason you do not trust me with everything that's going on?"

"I trust you a lot, sir. More than any man I ever have. But I trust you with what I think you will understand."

"You don't think you might try trusting me to see if I understand?"

"It's not your typical teenage stuff, if you know what I mean." Coupe thought for a moment, trying to decide whether he should say what he was thinking. He decided that he would. "Sir, I think that Cooper is going to need someone by his side giving him support and advice on things that no person has ever had to consider before. I'm gonna do my best to do that for him."

"And you don't think I have anything to contribute to that conversation?"

"Sir, with all due respect, and please believe me, I have a lot of respect for you, but I don't think you could even understand that conversation."

Coupe gathered up his books and went back into the house.

As Everett watched him leave, he had to reluctantly agree that Coupe was probably right. They were in uncharted waters about which he could only guess. It pained him to see the boys go it alone. He was, however, glad that Cooper was no longer alone in those waters.

CHAPTER 20

October meant apples for the Callisters. As farmers, their calendars were dedicated to the crops, and October meant apples. Everett, Evelyn, Cooper, Coupe, and the two dogs were spending the day picking apples from a small apple orchard they had on the farm. The path that led to it wound around the back of the farmhouse and through a few gated fields to a well-seasoned hilltop orchard of about five acres. Evelyn would use many of them for cooking. Others would be stored in the basement, for they kept well. They could also sell them at the farmer's market. Everett took the bruised ones and made a large barrel of cider that he enjoyed throughout the year. He would also allow some to remain to fall later in the year, usually about when deer season started.

Coupe was by far the quickest picker. His hands were a blur as he went up and down the branches. He would scale the tree to get those out of reach. He left the ones that were highest for Everett to get with a pole picker. He did not want to leave them, but Everett insisted that Cooper stop throwing Coupe up into the air so he could pick the high apples and then catching him as he came back down. Everett had to admit that it was impressive, especially when Coupe started adding in twists and somersaults. Still, accidents did happen, even with extra-talented kids, so he put a firm stop to it.

That many apples meant a lot of time picking, so the family dedicated the weekend to bringing in as many as they could. They did not return for lunch. Evelyn had packed a hamper, and they stopped at noontime to have sandwiches. The October air was crisp, just like the apples they were picking, but as a family they were warm sitting on a blanket next to a stone wall where the October sunshine gave them a little heat.

Coupe heard a car approach while they were eating their lunch. It was Chief Dale. Everett stood in front of Coupe as the car pulled to a stop.

"Chief," said Everett.

"Hello, Everett," he said, extending his hand. Everett took it but looked back unsmiling. "I know you asked me to call the next time I was going to come out here. I did try, but there was no answer, so I drove out to see if you were outside working. Then I saw your tire tracks leading back behind the house and followed them out here. I'm not here to ask any questions, Everett, just share news with you."

Coupe and the family stood behind Everett, listening. Bryn walked over to Chief Dale and stood just out of reach, giving him the watch eye.

"Is that one of Bronson's puppies? She's a big one!" Bryn had continued to grow rapidly and was now larger than Roscoe, much larger. He tried to reach over and pet her, but she slowly moved back out of reach, keeping her eyes on him.

"What do you want to talk with us about, Chief?"

"Father Hatem. He died last night over at the county jail."

"So, Coupe will not have to testify?"

"No need now. But that is not all I came to tell you. He called a priest out to the jail to hear his last confession yesterday. He also invited me to listen to that confession." The chief then looked at Coupe.

"Coupe, when you and I last spoke you had asked me to give him your message." The chief held up his hands in a double one-finger salute. "I kept my promise and I delivered it to him shortly after I left you last time. Coupe, when I told him you were going to testify and said I had a message from you, he looked at me. I gave him the double bird, and it was like I had punched him in the gut. He just sat back and put his head in his hands. I left him that way and didn't see him again until yesterday.

"You were not the only boy he hurt, Coupe. But there won't be any more now. Coupe, he told me the whole story about the church money. He told me he had used the same con in other parishes he had been assigned to. He told me he always looked for kids like you out there living on the fringe. 'Easy targets' he said."

The chief shook his head in disgust.

"Coupe, he confirmed everything you had told me, and more. He told me about the others, too. I am going to see the ones that I know about around here. But you were my first stop. I will put out the word that you did not steal the church money, but the rest of it will come out too. I wanted to know how you felt about it."

Coupe did not hesitate. "Tell anyone who will listen, Chief. Tell them that I did not steal that money; tell them what he did."

"Coupe, I know you have always been upset about that label, but if it all comes out, then . . . the other kids at high school . . . I know sometimes they can be mean. They may start teasing you about, well, about the other stuff too."

"Let 'em, Chief! I know how to deal with smart-mouth kids. I am one, remember? Hell, I didn't do those things; they were done to me! I'm not gonna wear any shame just because that twisted old man picked me as one of his *easy targets* when I was a helpless little kid. That's on him, not me. And you are right. I have always hated that label, so I would like to get rid of it, if you don't mind. It may not be much of a name, but it's mine. I own it and I want it back. I don't care who you tell. I'm standing here, the truth came out, and he's dead. I win."

With that, Coupe fired off a double-fisted single-finger salute up into the sky and walked away.

They all watched as he hobbled down amongst the trees. They knew to give him his space. Only Bryn followed after him. Cooper thought back to that day they had gone out to the jail. His face hid a look of secret satisfaction.

"I hope he's going to be okay," said the chief.

"He will be, Altus. It's good news for him, but I think it will take some time to settle in." Everett handed the chief an apple. "Thanks for coming out to tell us."

"No problem."

The chief got back into his car and drove away. Everett, Evelyn and Cooper went back to picking apples. Evelyn looked at Cooper as they worked, and once again he sensed her concerns.

"He's still here. He's fine," Cooper said, unprompted. "He's just taking it all in, is all. He'll be back when he's ready." He turned and looked at his mother. "I know you want to hug him, but don't. He's not ready for that."

Cooper was right. Coupe came wandering back in about half an hour later. He was quiet but looked content, like a weight had been taken from him. He went back to picking without saying anything.

"You okay?" Everett asked.

"I'm good, sir, thank you. That had been bothering me for a long time. Now it's gone. So, yeah, I'm good."

Everett just smiled, and they all turned back to their day's work.

CHAPTER 21

Word got around quickly about Father Hatem's death, and even more so about his confession. Back at school Coupe noticed that the teachers who had always eyed him with a little suspicion now appeared to be sympathetic. Most of the kids were good about it too. Cooper got a sense of what they were feeling and shared it with Coupe. *Most* kids, that was.

Cooper and Coupe were having lunch together in the cafeteria a few weeks after the news got out. Everything was fine when they sat, but soon Coupe could see that Cooper was getting upset.

"What's wrong?" asked Coupe.

"Some people aren't nice, Coupe. They're thinking mean things about you."

"Oh yeah? So let 'em."

"But it's not nice!"

"Cooper, you are not the thought police. People are entitled to have their thoughts, good and bad."

Just then, a group of boys, including the one that had punched Coupe on the first day of school, laughed while looking over at him. Cooper was getting more annoyed, and he would not let Coupe inside his head.

Coupe took a deep breath. "Hey, Cooper," he said quietly. "You've got a pretty special gift there, what with being able to sense what's going on in peoples' heads and all. But if you can't handle the bad stuff, the annoying stuff, the ugly stuff when you find it, you better just stop using it altogether. Now get out of his head!"

Cooper looked down at the table and took a deep breath. "I know you're right. Usually it doesn't bother me, but you've been through enough. You don't need that asshole piling on."

"Woah, easy on the language, big guy. Your mother will think I'm teaching you bad habits."

Cooper looked over at the group of boys. They were clearing up. Cooper scowled.

"He's gonna come over here," Cooper whispered.

"So let him."

"I can make him go away."

"Is he coming over here to hit me?"

"No, he's just coming over to give you a hard time."

"So let him. You can't punish people for having bad thoughts, Cooper. We'll just use our words, okay?"

As if on cue the kid came up behind him.

"Hey, Single! Sorry to hear about your boyfriend, but I bet you'll find someone new real quick, if you haven't already!" He shot a look at Cooper as he finished.

All the boys laughed.

"You're right, I already have, thanks!" replied Coupe. "Tell your ma I'll be a little late tonight!"

The boys laughed at the bully. He scowled and walked away.

"That guy really doesn't like your-mama jokes," Coupe said. "Low-hanging fruit I know, but I'll take it every time."

"I don't think he's done with you."

"Probably never will be, but hey, maybe we'll turn it around and become lifelong friends."

"What if he corners you and wants to beat you up?"

"If that happens *and* I can't handle it, you can think him away, but otherwise, save that stuff for special occasions, okay? It's powerful, and you need to realize that."

"Yeah, I know."

"I'm not sure you do, not enough at least. Remember what *you* taught *me*. They may seem big and grown up, but to you they're just four-year-olds doing what four-year-olds do. Remember that?"

Cooper took a bite out of his sandwich. Coupe could see Cooper was annoyed.

"Hey, Cooper. Lighten up. It's just me and you here, talking, like we're supposed to, like your dad taught me to when things need saying."

Coupe sensed his friend was easing up. "Good. I thought I was gonna have to hit you again there. Or put you in a headlock and give you a clownie. In front of all these people too. Imagine them all seeing you cry. What would that do for your rep?" Coupe winked at him and took another bite out of his sandwich. Cooper laughed and went back to eating his lunch.

CHAPTER 22

Home life at the Callister farm fell into a comfortable routine. The confession of Father Hatem was a turning point for Coupe. He was more relaxed around Everett and Evelynn. Cooper noticed that he had started sleeping all the way through the night without any help from him.

Cooper celebrated his fifteenth birthday on November 15, and since no one was really sure of Coupe's birthday, they celebrated as if it were his too. It was only the four of them, but they had a cake and some small gifts.

Coupe *really* enjoyed it. His face was animated, and he laughed and sang as loud as he could, leaning on Cooper with his arm around him even though the cake was for him too. Afterward he said it was the best birthday party he ever had. Evelyn chided him, saying it was just a simple thing, but Coupe insisted. He knew for a fact it was the best birthday party he ever had. It was the only birthday party he had ever had.

School also became easier for them. They were not exactly the popular kids, but they were certainly looked at in a different light, especially Coupe.

The weekend before Thanksgiving, Everett and Evelyn were sitting around the kitchen table. The two boys came in from playing ball wearing wide smiles. Everett had begun to notice that Coupe made eye contact and smiled longer.

"Good game, boys?"

"Yeah, Dad, I won," said Cooper.

"I let him win, sir. I saw he was going to cry, so I thought it was the right thing to do."

Coupe still persisted in calling him *sir*. Everett thought it was worth taking another shot at getting rid of that.

"That's good of you, Coupe. Say, Coupe, you've been here going on seven months now. Any chance you're ready to let go of the *sir* yet? It's just so formal."

Coupe usually would shut this conversation down right away. But this time he did not. "I don't know what else to call you. I can't call you *Everett*. That would be weird."

"How about *Dad*?" Coupe silently stared back at him, studying his face, then a quiet sniff. "I wouldn't mind it," Everett continued. "In fact, I think I would kind of like it. And I don't think Cooper would mind; would you, Cooper?"

"No, I don't mind. I think of Coupe as a brother anyway."

Coupe thought about it a moment longer but then shook his head. "You know, I never knew who my dad was, but he has to be out there somewhere. I have to save it for him. I mean, he is my biological dad, whoever he is. I mean, it's different for you and Cooper because you are his dad, so it makes sense. That's why it makes sense for me to wait, in case I ever find out who my dad is."

"If that was the way it worked, I wouldn't be able to call Everett 'Dad' either," Cooper interrupted. Coupe looked confused.

"Wait? What?" he asked.

"I mean, I think of him as my dad because he's all I've ever known, so he is my dad. But my mom and Everett didn't meet until I was about a year old."

"Really? Is that true, sir?"

"It is," replied Everett, smiling. "So, it's all the more reason for you to consider using it too. We're just one big blended family here."

"Wow," said Coupe, amazed. "How did I not pick up on that?"

"Like I said, 'cause I only think of him as my dad."

Evelyn had been sitting quietly but began to fidget.

"But haven't you ever wondered who your real . . . I mean, your biological dad is?"

"Not really. It's always been Everett. And Mom doesn't talk about it. She doesn't even like to think about it."

"That's right," said Evelyn, "because Everett *is* Cooper's dad and always will be."

"But what if Cooper wanted to know? Would you tell him?" asked Coupe.

"The answer would be *Everett*," she replied.

"Yeah, if you wanted to end the conversation it would be. But that's not an answer to the question. I mean, I thought we talked things out here—right, sir?"

Everett recognized his owns words coming back at him, but he also sensed that the conversation was going sideways. Evelyn had never even told *him* who Cooper's birth father was; he knew not to press it.

"Let it go, Coupe. That's a conversation for another day," Everett said, but Coupe had turned back to Evelyn and was studying her face.

"Coupe! Stop that right now!" she ordered.

But Coupe had fixed on Evelyn. Everett saw what he was doing, the way his eyes were darting all over Evelyn's face as he struggled to read her. Coupe sniffed, interpreting everything he had just seen and heard and intuiting out the truth.

"Holy shit!" said Coupe involuntarily. "He's—"

Coupe never finished the sentence. Evelyn jumped from her seat at the table and slapped him across the face. "Just stop!" she shouted at him. "Don't you say another word!"

It was not much of a slap, really. But it might as well have been a bat across Coupe's face. His hand shot up to his cheek. He immediately began backing up with his mouth open, eyes wide with shock.

"No ma'am, not another word!" he said, then turned and fled out the kitchen door and into the yard. Bryn scampered after him, barking.

Cooper looked at his parents, not knowing what to say or do. He had never seen his mother act violently. She had never struck him. He also had never felt such panic in her before. He did not know what to do.

"Evelyn!" said Everett in obvious anger. "Why did you hit him? Why? He's had more than his fair share of that in his life. He should not get it here. He *will not* get that here! The poor kid has been through too much already!"

Evelyn put her head in her hands and sighed as she sat back down at the table. "I know, I know. I don't know why I did it . . . it's just that—"

Cooper finished her sentence. "It's just that you didn't give birth to me, did you, Mom?"

Evelyn looked up, her eyes filled with tears. She hesitated for a moment and then said, "No, Cooper, no I didn't. But I'm still your mother!" She began sobbing.

Cooper came over and knelt next to his mother. He put his arms around her and gave her a hug.

"Of course you are, Mom. It's always going to be you. But can you at least tell me where I came from?"

She paused for a moment and looked deeply into his innocent blue eyes. He stared back at her in expectation. She took a deep breath.

"I adopted you, Cooper. When I was a young woman I learned that I couldn't have children. I was devastated by the news. More than anything else in the world I wanted to be a mom. I wanted to have a child of my own. I wanted to raise that child and guide them into adulthood, just like I have done with you. So I applied to adopt a child.

"It wasn't easy. Single moms are not prime candidates, and I was turned down so many times that I wanted to give up. But I didn't. I started including a letter with each application along with all the paperwork they wanted. It was a letter to my child, about how much I wanted to love them and help them grow up. It was about how wonderful their life would be with me. Still I got rejection after rejection. It broke my heart each time.

"Finally, my prayers were answered. I was accepted! And just a few months later I met you, not more than a week or two old.

"One of the conditions about the adoption was that I was not allowed to know anything about the birth parents. In fact, your birth certificate was delivered to me with my name on it as the biological mother. I thought that was wonderful too. I would never have to go through the awkward conversation we are having now. I convinced myself that I actually was your mom.

"I never wanted and never expected to have this conversation, but then Coupe . . . You know how well he can read people. I saw him looking at me, looking at my eyes, my face. And then he sniffed. *He knew!* And I was afraid he would blurt it out, but I didn't want you to know.

"I acted awfully. I thought my slap would stop him, stop this conversation. It was a mistake. I wasn't thinking. I just panicked!" She stopped looking at Cooper and looked over to the door through which Coupe had fled. "I need to apologize. Right now. I need to explain it to him and hope he will forgive me. You're right, Everett. I hit the one boy in the world that I could possibly do the most damage to with a single slap. I feel awful. We must find him."

Evelyn stood. They heard Bryn barking outside, so she knew he could not have gone too far, but then Cooper tensed up and looked alarmed.

"He's not here. He's gone. I mean, I can't sense him nearby."

"But I can hear the dog," said Everett.

"I know, it doesn't make sense. We need to find him," he said, rushing out of the house.

They found Bryn in the barn. Coupe had locked her in there, but he was nowhere to be found. The three of them looked all around, calling out his name, but there was no response.

"Do you think we should go check down by the river?" asked Everett.

"It's the only other place I can think of," replied Cooper.

Everett and Cooper climbed into the truck to check by the river. Hopefully they would pass him on the side of the road, if he hadn't tried to catch a lift.

When they got to the school Cooper quickly disappeared from Everett's view as he sped ahead. Everett eventually caught up with him at Coupe's old camp. Cooper was sitting on the ground in the middle of Coupe's old tent. It was obvious that no one had been there since they had last left, many months before. When Everett entered the tent he saw Cooper's shoulders. He was sobbing quietly.

"He's not here, Dad," he said. "He's gone. He left me behind."

Cooper turned into his father's arms and cried.

When the truck finally arrived back at the farm, Evelyn ran out on the porch in hopes that they had found him. But they were alone. Cooper pushed past her and went straight up to his room. She tried to stop him and console him, but he did not want consoling, at least not from Evelyn.

"Give him some space, Evelyn," Everett said when he came up onto the porch. "He's upset. He's *really* upset."

"With me?"

"With Coupe gone and . . . yes, with you."

Evelyn sat down on the porch. "I am so sorry, Everett. I just don't know what came over me."

"What came over you is that you have always put Cooper ahead of Coupe. And he sensed that. Hell, even I sensed that."

She pulled away from him. "That's not true! I have done everything I can to make our home his home."

"You have been good to him, Evelyn, without a doubt, very good to him, but he's always seen that you favor Cooper, Evelyn. You are not mean; you did not treat him badly. You are really good to him. But every time you questioned whether he was good or bad for Cooper, Coupe knew. He knew it was an assessment of him against Cooper and you looking out for Cooper first. You know how perceptive he is, even without reading your face. I am worried for him, Evelyn. I really am. *If* we get him back here, we are going to double down on letting him know he is home here, he is safe here, and there will never ever be any more hitting."

"No, of course not! I don't know why I acted that way."

"Your protection of Cooper! That's what came over you! You did not want Cooper to know that he was adopted, so you slapped Coupe. If we are going to be a successful family, you need to protect them both."

Evelyn hugged Everett hard.

"I want him back, I really do. I want to apologize."

Everett kissed her head. "I know you do, Evelyn. I know you do. I just hope we get the chance."

Afterward she went up to talk with Cooper. He had been sitting on his bed with his back to the door and initially refused to even acknowledge she was there. But she persevered and spoke with him quietly about how sorry she was for what she had done and how much she loved him and wanted both him and Coupe to be her sons. With that he turned and hugged her and held her tight.

"I see him like my brother, Mom, so we both have to be your sons."

Everett called Chief Dale to let him know that Coupe had run off after a family argument. He did not mention that Evelyn had slapped him, but stressed that they were all worried and wanted him back. The chief sent out cars looking for him in every direction. He contacted neighboring towns and immediately entered Coupe's name into the missing person database, but all to no avail. It was a very dismal Thanksgiving at the Callister farm.

CHAPTER 23

When school started after the Thanksgiving break, Cooper refused to attend. It was not until Wednesday that Everett and Evelyn could get him to return, and when he did go back he was no longer talking. His teachers were concerned. So were his parents. He would go to school and do his work. He would come home, do his chores and his homework, and then retreat into his bedroom. The only ones he wanted up there with him were Roscoe and Bryn. Bryn also missed Coupe. His blankets and pillows were still on the floor, and she spent most of her time lying on them.

Inside, Cooper was really suffering. He had come to rely upon Coupe more than he had realized. His success in school was in large part because of his friend. Either Cooper had just gotten used to it or did not realize it, but it was Coupe keeping him calm and in control during the day. He was the cool blue light in his head. Now with him gone, all the voices, all the feelings, all the thoughts came flooding back in, like a storm. It was too much. The pleasant blue light had been torn away, and he felt himself being buffeted each and every day like he was a young child all over again.

Weeks turned into a month. Soon Christmas was only a few days away. The intervening time had been tough on the Callisters, but Cooper started to come back out of his shell. Though he was not yet talking again at school, things had returned to normal at home, but Cooper was still quieter and did not laugh.

The time since Coupe had gone had allowed them to discuss the issue of Cooper's birth. Evelyn could really provide no other information than what she already had because she had received such limited information herself. She did produce Cooper's birth certificate. According to that record, he had been born in upstate New Hampshire. It listed Evelyn as his mother and the father only as *deceased*. It was a dead end as to any further information. The hospital where he had been born must have closed because they could find no information about it. Frankly, Cooper was not interested. Evelyn was his mother and Everett his dad.

Not giving up hope, they talked about what they would say if Coupe came back. Evelyn wanted to offer some explanation and ask for Coupe's forgiveness. They were also going to insist that he stop calling them "sir" and "ma'am." He needed to know he belonged and that he should never flee no matter what went wrong because families stuck together. Good families, that is.

But the day for the conversation grew distant. There was no sign of Coupe anywhere. Chief Dale gave them regular reports. He even asked nearby towns and even the closest larger towns to keep an eye out for him, though he would not share a photo. Everett was surprised and asked him why not. By way of explanation he showed Everett another photograph that he said was taken from a security video. This one was very clear. It showed Coupe running down a side street in dim light.

"This one was taken near the site of another abduction. This time it was a boy in his early twenties that went missing. This is why I don't want to put Coupe's picture out there. As soon as I do, there will be a lot more folks than just you and me looking for him. Don't worry. I know it's not him. I know that for certain now."

"How so, Altus?"

"This video was taken in Wilmington, North Carolina, on the same day I came out here to tell Coupe about Father Hatem's death. I'm his alibi now."

Everett shook his head with satisfaction. He could not help himself. "I told you it wasn't him, Altus."

"I know. I believe you. I should've believed you then, but, like I said, I've got a job to do. There's also another reason this kid can't be Coupe," he added.

"Oh yeah?"

"This photo came from a video that I watched. This kid was running, and I mean flying. The kind of speed that gets you a track scholarship. There's no way Coupe could do that with his bum foot."

"You are right there, Altus."

· · · · · · · · · · · · · · · · ·

Chief Dale called late on the morning of Christmas Eve. He had found Coupe. The boy had been injured in a robbery in Worcester, Massachusetts. According to Chief Dale, two punks came into a convenience store to rob it, and Coupe had appeared out of nowhere to protect the cashier. They had been armed with knives and he was stabbed. Apparently, the story was on the news with security video footage of the attack. He had been taken to a hospital for treatment, but it did not look promising. He had been stabbed in the torso multiple times and lost a lot of blood.

Cooper was sitting in the truck before Everett finished his conversation with Chief Dale. When Everett came out of the house he wondered for a moment if Cooper should stay, but he quickly dismissed the thought.

"Buckle up. We've got a long ride."

It would be at least two and a half hours, and there was no easy route. They met up with Chief Dale in town. He insisted on coming down with them to ensure there were no problems in getting to Coupe.

They followed Chief Dale in his squad car. He had his lights on for most of the journey, and they traveled at a healthy pace to get there. When they finally arrived, they learned that Coupe had been taken into surgery again. He had been stabbed in the liver and was bleeding internally. They had not been able to close it sufficiently when he was first brought in for emergency surgery.

Chief Dale had part of the police report pertaining to the robbery. He had the address of where it happened, and he suggested that they go over there to see what they might learn. As it turned out, it was a good idea. The woman on duty when Coupe had been stabbed was working when they arrived. By now she was used to seeing men in uniform wanting to question her, but she was surprised when she learned that the other two were Coupe's foster family.

"Coupe was fostered with me and my family when he was younger. My name is Vera," she explained with a slight Hispanic accent. Vera could not have been more than eighteen or nineteen herself. "I always liked him," she added, smiling. "He was always nice to me. He left like three years ago. Then there he was about a month ago standing outside my house. He couldn't come in, so I set him up as best I could in the storeroom out back. I usually work nights, you see, so it would give him a place to sleep when I was working. They just switched me to days, though, on account of the robbery. The boss was not happy that I let Coupe sleep in the back, but it was the best that I could do on account of . . ." She trailed off.

"On account of what?" asked Everett.

"Coupe and my dad didn't get on so well," she said, looking sad. "My dad is the reason that Coupe has that limp."

"What happened?" asked Everett.

"Coupe had a way about him. He was funny and quick witted back then. He used to drive my dad crazy. When he got out of line my dad was not shy about using his belt. The trouble was he could not always catch Coupe. He was just too fast. Coupe would say something to set him off, and he would jump out of his chair, and then Coupe was off! Sometimes he would bounce around the room before finding the door and shooting outside for safety.

"One weekend my dad had been drinking pretty steadily starting Saturday morning. Come Sunday afternoon he was well into it, and Coupe said something to set him off. My dad jumped out of his chair to belt him, and the chase was on, like usual. The problem was that my dad had locked all the doors, so he had nowhere to go. My dad caught him, dragged him over to the fireplace, put his foot on the hearth and stomped on it."

Vera became emotional.

"I can still hear the howl of pain coming from his little body. He lay there panting and breathing hard. My dad just went and sat down. I helped him upstairs and out of the way. We dressed it as best as we could. It was badly bent over, but we knew my parents wouldn't be taking him to the hospital. I stayed with him all night. His breathing was so heavy as he fought through the pain, but he never cried, not once. I did, enough for both of us, but he didn't.

"My parents kept him out of school for about a week and then got an old pair of crutches. He was told to tell anyone that asked that he sprained it. I thought it was broke real bad, but he got rid of those crutches and started walking on it about a week later. But the ankle was always bent over funny after that. A few months later my family lost their foster certification for . . . for other stuff, which was probably a good thing. He got taken out and I never saw him again until right after Thanksgiving. There he was standing on the corner. He said he was waiting for me. He was so different."

"How so?" asked Everett.

"Like I said, he used to be so funny and talkative. He was always a quick-witted kid. But when he came back, he barely said twenty words when asking for help. Then after I set him up in the back room I never heard him speak, unless he was sleeping. He always made a lot of noise when he slept, but you probably know that. It drove my parents crazy. I think that was another reason my dad did not like him. He woke him up with all his crazy dreams and screaming.

"The only thing I can remember him saying once he settled into the stockroom was after he had one of his nightmares. I was worried and wondered if I should go in. I walked to the back door and looked in on him. I heard him say, 'Cooper, I'm scared.' Then he went back to sleep. At least for a while."

"What happened the night before last, miss?" Chief Dale asked.

"It started out like every other overnight. You get the drunks that come in after the bars close. Most of them are good, some of them are belligerent, but you learn how to deal with them. My dad taught me that! It was about two in the morning and the place was dead. I was cleaning like I was supposed to when it was quiet like that. These two guys came into the store screaming at me. They were going to kill me if I didn't empty the register right away. They had knives and kept swinging them around. We're trained not to put up a fuss, and I wasn't gonna be no hero for a hundred bucks, so I went behind the counter and quickly gave them the money.

"But they didn't leave. One of them said they need more, they wanted a little *extra*, and he grabbed his crotch. I started to cry and plead with them to just take the money and leave, but he came behind the counter. That's when Coupe came flying out of the storeroom and hit him in the back. He started punching and punching. He was so fast, he was all over him.

"The guy didn't know how to react. But I don't think Coupe knew there were two of them. The other guy grabbed him from behind. Coupe tried to fight them off, but they had knives. They stabbed him up really bad and fled. I called the ambulance and I held him until they arrived. I tried to stop the bleeding but there was so much blood! They took him away. He wasn't conscious when he left. I'm really scared for him. I mean, he got stabbed protecting me."

The girl started to cry. Everett reached out to comfort her, but Cooper was holding her already. She put her head on his shoulder.

They went back to the hospital to learn that Coupe had come out of surgery. They spoke with the surgeon who was on his floor when they arrived.

"He had four stab wounds to the torso and multiple defense wounds to his arms. When we opened him up he wasn't as bad as they said he was yesterday. No active bleeders, and he seemed to be healing quick. Really quick. He'll be fine after a few weeks of rest. Tough patient, though."

"Why is that?"

"The anesthetic didn't seem to work on him overly well. Woke up almost immediately after we finished. Started freaking out. We had to restrain him."

"Wait! You tied him to a bed?" asked Everett.

"We had to, until he calms down. Don't worry; there's an attendant with him."

"What room is he in?"

The doctor pointed to room 508 around the corner.

When they entered they saw a large man leaning over a bed. They could see Coupe's legs thrashing back and forth.

"Just settle down, little man," they heard him say. He turned as he heard them come in the room. "Can I help you?"

"We're his foster family; we'll stay with him now."

"You should come back tomorrow, once he has settled down."

The attendant did not notice Cooper slipping behind him as he spoke with Everett and the chief. Cooper turned to look down at Coupe's eyes wide with panic. He had not needed to see him to sense what was going on inside his head. There were bandages across his chest, and both of his forearms were wrapped up. His wrists were being restrained to the rails of the bed with padded restraints.

"They're family," said the chief. "You should let them stay."

"But you probably don't want to see him like this."

The padded restraints came flying from behind him to land in the corner of the room.

"What the—"

The orderly turned to see Cooper leaning over Coupe in bed. The restraints had been "removed" by him. Cooper had his hand on Coupe's chest.

"You probably should not be touching him, young man."

Just then Coupe seemed to take a deep breath, and then fell asleep. His face now looked calm. The attendant lifted his wrist and took his pulse. It was steady.

"Looks like he finally fell asleep. But you should not have removed those restraints. You would be surprised how strong people can be coming out of anesthetic."

"I think he'll be fine now," said Everett.

The man thought for a moment and then said, "Good enough. I'll be here until twelve if you need me." He left.

Chief Dale came over to look at Coupe. He looked thin and pale, but it was Coupe, at last. He was concerned about his condition but content that they had found him. He knew he was in good hands now.

"I'm going to head back up to Riding," said the chief. "You give me a call if you need anything."

"Thanks for all you have done, Altus," replied Everett.

•••••••••••••••••

Once he left, Cooper and Everett settled down to spend the night with Coupe. He seemed to be resting peacefully. Whenever that peace seemed disturbed, Everett watched Cooper reach out his hand and put it on Coupe's chest. Coupe would immediately fall back to sleep. Everett knew that Cooper helped Coupe sleep through the night, but never knew how he did it. He was amazed.

"Care to share with me how you do that?"

"I just think him back to sleep," was all he said.

Everett thought back to his conversation with Coupe after the incident in the bathroom on the first day of school. He never really understood how Cooper got three upperclassmen looking for trouble to just leave when they were beating Coupe. Everett was beginning to suspect that Cooper could do more than just help Coupe sleep. Cooper turned and stared at him for a moment, then turned back to Coupe.

At about nine that evening Everett realized that neither he nor Cooper had eaten anything since they left that morning.

"You hungry, Cooper?" asked Everett

"Yeah."

"I'll go see if the cafeteria is open and grab us some sandwiches or something."

"Thanks, Dad."

Everett went down the hall and got in the elevator. He had seen the cafeteria down on the first floor across from the main entrance. As the bell dinged, Everett stepped out of the elevator into the main foyer of the hospital. There was a reception desk in its center. The woman seated at that desk was speaking with two men in suits. They looked like cops. As Everett walked by them on his way to the cafeteria, he saw that they were showing the receptionist a photograph. It was of Coupe, the same one that Chief Dale had shown him. Everett tapped his pockets like he was looking for something, feigning he could not find it. Then he abruptly turned and got back into the elevator.

Once back on Coupe's floor he quickly found a wheelchair. When he wheeled it into Coupe's room, Cooper had already picked Coupe up and was waiting to place him in the wheelchair. He had read Everett's thoughts as he approached. Everett found a blanket in the closet, and they wrapped it around Coupe, to both keep him warm and disguise him.

They found a service elevator on the opposite side of the wing. It stopped on the next floor down and a nurse got in. She told them they were not allowed to use the service elevator. Then she looked down at Coupe, wrapped up in a blanket and asleep in the wheelchair. She asked them what they were doing as the door closed. When it opened up again she was fast asleep and being held in Cooper's arms. He saw a small couch in the elevator vestibule and gently laid her on it.

Once outside, Cooper and Everett loaded Coupe into the back of the truck. Cooper stayed in the back with him to keep him safe. They left the hospital without ever seeing the two big men and, more importantly, without them seeing Coupe.

"Who were they?" asked Cooper once they were on the highway traveling home.

"I think they were cops looking for Coupe. They had his photo," replied Everett. "We just got him back. We're not going to let them take him. Now, let's get home for a family Christmas."

"Yeah, family Christmas," Cooper said quietly.

CHAPTER 24

When Everett pulled up to their house it was past midnight. Christmas lights were hanging from the porch, and he could see the tall tree lit with tiny multicolored lights through the living room window. Everett took Coupe out of the truck. He was still sleeping. Cooper made sure of that. Everett brought him inside, and Evelyn looked down on his sleeping form with concern.

"He'll be okay, Evelyn. Let's get him upstairs."

Evelyn spread out his blankets and pillows on the floor, next to Cooper's bed. Everett laid him down there. It felt odd putting him on the floor, but he knew it was what Coupe preferred. As soon as Everett stood, Bryn came in and sniffed at Coupe a few times, licked his face, and then curled up next to him with a satisfied grunt. Once certain he was resting comfortably, they all quickly got ready for bed and settled in, feeling whole once again after over a month of feeling like one piece was missing.

Coupe was the first to awaken on Christmas morning. He was unsure where he was; then he recognized the ceiling above him and the bed beside him. He felt the warmth of Bryn pressed to his side.

"Cooper? Is that you?" he asked.

Cooper was in the bed above. "You know it is."

"Am I . . . h-home? How did I get here?"

Cooper leaned over and could see Coupe was pale. He looked thin again. He also looked scared, like he needed reassuring.

"Yeah, you're home. Me and Dad went and got you from the hospital and brought you back to the place you never should have left. I am really mad at you, Coupe."

"I know," replied Coupe. "And we should talk it out like your dad says. But until that happens you have to stay out of my head, or I am going to get up and leave again."

"No, you will not!"

"I will if I have to, Cooper."

Cooper jumped out of bed and stood in front of him. "How are you going to do that if you have to get through me?" he challenged, raising his voice.

Cooper thrust his chin out and looked down at Coupe with balled fists.

"Then stay out of my head!" Coupe ordered.

"Fine!"

Coupe felt like a line had been cut between the two. He could not sense him at all, and he presumed it was the same for Cooper, who was still glaring down at him.

"Why don't you want me in your head?" Cooper asked.

"Because there's something you cannot see. I left to protect you from it. I don't want you banging around in my head and running into it, okay? It's not like I'm mad at you or anything . . . like you are clearly mad at me. I'm just trying to do what's right by you."

"Like getting stabbed in a knife fight? How's that good for me?"

"C'mon, Cooper. It's not like I planned that. I just didn't have anywhere to go when I left here and that's where I ended up."

"You shouldn't have left! This is your home! Mom was wrong to hit you, and she is real sorry, *real* sorry. You have to forgive her, Coupe. *Please.* It has to go back to the way it was."

"I'm sure your mom is sorry, and I got over that pretty quick, Cooper. I've been hit plenty harder than that. It just shocked me is all. I didn't expect it from her. But the more I thought about it, I realized she was just trying to protect you, and I'm okay with that. That's what I promised your parents I would do too. I couldn't do that if I stayed here."

Cooper's anger surged. "Yeah? Well, you shouldn't be okay with it if someone hits you, Coupe! It's not okay for people to hit you, and that includes my mom! You can't go running away anymore when something bad happens. It's bad for you! Look what happened to you!" Cooper was animated and breathing hard. Coupe had never seen him this upset. Cooper calmed himself.

"It's bad for you to leave, Coupe, but it's even worse for me. When you left everything came flooding back in. I didn't realize how much you had been helping me. And I had no one to talk to about it, because you're the only one that understands . . . this!" Cooper smacked himself in the head, harder than Coupe liked to see.

"Easy, Cooper."

"Easy? The one thing it has not been is easy."

"But I did it for you, Cooper."

"Yeah? Well, don't! Don't ever do it for me again!"

Cooper sat down on the corner of the bed. Coupe felt him reaching out, trying to sense him. Coupe pushed him back out.

"I said don't do it, Cooper."

"Why not? What is it you need so desperately to hide from me? I've seen your dreams, Coupe! I've seen what those terrible people did to you! What else is there left for you to hide from me? Is there something worse than that?"

"No, it's not like that. It's not a bad thing. I just need to protect you, is all."

Cooper had assumed that Coupe left because he had felt unwanted, unloved, cast out, even betrayed by Evelyn's slap. *If not those things, why did he leave?*

"I know my mom is not my birth mom. Is that why you left? You figured it out and you didn't want me to read it from you?"

Coupe looked surprised. "Yeah," he replied, slowly. "When did you find out?"

"About thirty seconds after you bolted out the door. I read it off Mom after she hit you."

"Son of a bitch. Then I left—"

"—for nothing, Coupe. Now do you see why you can't just run off anymore?"

"But I didn't think I had a choice, Cooper. What if you found that out from me? I mean, what would your mother think of me then?"

Cooper stared at him, choosing his words carefully. "She is *our* mother, Coupe. And she is waiting for you to open up to her. It's one of the things we talked about while waiting to get you back here. She knows that she made you feel you were second to me. She didn't mean to do it. She won't do it anymore, and if she does, you call her out for it. I'll call her out for it. Dad already has. Everyone here is ready to commit to you, Coupe. You already knew I was, until you kicked me out of your head, that is. So the question is, are you ready to commit to us? You want to be a family, or what?"

Coupe stared back up at Cooper. They locked eyes, and then Coupe's started darting all over Cooper's face. He sniffed. A few seconds after that Cooper sensed his shields coming down, and he could once again sense Coupe. Cooper got the answer to his question, but he was not letting Coupe off the hook.

"Say it, Coupe."

Coupe paused for a moment and then spoke quietly. "Yes."

"Yes, what?"

"Yes, I want to be part of your family."

"It's *our* family now. You have a mom and a dad and a brother, and you are going to start calling them that, right?"

"Yes."

Relieved, Cooper grinned happily and flopped back on the bed. "Good," said Cooper. "You should know that when I learn to talk more I'm going tell people that I'm your big brother, since I have to keep looking out for you and breaking you out of hospitals and everything."

"Well, we share the same birthday, so why don't we go with twins, and then I can explain you got extra food in the womb."

Cooper giggled. "Okay, if you want."

"So, what was that about breaking me out of the hospital? I don't know how I got here."

Cooper explained everything that happened since they found him. He told Coupe he knew how his foot got twisted.

"Yeah, another winner from my past. But what about these guys that wanted me? What did they look like?"

"Don't know. Dad saw them. When he was coming back up in the elevator he might as well have had police lights going off in his head. He was worried. We got you out of there, though, and Dad will deal with them if they show up here. So will I if they try to take you."

"Do I have to slap you again? Remember our chat?"

"I do, and I think about it a lot. But if they try to take you, I think that justifies me doing . . . something."

"We should talk about just what that something might be before you do it. And speaking of what you can do, would you please use your super strength to help me stand up? I don't think I've peed in three days—at least, it feels like that."

Cooper snickered as he bent to lift him up. He noticed Coupe was much lighter. He would need some fattening up at the Callister dinner table. Cooper placed him on his feet and steadied him. Coupe winced. He healed fast, but not that fast.

"C'mon, I'll steady you," said Cooper.

"Okay, but no peeking. I don't want you getting jealous."

Cooper snickered again and walked Coupe into the bathroom. Once he was sure he was steady, he left him alone. Outside in the hallway he found his parents waiting.

"Everything okay?" asked Everett.

"Yeah, he's just peeing."

"I get that. I'm talking about the raised voices I heard between you two. Clearing the air?"

"Yes, Dad. Everything's good."

"What happened?"

"We can all talk about it later. He won't be running off anymore. Mom, I told him how sorry you were about slapping him. That's not even why he left."

"Why then?" asked Evelyn.

"He left because he figured out you were not my birth mom and he didn't want me to find out from him."

"He's a good friend, Cooper."

"No, he isn't, Mom."

She looked back at him with confusion.

"He's a good *brother* now."

She smiled. "Of course he is, if that is what he wants to be."

The door to the bathroom opened and Coupe stepped out. He was wearing hospital pants and had no shirt, just the bandages wrapped around his chest. He saw Everett and Evelyn looking at him with concern.

"I guess it's going to be Mom and Dad from now on," he said. "Thanks for caring about me. Thanks for coming to get me. I won't ever leave again, I promise."

"I believe him," said Cooper, smiling.

They wrapped their arms around him and hugged him.

"Merry Christmas, son," is all Everett said.

TWO

CHAPTER 25

Even though the Callisters did not know if Coupe would be back for Christmas, they had planned as if he would. There would be time to explain and apologize later. Right now it was Christmas! Cooper helped Coupe down into the living room where he saw the Christmas tree with gifts piled beneath it.

"Whoa," he said as they got him comfortable on the couch. "I've only seen shit like this on TV." Then, "Oops, sorry, ma'am—I mean, Mom."

"It's Christmas, Coupe, so we are big on forgiveness," said Evelyn, smiling, "but see what you can do to rein it in."

"Yes, ma'am. I mean, Mom. Sorry, it's going to take me a while."

The morning unfolded with gifts for them all and breaks for coffee for Everett and Evelyn and food for the boys. Once done, Coupe asked for water, perhaps three times, and then fell asleep on the couch. Cooper sat next to him watching, and occasionally placed his hand gently on his chest. Evelyn grew concerned, but Cooper told her not to worry; it was just Coupe's way of healing.

Coupe awoke just in time for Christmas dinner. He looked much better, and stronger too. He was able to stand without help and walked to the dinner table where he started eating . . . and eating and eating. Evelyn continued to fill his plate for as long as he kept asking. Everett was the first to speak.

"Coupe, how did you disappear so quick, and how did you get down to Worcester?"

Coupe looked at him and smiled. "Well, *Dad,* first I ran as fast as my bum foot would carry me. I felt certain I would get tackled by Cooper and dragged back. Once I got to the road I started walking and thumbing. I got lucky and was picked up by someone heading down to Lebanon, New Hampshire. From there I worked my way to Concord, then Manchester, then Nashua, then Lowell and finally Worcester. I went looking for Vera. She helped me before. I hoped she would help me again. She did. Vera was always good to me, and she did her best to help me when I went back down there."

"Looks like you did your best to help her as well," Everett noted.

"Yeah," Coupe said, rubbing his gut. "It had to be done. I mean, the money was one thing, but what that guy was gonna do . . . it wasn't right."

"No it wasn't," Everett said. "You're a brave young man, Coupe."

"Thank you, sir."

Everett cleared his throat.

"I mean, Dad."

The phone rang and Everett went to answer it. Evelyn leaned over to Coupe.

"Coupe, I need to say how sorry I am for how I acted the day you left. It was unforgiveable for me to hit you. I just didn't know how else to stop you from doing that thing you do and figuring out what I was thinking."

"You are forgiven, *Mom*. But I have to admit it came as a shock, especially from you because you treated me so well. You treated me better than my real mother ever did. But I understand you were trying to protect Cooper. That's why I left. I didn't want him to sense me and find out."

"Coupe, that's just it. I should not be protecting one of you over the other; I should be protecting you both. I know that now, and I am going to do a better job of it. Cooper made it clear to me you are brother material. He is right, you are, so that means you are another son to me, and I will be the best mom I can be for you."

"Thank you," said Coupe, smiling.

Everett returned to the table. "That was Chief Dale. Coupe's disappearance from the hospital didn't go unnoticed. He got a call from the Worcester PD telling him what happened. I told Chief Dale we did not want Coupe to be held for those other cases. He understood. He said he would call them back and tell them we just wanted Coupe home for Christmas and that Coupe is doing fine. He'll let me know if he hears from the other cops that were there at the hospital. He doesn't think that they were from Worcester PD. He suspects they were feds. If he hears from them, he will tell them they've got the wrong boy, and he will also let us know *immediately*."

He looked over at Coupe. "So, how you doing, son?"

"I'm feeling a lot better, but I'm still tired. Rest will do me good." He popped out of his seat and walked back into the living room to lie down. The way he walked, no one would have suspected that he had been stabbed four times a few days earlier.

Everett walked over and put his hands on his wife's shoulders. "Heals fast," he said. "Hell, that kid heals on a timescale all his own."

"He's back, though, Everett. And I think he is here to stay. I'm so happy. Family of four now."

"Never would have expected it, but I sure as hell like it."

"Language, Everett," she chided, tapping his hand.

"Sorry, Evelyn."

CHAPTER 26

Christmas had fallen on a Saturday. The boys had the entire week off for the holiday break. Normally, they would have thrown themselves into activities, like sledding or skating and pond hockey. But with Coupe recovering from his injuries, the family decided to stay home. Coupe worked his way through a dozen books from Sunday to Wednesday. By Wednesday, however, he was not only feeling better, he was looking like he had never been injured. Evelyn removed the bandages from his arms, and he had nothing but pink scars where the knives had cut into his forearms and wrists. He would probably bear those all his life, but the wounds had healed. She removed the bandages from his torso, and it was the same with his abdomen.

It snowed heavily on Tuesday, so on Wednesday the boys were

eager to get out into the orchard and sled down the hill. Evelyn immediately said no. Everett was out snowplowing his way to the road and had not been part of the conversation, but the boys continued to plead with her. Finally, she deferred to Everett.

Everett finished the plowing around ten o'clock, and they both caught him at the door as he came back into the house. Evelyn stuck her head out of the kitchen door to listen to the conversation. After they made their case, Everett looked hard at Coupe.

"How are you really feeling, Coupe, and tell the truth or Cooper will know and let me know, won't you, Cooper?"

"Yes, Dad," he said obediently.

"I feel good. I mean, I want to get outside and do something. I like being outside. If I start to hurt, I will tell Cooper immediately."

Cooper laughed. Coupe changed his response.

"If I start to hurt, Cooper will immediately know. And then I will let him carry me back to the house and put cold compresses on my head."

Cooper laughed again. Coupe was beginning to remember he had an easy audience with him. Everett stared at Coupe for a moment longer, looked at Evelyn still watching from the kitchen, and then shrugged.

"He got stabbed a week ago!" she said sternly.

"Anybody else I would say absolutely not. But this is Coupe. Cooper has super strength. Coupe has super healing. I trust his judgment, and Cooper's senses. Go out and have some fun, boys, but don't overdo it. Your mother and I will go into town and replenish the shelves you two are emptying at lightning speed."

The two boys cheered and ran upstairs to put on some warm clothing and tore around the back of the house, sleds in hand, to work their way through the snow to the orchard. It would take them a few turns to knock down a run, but once it was in, it would be a good run for the entire winter. They locked the dogs in the barn so they would not follow and get in the way.

Once out in the orchard, they decided the best way to make the run was for Coupe to sit in the sled and for Cooper to push him. A normal kid would have pushed and stopped for a while, then pushed some more and eventually gotten to the bottom. With Cooper and Coupe, though, it was different. Once Coupe was seated in the sled, he saw both of Cooper's gloved hands clamp down on the sides.

"Hold on," is all Coupe heard; then he was charging down the hills as if he had a motor attached to the back of the sled. Snow flew up into his face. For half the ride he could not see as he shook it out of his eyes, but he knew he was *flying*! Coupe hooted and laughed all the way to the bottom. When they eventually reached the bottom of the long hill, Coupe fell out of the sled laughing.

"That was awesome, man," he said between laughs. "I mean, that was fucking awesome! I bet I am the first person on the entire planet to experience a superhuman-powered sled ride, *Whoopee!*" He shouted so it echoed off the hill.

In that moment he was a child again, enjoying the things a child ought to enjoy—the innocent pleasure of sliding down a hill in the backwoods of Vermont, through fresh white snow on a cold winter morning. Cooper sat down next to him and they both laughed.

Cooper thought of all the awful things Coupe had experienced and how much of his childhood he had really missed. It pained him. *But Coupe got to have today,* he thought, and he smiled at that.

"Happy to help, little bro!" said Cooper, lying back in the snow, leaving his imprint in the fresh snowfall, then spreading his arms to make a snow angel. He had just finished pushing Coupe down the hill across two acres of heavy snow, yet he wasn't even breathing heavily.

"Okay, the run is packed. It's your turn next!" said Coupe with obvious excitement.

"Okay, but you sit in the sled. I'm pulling you back up."

"No way, man! I feel good!"

With that, Coupe started bounding back up the hill with surprising speed, despite his twisted foot. Cooper let him get a good head start before he caught up to him, grabbed him, and then hauled him to the top of the hill.

The boys spent a good hour and a half going up and down the hill until Cooper started to sense Coupe's fatigue. Coupe wanted to keep going. He was having too much fun to stop. But Cooper refused. He knew he was being overprotective, but he also had good reason to be. Coupe finally relented and they walked back.

When they got within a hundred yards of the house, Coupe proposed a race. Cooper had to give him a fifty-yard head start, on account of him being injured and all, and then see if he could catch him. The loser had to make peanut butter sandwiches. Cooper grinned confidently. Coupe was fast, but not over distance and certainly not through snow.

"Go ahead, little bro. I will count down from three. Three, two, one . . ."

Cooper watched his new little brother hobbling as fast as he could toward the house. Granted he was fast, but his bum foot slowed him down significantly. Cooper felt a pang of guilt but knew Coupe would sense that and be all over him. He then dug in and took off after him.

Cooper caught him near the back porch, picked him up over his shoulder, and carried him over the last few yards, both of them laughing as Cooper jumped onto the porch from five yards away and opened the kitchen door to get back inside into the warmth. The fact that they had been so focused on their foot race explained why they did not sense the two men in suits sitting at their kitchen table. But as soon as they entered the room, they knew they were there. One of them stood and smiled. He looked at them both and then back at Cooper.

"You must be Cooper, the strong one," the man said. He pulled a gun out of his coat and shot him in the chest.

CHAPTER 27

Coupe screamed and jumped at the man, but the other one grabbed him in a bear hug. "Hold still!"

Coupe quickly threw his head back, striking the man in the face with the back of his head, but the man did not let go. The other man approached and put the gun in his chest.

"You want it too?" he asked. "It'll hurt you a lot more than it hurt him."

Coupe looked back at Cooper to see what the gunshot had done. He had no idea if a gun could hurt his brother, and he earnestly hoped that it could not. But Cooper was struggling to keep on his feet. It was clear the shot was having some effect. Coupe watched in horror as Cooper, breathing heavily, toppled onto his back. It was only then that Coupe saw the dart sticking out of his chest. Coupe stopped struggling, unsure just what was happening.

Cooper was not done, though. He was still conscious, and even though he could not stand, he reached over and grabbed the leg of the man who had shot him. The man howled in pain. Cooper then threw the man at the kitchen door with such force that the man's body slammed into the door and shattered it. Cooper turned and started to crawl toward the other man, whose arms snaked around Coupe's neck and tightened.

"Stop! You come near me and I will snap his neck!"

Cooper stopped moving.

"That's better. Now listen up, both of you. We are all going to get up and get in the van that is parked outside. We are going to do it quickly. You want us to do it quickly because if we are not out of here before your parents come back, Cooper, I'm going to have to shoot them too. And my gun doesn't shoot darts."

Outside, the other man was rousing himself.

"Can you walk?" the one inside called to him.

"I think so," he replied.

"Then go get the van."

The man got up and hobbled off around the side of the house. On the floor Cooper rolled onto his back and pulled the dart out of his chest.

"That should have knocked you out, strong man, but at least it will keep you dopey for a few hours."

Coupe sensed that Cooper's thoughts were being dulled by whatever drug had been pumped into him. He was also perplexed as to how the man knew of Cooper's unusual strength.

"See if you can stand up," the man said to Cooper.

Cooper sat up and rolled onto his knees. He grabbed hold of the kitchen table and pulled himself up. He was wobbly, but upright. The van appeared at the back door.

"Okay, let's go. Get in!"

Cooper staggered toward the door, catching hold of the door frame to steady himself, and stepped inside the van. Coupe was shoved in behind him. The kidnappers quickly zip-tied the boys' feet and hands and left them sprawled on the van floor.

"I don't want any problems with you two, understand? If you cause any problems, I'm going to come back here and burn this place down myself. No talking, no moving. Just sit there and everything will be okay. Got it?"

The boys nodded.

"Good," said the man, and he slammed the door shut. A few moments later they drove away from the farm. Coupe felt Cooper's relief as he realized they were now on a main road and had not been stopped by their parents returning from shopping. Their parents were safe.

Cooper's mind was suppressed by the drug injected into him. He could not sense in the way he normally did. He wanted to reach out to the two men and make them stop and tie their own hands together, but he simply could not bring his mind into sharp enough focus to do so.

Coupe immediately tried to get into Cooper's mind to see if he was okay. It was obvious he was not. Cooper did not even know Coupe was trying to communicate with him. Coupe wondered how long the drug would last and also how long they would be in the van. He shuffled his body over toward Cooper and leaned up against him.

It was cold in the van, even with their winter clothes, which were now damp from their sledding. Even though he had been drugged, Cooper felt Coupe shivering next to him. The smaller boy may have been a quick healer, but their sledding and this ordeal was taking a toll. Cooper pulled Coupe to his side for warmth and then lost consciousness. The back of the van finally started to warm after about a half hour.

After about four hours, the van began to slow down. Coupe heard a gate opening, and the van started moving again. There were at least

two more stops, and then Coupe heard a garage door opening. The
van pulled forward slowly. He heard the door close behind them, and
the van was shut off. The two men got out, and the side door to the
van opened. Coupe blinked as light flooded in from a well-lit garage
bay. Cooper was still sleeping.

"Let's get him moved," said one of the men, pointing at Cooper.
Two other men reached in and pulled Cooper's unconscious body
out of the van. There was a waiting stretcher. He was placed upon it
and wheeled away, out of Coupe's sight.

"Okay, little guy," the man said to Coupe, "scooch your ass over
to this door."

Coupe did as he was told. Once his feet were hanging out the
door, the plastic tie holding his legs was cut. Coupe held out his
hands.

"Not yet," said the man in the suit, pulling Coupe forward to
stand with his hands still bound. He was handed off to two other
attendants. "Be careful with this one. He's fast, even with that bum
foot."

Coupe quickly looked around. He could now see he was in a
garage bay built for about ten vehicles. There were three other vans in
the bay already. The two attendants that now took possession of him
were just as big and bulky as the two men in suits that had abducted
them from the farm. One of the men in suits was limping badly, and
Coupe smiled when he saw it.

"Little punk!" he shouted at Coupe. He looked at the other men.
"I'm going over to the medical building." He hobbled off.

Coupe was led through a series of heavy security doors deeper
into the building. The men held his arms on either side, but they need
not have bothered. It was pointless to attempt to flee now. They came
to a final heavy steel door that needed a special card to open. The
man pulled it from his side where it was attached by a retractable
cord. He waved it over a sensor, and the door clicked and buzzed.
He pushed it open, and they entered a hallway with one door and

two large windows on the left. Coupe was taken to the door, spun around, and the plastic restraint was removed. The man then used the card to open the door.

"Go on in, Coupe. It's your new home, for now," said the attendant.

Coupe said nothing. He just stepped into the room, and the man pulled the heavy steel door closed behind him. It was obvious it was a holding cell, but pretty comfortable compared to others he had been in. In the corner was a desk with a computer. A door next to it appeared to lead to a bathroom. Directly in front of him were two comfortable-looking chairs. They were directly in front of the large glass window that was only a mirror on this side. In the far corner was a set of bunk beds with lights over the heads. It was only then that Coupe noticed the body in the lower bunk.

"Cooper!" he shouted and hobbled over to him. He was laid out on his back, still sleeping. Coupe went into the bathroom and found a towel and wet it down. He took it back over to Cooper and wiped down his face. "Cooper!"

Cooper's eyelids flickered, then opened. He looked momentarily disoriented, and then his eyes, and his mind, locked onto Coupe.

"I don't know," Coupe replied to the unspoken question. "We drove for nearly four hours, then we turned onto what sounded like a dirt road. I could smell trees, so I think we were driving into a forest. We drove that way for a while and then stopped at a couple of security gates. Only the second was manned, I think. Then they brought us into a big garage and down a few hallways through thick security doors and put us in here. How's your chest?" asked Coupe.

"I dunno," responded Cooper, sitting up and lifting his shirt. Coupe turned on the light to get a look at what the dart had done. Cooper had been hit just below his collarbone, halfway between his neck and his shoulder. There was a small hole with a small bruise. "Wow," he said.

"No big deal; it'll heal in no time. I don't think I've ever seen you hurt before."

"I remember I got kicked by a horse once when I was five. That hurt. And I burned my hand on the woodstove once; that really hurt!"

"No doubt. You've been lucky, though."

"You haven't."

"The story of our lives, Cooper."

"What time is it?"

"Dunno. Probably late afternoon. I'm hungry."

Coupe sat on the bunk next to Cooper and took another look around. The desk had no drawers. Coupe looked over at the mirrored glass and wondered if they were being watched. Then he noticed a round object in the far upper corner of the room. It looked like a surveillance camera. He turned his gaze to the ceiling. There were round, cloth-covered openings in four areas. Coupe was pretty sure they were microphones. As he thought it, he saw Cooper look at the ceiling too. He sensed Cooper urging him not to say anything they wanted to keep private, but Coupe had the same thought himself.

Coupe got off the bed and stood in the center of the room and waved his hands at the camera. "Hey! Any chance we can get some food, and perhaps, oh—I don't know—an explanation for why we are here?"

They would get the food, but no explanation. About twenty minutes later they heard the door click, and the same attendant that had shown Coupe into the room came in with the same smile.

"We were not sure what you would like, so there are some turkey sandwiches, some roast beef sandwiches, and some peanut butter and jelly sandwiches . . . just for you, Coupe." He gave him a wink like he knew him. "When you are done just push the trolley over by the door and we will come get it, okay?" He did not wait for an answer. He left, shutting the door firmly behind him. Again, Coupe did not get a sense of animosity from the man.

"What did you get off of him, Cooper?" he asked.

"Nothing bad," replied Cooper. "Kind of nice. Should we trust the sandwiches?"

"I suppose if they wanted to kill us, they could have done it by now. Eat up."

Coupe pushed the cart over to the bed, and the two of them sat and ate their fill. True to form, Coupe went for the PB&Js. Cooper ate pretty much everything else. With the meal was a plastic pitcher of water, which Coupe was plenty glad for. He still seemed to need a lot of water to help him heal.

After they were done eating, Coupe went over to the desk to look at the computer. He turned it on to see if it had an internet link. It did not. But it was full of e-books. Since there was nothing else to do, Coupe opened one of the books and began to read. Soon he felt Cooper in his head following along. They passed the rest of the evening that way until the lights flashed. They did not speak out loud since they knew that the microphones would pick up their conversation. The lights flashed on and off again at nine that evening. There was, at least, a clock on the computer. Once the lights finished flashing, the computer turned itself off.

"Looks like they want us to go to bed, Cooper," said Coupe, the first words he had spoken for perhaps two hours.

They found clothes in the bathroom, including stuff for them to wear to bed—two sizes, one that fit Cooper and one that fit Coupe. The boys changed and the lights flashed again, stayed on for a minute longer, and then went out. Coupe checked the lights over the bed. Those still worked, so he turned one on. Without Coupe having to ask, Cooper pulled the bedding off of the top bunk and onto the floor next to the lower one.

"Will this work?" he asked.

"Yeah, thanks, Cooper."

Coupe was worried about sleeping, especially since he knew that they were being watched and would likely be watched through the night. But on the floor next to Cooper would work. Cooper got into bed and Coupe settled into his bedding before Cooper reached over and put his fist in his chest. There was a sharp intake of breath and then Coupe fell asleep.

Cooper had not done that in a long time, but he sensed Coupe needed it given all that had happened. He was right. He had to do it twice more during the night.

CHAPTER 28

The lights and the computer came back on at seven in the morning. The boys were not sure what they were supposed to do, but they did not have to wait very long. Shortly afterward, the door opened again. The two attendants from yesterday came in with one of the men who had abducted them.

"Where's your buddy from yesterday, big guy?" asked Coupe. "Walking like me now?"

"Cooper broke his ankle," he said quietly, looking at Cooper. Cooper simply stared back at him impassively. "He's recovering."

"Go around kidnapping people, lucky that's all you get."

The man did not take the bait. "We need to transport you to another part of the facility. We can do it the easy way, or"—he pulled the dart gun out from a holster on the back of his belt—"we can do it this way."

"Please allow me to speak for both of us here," said Coupe. "Easy way."

"Very wise," said the man. "Okay, follow me, boys."

They were led out of the room, surrounded by the three men, and into the garage, where they met a fourth waiting in a van to drive them. This van was different. It had three rows of seats. Cooper and Coupe were directed to the middle, and two of the attendants sat behind them, the other two in front.

The van pulled out of the garage, and the two boys got their first good look at where they had been brought. The building they had been housed in appeared to be a two-story building of industrial design. They were on the edge of a campus of buildings surrounded by a fence, surrounded by woods—lots of woods. The woods rolled into hills that appeared to roll into the distance without any other sign of civilization to be seen. The building they were leaving was set away from the rest.

"Where are we?" asked Coupe, looking around.

"You are in the ass end of nowhere in the middle of the deep woods of Maine. You try to run and you will die of starvation or exposure before you hit the nearest backwoods town," replied their abductor. "So don't try. You're safe here."

The buildings around them looked as if this was once some sort of small school campus. Some old brick and white clapboard buildings stood at the center, surrounded by newer, more modern buildings. The one directly in front of them was four stories and built of reflective glass. It looked out of place, but also appeared to be the new hub of the campus.

The van rolled down a ramp and through a sally port to enter the basement of the glass-sided building. They were once again in a garage. This time they were taken to an elevator. Surrounded, they were shepherded inside, and their friend from yesterday pressed for the third floor.

When the door opened they were taken down a very imposing hallway with dark-paneled walls. They were then led into a large room. It had books, lots and lots of books, stacked on two levels on three of the four walls. A library—a very lavish one. The fourth wall faced outside and was all glass. It looked out onto the campus and a small lake. The wall of windows extended up to the fourth floor of the building. The library comprised two floors, with a second floor of books accessible by a spiral staircase and a wide platform circling along the wall.

As they looked around, Coupe's eyes came to rest upon a man standing on the platform. Cooper looked up too. The man's thick straight hair was iron grey and slicked back. He had a hawkish nose and sharp eyes that stared at them through thin, rimless glasses. He was wearing a white lab coat and had his hands on the rails. He looked down at them, smiling.

"Boys!" he stated, grandiosely. "Welcome home!"

The grinning man brought his hands back down to the handrail in front of him and continued to smile at the boys.

"I am sure you have many questions," he said, "so why don't you go ahead and ask. I will do my best to answer them."

Coupe felt Cooper's questions but knew he would not ask them. Coupe took the lead.

"Okay. Why are we here?"

"For your own safety," replied the man. "It was very likely you were both about to be abducted—by someone other than me—and then killed. I did not want that to happen. I have devoted years of research and considerable assets for you to exist, and I did not want that to stop, a sentiment you no doubt share. So, I had you brought back here to keep you safe. I sent out my best security members to help you, one of whom now has a broken ankle." The man wagged a finger at Cooper. "But here you are—safe!"

"What about our parents?"

"Yes! *Your* parents are safe! Now that you are no longer with them, they will be of no interest and they will be left alone. But still, I do have people keeping an eye on them just to be sure."

Both boys were confused. "Who wants us dead?" continued Coupe.

"You do, Coupe!" The man smiled.

"What?" asked Coupe. "That makes no sense. I would never hurt Cooper... or our parents. They are the kindest people I have ever met."

"I know you wouldn't, Coupe, but you don't know what I know. So here you both are. I had not expected bringing you back like this, but, surprise!" He grinned. "I must say, I am so very impressed with both of you. I really am. You have developed beyond my wildest expectations. I think we should have a chat, a very long chat. But first things first."

The man in the lab coat moved to the spiral staircase at the end of the platform. As he descended the stairs, they noticed he was being followed by a boy who had been standing behind the man. He looked to be the same age as them, about fifteen or so. As the two strangers reached the bottom of the stairs, they saw the boy more closely. He was staring at Cooper with interest. Cooper stared back at him, his mouth hanging open in complete shock. They were exactly the same in appearance and build. Cooper had a twin.

The boy looked at Coupe, and the expression on his face soured to deep suspicion. *Story of my life*, thought Coupe.

The man now stood before them, and he smiled at the look on the two boys' faces. "You have even more questions now, and I will be happy to answer them, but first we must come to some terms. I am well aware of the special qualities you both possess. I have no doubt that if you wanted to, you would find a way to leave our happy campus and return to your parents. The staff here have been instructed to stop you from doing that, but I would prefer that they did not have to worry about keeping you here."

"Why should we want to stay here, wherever *here* is?" asked Coupe.

"Because right now it is the safest place for you. It is also the safest place for you to be for your parents' sake. I will make this promise to you both. For so long as you stay here, I will use all my efforts and assets to ensure that your parents remain safe. Should you choose to defy my requests and leave, well, should that happen, I will no longer be able to guarantee their safety, and who knows what would happen to them."

Coupe was unsure if it was a threat or not. The man's face was difficult to read. He reached out for Cooper to get his sense of him, but Cooper's sense was confused. The man did not want to do them any harm, but at the same time this man would do them harm if he had to.

The boy who looked exactly like Cooper came and stood next to the man.

"Corwin, meet your brothers, Cooper and Coupe."

Corwin looked at them both momentarily and nodded. His face betrayed no emotion that he had not previously revealed. Interest in Cooper and a fleeting impression of suspicion, sadness and frustration when looking at Coupe.

The man turned back to them. "My name is Dr. Steven Stein and I am"—he threw his arms in the air again and walked about theatrically—"your father!"

"What do you mean?" Coupe blurted. "We are all brothers? I mean, I can understand those two—look at 'em. But what about me? How come you gave them all the gravy?"

The man laughed. "Ah, Coupe, such the charmer! I was hoping that would occur as part of your development. Very satisfying to see, very satisfying." He came over to stand in front of Coupe. "You should know, Coupe, you were my biggest risk, my biggest gamble! But I also knew the return could be the greatest. So far, you have not disappointed."

Coupe hobbled a step back from the man.

"I was also very upset to learn about that injury to your foot. What happened?"

"I broke my foot," replied Coupe, showing his usual evasion.

"I was hoping you might be willing to share more than just that. It would seem to me that a comeuppance may be overdue."

Coupe searched his face. Despite his odd and eccentric manner, he appeared to be sincere.

"Well, Doc, where I've been is good and gone. You weren't there to stop it, so don't act like you're all offended now."

Dr. Stein smirked. "True, true," remarked Dr. Stein, inwardly pleased to note that Coupe had not developed any exaggerated need for vengeance given the events of his life. "Nevertheless, we can certainly improve your future. I don't like it when other people break my toys. I'll arrange for it to be fixed right away."

"Fixed?"

Dr. Stein nodded quickly, smiling, his eyes opening wide. Coupe searched his face again. He was a tough one to read. The man who had them kidnapped—for their safety—and whose men threatened to kill their parents—to keep *them* safe—wanted to help? Coupe quickly sniffed to confirm his instincts. Dr. Stein stared back at him just as intently.

"Fascinating. Coupe, you are fascinating. I so look forward to learning more about you and your development outside of our institution. You have been so successful. I mean, you really have no idea how successful."

Up until a few months ago, when the Callisters had taken him in, *successful* was not a word he would have chosen to describe his life thus far.

"Come, all of you. Let's sit by the window," said Dr. Stein, ushering them toward some chairs and a couch arranged in front of the wall of windows providing a commanding view of the campus and its surrounding environment. Directly in front of the building was a gradual sloping hill that led down to a lake. There was a scattering of buildings on its closest shore, but nothing else on the rest of the lake. They saw several other more modern buildings like the one they were in, although smaller, with the older buildings mixed in. To the left of the lake was an old playing field with a track going around it and a fieldhouse beside it.

"What is this place?" asked Coupe.

Dr. Stein sat and Corwin stood just behind his chair. "It has no official name, but I understand others like to call it Deep Woods Academy. It has a certain charm to it, so I allow it to be called by that name. Now, please, sit. I don't like to repeat myself."

It appeared that Dr. Stein liked things done his way.

As they sat, Coupe asked, "So again, Doc, why are we here?"

Dr. Stein smiled and looked out the windows. "Why are you here! Why are we here? There are so many ways I could answer that question, young man. From a spiritual perspective, perhaps, or maybe philosophical? Perhaps as a history of biology, the ontology of our very being!" He grinned smugly. "Perhaps you are speaking in a more existential frame of mind?"

Cooper turned to look at Coupe. He spoke for the first time since they had entered the room. "Coupe, I have no idea what he is talking about."

"Let me try to figure it out." Then to Dr. Stein, "Yeah, Doc, let's talk existentially and leave all the theoretical conversations for those who care. Right now, we don't. Why did you bring us to your secret lair?"

"Lair, yes!" Dr. Stein grinned. "Because you were being hunted."

"What? Wait, who was hunting us?" asked Coupe.

"As I said before, Coupe. You were hunting you."

"Yeah, you said that before and it makes no more sense now, so what do you mean?" As he spoke, Coupe had been studying the doctor's face, and Corwin's, who was still standing behind Dr. Stein's chair. They were the clues that made all the facts fall into place. He thought back to the photos that Chief Dale had shown him.

"Wait a minute. There are two Coopers. Are there two of me?"

"Precisely," said the doctor. "You got there much more quickly than I expected. You are so perceptive! Your intuitive powers need to be measured right away!"

"Save the praise, Dr. Stein," said Coupe. "What you're saying is that there is another person, just like me, out there abducting people."

"What I am trying to convey to you is that there is someone else out there *exactly* like you, genetically of course, abducting and then likely killing people."

Cooper's hands flew to the sides of his head, and he grimaced in pain. "Coupe, we need to get out of here. This is a bad place."

Coupe searched Cooper's mind and realized he had delved into Dr. Stein's mind. He had not liked it. Coupe tried to see what Cooper had sensed. Behind Dr. Stein's chair Corwin appeared to be catching on to what had happened. Apparently, he had some special sensing abilities too, though maybe not as strong as Cooper's. Coupe then felt Corwin's presence reaching out to his mind. They may have looked alike, but in Coupe's head Cooper and Corwin were distinctly different. Coupe threw up his wall and blocked him out. As he shut out Corwin, Corwin pointed at Coupe.

"That one is using the other to read you!" he said to Dr. Stein.

"Really? Block them both out, right now!" he ordered.

Corwin struggled but failed to block Cooper's sensing. The years Cooper had spent sitting in classrooms with the thoughts of all the other students in his head had strengthened his sensing abilities, making them much stronger than Corwin's. His communications with Coupe further heightened his abilities. Corwin could not put up much of a defense if Cooper wanted to push through and sense him. It was like wading through a low snowdrift. It slowed him down momentarily, but once again he was able to sense Dr. Stein, albeit with Corwin trying to stop him, like a child pulling on his arm.

"I can't!" Corwin said.

Dr. Stein came over and stood in front of Cooper. "Stop it right now or I will have my staff come in here and tranquilize you, just like they did yesterday. I will have order in my domain, and that order starts with you following my instructions, whether you like them or not. Now stop it."

Cooper continued to search the doctor's mind, trying to learn as much as he could.

"He is still doing it!" shouted Corwin.

Dr. Stein went to a desk over by the wall and picked up a phone. "Stop it now or you will be drugged and taken back to your room."

Cooper hesitated a moment and then withdrew. He had sensed much, but knew there was much more there to be read. He retreated back into his own mind, refusing to share what he had learned even with Coupe, who looked over at him searchingly. He got no response.

"He stopped," said Corwin.

Dr. Stein put the phone down and his demeanor once again relaxed. "Thank you, Cooper, for obeying my instructions. I am very much interested in what you are capable of, but we must have order here for us to accomplish the goals we wish to achieve. Your abilities were very much one of those goals, and it appears that they are more potent than I ever could have expected. But it was I who gave them to you, and I expect you to respect that and show that respect by not utilizing them against me.

"And, Coupe," he said, turning to look at him. "I knew you would have some enhanced telesthesia, but not to that extent. Cooper would—I expected to see that development in him as he grew up. But you, Coupe?" Once again the doctor smiled widely. He ruffled Coupe's hair. "Coupe, you amaze me. Tell me, can you do it on your own, or do you need Cooper's help?"

The doctor seemed to know more about him already, and since Coupe would be looking for many answers of his own, he decided to answer his question.

"No, Cooper's the one with that special talent. I just get to sense what he senses, when he lets me. But we've sort of grown to stay connected whenever we're around each other. Most of the time, that is," he added, again looking over at Cooper, who continued to block him out.

"So you can use Cooper's ability as a conduit for yourself then? Fascinating. A telepathic vinculum. I never would have predicted that outcome, or its extent at least." Dr. Stein seemed very pleased as he mused to himself. He turned back to Coupe. "Tell me, when did you two become aware of each other in this regard?"

·················

Coupe spent the next hour detailing his relationship with Cooper and how the boys came to be so bonded. He told Dr. Stein about how they protected each other, and their ability to calm each other.

"It was anticipated that this particular quality that both Cooper and Corwin shared would not begin to develop until they reached adolescence, so the timing does not surprise me. However, the fact that you are aware of his abilities and apparently have created some sort of symbiosis . . . well, that, quite frankly is, momentous. Wholly unanticipated. Tell me, can you use Corwin's telesthesia in the same way you use Cooper's?"

"Dunno. I only just met the kid and right now I am shutting him out. I expect he's doing the same to me. And I don't *use* Cooper. We just share a lot."

"It would appear that you do." Dr. Stein turned to look at Corwin. "Let him in, right now."

Corwin looked slightly annoyed by the request, but did as he was told. "Yes, sir," he replied.

"Okay, Coupe, I am thinking of something and Corwin is going to use his abilities to sense what it is," Dr. Stein said. "See if you can sense it too."

"It doesn't work like that. I can't go over into his head like he can to you. He has to establish the contact, not me."

"Fair enough. Corwin, establish the contact."

As commanded, Coupe felt Corwin reaching out to him. Just like last time it felt entirely different from what Cooper felt like in his head. His abilities seemed rudimentary compared to Cooper's, like a child just learning to speak. Coupe quickly sensed what Corwin was sensing. He also tried to get a sense of just what sort of a person Corwin was while he was doing it. He sensed that Corwin lacked something. If Cooper was an oil painting, Corwin was like a black-and-white snapshot.

"He's trying to read me too!" blurted out Corwin. He severed their contact.

"Interesting," said the doctor. "Coupe, were you able to see what I was thinking?"

"I think so. I got the impression of a man standing outside in the rain with an umbrella. He was in a big city somewhere and looking for an address he could not find. I get the sense it might have been you, only when you were younger."

"Very good, Coupe, very good. That is precisely right. Oh, I cannot wait to study what else you can do." He turned to look at Cooper, who, as usual, was sitting quietly.

"Don't worry, Cooper. I haven't forgotten about you! You and I will have long chats as well. I am particularly interested in how you appeared to put Coupe to sleep last night. That's something else I did not anticipate, something else I could not have predicted! Tell me how you do it."

Cooper just stared back at him impassively. Coupe knew the wall was up, and he also knew the more the doctor pushed, the more he would withdraw. Coupe started thinking about the color blue. As he did, he felt Cooper reach out to him to share in its calming qualities. They both felt Corwin reaching out to see what they were doing, and they quickly blocked him out but maintained their own contact.

"They're doing it again! They're communicating with each other, and this time they have blocked me out!" cried Corwin.

"Do you know how he does it, Coupe?"

"How about a little *quid pro quo* here, Doc? I'm answering all the questions and you're asking them all."

The doctor smirked. "Very well, Coupe. I will answer some of your questions. You are entitled to that. Both of you are entitled to that. But before I answer any of your questions, let me give you this warning. Whatever *additional* skills you two have developed, do not use them in here to somehow get away or thwart our studies of you. You are here for your safety—and the safety of others you have left behind. Do I make myself clear?"

Both boys stared at him, quietly absorbing the import of his words. Then Coupe said, "Yes, Dr. Stein, you do."

"I'll have an answer from both of you on this point. Cooper, do you understand as well?"

Wildly alarmed by the doctor's veiled threats concerning his parents, Cooper stood and took a step toward him. The doctor retreated. Corwin came from behind the chair to stand before the doctor. Cooper stared first at Corwin and then at Dr. Stein.

"He's trying to read you!"

"Well, keep him out."

"I'm trying!"

"Cooper," said Dr. Stein, "think very carefully on your next move. I truly want you to succeed and thrive here and for everyone elsewhere to do the same. But, as you can see, I already have one of you, so if you cannot agree to my demands and live within the structure I intend to provide for you, well, I have alternatives. Your time here could become very tedious."

Cooper took another step toward him, and Corwin put his hands on his chest to stop him. Cooper tried to push them away. While Cooper may have had the stronger telepathic abilities, Corwin was physically stronger. Cooper took a step backward, then went back to his seat and looked over at Dr. Stein, who was still eyeing him suspiciously.

"You are a bad man," said Cooper quietly, "but yes, I understand what you have said."

Dr. Stein appeared relieved and took his own seat again. Corwin went back to stand behind his chair.

"I am not as bad as you may think, Cooper. Hopefully, you will learn that I have some positive qualities that may moderate your opinion of me."

Cooper stared at him blankly. Dr Stein did not expect any response. He was fully aware of Cooper's history. He was surprised when Cooper then spoke to him.

"Tell Coupe who his mother is—and I don't mean the machines you grew us in."

Dr. Stein was shocked. Cooper had only been able to access his mind for a brief period, but he had perceived far more than he would have expected.

"Wait, what? Machines?" said Coupe. "Tell me."

"No," replied Cooper. "He has to tell you. He needs to tell you what we are and what he did to you."

Dr. Stein bristled. "I made him what he is today, perhaps the greatest creation that has ever come out of this facility!"

"Then tell him how you did it!" shouted Cooper.

"Very well!" said the doctor. "I will tell you, but I will tell you in my own words the way I want you to hear it. Not just from Cooper's brief glimpse into my memory. Because a partial memory is not a real memory, and you both need to have the whole history to fully understand just how remarkable all three of you really are. Corwin, sit down too. I know that you are well aware of your history, but I do not think Cooper is going to do anything rash."

CHAPTER 29

When the three boys were settled and calm, the doctor began.

"Cooper, Coupe, consider this your Book of Genesis, but written by me. I am a geneticist. Not just some geneticist, mind you. I am a brilliant geneticist! Even when I was an undergraduate student, I looked beyond the horizon of what the field of genetics could do and beyond the thoughts and theories of other geneticists of the time. I challenged the limitations of those times. I *knew* there was so much more we could accomplish if only we had the moral courage to explore genetically. We could rewrite the whole human genome, which to my mind was a mess. Our genome looks like we were thrown together in God's garage. It made us smart and got us working, but is replete with what I can only conclude are errors, of a sort.

"Do you know that humans have many times more genetically induced conditions and diseases than any other species on the planet? Have you ever seen a chimp with Down's syndrome? A moose with cystic fibrosis? No! Not the way humankind has been afflicted, that is. Early in my career I made it my goal to make humans better by making better humans. I knew there was more that could be done to advance humankind.

"At first I thought in terms of ridding our race of genetic diseases, but then I began to think it would be much more practicable to just make a better genome. So I did!"

Dr. Stein was now warming up to his audience. He turned to look out the window before continuing.

"As expected, the start was slow. The funding was limited. But the work I did back in those early days caught the attention of the right people. The scientific community was elated when it unraveled the human genome. But I said it was not the end of the job; it was just the beginning because now that we had the building blocks, we could start to build something really spectacular, so much better than pathetic ape-like creatures with all their defects. We could reshape those building blocks, not only to do away with genetic disorders and make us immune to other diseases, but also enhance our good qualities, reduce or extinguish our weaker ones. My theories and early research caught the attention of powerful people, both inside the government and out.

"Coupe, that scene you were able to see so easily was of me, some thirty-five years ago. I had been invited to present my research to some unnamed but well-funded board that was interested in my results. I was in Washington, DC, for the first time in my life, and I had gotten lost on a rainy day. Thankfully, a car was sent for me and I was found. And I presented my research about what I thought might be possible. From that meeting this campus was born.

"Obviously, it was not a quick transformation to what you see around you. Like Sisyphus, I was given a task that many thought could never be accomplished, doomed to failure after failure. And in the beginning that is exactly what it was. But then there were small successes. We took those small successes and we gathered them together for a slightly larger success. There were many failures, many false starts and wrong turns. But we learned from them too.

"The road was long, and those successes at times seemed too few. But we did not waver. In fact, we persevered! We knew that our goal was humankind in a state of greatness. That was our goal—to improve humankind. Make it better than it had ever been. Make it greater than it could ever expect. And in so doing create a better society. I was given the task of Sisyphus, to forever push a boulder up a hill. But unlike Sisyphus, I reached the top of that hill. And the view is grand, my boys. The view is grand!"

Dr. Stein did not notice—or did not care to notice—that his audience was not as impressed with him as he was with himself.

"In my lab, we analyzed the genes of not only humans but many other creatures as well. Cooper, your uncommon strength has its beginnings in the DNA of chimpanzees!"

"You mean I'm a monkey?" asked Cooper. The doctor gave a quick laugh.

"No, no you're not, Cooper. Nothing of the sort. I'm an ape, or at least a member of the ape family. I carry that in my DNA; it limits my strength to that of mere mortal man. But it is not in yours, Cooper. Not one bit. Your strength comes from something much more special."

"So, what am I then?"

"You are what I made you to be. Your DNA was synthesized. Granted, it has been placed into a hominid frame, but there is no other creature with your DNA, except for Corwin here. The same goes for you too, Coupe, and all of your siblings that were created here at this campus. We analyzed the genes of other creatures, but we did not use them. We synthesized our own genes to enhance what we studied, make those genes create a more robust form of human being. And then we combined them for different qualities. Then we enhanced their functions by creating synthetic hormones and synthetic proteins to be utilized by the synthetic DNA, all to create your unique physical attributes like nothing ever before.

"Cooper, that is in large part what made your telesthesia possible. Coupe, you have some similar ability, but not as pronounced as it was developed to be for Cooper."

Coupe was now curious. There had been so many things about himself he knew were odd, like his sniffing.

"Dr. Stein, my sense of smell. Did you do anything to enhance that?"

"We most certainly did! Your sense of smell, your sense of hearing, your eyesight, even your amazing quickness and dexterity. All of them are far superior to that of any normal human. Your ability to regenerate, to heal yourself rapidly, is something I worked on for a very long time. Your sense of smell is closer to that of a dog or a bear than it is to a human. You have better eyesight than an eagle and ears sensitive enough to hear a mouse walking through grass! You all have greatly delayed senescence. Each one of you represents the very bright future of humankind."

Dr. Stein stood and approached Coupe, who was seated. "I suspect that it was pretty overwhelming for you at first, Coupe. Just as Cooper's telesthesia was for him, until just recently. I have learned that Cooper has started to overcome all the noise in his head with your help. But I also tried to give you tools to deal with your enhanced senses, Coupe. I tried to enhance your intuitive abilities and most of all . . . your intelligence."

"You made me smart? How smart?"

"I designed you to be capable of a very high intellect, but with limitations."

"What sort of limitations?"

"Our prior experiments showed us that the higher we increased intellectual ability, the more often our test subjects would be prone to varying degrees of mental instability. It was a problem we tried again and again to overcome. But we could not. Ultimately, we had to find the happy medium. Enhance intelligence as much as we could without catalyzing symptoms of mental illness. With you we appear to have struck that balance. The reason you are here is because we failed to strike that balance with your twin, who was known here as Chase."

"Is that the kid in the photographs Chief Dale showed me? He has been abducting other kids?"

"Yes, I expect that is he, Coupe. He left us about two years ago. In that time he has been hunting down and killing, not just abducting, other enhanced individuals such as yourself and Cooper. We are not really sure how he is finding them, but then again, he is very smart. Smarter than both you and me."

"How can he be smarter than me if he is the same as me? And why am I not going nuts too?"

"Good questions, Coupe. Genetics plays a large part in what we all become, but it is not the only factor. Environment is also a very significant factor. Nutrition is a significant factor. Even subtle variations in the gestational environment can have significant impacts on subsequent development.

"Your counterpart, the one that is out there destroying all my good work, his intelligence was exceptionally high. As it continued to improve, he began to show the telltale signs of mental compromise. Ultimately it became clear he could no longer think coherently. He became paranoid and delusional. He had once been our brightest star, but he became something else entirely. He decided that our entire program was corrupt and compromised and that it had to be ended.

"One night about two years ago, he set a trap for his brothers and sisters and myself. He killed one of them while trying to kill all of us and then escaped. Since then he has been hunting down and killing our environmental test subjects. That is why we brought you and Cooper back here.

"You made the news, Coupe, when you were stabbed in that

robbery in Massachusetts. Your actions in protecting that young woman were commendable. It was deeply gratifying to see your moral foundations so well developed.

"But there could be no doubt Chase would recognize his own twin and would soon be hunting you too. I expect he would have an added zeal in bringing you down given that you are his twin. We could not allow that to happen, so I ordered your return to us here, where we could protect you."

Each time the doctor answered one of Coupe's questions, it spawned others. But there was one area that piqued his interest most.

"What do you mean by environmental test subjects, Doc?"

Dr. Stein knew he had to be careful answering this question. "Coupe, in a typical scientific experiment there are generally two types of test subjects, a control group and then the test group. As you have already seen, there are two of you. In your test round there were actually twelve of you—six matched pairs. One set of those matched pairs was kept here as the control group, which was carefully monitored, carefully nurtured, and exposed only to those things to which we wished them to be exposed.

"The environmental test group, however, was placed out into the general community under various conditions to see just how they responded to the environments they would typically experience growing and living without any controls. Both you and Cooper were part of that group. It was important for us to learn just how our genetically enhanced subjects would interact with the real world. In fact, it was vitally important. History is replete with examples of good-intentioned scientists introducing a new species to a new environment in an effort to improve the quality of that environment only to have it go disastrously wrong. To avoid that result we decided to start testing our genetically enhanced subjects on a very limited scale to ensure that any untoward results could be controlled, if necessary."

"Why make us at all?" asked Coupe.

"Think of the ramifications! It would advance our potential evolution by thousands of years, create people with abilities far beyond what nature could produce in any given generation—if at all. Do away with disease, genetic deficiencies. People might stop getting sick. If people do get injured, they heal in a tenth of the time. Hospitals would be empty. Life itself could be enhanced."

Cooper was getting impatient with the doctor. Suddenly he blurted, "Tell him who is mother is!"

Dr. Stein looked annoyed, but he could also see that Coupe was now studying his face. "Well, Doc? What is it that you're holding back?"

Dr. Stein sighed and began to explain. "None of you had any real mother or father. Your DNA was synthesized, and your creation was orchestrated in a laboratory. Your prenatal development was conducted in biological incubators that allowed you to grow until you were ready to survive on your own. The control subjects did not need people to act as a mother or father. The staff members here provided everything we wanted them to have. But those subjects that we placed in the outside environment, well, we needed to find suitable people to act in those roles.

"Cooper, your mother did not know it, but she adopted you from us. For you we wanted someone who could be especially nurturing. The proper and maximal growth of your empathic powers absolutely depended on a loving and nurturing environment. The letter that your mother included in her application set her apart from all the other applicants. We chose her for you because of the love we knew she could give to you. And then when she met Everett, we thoroughly investigated him. He was a very satisfactory addition and we allowed the relationship to continue. Of course, all of this was done without either one of them ever knowing about it or knowing about this institution." Dr. Stein smiled at Cooper, who was still frowning heavily. "Cooper, I still have that letter your mother wrote. Would you like to see it?"

"Tell Coupe about his mother!"

"Yes, yes, very well," said Dr. Stein impatiently. "Coupe, your environment was carefully chosen as well. But different choices for different reasons. Because of the enhancements we had designed into you—especially your increased intelligence and intuitive powers—and because we had issues with mental instability in prior iterations, we needed to see just what would happen if a person with your unique abilities was raised in a negative environment. We needed to test your mental durability. After all, the last result we wanted was to produce a near genius psychopath and let him loose into the world at large."

Coupe chose not to point out that was, in fact, precisely what Dr. Stein had done with Chase. Right now he felt a growing concern as to what Dr. Stein was revealing about his own hostile childhood.

"We needed to see just how your particular genetic makeup would survive in a hostile and marginalized environment," Dr. Stein continued. "To be quite honest, Coupe, I was surprised at how well you have done. I was all but convinced that the things that you have been exposed to would have caused significant mental instability. But instead you have thrived! And to our complete surprise, it was our control subject that suffered the mental degradation. The results were completely the opposite of what we expected. Though, that is why we conduct experiments. We see what works and what does not."

Coupe had been listening to this with ever greater concern and anger. "My environment was controlled, just like Cooper's? Except instead of placing me with a loving and nurturing family like his, you let me be adopted by a boozing drugging deadbeat mom who let her boyfriends abuse me?"

"She never adopted you, Coupe. She was hired to act as your mother, paid a modest monthly stipend to care for you—in her own way. Of course, she never knew about your special qualities either, or where the money was coming from. It was presented as a sort of quasi-governmental welfare that she would receive so long as you were in her care. It was enough for her to want to keep you around, but not enough to live on comfortably. We wanted her to continue in the quasi-transient environment in which we found her. She was required to provide us with monthly reports of your activities, though truth be told, we had our own technicians gathering data all along, occasionally making observations to confirm what we learned."

"Do you know what happened to me?" Coupe asked, anger boiling behind his words.

Dr. Stein met Coupe's fiery gaze. He paused before he spoke, but he did not flinch from answering the question.

"Yes, Coupe. I know everything that has happened to you. Some of it was expected. Much of it was not. But all the horrible things that have happened to you are what we believe has made you the most exceptional subject we have ever produced. Your suffering has caused you to become . . . exceptional."

Coupe stood and walked to the window to look out on the scene below. Cooper knew what was brewing in Coupe's mind. He stood in anticipation. Corwin sensed something too and also stood. He went to guard Dr. Stein. In a moment of astounding agility Coupe turned and lunged, hobbled foot in tow, at Dr. Stein. His first step was incredibly quick, but was blocked by the other two boys, who stood in front of the doctor like linemen. Coupe was able to knock the glasses off of Dr. Stein's face but nothing more. Cooper and Corwin easily prevented Coupe from doing anything further.

Coupe stumbled back to the window to settle himself. Cooper approached, but Coupe turned away. Cooper turned him around and pulled him to his shoulder and held him there. Coupe took a long, deep breath. He stayed like that for a few moments and then pulled back. He stared at Cooper, and it was obvious they were having another one of their silent conversations. Corwin attempted to sense what they were doing, but he was quickly blocked out.

Dr. Stein retrieved his glasses and studied the silent conversation between his two creations. Their silent interactions fascinated him. He had to know more of just what they could do.

Eventually, whatever communication the two boys had led to Coupe settling down enough to allow the conversation with Dr. Stein to continue. Corwin was planted firmly in front of the doctor now.

"I am sorry I did that, Dr. Stein. I shouldn't have. But I am really, really mad right now."

Dr. Stein was surprised by the apology and wondered what had prompted it. Nonetheless, he knew Coupe possessed good manners and a forgiving nature from reports he had read.

"I do not think that there is anything I can say that would lead to you forgiving me, Coupe. But then again, I am not looking for forgiveness. At my core, I am a man of science. The terrible, terrible things that happened to you were, for the good of all mankind, a necessary predicate to determine if indeed your particular genomic arrangement was viable. You have proven that it is—under the right circumstances.

"I know you will not understand this, but you should take immense satisfaction in your survival, in your resilience, in your ability to thrive where all others would likely have foundered. It was those profoundly disturbing experiences that molded you, strengthened you, made you capable of controlling the tremendous gifts you possess. I believe that without those experiences and your struggle to survive through them, you would not have been forced to tap into the depths of what is inside you. But you did it, and it has made you stronger. Perhaps not as intelligent as your analogue, but stronger in many other ways that allowed you to control your gifts and not to succumb to them as Chase did."

Coupe was silent for a moment. He did not want to ask, but he had to know. "What about Keith and Father Hatem? Did you send them?"

"No, we did not, and we obviously did not cause it. We would have stopped it had we known. But once it was over we learned just what you were capable of withstanding and learned how such events would impact you, and perhaps others that came after you. We wanted a stable genome, and you withstood perhaps the most rigorous attack on that genome. You not only survived, you *thrived* because of it."

"Yeah? Well, I don't feel any stronger, and you don't know if I would have been this way or not if you stopped those things."

"But I do, Coupe. Your control counterpart proves that."

Coupe dismissed the doctor's explanation. He felt nothing but contempt for the man who had intended for his childhood to be rough and tumultuous and then did nothing but study the effects when it slipped into something entirely more pernicious. He tried to think of what he might have been like if he had been raised by Everett and Evelyn, just like Cooper had. But he could not. It was too painful, so he simply changed subjects.

"So, my mom, she's not blood to me at all?"

"None at all, Coupe. A hired attendant that kept us apprised of your progress. Admittedly, she moved you around more than we would have liked, but your mother always let us know where she went. She wanted her check."

"I'd appreciate it if you did not call her my mother anymore. I at least thought I had a blood bond with her, even if she usually didn't give more than two thoughts for me in a day. Now I know better. No mom, no dad, no family."

"That's not true, Coupe. You may have had no mother or father, but you have siblings. In many ways Cooper really is your brother. So is Corwin here, Chase, wherever he is, and the others that were in your iteration. You were all created on the same day, and you were all initiated—born, if you will—on the same date. You all share the same basic framework."

"So how many of us are there, and what did you mean by *iteration*?"

"Sorry, perhaps not the best word for you to hear. I used iteration because you began as a group of genetically modified viable eggs, which had been predicated on prior versions, each time modified, tweaked, to make the outcome more successful. It is a vernacular perhaps peculiar to this place. But to answer your question, there were six successful paired iterations—genacies, to be technical—in your group. You were designated *Omicron, Group C.* Over time I just began referring to you and your siblings as the Omicron Six."

"Omicron?"

Dr. Stein smiled at the question. "You will have to forgive my classical education. Omicron is the fifteenth letter of the Greek alphabet. There were fourteen attempted genacies before we were finally successful. You are Group C because there were two groups before yours. There were eight viable genacies in Group A. They were not paired. There were six in Group B, again unpaired. But Chase has been busy, as you know.

"And until we capture him, it is best for you to stay here and be safe. You will have the opportunity to meet your siblings! This place may be remote, but it is also beautiful, with remarkable resources. And you will want for nothing. Please believe me when I say you will be made most comfortable while you are here, so long as you conform to our expectations."

"How long are you going to keep us here?" asked Cooper.

"For as long as I deem it necessary to keep you safe. I will also use the time that has been afforded to us to learn more about you two. I am very disquisitive, and want to study your unique abilities to interact with one another."

"What about our parents?" Cooper asked. "Do you know what they think happened to us?"

"Right now, they believe you have been kidnapped. Chief Dale firmly believes that Chase was behind your abduction. He has been aware of the similarity between Chase and Coupe for some time. He appears to know that Chase was involved in other abductions and he has presumed that he was responsible for yours. His trail will likely run cold after that, but should he by some miracle be able to arrest and detain Chase, well, that will make all of our lives much easier.

"But your parents will not be left to suffer for much longer, rest assured. This place is funded by some very powerful people. As we speak, representatives of the Consortium that funds this academy are on their way to your parents. They will explain that you have been taken to protect you from Chase. Other members of the Consortium will reach out to Chief Dale to provide a similar report. Your disappearance will then be regarded as you two on a lark, heading for warmer weather when the snow arrived. A thin cover story, I admit, but it is one that allows us to bring your parents into the fold and to manage your disappearance."

"But Chase for sure knows he did not take us," said Coupe. "Once he realizes we are gone, he will know that somebody else took us. It's not much of a leap for him to think that you did it, Dr. Stein."

"You are quick, Coupe, very quick!" he said, smiling broadly. "That is precisely what I expect he will think!"

"So, we're bait?"

"Very valuable bait, Coupe! Bait I intend to expend every resource to protect, though I expect both of you would be better suited to that task than anything I could do! But nevertheless, you are here for your own protection. Though I must concede it does present a very desirable target to your missing brother!"

"So you are just going to lock us away in our little cell until he comes and hope you can stop him?"

"Not at all. Those accommodations were for your first night only. Until we could have this chat. You are free to wander the campus going forward, but stay within the fence line; that is my only restriction on your freedom. I trust you will honor your word, if I should grant you this parole; otherwise . . ." Dr. Stein trailed off.

"You have met Corwin. You now have the opportunity to meet your three other siblings that are still here on campus. They too can share a great deal of information with you. They can tell you about our community here and what it has been like for them to grow up here.

"I have given you a great deal to think about. I expect it will generate many questions. For now, however, I will allow you to digest what you have learned so far. And I will arrange for your ankle to be repaired tomorrow, Coupe. Now take this opportunity to explore your new home."

Dr. Stein pressed a button on his phone, and the door to the library opened. One of the caretakers held it open, and Cooper and Coupe knew they were being dismissed. Corwin remained at the doctor's side, but Dr. Stein motioned them toward the now open door.

"Have a look around," he said. "This man's name is Stanley. He should be able to help with your day-to-day needs."

It was the man who had let them into their secure room the night before, and wearing the same gentle smile.

"C'mon, Cooper," said Coupe. "Our audience is over." He hobbled toward the door. Cooper got up and obediently followed, giving a final glance at Dr. Stein. Stanley closed the door firmly behind them as they left.

"You have been given free run over the campus, boys," he said. "I printed out these maps to give you some sense of your surroundings. If the door is unlocked, you can enter. If not, well, find another building." He handed them the maps. "I highlighted the dining hall in yellow. You will want to be there between twelve and one for lunch and five and six for dinner. If you need me, pick up a campus phone and dial twelve.

"You will be assigned rooms in the regular dormitory for this evening. I will show you to your rooms later. Meanwhile, if you go back to the rooms you stayed in last night, you will find fresh clothes and winter jackets. Dr. Stein has assigned me to your care. I take that seriously. Like I said, if you need anything, just dial twelve."

"Thank you, Stanley," replied Coupe. "We will make our own way back to the room and call you if we need you."

Stanley nodded and quickly disappeared down the hallway.

CHAPTER 30

The two boys made their way back to the room they had stayed in the previous evening. All doors leading to it now appeared to be unlocked. Out of curiosity, Coupe tried the one that led toward the garage where the vans were kept. It was locked.

In their room they found more clothes in their sizes. Among the selection were down-filled winter coats appropriate for a New England winter. On the left breast of each coat was a simple crest. Inside the crest was a representation of a pine tree with a double-helix ouroboros overlaying it. Above the crest it read *Deep Woods*; below it was inscribed *Academy*. Coupe laughed. It seemed pretentious but he liked it. It provided him status. He wondered if he would be allowed to take it home—if and when they were allowed to leave.

"I wonder if we'll make the basketball team?" joked Coupe, and Cooper smiled, the first in a long time.

They changed and put on their warm winter coats before heading back outside to explore the campus that was their new forced home.

Coupe pulled the map out of his pocket and oriented it to the library building in which they had met with Dr. Stein. All of the main buildings were perched on a shallow hill leading down to the tree-lined lake that bordered the campus' southern edge. At the top of the hill was a solitary water tower, looking down upon the campus. Without a word the boys walked toward the lake. There they would have a better view of the various buildings on the campus. Besides, the dining hall appeared to be next to the lake anyway, so they would be able to get something to eat once they were down there.

They noted a few people walking about the campus, but they were adults. None appeared to be the other young genetic experiments. There were several people wearing security uniforms. Others wore lab coats or smocks.

Cooper and Coupe did not speak as they walked along the quiet paths between the buildings and down to the lake. They were conversing in their special way, doing their best to figure out how to handle their present situation. They did not sense any present danger but suspected they were being closely watched.

Their silent conversation eventually brought them down to the shore of the lake. It had a wide sandy beach, which in the summer would be an attractive place to spend time. Now, however, the lake was covered by a thin sheet of ice.

The two walked toward a long wooden dock that jutted out into the lake. Beyond that was an old boathouse, closed tight against the winter. No doubt during the summer boats would have been tied to it.

About halfway along the dock Cooper stopped walking and began looking around, as if looking for someone.

"What's the matter?" asked Coupe out loud. He could feel Cooper sensing for something.

"I don't know," he said. "I can feel someone else is with us, like when someone comes into a room. But I can't see anyone to explain it."

The two boys looked around. The closest person that Coupe could see was a man standing near where the sand started and the path had ended. He was likely assigned to keep an eye on them both. He was at least a hundred yards away and well beyond Cooper's ability to sense his presence.

"I can't see anyone except for that guy that is probably following us," said Coupe.

"He is," he said. "I got a sense of him when we left the building where they held us last night. But it's not him. He's too far away."

The two boys stood on the dock trying to locate the supposed spy. Their conversation once again slipped into silent mode as they worked their way to the end of the dock. At the end of the dock they spotted a hole cut into the ice near a ladder leading into the water. Being from Vermont they knew it was not for ice fishing. The ice was too thin and the hole was too big.

"What do you suppose that's for?" asked Coupe.

"No clue," responded Cooper.

In answer to their question a head suddenly popped out of the hole, breaking a thin sheen of ice that had formed over it. It was the head of a teenage girl. The two boys were momentarily shocked and then looked around for something to throw in to help her.

"Hang on!" shouted Coupe. "We'll help you!"

There was nothing on the end of the dock that they could throw to pull her out, but they need not have bothered. The stocky young girl simply pulled herself out of the hole in the ice and walked over to the ladder, grabbed a robe that was hanging on it, and got up on the dock. Her robe had the same crest as their jackets.

"You two must be Cooper and Coupe," she said. "I've been expecting you. I'm Cotovatre."

Shocked, Coupe said, "Aren't you cold?"

"A little bit. But I can warm up in the dining hall. C'mon, we can have lunch together," she said as she walked past them and started down the dock. "By the way, I'm your sister," she added over her shoulder.

"How about that, Cooper? We have a sister, and she is part fish."

"My DNA is based on dolphins and other aquatic mammals, not fish," she huffed and kept walking. "C'mon, today is Thursday. That means the haddock special."

"Are you sure that isn't cannibalism?" quipped Coupe.

She paused to look back at them, smiled, barked remarkably like a seal, and then turned and left them behind.

The two boys quickly caught up to her. But she remained silent, leading the way to the dining hall. Cooper could sense—and Coupe quickly read—that she was just as interested in them as they were in her. For now, however, she was trying to act aloof; that is, until Cooper called her on it.

"I don't know why you are pretending you are not as interested in us as we are in you," he said. "I can sense your curiosity, you know."

Cotovatre stopped and turned. "That's right. Franklin told us you had empathic abilities that were pretty amazing. Tell me, what am I thinking about now?"

"The number seven," replied Cooper. "And who is Franklin?"

"Wow. That's pretty impressive. And I'm talking about Dr. Stein."

"Why do you call him Franklin?"

Coupe let out a short hoot of a laugh. Cotovatre looked at him. He smiled. "I read more than he does. That's funny; that's good."

"I don't get it," said Cooper. Then he reached into Coupe's mind and he started smiling too. "Oh, now I get it. That is funny!"

· · · · · · · · · · · · · · · · ·

With the ice broken, the three walked into the dining hall. Cotovatre was right. There was a haddock special, and she helped herself to it. There was a whole serving line of dishes to choose from along with a sandwich bar. The boys could see nowhere to pay, and no one was looking for money, so they dug in and got sandwiches with fries. They found seats with Cotovatre, sitting across from her.

"What?" asked Coupe, seeing Cotovatre stare at them.

"She's still trying to figure us out," replied Cooper, not looking up from his sandwich, stuffing one of the fries into his mouth. "You remind her of Chase, and she used to like him, for a while. Then he changed. Me, she doesn't trust at all. I remind her of Corwin, and I get the sense she and him don't get on. Well, at least as well as Corwin wanted them to. He sorta liked her, but she didn't feel the same way, even though they were kids together and grew up together."

Cotovatre looked at Cooper with wide eyes. "Okay, Cooper, that's impressive, but let's set some ground rules here. Can you not do that? I am happy to answer your questions. You just have to give me the chance. If I know the answer, I'll tell you the truth."

Coupe smiled again. "If you don't, he will know," he said, nodding at Cooper.

"Yeah, I get that. It's kinda spooky."

"You'll get used to it. He's got a good heart. You'll see that if you don't confuse him with Dr. Stein's pet. Give him a chance," said Coupe.

Cooper smiled at her. "Sorry," he said. "I'll try not to answer for you again."

"So, how long have you been here?" asked Coupe.

"All my life. This has always been my home—the people here, my family. This place started out as a private boarding school. It had an excellent academic reputation, but the location proved to be too remote for anyone other than the most hardcore students, so that school eventually closed. Dr. Stein was one of its last graduates. Then the Consortium purchased it for Dr. Stein about thirty years ago, and he turned it into a thriving scientific community."

"The Consortium?" asked Coupe.

"That's what Dr. Stein calls the various groups and agencies that support his research and our community here. I once asked just who they all were, but he gave me a vague answer. It appears to be a bunch of different groups and people that are interested in just what he can do. It looks like they're all pretty happy with the outcome so far, because there is no shortage of funds. If Dr. Stein wants a new building or new equipment, he simply requisitions it and he gets it."

"All the guards, are they with the Consortium?"

"Guards?" asked Cotovatre, obviously concerned.

"The goons that keep you in here, like the one that shot Cooper yesterday when they dragged us in here."

Cotovatre looked a Cooper for a moment before answering. "Well, I don't know anything about you getting shot, Cooper, and you look pretty healthy to me, but they are not guards. They're here to protect us. And you were brought here so they could protect you as well."

"How do you know?"

"We had a meeting about it last week sometime. Dr. Stein informed us that you two were in danger because you, Coupe, had been in the news and it was very likely Chase would hunt you down, find you. He did not want that to happen, so he informed everyone you would be coming back. I must tell you, I was excited. I wanted to meet you and find out what it's like out there. He also told us what you did, Coupe. I was really impressed. You are very brave. Of course, Dr. Stein likely designed you to be that way. You have absolutely thrived in the outside world."

"What? Outside world? If you're interested in it, why haven't you just left and found out for yourself?"

"Leave? I don't want to. At least, not right now. I will go when Dr. Stein tells me I'm ready. I know I've mocked him a little bit in speaking with you, but that does not mean I don't believe in what he is doing. When it's my time, I will be introduced into the outside environment. Dr. Stein and I have already started talking about that day. He wants me to go college and continue my education. Just like the Alphas and the Betas did. But not yet for me. I'm not ready. And not while Chase is still out there."

Cotovatre thought back to when the campus was full. "The place used to be busy. We were the third group of kids that Dr. Stein produced. There was eight with Alpha group and another six with Beta, each about four years apart. Each group started as a test group of ten, but not all of the genacies were viable. The Alphas will be in their twenties now, hopefully. There were six in our group, but we were twinned. C group was the only twinned group. Dr. Stein was getting closer to his desired outcome, so tests beyond this facility were determined necessary. That's where our group came in. Half of us were raised here, and the other half, well, you know. So as a kid this place was really hopping. There were twenty of us at one point. It's so quiet now, but they do come back from time to time, so it picks up then."

"How do you know so much about it?" asked Coupe, surprised by the extent of her knowledge concerning Dr. Stein's experiments.

Cotovatre seemed surprised by the question. "Because we were told all about it. We were instructed in what we were, how we were different, how we were to change the world. Dr. Stein was very proud of his accomplishments, and he wanted us to share in that as well. He wanted us to know what we represented to humankind and how we could change it."

"Yeah, so how did the good doctor tell you to *change* the world?"

"No, not that way. We were not created with some sort of mission to change the world, just to improve the human condition. Make humans stronger, healthier, live longer lives. To help and support each other during our time. We have all that promise inside of us.

"Say what you will about Franklin—and I say a lot, believe me— but he has given each of us unique abilities that we were taught to treasure and utilize for not just ourselves but the improvement of everyone, like you did for that girl you saved. Dr. Stein may be amoral by your standards, but he is not immoral. I can see now how others might see him like a mad scientist. But I am one of his monsters, and I like who I am, what he made me to be."

"Just what did he make you to be?" asked Coupe.

"Me? I am the underwater specialist." She beamed. "I can stay underwater for thirty to forty minutes at a time, depending on what I'm doing. I can see clearly underwater. I can find things underwater in sort of the same way a dolphin does, but not exactly. I can swim like a seal; I broke every single world record for swimming by the time I was ten. And the cold doesn't bother me much. Neither does heat for that matter, but that was just a happy accident, according to Dr. Stein.

"The Alphas and Betas had enhanced capabilities too, but not like us. Some of them had similar strengths, but Dr. Stein modified them with each genacy until he arrived at what he wanted. We were the first synthetic DNA subjects. The Alphas and Betas were enhanced natural DNA. That is what ultimately led to us. Improvement on natural DNA by discarding and synthesizing exactly what was needed. That was us. That *is* us. There's you, Cooper, with your strength and empathic abilities. Cory is your genetic match."

"Cory?" asked Coupe.

"Corwin, but only Franklin calls him that. He's nice enough, as you will get to learn, but he is definitely the teacher's pet, so be careful what you say to him."

"Yeah, we've already met Corwin," Coupe said. "Definitely Dr. Stein's pride and joy."

"Maybe, but not as much as you are, Coupe, or at least as much as Chase was before he . . . did what he did. Coupe, Dr. Stein put everything he had learned and tested into you and Chase. You were designed to have speed and dexterity with heightened senses, and you were made to be really smart. Your body knows how to heal itself super quick too. Dr. Stein always considered your genetic design to be his greatest achievement.

"There was Calix, too. She could not only heal herself really quickly, but others too. She was so sweet." Cotovatre briefly looked wistful before returning to her story. "She was killed on the night that

Chase fled. I don't know if her twin is still alive. Dr. Stein hasn't said anything about her one way or the other, but we know what Chase is doing. He is hunting us down. Not only C Group, but the Alphas and Betas that are out there too. He wants to wipe out all of us. I hope he hasn't gotten her. I do know my twin has gone missing. I expect that was Chase's work. Dr. Stein was arranging for her to be brought back here once he realized she was in danger, but it was too late. It's sad. I will never get to meet my twin, and I spent a lifetime thinking about the day it would happen, too."

Cotovatre looked down at her plate for a moment, feeling the pain of her loss. Cooper immediately sensed her pain and tried to comfort her.

"I'm sorry you lost your sister . . . I guess *our* sister. But you did get to meet us, and we are happy to meet you. I hope that helps a little," Cooper said.

Cotovatre looked up and a thin smile crept back slowly. She again realized how different Cooper and Cory were despite that identical appearance. Cory would never have offered comfort in the way that Cooper had. But then Cory had not been exposed to a normal family upbringing.

"Thank you, Cooper. Thank you both. It is good to meet you both. It's sort of like a family reunion. Only it would have been nice to have Caroline here too."

"Was that her name?" asked Coupe. Cotovatre nodded. "I'm sorry too," he continued. "I can see that she meant a lot to you, even if you never got the chance to meet her."

"You also have another sister, Cassiopeia, though we just call her Cassie. She usually tears herself away from the arts building for lunch, so hopefully you will get to meet her soon too. With Cassie, Dr. Stein tried to design someone who could excel in something other than physical abilities. Cassie is our resident artist. Dr. Stein designed her to have a keen ear and a catching eye. She has learned to play every musical instrument they have given her, and she has a beautiful voice. Not surprisingly she excels at the other arts as well. When the rest of us were just pasting macaroni on paper, she was copying Van Gogh."

Coupe thought it was an odd addition to Dr. Stein's collection of synthetic DNA, but he was beginning to see he did not know enough about Dr. Stein to form a reliable opinion about him. Obviously, his vision for the enrichment of humankind went beyond just strength and perception. He had given some thought to the arts as well.

"So, is she . . . snobby?" asked Coupe, expecting her to have that sort of temperament.

"Hardly," replied Cotovatre. "You will see when you get to meet her."

"And finally there is Carrick. He's around here someplace. I'll let him explain himself to you, if you can find him. He's good at hiding. He could be sitting right next to you and you would not know, so if he is, I am not going to let him catch me talking about him."

"Don't worry. He's not here," Cooper said.

"How do you know?"

"I just do."

"Hah! Carrick's not going to like that. Funny, Cory can't sense him like you do," she said.

"I am not Cory."

Just then the door to the dining area opened and a teenage girl walked in. It seemed to Coupe that she more floated through the door than walked, as her movements appeared to be effortless. She was their age, with long blond hair. On each side of her head she had made two long, thin braids and then used them to tie back the rest of her hair. As if sensing the eyes on her, she turned and then smiled. Two piercing blue eyes looked over at them. Coupe felt his heart jump. To him, she was the most beautiful person he had ever seen.

Seeing the two new arrivals, her smiled broadened, and she walked over to them.

"You two must be Cooper and Coupe! I'm Cassie."

For once it was Coupe who was speechless. He simply stared with a look of near stupefaction on his face.

"Hi, I'm Cooper and this is my little brother Coupe. Usually he does most of the talking, but I think he became speechless when you walked in."

"Aw, that is so sweet," she replied, looking at Coupe, reaching out and squeezing his shoulder.

Finally, he found his tongue. "Yeah, hi, I'm Coupe." It was all he could manage.

"Dr. Stein told us how you got hurt saving that girl. We were all really impressed." Cassiopeia squeezed his shoulder again. Coupe immediately blushed, and Cooper started smiling broadly. "I'm going to grab something to eat and I'll come back and join you."

Coupe watched her float away. In the brief time she had been with them he had found her eyes almost captivating, like Dr. Stein had somehow devised a way to genetically inject the ability to mesmerize into her DNA. But as he looked around, no one else seemed to be so smitten as he. Cooper stared at him, grinning. *You really like her, little bro*, he thought. Coupe gave him a quick smile and looked back to his lunch.

The door to the dining area opened again. Corwin walked in, alone. He looked around and saw them all sitting together. Coupe raised his hand in a half-hearted wave. Corwin curtly nodded and then turned to get some food.

"He doesn't like you, Coupe," said Cooper.

"Yeah, I get that, but I can't figure out why. I only just met him. Usually people have to get to know me before they decide not to like me. With him I got fast tracked."

"I expect you remind him of Chase. That's probably why he's being cold to you," said Cotovatre.

"They didn't get along?" asked Coupe.

"Exact opposite. They were the best of friends—sort of like you and Cooper. But then when Chase lost it, he tried to kill Cory before he left. He nearly did. He felt that betrayal deeply. I expect you remind him of that. But give him a chance. He's not that bad."

"He likes you," stated Cooper.

"Yeah, I thought we agreed that you were going to stay out of my head?"

"Sorry, but you just thought it so strong, I couldn't help it," replied Cooper. "So, what happened? You don't like him?"

"I do like him, just not in that way. I see him as an annoying brother. He saw me as something more than that, and I had to make it clear that I saw our relationship as something different. He did not take it well."

"Yeah, the high school dances must be a little creepy around here," said Coupe.

Cotovatre laughed quietly. "Our community is unique, without a doubt. It may not be a perfect match for what you get outside of here, but it's still pretty good. As for the dating scene, well, I know some of the Alphas and Betas dated each other. Dr. Stein never objected, though he kept a keen eye on it. But I never saw any of the other kids here that way—especially from C Group. We grew up together, and I just always saw us as siblings, even though technically we are not. Cory, on the other hand—"

"He's coming over and he is trying to sense you right now," said Cooper. "Do you want me to block him out?"

"You can do that?" she asked. Cooper nodded. "Please do. It's probably a good idea given what we're talking about. I don't want to embarrass him."

Cooper used his abilities to block out Cory's attempts to sense her. Cory immediately sensed Cooper's presence and stared at him with irritation, but withdrew his attempts to sense any of them. Instead he came over to the table.

"Do you mind if I sit down with you?" Corwin asked.

"Of course not," replied Coupe. "Cotovatre was describing the history of this place."

"Coty would know the most," replied Corwin, taking a seat next to her and across from Cooper. "She's sort of the leader of our group here." He spoke to the table in general. He would not look at Coupe. Corwin picked up his sandwich and began to eat. Their prior conversation was replaced with an awkward silence. Coupe tried to read Corwin's face, but he would not look up. Nonetheless, Coupe's eyes darted around as best they could, and then he sniffed. As he did so Corwin's head snapped up, and he stared intently at Coupe.

"You just scared him," said Cooper, finishing up his own sandwich. "When you just sniffed you reminded him of Chase and he's still really mad at him, so now he's kinda mad at you, though he knows that he shouldn't be."

"Stay out of my head!" snapped Corwin.

"Sorry," replied Cooper, "But for some reason you are the easiest person to read that I have ever met. I guess it's because we're the same."

"Then why can't I do that to you? I try and all I can sense is the color blue."

"Because I'm blocking you and you can't do it like I can. The blue is Coupe."

Corwin looked over at Coupe, confused, but Coupe understood completely.

"Looks like going to school and having to sit in a room with thirty kids all day paid off for you, Cooper," said Coupe. "It made your blocking abilities stronger."

"That and you and your blue light."

Corwin began to eat. He had no intention of participating in their conversation; he just wanted to listen and sense what people were thinking. Today, however, he was not able to do that. Thankfully, Cassiopeia then joined them with her lunch. She sat next to Coupe.

Coupe smiled broadly, the gap in his teeth showing. Cassiopeia smiled back.

"What happened to your tooth?" she asked, showing genuine concern.

"Oh, that?" Coupe held his hand up to his mouth. "I must have forgotten to put that one in this morning," Coupe said, showing his usual charm and evasiveness. But Cooper was not going to let him get away with it. He wanted Cassiopeia to know what sort of person Coupe really was.

"It got knocked out when Coupe got in a fight, trying to protect me," he said.

It was Corwin who asked the obvious question. "Why would he need to protect you? I mean, you've got the same type of strength as I do. Well, almost."

"I wasn't allowed to use my strength. And back then Coupe didn't even know what I could do. He just jumped in to help me out."

"So you're violent, just like Chase," replied Corwin, staring back at Coupe. The group fell silent after Corwin's awkward comment. Coupe tried to get them talking again, and given that Corwin had raised the subject, he decided to ask about Chase.

"Can any of you tell me what happened with Chase? I mean, I am his genetic equivalent. I kinda want to know what might be in my future."

"Coty can tell you," said Corwin. "I don't like to think back about it."

"Really?" she replied. "I don't want to get you all worked up."

"They should know what happened."

"Okay. Like I was saying before, growing up here was not a bad experience for me, or for Cory or for any of us, really," Cotovatre said. "Our childhood here was not by any means normal, but it wasn't in any way deprived, either. We were given attention, affection by the staff assigned to us. All our physical needs were met, meaning we always had food to eat—" She shot a glance at Coupe as she said this. "And we had a beautiful place to live. We have been given a great education and all sorts of other things to help us learn and grow.

"When we started our fifth year of education, Dr. Stein began to introduce our history to us, meaning what we were and how we had come to be. The following year he explained how we were not alone, meaning that we had twins and that they lived outside of Deep Woods. I think it was this revelation that triggered Chase.

"After it all happened we found out that Chase had taken a cell phone from one of the staff members and had been accessing the outside environment through unfiltered access to the internet. Dr. Stein filters what we are allowed to see. If it comes to us via the internet, it means that it has been reviewed and judged to be accurate.

"Chase was sweet growing up. He had a wonderful smile and always seemed to know when to say the right thing. But he had always been sort of high strung too, sort of twitchy, always asking one question too many of Dr. Stein. When Chase learned the full extent of what Dr. Stein was doing and that we were intended to be the *new* generation of human beings, he just sort of melted. He could not accept it. When he got the cell phone he tried to find information about what Dr. Stein was doing but couldn't. All he could find was a bunch of sites that confused him and made him angry. He latched on to some preachers that talked about the Bible and how it had to be followed to the letter because it was the word of God.

"Dr. Stein had given us a good education in science, but he had never taught us much about God or religion. It was all new to Chase. He thought it was fundamentally wrong that Dr. Stein was dabbling in what ought to be left to God and nature. It was pride, and pride was a sin. Dr. Stein was the living embodiment of pride, he would say. I didn't understand how pride could be a sin. It's good to take satisfaction in accomplishments, I thought. He saw pride as something different.

"He began to challenge Dr. Stein in classes. Eventually he challenged his own right to existence. He challenged all of our rights to exist. He started to frighten me. I couldn't understand why he was threatening my very existence. The others felt just as concerned as I did—well, except for Corwin."

Cotovatre looked down the table at Corwin. He had put his food down and was staring intently at his hands, which were folded on the table.

"You have to understand," continued Cotovatre, "that Corwin and Chase were nearly inseparable from the time they could crawl. They seemed to share a natural affinity, sort of the way that you and Cooper appear to. They were always together, sometimes studying together or giggling off in a corner.

"It came to us as a shock when Dr. Stein announced that Chase would no longer be attending classes and had been moved to the medical building where he was restricted. Cory was able to keep in contact with him, but did so secretly."

Corwin stared into his lap, motionless.

"What happened next changed us all, forever. I'll never forget it. I wish I could forget it. It was two years ago, last summer," she said. "Classes had ended about a week earlier when all of C Group got a message to meet in the gym for a surprise at nine. I thought it was something that Dr. Stein had put together. He often arranged activities or events for us. Since we had just finished the school year, I figured he was behind it. Calix and I arrived first, then Carrick and Cassie. Then Dr. Stein came in. But when he got there he started asking what was going on. It was then I realized the surprise was not Dr. Stein's idea.

"Then Chase and Corwin walked in and Chase shouted *Surprise!* At first I was delighted. I thought we were there to celebrate Chase being released from the medical building. Then I saw Dr. Stein's face and I knew that couldn't be the case.

"Chase and Corwin both had big grins. Later I learned that Corwin had no idea what Chase was planning. Chase had told him he had been released. Chase had convinced him that he was fine and that we all needed a big end-of-the-school-year party. Chase was just using him to set up his plan to end us all.

"I remember squealing in delight when I saw Chase. I can still see him standing in the doorway of the gym. We were all inside. Cory had arrived with him but walked ahead of Chase to join us. I remember the smile on his face. Chase was smiling and waving at us all. Then he reached inside his jacket, pulled out a metal bar, and smashed it down on Cory's head. Cory fell down onto the ground and didn't move. All his super strength couldn't protect him from the betrayal by his best friend and brother."

Cotovatre began to cry as she remembered that evening. Corwin now held on to the edges of the table as if to steady himself as Cotovatre told her tale. Cotovatre composed herself and continued.

"'*We should not be here!*' Chase shouted at us. '*None of us should exist! We have no right to exist!*' I remember his words echoing in the gym as he screamed at us. His smile was gone. Spit flew from his mouth as he screamed at us. He looked at us with nothing but hatred. We had been born together, grown up together, laughed and cried together, played and even fought together. But nothing like this. Now he wanted us all dead. We were not fit to be alive because we had not been born like everyone else, because our DNA was different from that of everyone else."

Now Cotovatre began to get angry.

"We hadn't done anything wrong. It's not even as if Dr. Stein was training us to go out and hurt other people—to take over the world, or something equally stupid. He just wanted a better world, and our sin was that we were his vision of that better world.

"Calix had run over to Cory to help him. I pleaded with Chase to think about what he was doing, but he just stared at me and screamed so hard his nose began to bleed. He was terrifying. He started speaking so quickly no one could understand what he was saying. Then he turned and fled out of the gym.

"As soon as he was gone we all ran over to Cory and Calix, except for Dr. Stein, who ran after Chase. Cory was in a bad way. Dr. Stein came back and told us that Chase had locked us all in. Then a few moments later we saw smoke.

"The smoke started right at the door that Chase had fled through; he was trying to burn us alive. Soon the gym was full of smoke and it was starting to get hot.

"Dr. Stein turned to Calix and asked what she could do. He said she had to revive Corwin because only he had the strength to break down the door. Calix knew that Dr. Stein was telling her she needed to heal Cory even if it meant sacrificing herself. I remember her eyes being wide with fear. But then she swallowed hard and nodded. She turned to Cory and took his head in her hands and she started doing what she did so well. She started healing him.

"I could see the strain it was putting on her. I could see the pain on her own face, but she didn't stop or slow down. Soon there were tears rolling from her eyes and she began to sob heavily. I went over to comfort her, but Dr. Stein held me back. Just then Calix gasped and slumped down beside Cory. A moment later he took in a sharp breath and sat up. He looked around confused, but Dr. Stein didn't give him a chance to ask any questions. Dr. Stein ordered Cory to break down the doors.

"Cory looked at Dr. Stein for a brief moment, saw that the room was full of smoke. He got up, went over to the door, and ripped it off its hinges. Flames roared in, but the outside doors were only twenty feet away. Dr. Stein ordered us all through the flames. We knew it was our only chance and we took it. It was hot but we made it; we were all alive. Cory, Carrick, Cassie and Dr. Stein had gotten some burns, but we were alive. All except Calix. Carrick and I had grabbed her as we fled. Cassie helped too. We dragged her to Cory, who picked her up and carried her through the flaming doors. But she was gone. I only realized when we were outside. I screamed her name and held her tight, but Dr. Stein grabbed me and gently pulled me away."

Cotovatre and Corwin had tears slowly dripping down their faces. Cassie had covered her face.

All was quiet until Coupe spoke.

"You guys okay?" he asked.

"We will be," replied Cotovatre. "But if you get funny looks from people around here, Coupe, now you might understand why."

"Yeah, I get it," said Coupe. "Trust me, I'm used to getting funny looks. Same shit, different place. It never ends.

"So, my twin—my clone, whatever the hell he is—went completely nuts when he was about twelve. We are exactly the same, but here I am. Maybe not perfectly sane," he said, sniffing, "but I ain't anywhere close to being a homicidal maniac."

....

Despite the painful revelations that Cotovatre had shared, Coupe was relieved and pleased that his fate was manifestly different. He felt Cooper sensing the same thing. And in that moment it raised a question.

"I'm wondering, Cory," he said, "how it was that Chase got out of the medical unit and you didn't know he had some bad thoughts running around inside his head."

Corwin kept his eyes down. "Chase tricked me. I had still been visiting him in the medical ward. He was kept in a special room that was secured with a magnetic strip card and a code. He told me he had been cleared and that Dr. Stein had planned a big surprise to let everyone know to meet in the gym, but not to let anyone know about him. He told me when to come get him and I did. He had the strip card and slipped it under the door to me and then he told me the code.

"It wasn't until later we learned he had taken the card from Dr. Stein and somehow stolen the code too. But he was clever that way. He always was. I let him out. It's as simple as that. I let him out and he killed Calix."

Cotovatre came to his support. "You didn't know what he was going to do, Cory. It wasn't your fault."

"Yeah, it wasn't your fault," agreed Coupe, "but how was it you didn't know what he was up to? How come you didn't sense it?"

"He wouldn't have been able to." It was Cooper who had responded, surprising Corwin. "If Cory is like me, his powers would only have just started back then. He wouldn't have started getting real strong senses of people and what was going on inside their heads until he was a year older. That was the way it was for me. Before that it was a bunch of deafening noise."

Corwin looked at Cooper with a sense of relief. Then Cooper spoke up again.

"Just come sit down. I know you're there, and I know you listened to everything we have just said. I sensed you come in behind Corwin."

Cotovatre snickered. "He can sense your presence, Carrick. Cooper doesn't have to see you to know that you're there."

At that moment the wall sprouted eyes and looked at Cotovatre. Then it blinked and looked at Coupe and then Cooper. Then part of the wall seemed to morph into the shape of a body. Then that body stepped away from the wall and took on the shape of a teen boy. A naked one.

"Whoa," Coupe said quietly. "That's super impressive."

"Thanks," replied Carrick, smiling. "I'm just as fast as you are too."

"Probably a lot faster," he said, knowing his bad foot put him at a speed disadvantage.

"Yeah, probably." Carrick grinned. "Can I sit with you guys?"

"Umm, why don't you put your clothes back on first?" suggested Cotovatre.

"Oh, yeah, I'll be right back." The group was then treated to the sight of Carrick's naked behind sprinting out the main doorway.

Cotovatre rolled her eyes. "Carrick is our resident exhibitionist. His super cool ability to blend in only works if he's naked!"

After a few moments he returned, still slipping his sneakers back on his feet. When not naked and camouflaged, Carrick was a pleasant-looking boy, with brown hair, brown eyes and brown-toned skin. He was about the same size as Cooper and Cory, but he had a thinner frame than anyone. His arms seemed to be unusually long as well, as did his fingers. They would later learn that he was an excellent climber, and, like Cotovatre, had a high threshold for extremes of both cold and heat. He made his way to the food line and then came over and sat down with them. After introductions were made, Coupe tried to satisfy his curiosity.

"You have a twin too?" he asked.

"Yeah, but I haven't met him yet."

"I've gotta ask, with your special talents, how is it I haven't seen your face plastered across the news or on the internet somewhere, you know, *Human Squid Boy Spotted at Local Mall,* or something like that?"

"First off, my design was based upon octopus DNA, not squid," he said, acting slightly offended. "Second, my twin isn't roaming freely in the outside environment like you two were. His activities are more restricted."

"Yeah? How so?"

"He has grown up at a military installation somewhere. That way he can be protected as necessary but still be given exposure to the outside world. But if anything should happen, well, there would at least be some control to stop things happening like what you were thinking."

"So, you were designed with military applications in mind?" asked Coupe.

Carrick grinned. "Yeah."

"How's your eyesight?"

"Just as good as yours."

It did not come as much of a surprise to learn the Dr. Stein had designed one of his test subjects to specifications likely provided to him by some government-led contingent of the Consortium. Dr. Stein had designed the perfect spy, or soldier.

Coupe felt disquieted by the direction Dr. Stein's genius had led him. Carrick represented less of the genetic ideal and more of a pragmatic and utilitarian manipulation of the human genome for some strategic advantage. Coupe wanted to learn more about Carrick in the future.

CHAPTER 31

The group sat at the table talking well after the lunch was finished. Cooper and Coupe had many questions for their four new siblings, and, in turn, they were just as interested in Cooper and Coupe and what their lives outside of the facility had been like. The teens talked for so long that the staff were starting to get the dining hall ready for dinner. Two attendants walked through the door and came over to their table. As they drew closer Coupe turned to see they were staring at him. One of them was Stanley, their designated host.

"Hello, Stanley," said Coupe.

"Hello, Coupe. I'm afraid there's no dinner for you tonight."

"Oh yeah? Why is that?"

"Dr. Stein has arranged for you to have surgery tomorrow

morning to fix your ankle. You have to come with me now to get you ready."

Coupe looked over at Cooper. Stanley was being truthful. Coupe thought it would have been nice to be asked, but, that being said, the answer would have been *yes,* so he got up to leave. Cooper stood to join Coupe.

"Just Coupe, this time," said Stanley.

Cooper and Coupe stood staring at each other for a few moments. As the time stretched on, Cotovatre became confused by their silence. "What's going on?" she asked.

It was Corwin who replied. "They're talking to each other. They can do it all inside their heads."

"Really?" asked Cotovatre, her eyebrows shooting up incredulously. "They can do that?"

"Yes," replied Corwin flatly.

"Can you do that?" she asked.

"No, not yet."

Just then Cooper looked over at Corwin. As he did so, Corwin's eyebrows shot up in surprise. Cooper had reached out to him so he could join their silent conversation. "Yes, you can," he said to Cooper and Coupe. Then to the others at the table he said with some pride, "They're trying to figure out if they should trust Stanley and Dr. Stein."

Cotovatre turned and spoke to the two newcomers. "Dr. Stein may have his faults, but he's not going to kill you or do anything bad to you, Coupe. He made you. He wants to fix you. And Stanley here is a teddy bear. He'll take good care of you." Stanley smiled and winked in response.

Coupe looked at them all and then said, "Thanks." Then to Cooper, "I'll take it from here, big guy. We'll catch up later. I'll be fine, and you can learn more about our new family. Maybe you and Cory can arm wrestle; that could be fun."

"I would win," replied Corwin.

"Yeah? Don't be so sure, Cory," said Coupe. "Cooper here has some hidden talents. On second thought, no arm wrestling until I get back. I wanna watch."

With that, Coupe reached out and gave Cooper a brief hug. He then turned and left with the two men.

....

Coupe felt groggy, like his mind was full of sludge. But he also felt he was not alone. He opened his eyes and saw Dr. Stein sitting beside his bed. Coupe was lying on the floor next to the bed in a nest of blankets and pillows.

"Good morning, Coupe!" said Dr. Stein.

"Doc. To what do I owe the pleasure?"

"Well, I came to check how your surgery went and I am told it went very well. You will be walking and running as if it were never broken in a matter of weeks. But I also thought it would be an opportunity for you and me to have more father-son time together."

"You do realize that line does not work for you one little bit."

Dr. Stein looked disappointed. "Not even a little? I mean, I did create you. I did give you all the attributes you now possess."

"And you left me to a childhood of neglect and abuse."

Dr. Stein looked a little deflated. "I admit there is *that*. But, Coupe, I don't think you understand yet just how *special* you are and how your unfortunate childhood likely contributed to your adaptation to your special skill set. Chase was unable to handle it, but you . . . you have excelled!"

"I admit I'm doing better than my twin, but how do you know that it's because of all the bad things that happened to me? How do you know it wasn't because I finally found the Callisters? That I found Cooper? I think you are ignoring just what he has done for me. I was pretty much down and out when he entered my life and propped me back up. Who knows? Without him, I might have ended it all by now."

"Perhaps," said Dr. Stein, "but doubtful."

"Oh yeah? And why is that exactly?"

"Because your twin, Chase, began to exhibit his unstable mindset when he was about twelve years old. You did not. You were able to cope. The fact that you found the Callisters has had a positive effect on you, without a doubt. But by then, you had been through the mental and emotional crucible that had provided you with the mental and emotional capacity to survive things that Chase simply could not."

Coupe had to admit that the doctor's analysis seemed to be better than his own. Despite his resentment and hurt at what the doctor had allowed to happen, he was beginning to respect his intellect. He decided not to give him too much of a hard time.

"So, what is it that you want, *Franklin*? Time for another debriefing?"

Dr. Stein bristled at the use of his nickname.

"I see that Cotovatre has shared her pithy little nickname for me—very droll, very jocular, I am sure. But you are right, Coupe. I am fascinated by what you have become. I am equally fascinated by the relationship, the symbiosis, that you and Cooper have established. I am especially interested to learn more about that. I tried speaking with Cooper earlier, but he just stared off into the distance. I know he was nonverbal for a long period of time, but I am not sure if his silence was an extension of his natural silence or if he was willfully refusing to answer me."

"It could have been both, Dr. Stein," he said. "If I was out, he kind of shuts down to a certain extent. But you should also know that Cooper is sort of like a moral compass. If he has decided he does not trust you or that you might be a *bad man*—and I think he has—well then, you have some ground to make up if you want him to work with you. My takeaway from our first conversation was that he was *not* pleased that you had let me suffer. That is going to take some effort for him to get past."

"I appreciate that, which is why I am here speaking to you instead. You have shown yourself to be more inclined to share with me. I am hoping that you can convince Cooper to be more open as well. I find it strangely frustrating because my own Corwin is very fond of me."

"Well, my own Cooper is not."

"Mmm, yes." Dr. Stein looked at Coupe's bandaged foot. "Are you having any pain?" he asked, changing the subject.

"Some, but nowhere near as bad as when it got broke the first time."

"*Was broken*, Coupe," corrected Dr. Stein. "You have a hyper-genius IQ. You should speak correctly."

Coupe noted how prickly Dr. Stein could be, and how easy it would be to prick the good doctor should the mood take him. But as the thought passed, he replied, "Thank you for that, sir. I will endeavor to speak properly in the future when I am in your company."

Dr. Stein recognized the rebuke in Coupe's response. "You will have to forgive me, Coupe. I have been responsible for the care and upbringing of many special young people here at Deep Woods. I have cast myself in the roll of educator for so long it has become second nature to me. On top of that you remind me so much of Chase. I watched him grow up from his infancy. I cannot help but transfer some of that history into my interactions with you."

"Well, I am not Chase."

"I understand that and will endeavor to separate the two of you in my mind." Dr. Stein steered the conversation back to Coupe's foot. "Would you like something for the pain?"

"I'm good for now. What did you do to it, anyway?"

"I did nothing more than order its repair. I had an orthopedic surgeon flown in here this morning. I spoke with her before she left. As you probably suspected, it had been brok*en* when someone you will not name, but I know anyway, stomped on it. The bones had healed, but they healed without being set in the proper position, leaving you with that fixed inward curvature and lack of proper range of motion. The doctor rebroke it and then set the bones in their proper positions. Your foot is now aligned, and I expect with some physical therapy you will have full strength and range of motion very quickly."

"Yeah?" Coupe looked down at his foot. He was excited to see what it would be like to walk without his gimpy limp. "Thanks, Doc. How long until I am up and running again?"

"Anyone else, six to eight weeks. You? One, maybe two weeks at the outside. You were designed to heal very quickly, Coupe."

"Yeah, I've seen that. You'll have a hard time telling me and Chase apart if he comes back."

"That thought had crossed my mind."

"Don't let it worry you. Cooper will have no problem telling us apart."

"I considered that too. With his sense of people, can he tell them apart just from those psychic impressions?"

"Just as easy as looking at you. I got a sense of Cory yesterday. I know they look alike—identical—but in my mind they were just as different as you and me."

"That sensing that goes on between you and Cooper—I note that you communicate quite readily without saying a word. Just how does that work? You explained that Cooper has to establish the link, but once that is done, is it like he is inside your thoughts?"

"No, not really. It's something entirely different. Now he's just usually present . . . with me. And I am with him. When it first started, he would establish the link, but it sort of morphed into more than that now. Generally, if we are in sensing range of each other, our minds just automatically link up. It would be unnatural if we didn't. In fact, if one of us shuts the other out, it generally makes the other one suspicious. These days, if we weren't linked up and he was nearby, well, it would be like listening to music in only one ear or reading with one eye closed. Know what I mean?"

"I think I do. You two have grown to rely upon each other to such an extent that when you are not psychically linked you feel like part of you is missing. That is a profound symbiosis."

"Yeah, I mean, we can survive without each other. And we do whenever we are apart, like now. But when we're together it just makes sense to stay hooked up. We decide together what to do, we stop each other from making mistakes, we think things through together."

Dr. Stein shifted the conversation to something else he wanted to learn, something that really intrigued him.

"Coupe, the first night you were here, I observed Cooper place his fist on your chest and you fell asleep almost immediately. What does he do to you, and why?"

Coupe stared at Dr. Stein for quite some time, contemplating how to answer. He decided to be vague.

"He helps me sleep, sir," he replied.

Dr. Stein ignored the deflection and pressed his question. "I saw that, but how?"

Coupe knew he had to tell him or refuse to tell. In that moment he chose to reveal some of what Cooper could do.

"I'm not sure exactly. He just can," Coupe said. "All I can tell you is that I hadn't slept through the whole night for years. I would wake up screaming. In my dreams I would relive all the crap that had been done to me . . . all the stuff that *you* let happen to me."

"Night terrors," diagnosed Dr. Stein, ignoring the accusation in the revelation. "I would not be surprised to learn they acted as some sort of mental relief valve to stop you from falling down the same rabbit hole of madness that Chase did. When Chase started exhibiting his instability he had stopped sleeping altogether, so he lost the opportunity to experience night terrors and the relief they may have given him."

"Yeah, jeez, lucky for me," replied Coupe. "Anyway, sleeping for me was pretty tough for a few years. Then along comes Cooper Callister with his magic fist. He plants it square in my chest and I immediately fall asleep. If I wake up in the night, he's there for me to take it all away and put me back to sleep. He not only puts me to sleep, he chases them away, those things in my head. You call me the special one, Doc. You're wrong. It's Cooper Callister. He's the only reason I'm still here. I'm sure of that."

"I applaud your devotion to your brother, Coupe. I really do. Your bond with him is something I would have thoroughly encouraged if you two had been here. I urge you to continue developing that bond. Tell me, does he have to touch you to put you to sleep?"

"Yes," replied Coupe. A lie. He was not sure why. "You encourage this bond between me and Cooper. What about with Corwin and Chase?"

"If he had been here when Corwin developed these abilities, I would absolutely have encouraged it. But he left before Corwin became extra sentient. Nonetheless, those two developed a strong bond even without the abilities that you and Cooper share."

"Yeah, so strong that Chase tried to kill him with a steel bar."

Dr. Stein winced. "A very unfortunate outcome and one for which I accept the full blame. I should have anticipated Chase's ability to manipulate our security. I assure you, I will not let it happen again."

"I sure hope so. Tell me, Doc, since we are here as your bait, how do you think Chase will come for us?"

"An excellent question, Coupe!" replied Dr. Stein "Tell me, how do *you* think he will come? After all, you are the same as him, genetically."

Coupe eased back in the nest of blankets and looked out the window. He remained quiet for quite some time.

"I suppose if I was alone and wanted to do as much damage as possible, I would attack the water and food supply," said Coupe. "One teenage boy is not going to defeat your security in an open assault on this facility. He would need to attack covertly and attack in a way that would get us all, or as many as he could. The common thread would then be our food and water, maybe our air, but I don't see that happening."

"Precisely!" said Dr. Stein.

"Of course, if he is as smart as you say, he would know that we would be lookin' for him there and come up with another plan. Or use our focus on those areas as a fake out. So that means you have to be ready for anything, really, but keep an eye on the food and water. How secure are they?"

"The water for this facility is from a series of wells that pump into a large water tank at the top of the hill on the north end of the campus. All the sources and access points have been sealed and alarmed. It will be near impossible for him to tamper with it now. Security cameras have been mounted throughout the campus. Our food supply is secure. It comes from a . . . very secure source."

"What is it you don't want me to know about the food?"

"It's not that I don't want to tell you, Coupe. You just don't have the requisite clearance. But if the food supply to the US Congress and the White House is secure, so is ours."

"Wow. Important friends," noted Coupe. "So, what makes you think he is going to come here after Cooper and me instead of picking off more of your Alphas and Betas, or any of our remaining twins?"

"If he saw your image on the news—and I am almost certain he did as he would have been looking for any leads to any of my creations—he would have put you and Cooper at the top of his list."

"Why?"

"Because you are he and he is you, Coupe. He already thinks he has killed Corwin. He only needs to rid the world of Cooper, and that genetic constellation will be extinguished. So too for you."

"What is your plan, Doc?"

"For now, it is for you to heal, and for us to keep a strong watch along our fence line and beyond. I am hopeful he will come back to us. If not, then maybe we will have to go looking for him, but I do not think that will be necessary. In the meantime, relax and get better, Coupe. I hope to have many more conversations with you, but for today, I will let you relax and heal.

"I expect you will find the amenities satisfactory. There are a set of crutches here for you. When you are ready, you may get up and explore. I request that you do not go beyond this building as we are still monitoring you medically. Tomorrow we will return you to the others."

"I will do as you say, Doc. And thank you for fixing my foot."

Dr. Stein smiled down at Coupe as he got up to leave. "You are entirely welcome, Coupe. It was the least that I could have done for you."

After Dr. Stein left, Coupe fell asleep again. He awoke a few hours later to find Cooper sitting where Dr. Stein had been sitting earlier.

"How are you feeling, Coupe?"

"Good. How long have you been here?"

Cooper kind of shrugged as if to avoid the question, but Coupe immediately knew that Cooper had been sitting there patiently for hours waiting for him to wake up.

"What have you been doing?" he asked.

"Hanging out with Coty, looking around this place. It's pretty big, but she's a good guide. Are you allowed out yet?"

"Not until tomorrow. The doctor told me I could wander around in this building. There's some sort of common room up here. I think we can get food there, and I'm hungry. You wanna eat?"

"Sure."

Coupe started to scoot over to the crutches that had been left for him, but Cooper grabbed them for him and then helped Coupe stand.

"Thanks, but I could have done that."

"I know. It's just you just had surgery."

"Always lookin' out for me, big brother."

The two exited the room and started down the hall to where Coupe thought they would find the common room. "You know, Cooper, we should ask Dr. Stein which one of us was born first. It may be that I am *your* older brother."

Cooper laughed. "I doubt it. I am definitely the big brother."

The two boys were still giggling about it when they entered the common room. The room was not empty. Sitting near the window with a foot propped up on pillows was one of the men that had taken them from their home only a few days before. There was a moment of silence as they all recognized each other.

"Look, Cooper, it's one of the guys that kidnapped us," said Coupe.

The man looked at them both before replying. "Hey look, it's the kid that broke my leg, and the other kid who laughed about it." There was a moment of awkward silence before the man reached over and extended his hand. "My name is Sammy," he said.

Cooper said nothing but shook the man's hand. Coupe did the same.

"Pleased to meet you," said Coupe. "And sorry for laughing about your leg. I kinda feel for you right now, if you get my drift."

"Yeah, we're sort of in the same boat. The same surgeon that fixed your leg fixed mine too. Listen, boys, I know we didn't get off on the right foot, so to speak, but I want you both to know, it wasn't our intention to hurt you. In fact, we wanted to make sure you didn't get hurt."

"But you shot me," Cooper protested.

"We were given orders on just how to bring you back here by Dr. Stein. Cooper, we had to get control of you before that super strength of yours turned me and the other man with me, Severus, into pounded dust. It was the quickest way to get you under control. I just want you to know that we will probably see a lot of each other around here from now on. We are here to protect you. In fact, Severus is in charge of security here. It says something that he went out personally to get you two."

"Thanks, I guess," replied Coupe. He was uncomfortable in the man's company, despite his assuring words. After all, Severus had threatened to break his neck. "Is there any place to eat here?"

"There's a cafeteria on the ground floor."

The two boys quickly left in search of the cafeteria.

"So, what sense did you get of him?" asked Coupe once they were seated in the cafeteria.

"I think he will try to protect us, but only so long as he is ordered to protect us. I also think he would hunt us down if that's what he was ordered to do," replied Cooper.

"Yeah, I got that impression too. So who can we trust here?"

"So far, Cotovatre is the only one that I get a real strong sense from. Maybe Carrick and Cassie, but I haven't spent enough time with them yet."

"I think Cassie seems trustworthy," offered Coupe.

Cooper grinned at him.

"What?" asked Coupe, feigning ignorance.

"Don't forget I'm up in that head of yours, little bro. I sensed your heart melt when she walked into the dining hall. First time I have ever seen *you* speechless."

"Well, she is pretty."

"She thinks you're sweet on account of the brave things you've done."

"Tried to do. By my count I'm 0 for 2."

"I don't think other people are keeping score the same way that you do, Coupe."

"Yeah, well, we won't be here long enough for anything to come of it. Besides, the more she gets to know me . . . well, you know."

"What do I know, Coupe? You are always going on about how you're unlikeable. You're not; it's just you had a crappy childhood and you're not used to people being nice to you."

"That's me, damaged goods."

"You need to stop saying that."

"What? Damaged goods? Would we be having this conversation if I weren't? I accept who I am, Cooper."

Cooper looked frustrated. "You may be right that you got damaged. Doesn't mean you can't be fixed, just like your foot."

"Yeah, maybe."

They finished their meal in silence—at least, that's what it would have looked like if anyone else had been watching, but their conversation continued, just not verbally. Once done eating, Coupe felt tired.

Cooper was allowed to visit, though he could not stay overnight. He was expected to stay in his new room in the dormitory, which was staffed with proper security. Without his help Coupe spent a restless night sleeping on the floor next to his bed, but he managed not to awaken everyone in the small hours of the night with one of his night terrors. Coupe wondered if they were becoming a thing of his past. He certainly hoped so.

CHAPTER 32

The following day Coupe could leave the medical building. Stanley arrived and took him to his new room in the academy's dormitory, one of the older buildings. It was a three-story and brick with large white-framed windows, typical of New England colleges and prep schools. Coupe smiled when he saw that the name of the building was *Omicron*. It appeared that Dr. Stein had allowed the community to develop a Greek system all its own.

Inside the main doors was a spacious foyer comprised of a long oak counter with a small office behind it. The wall behind the counter was covered in pigeonholes and cubbies of all sizes. An academy security officer sat behind the counter and watched them approach. He was large, wearing a dark sport coat and a dark turtleneck. A curly wire appeared at his collar and climbed up to disappear behind his ear. He gave Stanley a nod when they entered.

"There will always be security in this building. That man's name is Jay. They will be at the door and monitoring you by security cameras as well. You will be safe here," said Stanley. "The elevator is over here. You are on the third floor with the rest of C Group."

Stanley led him to the other side of the foyer where there was an elevator with oak-paneled doors. Beside it was a wide staircase, but since he had surgery only yesterday, Coupe was happy to use the elevator. Despite the age of the building, its interior was surprisingly modern and well maintained.

The elevator door opened on the main hall of the third floor with a *bing*. On each side of the hallway were four doors. Coupe immediately felt Cooper's presence. Just then, one of the doors opened and Cooper stepped into the hallway with a welcoming smile. A moment later, Cotovatre stepped out of the room as well. She too was smiling.

"Welcome to your new home, Coupe!" she declared.

"We're down at the end," added Cooper. "C'mon, I'll show you."

Coupe hobbled after Cooper, and Stanley and Cotovatre followed. Coupe looked inside and saw it was a large, high-ceilinged room with two wide, near-floor-to-ceiling windows on its far wall. Against the nearest wall was a set of bunk beds. As expected, Cooper had pulled the bedding off of the top bunk and put it on the floor next to the lower one.

"Usually each person gets their own room, but Cooper suggested you two would be better off sharing a room," said Stanley.

"Works best for me," replied Coupe. Cooper simply nodded.

"I had some things brought over for you. You will find everything you need in that dresser and the closet over there." Stanley pointed to a door to Coupe's right. "If you don't need anything else, I will leave you to get settled in."

"Thanks, Stanley," replied Coupe.

Cotovatre followed Stanley. "Come down and see me once you get settled in," she said, smiling again and closing the door.

Cooper smiled back at her. "She's really nice."

Coupe sensed that Cooper was really taken with Cotovatre. "Yeah, I'm getting that impression from you," he said. "So, what did I miss while I was gone?"

"I got moved in here when you went to have surgery. We are all up on this floor. Carrick is nice, too, but Cory doesn't like me much. Still, I'm trying to be nice to him. Cassie played the guitar last night. You are really gonna like that. We spent most of the day just talking and walking around outside. How's your foot?"

"Right now, immobilized, but Franklin said it might be better in as little as one or two weeks on account of me healing quick. This boot comes off tomorrow if the X-rays look good. So, you and Cotovatre, how's that going?" asked Coupe, smiling.

Cooper grinned sheepishly. "It's nothing like that," he replied.

"Yes it is. You forget I get to see right into you too. Well, at least when you let me."

"Yeah, I know, but isn't she sort of like my sister—you know, like she sees Corwin?"

"Trust me on this: the only one you share any genetic relationship with is Corwin. We may have all been hatched at the same time, but according to Dr. Stein we are all unique, other than our twin of course. She only sees Corwin like a brother because they grew up together. But she didn't grow up with you. And I expect the more time you spend with her, the more she will realize you are a lot different than Corwin. C'mon, you have to have gotten some sense of how she is feeling toward you by now."

Cooper blushed and looked at his feet. "A little, but I'm trying not to do that, but sometimes it just slips through. She likes us both. But I think she likes me a little more . . . and differently," he said, smiling.

"I'm crushed," Coupe replied, smiling back.

Just then Cooper turned his head slightly, listening in his special way.

"Cory's back," he said. "He wants to talk to Coty. I think he's jealous about the time I spent with her yesterday . . . and today."

Coupe heard someone knocking on one of the doors out in the hallway. He assumed it was Corwin knocking on Cotovatre's door. He heard muffled voices. Coupe looked over at Cooper, who obviously sensed what was going on. Soon Coupe sensed it from Cooper. The voices got louder.

Coupe heard Cotovatre say, "I can talk to whomever I want, Cory. It's not like they're dangerous. Coupe doesn't seem to be anything like Chase was when he left. And Cooper's a sweetheart."

"Cory didn't like hearing that," Cooper said. "C'mon."

He walked out of the room. Coupe hobbled after him. In the hallway Cotovatre and Corwin had stopped arguing, both turning their attention to Cooper as he approached. Cory scowled.

"Cory," started Cooper, "I know you are not happy about me and Coupe being here, probably for a bunch of reasons. You don't trust Coupe after what happened with you and Chase, and you don't like me talking with Coty."

"That's not true," Corwin snarled.

Cooper rolled his eyes. "Yes, it is. I can sense it from you."

"I told you to stay out of my head!" Corwin shouted.

"I'm trying, but you might as well tell me to walk around with my eyes closed all the time. I just can't do it. But I want to get along with you. I mean, we're twins after all. Just different upbringings."

"Listen to you, the bigshot that can't help but read everybody's minds just because you got to live in the outside world while we got stuck in here. I'm gonna learn how to do it, Cooper, and when I do I'm going to crawl up inside your head and start moving things around!"

"Cory, lighten up," interrupted Coupe. Cory's eyes flared with anger. "I mean, it's not like we're here by choice. And if you don't like the competition now, you're definitely not going to do well outside of this place."

In an instant Corwin was at him with his hand under his chin, grabbing his throat. Coupe's crutches went clattering to the floor. Corwin cocked his fist, and Coupe knew if that fist landed it would likely kill him. But it never landed. Instead, Cooper grabbed Corwin's arm and pulled him off of Coupe.

Corwin grabbed hold of Cooper and pushed him back against the wall, crushing the plaster and supporting wall studs. Corwin was clearly stronger than Cooper.

"Cory!" Cotovatre shouted. "What has gotten into you? Stop it! Stop it! Right now!"

He relented, letting go of Cooper and taking a step back and then, oddly, bending to retie his shoelaces.

"I'm not sure why I went off like that." He looked at all three of them in turn and then said, "I apologize." He turned and left.

Cotovatre turned to Cooper. "Are you okay?" she asked.

"Yeah, I'm fine. How about you, Coupe?"

"I'm fine too," he replied, retrieving his crutches. "Has he always had a temper?"

"No, never. I don't understand it."

"I do," said Cooper. "I know he doesn't like me to sense him, but he was just about shining like a search light just then. Coupe reminds him of Chase and he still remembers what Chase did to him. But he is most annoyed that Dr. Stein is paying so much attention to me and Coupe. Apparently, he has been talking nonstop about us to Cory, and he thinks he has been replaced as the doctor's favorite. That really hurts him. Then to cap things off he sees you and me talking and laughing and he wants it to be him you like, not me."

"But I do like him," protested Cotovatre.

"You know what I mean," replied Cooper.

She was about to protest again, but then looked at Cooper and knew there was no point. "Yeah, I can see how that sensing might get a little annoying after a while."

"Sorry," replied Cooper.

Cotovatre turned to look at Coupe. "Doesn't it bother you at all, you know, when Cooper's inside your head, sensing you?"

"No, I've just grown used to it. He knows all my secrets now. We kind of feed off each other."

"What about his secrets?"

"Cooper? He doesn't have any. What you see is what you get. He's my Percival," added Coupe, making a literary reference that fell flat.

"But you can feel his presence in your head, right? You know when he's there?"

"He's pretty much always there when we're together."

"But you can close him out, when you want to?"

"I can, but usually don't."

"Why not?"

"Because it helps me. Cooper has helped me deal with a lot of things. Who knows, if it weren't for Cooper, I might have gone down the same road as Chase, or something like it. Cooper picked me up when I was down and has been there for me ever since."

"So what does Cooper get out of the deal?" she asked.

Coupe thought for a few moments before responding. "Before we met, Cooper would get overwhelmed by people when he was around them. They weren't consciously doing anything to him; it's just their presence to him was like someone screaming in his head. The more people, the more screams. School was awful for him. He would just shut down. He didn't even speak in school until this past year.

"After we realized we were somehow linked, we started working together. He helped me and I helped him. I help him by acting like a filter for all that noise in his head. I think I help him focus his abilities more. He can control them now rather than the way it was before. Once he started controlling it, he learned just how much more he could do."

"How much more can he do?" she asked.

Cooper and Coupe looked at each other, trying to decide how much to reveal.

"You two are talking to each other inside your heads, aren't you?"

Coupe smiled. "Yeah, just trying to decide how best to answer your question. Cooper's going to let me answer for him. So, how much of what we tell you are you going to go tell Dr. Stein?"

"None, if you don't want me to. Why? What is it?"

Cooper looked at Coupe and nodded.

"Okay, but just between us for now. Dr. Stein seems to think I am the star of the show, but he's wrong. It should be Cooper. Cooper's empathic . . . telepathic . . . telesthetic—hell, whatever Dr. Stein wants to call them—well, those powers are more than just impressive. They are scary impressive.

"Just now, when Cory was about to hit him, he changed his mind, stepped back and tied his shoe. Cory didn't decide to do that. Cooper got in his head and made him do it. He didn't even realize that Cooper had done it either!"

"No way! Really?" asked Cotovatre, incredulously. "Do it to me," she demanded, looking at Cooper.

Cooper and Coupe looked at each other once again, and Coupe shrugged and then nodded. Cotovatre looked expectantly at them both wondering if indeed Cooper would demonstrate his abilities. It was only then she realized she had bent down and was tying her shoelace—even though she was not wearing shoes.

"That's incredible," she said, staring at her foot. Cooper and Coupe stepped over and helped her up. "So you can make people do whatever you want, and they wouldn't even know you were doing it?"

"Well, so far it has been limited to shoe-tying, making people walk away, and helping me sleep, but yeah, I think he has that potential," replied Coupe.

"So what's to stop you from making me do whatever you want and me never knowing?" she asked Cooper.

"Because I would not do that," replied Cooper quietly. "I wouldn't do it for bad things."

"He's right. He wouldn't. And I would know because I am inside his head. If he ever did something like that, he would have to deal with me about it, and he knows it's a sensitive subject for me. There'd be consequences." Coupe had grown quite forceful in his response, but then tried to lighten up a little. "I'd put him in a headlock and give him a clownie."

Cotovatre was silent for a moment, thinking back to Corwin's recent outburst. "What about Cory? Can he do that?"

"No," they said in unison.

"Why not?"

"Because he grew up here," responded Coupe. "He didn't have to grow up with the sounds of thirty other kids in his head all day long each time he went to school. He didn't have to suffer through a playground full of kids all screaming into his head like Cooper did. I know it was tough for him, but it's also what helped him learn to control his abilities, find a way to funnel them. Without going through that experience, Cory is never going to learn how to use what he has. And if he is going to start pushing people around as soon as he gets frustrated, perhaps this is the best place for him, serving as Dr. Stein's personal on-campus bodyguard."

After a moment Cooper spoke up, quietly. "Cory doesn't have Coupe to help him either. I don't think I would be able to do the things I can do if not for Coupe. He focuses me. Coupe helped me turn all that noise into something else. Cory lost Chase before they could ever figure out what they could be together."

"You should know, Coty," offered Cooper, "Cory isn't a bad person. He was just angry, and hurt. I may have made him back off and tie his shoe, but I never made him say sorry. That was him."

CHAPTER 33

After the confrontation in the dormitory there were no further incidents between the three. The wall was fixed, and the boys were summoned to Dr. Stein's office where they were officially *remonstrated*, as Dr. Stein put it. It was obviously a role in which Dr. Stein was uncomfortable and had little previous experience, but he let them know that such behavior was not acceptable and that there would be consequences should it continue. Cooper and Coupe knew that Corwin got a more serious talking to by Dr. Stein. They read it off him when he returned.

They tolerated each other's presence, Cooper and Coupe more so than Corwin. They were willing to engage with Corwin, but it was not readily reciprocated. As a group, the six of them would eat together and sometimes hang out together, but there was always a tension between Cooper, Coupe and Corwin.

Cooper and Cotovatre started spending more time with each other. Coupe found himself spending more time with Carrick and Cassie. He quickly learned that Carrick was a rascal. Coupe found him to be funny and quick witted. Carrick saw himself as a legitimate competitor for Coupe and his skill set. Carrick was always asking just what Coupe could do and then telling him he could do it better. Thankfully, he did it with a smile. Coupe sensed that Carrick truly wanted to know how he measured up against Coupe.

Coupe still found himself tongue tied around Cassie, but it did not stop them from spending time together. Cooper was right. For some reason she had found a special place in his heart in a way no one else ever had. Coupe loved listening to Cassie sing and play the guitar in the evenings. Listening to Cassie play and sing in the hallway became part of the evening routine.

On some occasions Coupe would ask her to play just one more song, after the lights were out and after everyone else had gone to their rooms. To him those songs were the most special as he pretended she was singing just to him. Her voice was sweet and so soft it carried him places in his mind. He was thankful that the lights were dimmed because sometimes he would finish the evening in tears. He always thanked her for those special songs. He could see her smiling at him kindly in the dim light as she got up to go to bed, those blue eyes holding him in their soothing gaze.

"You are always welcome, Coupe. Good night," she would say as she glided down the hallway to her room.

Coupe found his sleep being interrupted less and less by his night terrors thanks in part to Cassie's soothing songs. It made Cooper's job all the easier. Coupe still slept on the floor next to Cooper, though. Just in case.

After their first week, Cooper and Coupe found out that their four new siblings were on a winter break and would return to classes the following week.

Deep Woods Academy was teaching at a very accelerated rate. Not surprisingly, the coursework was heavily geared to STEM. Dr. Stein arranged for both Cooper and Coupe to better identify their academic strengths and needs. The classes were obviously tailored, as there were only six students. The boys noted that the school the six were now attending had the facilities of a large, well-funded private prep school. They even had uniforms, of a sort, with the Deep Woods crest on their sweaters or sweatshirts.

Dr. Stein began testing Cooper and Coupe's telepathic abilities. Generally those tests involved hooking wires to their heads and conducting simultaneous EEGs or some special modifications to those tests. Dr. Stein could see obvious signs of communication between the two boys' brains, but he could not determine just how it was happening. The mechanism of communication was elusive. Dr. Stein was not even sure if he had equipment capable of measuring what they were doing. He was undaunted, assigning a team of researchers to design just such a machine.

As expected, Coupe's foot healed at a remarkable speed. He was out of his protective boot within three days of surgery and back to normal walking after a week. He was assigned a physical therapist, but there was no need. After the second week it felt like he had never had surgery at all.

Dr. Stein arranged for him to meet him in the athletic complex on the twenty-first day of their compulsory admission to Deep Woods Academy. Dr. Stein wanted to assess the viability of the repairs to Coupe's ankle. Cooper came along, as usual.

The two boys found Dr. Stein waiting for them at the indoor track. He was with several other people from his team of experts. Dr. Stein smiled widely when he saw the two enter the track.

"Welcome, Coupe! You too, Cooper! Now come on over here so

we can get started. Let's find out if we have put you back together properly."

"And if you didn't?" asked Coupe.

"We'd do it again!" Dr. Stein beamed. "But I doubt that will be necessary. The surgeon I selected was one of the best in the Northeast. She knew what she was doing. Now, let's get you suited up."

Under his coat Coupe wore sweatpants and a T-shirt as he expected he would be running. Dr. Stein provided him with a fine pair of running shoes, which fit as if they had been made for him. They even had the DNA ouroboros on the side. He was then trussed up with a series of electrodes running to a small harness attached to his waist with a belt.

"The wires are to monitor your heartbeat, respiration, and so forth as we put you through your paces," offered Dr. Stein by way of explanation.

"I know," replied Coupe. "Cooper already told me."

Dr. Stein looked confused and then gazed at Cooper in realization. Cooper raised his eyebrows and shrugged.

After allowing Coupe to warm up and do a few stretches, Dr. Stein directed him to the track. He was going to have him run 1,500 meters, rest; 400 meters, rest; and finally 100 meters. Dr. Stein and his assistants stood inside the track along with Cooper as Coupe began.

There could be no argument. Coupe was fast—chin-dropping, eyebrow-raising, eyeball-popping fast. As Coupe finished the first lap he winked as he whizzed by. Cooper felt a breeze in his friend's wake. Dr. Stein looked down at his stopwatch and smiled. Coupe ran the following two laps with equal celerity. For the final lap, Coupe seemed to find hidden reserves, and he simply blasted around the track, leaving everyone amazed. As he crossed the finish line Dr. Stein's assistants started to applaud. Coupe came to a slow halt and then circled back to Dr. Stein.

"So, Doc, how did I do?"

"Well, Coupe, let's just say there is a new world record, a record that no one other than you or perhaps Chase could ever break."

"For now. Got any more babies cooking back in that lab of yours, Doc?" asked Coupe.

"No, Coupe," replied the doctor. "Not presently."

"What about Carrick?"

"I'll admit he is fast, but he was not designed to have your speed."

"Well, don't tell him. It'll break his heart."

One of Dr. Stein's assistants approached them. "Pulse and respiration are back to normal."

"Amazing," said Dr. Stein quietly.

Coupe's 400 meter run was equally impressive, but it was his 100 meter time that left them all in outright awe. Coupe slowly jogged back to the doctor after finishing. He was standing with his assistants along with Cooper, who was grinning. They were all looking at a radar gun. As he reached them, Dr. Stein turned it around.

"Forty-four miles per hour, Coupe," he said. "Science has theorized that a man could run at that speed, but no one has ever done it. No one has even come close. But you did it, easily. Tell me, Coupe, how long do you think you could have kept up that pace?"

"I dunno. Maybe twice as far? Three times? I dunno," he replied. "Want me to try?"

"No, at least not today. We will let you have a few more weeks of healing before trying it again. The results are impressive though, Coupe."

"Yeah, about that *few more weeks*, Doc. Me and Cooper—"

"*Cooper and I.*"

"Oops, sorry about that. *Cooper and I* are wondering just how long we will be here and if you would let us at least call our parents and let them know we are okay. We worry about their worrying."

Cooper and Coupe had persisted with this request every few days but always got the same reply. But now their stay was stretching into weeks.

"Not yet, Coupe," replied Dr. Stein. "You help me keep them safe by remaining here and out of contact."

"You said if we stayed here, you would keep them safe." Cooper glowered. Dr. Stein did not like the look of distrust in his eyes. He suddenly wished that he had brought Corwin with him. But he need not have worried.

"I am, Cooper, and I will endeavor to keep them safe, but I must have your assistance in this regard. Calling them would be detrimental to that shared objective."

The two boys looked at each other for several moments.

"You're talking to each other, aren't you?" asked Dr. Stein.

"Yeah, kinda sorta. Trying to figure out what to make of you," replied Coupe.

Dr. Stein appeared to be unconcerned for his safety and more interested in the mechanics of their communications. "Tell me. Is it like you hear each other talking in your heads?"

"No, it's not like that. There are no words, no sentences. Just thoughts, impressions. I guess the things that lead to words when you have to talk. We just never have to get to that step, at least anymore. He thinks, I understand. I think, he understands. It's that quick."

"Fascinating. I really need to learn how to measure it, quantify it."

Coupe smiled, sensing opportunity. "I tell you what, Doc. You let us contact our parents and you can hook us up to any machine you've got right now!"

The doctor's face lit up with his trademark smile, and he barked out a quick laugh. "Ha! Ever the dealmaker, Coupe. The outside world has made you street savvy and sly in your negotiating style. I like it! But the answer remains the same. Once it is safe to do so, we will revisit that question."

The conversation ended after that and the two boys left, dissatisfied. They wondered just how long they could continue to be patient.

CHAPTER 34

As their time at Deep Woods Academy increased, the boys started to enjoy their schoolwork, especially Coupe, who was being challenged in ways he had never experienced in the past. Coupe's experience in school had always been as the student that teachers sought to overlook, but here he found he had individual tutors. Dr. Stein was very hands on with all the members of the Omicron Six, and he purposefully sought out Coupe with projects and assignments designed to challenge and expand his intellect. Coupe begrudged all the extra work to begin with, but then realized he could do it and enjoyed exceeding expectations. Gone were the days of under-the-radar 80 percent.

Cooper was equally challenged academically, but according to his own abilities. His workload was lighter, which was just fine because it gave him the opportunity to spend more time with Cotovatre. She had decided she was going to improve his swimming skills. He was better at sinking than swimming, she would tease. Coupe would smile when he saw the two of them heading down to the pool for their daily lessons. Corwin was not so impressed, but there had been no further outbursts since his initial attempt to push Cooper through a wall.

The group fell into a more comfortable attitude. The routine was the same during the week. They would attend classes together. After classes they would each pursue those activities that interested them personally. They would eat their meals together, and in the evening they would all gather in the dorm to chat and socialize in the hallway. Despite not being able to contact their parents, the two boys were adjusting well, and Deep Woods began to be an acceptable second home, at least under protest.

While Coupe's free time was limited, he still had some opportunity to explore on his own. He quickly found the fine arts building where Cassie spent most afternoons playing the instrument that captured her interest that day, often making up her music as she went along. Coupe liked to sit outside the large window of the presentation room and listen to her play. It was cold, but her music kept him warm. It carried him away like nothing he had experienced before. One day, a few weeks after Coupe had been eavesdropping, she suddenly stopped. He saw the door open, and Cassie came over to him still wearing her gentle smile.

"It's warmer inside if you would like to listen," she offered.

Coupe realized he had been busted. "It won't bother you? Distract you?"

"No, I like to have an audience. I play better when I do. I especially like having you as my audience, Coupe. You really seem to appreciate my music."

Cassie offered him her hand, and she helped him up and led

him inside. From then on, he always listened in the first seat in the front. He started to find his voice with her too, and he was not afraid to show his feelings when her music moved him, which was often.

One particular afternoon, as the cold winter sun was quickly setting behind the pine trees of Deep Woods Academy, Cassie had just finished playing a tempestuous and passionate piece for the piano in the darkening presentation room. It rose thunderous in parts, then quieted to the slightest touches of the keys in others. It finished with such a collaboration of sounds that Coupe found his head swimming with impressions that the notes seemed to create and inject directly into his senses. He knew she had just made it up. She had created it to suit the sky, to suit the season, to suit the two of them in that room together. To him it was profound. Perhaps no one else would ever hear it. Perhaps he would never hear it again. But he had heard it on that day and it left him changed, elevated, and in awe.

As the last notes drifted away, the two allowed the silence to float back into the room. After a while, Coupe spoke.

"If Dr. Stein wants to make humankind better, all he has to do is keep making copies of you, Cassie."

"Oh, Coupe, thank you," she responded from the darkness.

Coupe was silent for a moment longer as he decided whether to say more or not. And then he did.

"My childhood wasn't that great; you know that. I'm sorta damaged goods on account of that. But you, Cassie, you're undamaging me, so . . . thank *you*."

Coupe then got up and quickly walked out of the presentation room, anxious he had said too much. He need not have worried.

· · · · · · · · · · · · · · · · ·

Around nine one evening the lights flicked on and off, which was the staff's way of telling the six students it was time to go to bed. All seemed routine until Carrick was awoken by the rattle of his doorknob. His clock read 2:30 a.m. The doorknob rattled again. Carrick got out of bed and darted into the darkest corner of the room, where he instantly blended in. Suddenly there was a tremendous crash as the door splintered and came crashing inward.

A few doors down Cooper had awoken feeling alarmed just a few moments before. He reached down to the floor where Coupe was asleep and placed his hand on his chest. Coupe awoke with a sharp gasp.

"What is it?" he asked.

"There is someone else here," Cooper whispered. "I can sense someone, and it isn't anyone of us or any of the people that work here, at least none that I have sensed yet. And there's more to it than just that."

"Why? What is it?"

"It's what I'm sensing. It's . . ." Cooper struggled to put his thoughts into words. "It's all mixed up and unreadable. Whatever is going on inside their head is whirling around superfast. I can't get a hold on anything. I can't sense them like I would anybody else. I think it's—"

"Chase," said Coupe.

"I think so," Cooper replied.

"Where?"

"Up here somewhere."

Just then they heard the crash of Carrick's door splintering.

"C'mon!" said Coupe as he jumped to go investigate. Cooper followed.

They opened their door and went out into the dim lights of the hall. They heard someone shouting in Carrick's room. His door was wide open and his light flicked on, flooding out into the shadowy hallway.

"Come on out, Carrick!" they heard from inside Carrick's room. "I know you're in here! I might not be able to see you, but I can smell you! Remember?"

Cooper and Coupe ran down to Carrick's room. As they passed Cotovatre's room her door flew open.

"What's going on?" she asked.

"Don't know!" Coupe replied. "Go get Corwin and Cassie!"

Coupe was the first to reach Carrick's room, and he froze in the doorway. He found himself staring at his double. It was indeed Chase, and it was obvious that they were genetically identical.

A lifetime with a good diet had left Chase an inch or two taller, perhaps a little more muscular. Chase's hair was longer than Coupe's close-cropped cut. Chase's hair was also dirty, and unkempt. As Chase stared back at Coupe, he flashed an insidious smile, a sort of poorly constrained rictus.

Chase's eyes darted all over Coupe's face. Then he sniffed. Having never been on the receiving end of it, Coupe was unnerved. Then Chase's face began to twitch as he attempted to speak.

"Hello, Coupe," he said with the disturbing smile still spread across his face. "I have come here to destroy you, to destroy me, to end us all."

Chase was holding a fire axe, the tool he had used to force his way into Carrick's room. Its sharp edge gleamed in the light of the room. At that moment Cotovatre, Cassiopeia, and Corwin arrived at the doorway and stood beside Cooper. The four of them entered the room, flanking Coupe. Chase noticed there were two Corwins—one being Cooper.

"You lived!" he said, astonished and angry.

Coupe took a step forward, mindful to stay out of reach should Chase decide to swing his axe.

"It's nice to meet you, Chase," Coupe said. "I've only just learned of your existence, and I have spent a lot of time thinking about what it would be like to meet you. You know, to spend time with you and talk about just what our lives have been like so far given that we are identical but for how we grew up. Since we have only just met, I don't understand why you would want to kill me."

"It is very simple. You should not exist. None of us should exist!"

Chase's face began to spasm, and his lips pulled back tight, showing his gleaming teeth.

"We should never have been created and we should be destroyed. The Alphas should be destroyed! The Betas should be destroyed! Dr. Stein and all his work here should be destroyed! I must undo all of the evil that has been done here! It is my obligation to humankind!"

Chase looked at his brothers and sisters with eyes that betrayed his wildly unstable mind. Then Corwin stepped forward.

"Chase," he said, his voice low, "we used to be best friends. We did everything together. We grew up together. We learned together. We played together. You were my best friend. And then you tried to kill me. I would have died if not for Calix. She died saving me, so *you* killed Calix! She was one of us! She was our sister!" Corwin shouted.

"Chase, we can help you," urged Coupe.

"Yes, we can help," encouraged Cassiopeia, staring at him with compassion radiating from her hypnotic eyes, hoping to calm him. It had none of the effect it had on Coupe.

"Help him?" asked Corwin, turning on Coupe and Cassiopeia. "Help him to do what, kill more of us? I don't want to help *him*!" He took a step toward Chase. "I'm gonna help *us*! Keep *us* safe from *him*!"

Coupe's intent was lost on Corwin. Instead of calming the situation, Corwin was enflaming it. Corwin knew he was stronger than Chase, but he also knew he had to be able to grab him before he could swing his axe. Coupe looked over at Cooper expectantly. In his head he kept repeating to Cooper, *Tie his shoes, tie his shoes.* But in response Cooper just shrugged. Cooper could not get a fix on Chase's mind.

There was movement in the corner of the room. Suddenly Carrick crept out of the corner and moved to stand next to the others. Chase had been right. He should have thrown his axe into the corner as he thought. There would have been one less of them now.

Carrick alone was an easy target. But the six teens were more than his heightened skills could overcome. He looked at them each in turn, trying to sense a weak link. There was none.

With a mighty scream Chase hefted the axe over his head and threw it wildly at them with amazing speed. Even though he had not aimed at any one of them, the axe went hurtling toward Cotovatre, heading straight for the center of her chest. It would have struck her, too, if not for Coupe's hyper-quick reflexes. As it left Chase's hand, Coupe tracked its movement and its ultimate target. Before it could get there, he lunged forward and snatched it out of the air, just inches from Cotovatre's chest. She gasped, and Cooper pulled her toward him.

"Chase, let this be the end of it," pleaded Coupe, throwing the axe on the floor behind him.

But Chase screamed again, lunged forward, and grabbed the chair from Carrick's desk. Then he swung it around and threw it at one of the large floor-to-ceiling windows in Carrick's room. It shattered immediately. Broken glass could be heard falling to the ground three stories below. Just as quickly as the glass had shattered, Chase jumped out after it.

CHAPTER 35

The six teens quickly ran to the window to see what had befallen their brother after his ill-advised leap into the air from three stories up. A strong breeze was blowing outside, and they felt the cold night air crisp against their skin. They scanned the ground for Chase. But instead of looking down on his broken body, they saw Chase scrambling, spider-like, down the brick facing of the building. Near the bottom he turned and looked back up at them. He seemed to growl, his face twitching wildly. Then, he turned and completed his descent into the darkness and to the ground below.

As Chase rounded the building and disappeared, the six teens ran down the stairs into the foyer where they found Andrea, the night security staffer behind the desk. She was folded over on top of it, the back of her skull broken open by Chase's axe. Cotovatre reached over the counter to hit a large red button on the console in front of Andrea, and then they ran out the front door of the foyer. Once outside, the group stopped.

"Which way did he go?" asked Carrick.

The path in front of them was one of the main campus thoroughfares. It ran from the lake at the southern edge, all the way to the top of the hill where the water tower was located.

"Cooper, you, Cassie, and Cotovatre go see if he is heading down to the lake. Me, Corwin and Carrick will head up toward the water tower to see if we can see him up there."

Inwardly, Coupe was dubious as to their chances of finding Chase. There were many small paths off the main roads Chase could have taken. Cooper had the best chance of finding him if he could sense him nearby. The stiff breeze limited Coupe's ability to either hear or scent which way Chase had fled. Coupe hoped to climb up the water tower to see if he could spot him from that vantage point, but he knew if Chase was determined to get away, the odds were with him.

Campus security would soon converge to assist with the search. Coupe sped ahead of Corwin and Carrick and quickly arrived at the water tower. He scooted up the steel ladder attached to the tower's frame. The tower was roughly seventy-five feet high and surrounded by a gangway with a metal railing to protect workers using the gangplank. Coupe swiftly reached the top of the ladder and pulled himself onto the gangway.

He looked down at the campus below him. The wind whipped about him, howling softly at this height. He saw Carrick and then Corwin arriving and shouted down to them so they could see him. He could barely make out Cassiopeia, Cotovatre and Cooper down by the lake, but he could not see anyone on any of the footpaths, lit with occasional lampposts. He saw Dr. Stein and six of the security staff approach from the main path.

"I thought you would come up here. It's what I would have done."

Coupe whipped around. Chase stood next to the water tank just behind him. He had been hiding around the back. Coupe looked over to the gap in the railing where the ladder ended. Chase grabbed hold of him in a tight bear hug.

"Thinking of making a break for it? I thought of that too. You and I think very much alike." Chase's face was right in his. It was like looking into a mirror, but too closely. Coupe saw his own features reflected back at him, only now it was twitching, the smile stretched unnaturally. They were alike, but very much different. Chase even smelled different, giving off a sweet, sickly odor. Coupe tried to escape, but Chase's grip instantly tightened.

"Keep on struggling, Coupe. I'll take us both over the railing. I'm the one that wants us gone, remember?"

Coupe stopped struggling, realizing that Chase's threat was real. He could easily take them over the railing and down to the ground far below.

"That's better. I'm going to turn you around now."

With incredible speed, Chase spun around so that he was now at Coupe's back. His arm snaked quickly around his neck to hold him tight. The other grabbed Coupe's arms behind his back to stop him from attempting to spin free.

"Look, the gang's all here—well, almost all the gang," Chase whispered into his ear. "Call out to them. Let them know I am up here with you."

"What?" asked Coupe.

"You heard me. Call down to them; tell them I am here. They cannot see like you and I. It's too far and it's too dark."

Coupe hesitated and Chase tightened his grip. He pushed him into the railing.

"Do it!" he hissed.

Still he hesitated. If Chase had been trying to hide, why would he want them to know where he was? Unless he was not trying to hide. Chase was up to something, and Coupe could not figure out what it was.

"Go fuck yourself," Coupe hissed back.

Chase pushed Coupe's body toward the rail. Coupe felt it strike him in the waist; he felt his body folding over it. But Chase did not push him over entirely. He simply held him in that precarious position with his own body and then shouted down to the crowd below.

"Dr. Stein! It's me, Chase! I'm up here with Coupe!"

Suddenly powerful lights illuminated Chase holding Coupe by the tower's edge.

"Chase!" shouted Dr. Stein. "What are you doing? Come down. We can help you!"

"I don't need *your* help, Dr. Stein! *No one* needs your help! *Everyone* needs to be protected *from* you, Dr. Stein, and the evil you have done!" Chase was now leaning dangerously over the railing with Coupe. Coupe had very real concerns that he and Chase would go over the railing inadvertently as Chase continued ranting. "That's why I am here, Dr. Stein! I am going to erase everything that you have done! I'm going to make the world safe again! You will see it all, the destruction of all your work!"

"Chase, come down! You are confused! I can help you with that!" pled Dr. Stein.

"In time, Dr. Stein! In time we will both be down!"

Coupe's mind whirled. He knew that if Chase wanted Carrick dead, he could have easily killed him in his room. He could have easily killed at least one more of them before bolting out the shattered window. If he had wanted to escape, he easily could have. He had figured out a way to sneak onto the campus. He would obviously be able to sneak back off. If he had wanted to hide, he could have kept quiet on the other side of the water tower. If he had wanted Coupe dead, he could have pushed him over the railing. He had not. What was he up to? Coupe pushed back from hanging over the rail. Surprisingly, Chase did not stop him.

"What are you doing, Chase?"

"You will soon find out, Coupe."

"If we are supposed to be so much alike, why are we so different, Chase? I mean, we basically came from the same test tube. Here I am enjoying life, and here you are trying to destroy it all. I mean, what the fuck?"

To his surprise, Chase gave his question serious consideration. His affect was now much calmer than it had been in Carrick's room. Coupe's question appeared to be one he had previously pondered. "That's a good question, Coupe," he replied. "I think the best analogy is that we are like templates. We have our original initiating biostructure, provided to us by the good Dr. Franklin Stein. It is like our basic framework, upon which anything can be added. From that basic structure we grow in uncounted different ways, like crystals, like snowflakes."

Chase was keeping a watchful eye on the assembled crowd below. Four more security staff had joined the others. Coupe still could not sense Cooper, but he kept reaching out for him. He needed Chase to go to sleep or tie his shoes.

Chase looked at him and quietly laughed, like he knew what Coupe was thinking. Perhaps he did. They had the same templates, after all. But they were different. Coupe could sense that Chase was intelligent, much more so than he. His education had nurtured his intelligence. But there was a whole bunch of other stuff added to his template that somehow had made him unstable.

"We may have started out the same, Coupe, but we are not the same now. Not even close."

Thank God, thought Coupe.

"I know what you're thinking, that I have gone mad. I can understand why you would think that."

"You mean with you trying to kill us all? Why wouldn't I think you are nuts?"

"Because from your limited capacity to understand, my desire to destroy that which should never have been created would appear to be just that. But it's not.

"I have considered our existence, Coupe. I have considered what it means to each of us. I have considered what it means to the real humans who populate this world and what it would mean to the future of those people and their natural descendants. We have no place among them. We have no right to share this world with them. We are an infection that will slowly and inescapably drive them to extinction. We have no right to do that. Dr. Stein had no right to set such a course in motion, and it must be stopped now. It must be stopped, before it is too late."

"Yeah, a whole lot of thought, but perhaps you're not thinking with a clear mind."

"You think I lack clarity of thought? What would you know of it?"

"I'm thinkin' that might be one area where I have the edge on you. I mean, have you looked in the mirror, Chase? Your face is a mass of twitches. You can't talk without it contorting into manic grins. You rant uncontrollably once you get started. You're pulling out your own hair. Hell, you even *smell* crazy!"

"No, Coupe! You are wrong!"

"Wrong? Look in the mirror and tell me I'm wrong!"

"But you presume that my altered mental state came first. It *didn't*. All those things you have recognized started after I had my personal revelations about the consequences of our existence."

"Yeah, about those *personal revelations.* How can you be so sure that we are bad for mankind? I mean, have you seen what they're doing to the planet? It seems to me that they could use some super-enhanced help right now."

"That didn't take long."

"What?"

"Did you hear what you just said, Coupe? You just called the rest of humankind *they*. You have only been here, what, a few weeks? And already you see yourself as different from *them*. Not *we*, Coupe; you said *they*. You have already culled them out in your own mind. You have been pre-programmed to destroy humankind and you don't even know it."

"Or I have been pre-programmed to help them. You have no fucking clue which, and you are willing to destroy us all based on your own crazy assumption. You know what that is, Chase? That is bat-shit crazy. You need to come down from your I'm-right-and-everyone-else-is-wrong high and get some serious fucking help."

"You swear a lot."

"Yeah? Well, that would be part of the overlays on *my* original initiating biostructure."

"Hah! You're clever, Coupe. But you are not as smart as me. You still have not figured out what's going on."

"What do you mean?"

"In time, Coupe, in time. I may be mentally compromised, but I have not completely lost my senses. In fact, you are about to learn they are better than anyone has given them credit."

"What are you talking about?"

Cooper, Cassiopeia, and Cotovatre appeared at the far end of the main road that led up to the water tower. Coupe felt Chase tense up behind him. He tried to reach out to Cooper, but he was still too far away.

"We are an abomination on this earth, Coupe. We must be extinguished."

"Yeah, you've said that already."

"I know, but now it is time."

"Wait, what?"

Coupe sensed that something had changed in Chase. He suddenly seemed to have complete focus.

"Perfect. It's just perfect, Coupe. So perfect. We are all so entirely predictable. It's been nice knowing you, Coupe. I would have loved to know you under normal circumstances, but—"

"You and I are not normal."

Suddenly, Chase shouted in a loud and terrible voice, "Now! My brothers! Now!"

Just as quickly Coupe realzied what was about to happen. "It's a trap! It's a trap!" Coupe screamed down to the assembled crowd below.

CHAPTER 36

Amoment after Coupe shouted his warning, the grass on the hill just beside the water tower began to move. Then the grass took shapes, six shapes, those of men wearing highly camouflaged ground suits. They stood up with automatic weapons and opened fire on the group at the bottom of the water tower.

"*Kill them! Kill them all!* It is time for God's work, my brothers!" screamed Chase.

But Coupe's warning had not been in vain. Cooper jumped on top of Cassiopeia and Cotovatre, pulling them to the ground and protecting them from the hail of bullets whooshing just above their heads. Corwin had also jumped on Dr. Stein and dragged him down, saving him.

Coupe began struggling with Chase, but his grip had now tightened again. Coupe kept searching for Cooper in his mind. If ever there was a time for people to tie their shoes, it was now. But he could not sense Cooper and tell him to do it. He was too far away.

"Tie their shoes, Cooper!" he shouted as loud as he could over the gunfire.

Coupe continued to struggle. Chase grabbed him by the hair and pushed him against the railing much more forcefully.

"It's our time too, Coupe!" he shouted. "Do you think my friends down there have orders to spare me? You are wrong! I am part of Dr. Stein's grand mistake too! Tonight we all die!"

Coupe grabbed the railing as Chase tried to lift him over it. Down below the bullets continued to fly. Dr. Stein's security forces were now returning fire. But they were outgunned. They had handguns and tasers. Chase's followers had come armed with assault rifles.

To Coupe, however, these observations were nothing more than distractions. He was fighting to stay on the right side of the railing. Coupe lowered his hips to make it more difficult for Chase to lift him over it. Chase seemed to sense his intent and in response reached down under his crotch and started to lift him up over the railing. Panic filled Coupe's thoughts. He knew he could not stop Chase. His feet left the ground. His arms buckled as he lost his leverage. He was going over.

Then he felt Cooper's presence in his mind. In that moment, the automatic gunfire stopped. Chase hesitated. He peered over the railing to see why they had stopped. His followers now appeared to be tying their shoes.

"Noooo!" Chase screamed. "What are you doing? Now is the time! Shoot them! Kill them! It is God's work!"

His words were ignored. They did nothing but stoop to their feet, their weapons discarded. Chase was enraged. Somehow his plan had been frustrated. But he knew he could at least claim one prize. He redoubled his efforts and tossed Coupe over the railing.

Coupe felt himself tumbling over, but he was not willing to give up that easily. Tenaciously, he held on to the railing, but now from the wrong side. His legs swung freely seventy-five feet above the ground. Chase immediately tried to dislodge him by ripping at his hands. Coupe was not willing to let go for anything. Sensing his desperation, Chase bent down and started biting Coupe's hands. Coupe tried to hold on, but one of his hands broke free, and Chase immediately turned his attention to the other. One by one Coupe's fingers began to loosen.

Just as he realized it was hopeless, Coupe sensed Cooper in his head, stronger than he had ever felt him before, stronger by far than the day he had made him tie his shoes in the boys' bathroom. *Help him sleep!*

Without any further thought, Coupe reached through the railing and stuck his fist into Chase's chest. He had one thought and one thought only in his mind, propelled by Cooper's thoughts below him—*Go to sleep!*

Chase took a quick sudden breath and then collapsed onto the gangway. He was asleep. It was the last thing that Coupe saw as he lost his grip and began falling to the ground far below him.

Coupe screamed in frenzied fear as he hurtled through empty space. He swung his arms wildly as if he could somehow prevent the imminent impact, but he knew his efforts were futile. He was about to die.

He need not have worried. Some twenty feet above the ground, Cooper caught him, and they landed together, safely.

"Just like picking apples," said Cooper, smiling with more than a little concern on his face. He put Coupe down and steadied him as he got his feet underneath him.

"You caught me," said Coupe, stating the obvious.

"Yes. It seemed like the right thing to do."

"Yes, yes," replied Coupe, still trying to fully comprehend his miraculous escape. Then he turned and looked at Cooper, realizing, and not for the first time, that he would always have his back. He put his hand on Cooper's strong shoulder. "Thank you for that."

"You're welcome, little brother," Cooper replied, smiling more easily now as he sensed Coupe returning to his own senses.

Coupe looked around. Dr. Stein had directed the security staff to round up the men who had just been shooting at them but were now dedicated solely to the task of tying shoes and easily rounded up.

"Why did you wait so long to make them stop to tie their shoes?" asked Coupe.

"I didn't. I kept trying to do it as soon as they started shooting but it didn't work. Then I figured I had to find you. Once we linked up, I tried it again and they all stopped. I don't think I can do it without you, Coupe."

Coupe was surprised. He had always thought this talent was peculiarly Cooper's, but apparently it was only possible when they worked together.

Coupe looked around and saw Corwin, Cassiopeia, and Cotovatre kneeling over Carrick. Noting their concern, he quickly realized that Carrick had been hit. They both ran over.

Carrick was on the ground breathing heavily with an obvious gunshot to his side. Coupe looked around to see if anyone else had been injured. Two of the security staff were also on the ground. One had a wound to his arm, but he seemed to be okay. The other one was not so lucky. Coupe could see he had been shot in the head.

Cooper knelt beside Carrick. The injured boy grimaced.

"It hurts, Cooper," he said.

"I know it does, Carrick," he replied. He sensed Carrick's pain and the disquiet it was causing him. He felt for him and wished there was something he could do. He thought for a moment and then stretched out his hand and placed it on Carrick's chest. Shortly after doing so, Carrick's breathing slowed to normal. "Is that better?" he asked.

"Yeah, Cooper. I feel better. Did you heal me?"

"No, Carrick. I can't do that. I just helped you to stop feeling the pain."

Dr. Stein appeared and knelt beside Carrick. His look of concern was genuine. It was clear that Dr. Stein did see them all as his children, of a sort. He bent down to scrutinize the wound.

"This might hurt," he said as he gently rolled Carrick over to look at his back for an exit wound. He quickly rolled him back. "Did that hurt?" he asked.

"Not really, but Cooper did something to make it *not* hurt."

"Cooper appears to have all sorts of unique skills that he has been keeping from me," replied Dr. Stein, glancing up at him. "Carrick, the bullet has gone straight through. Right now your biggest danger is blood loss. I am going to make a pressure bandage, and I expect that will hurt, but it is necessary to keep you ali—to help you." With that he took off his shirt and wrapped it tightly around Carrick's torso. He then placed his hands on either side of the wound and pressed down firmly. Carrick let out a gasp but did not appear to feel any pain. Carrick smiled at Cooper and gave him a thumbs-up. Dr. Stein looked both astonished and intrigued.

Coupe heard vehicles coming up the roadway and then saw two of the campus vans. One went toward the security staff and their new prisoners. The other headed for them. As it arrived Dr. Stein called over one of the security staff. Coupe recognized him as the other man who had kidnapped them, Severus. He appeared to be in charge as Dr. Stein spoke to him.

"Get those men down to the security building. I am taking Carrick to the medical building and I will be busy patching him up for a while. But I want to speak with those men and find out just who they are. And figure out a way to get Chase down from the tower."

"He's asleep. I'll go up and bring him down," replied Cooper.

Dr. Stein looked at the two of them with some surprise. He thought they had killed Chase. Then he considered Cooper's offer to get Chase down and frowned.

"No, Cooper, it's too dangerous. I don't want you falling and getting hurt."

"I'm pretty sure he could just jump off the top of that tower and not get hurt," replied Coupe. "He just caught me as I fell off. You are the one that gave him all these super strengths. Why not let him use them?"

Dr. Stein considered Coupe's words for a moment and then slowly nodded. "Okay. Severus, go with him."

"Do you want me to go too?" asked Corwin.

"No, you stay here with me," replied Dr. Stein. Corwin looked disappointed. "And Corwin?" Dr. Stein added. "Thank you for saving my life. If you had not pulled me down so quickly, I am sure I would have been struck."

Corwin brightened at the doctor's words.

Dr. Stein loaded Carrick into the van and climbed in after him. They quickly left to go to the medical building, and the others followed. Coupe trotted over to the water tower.

As he approached, Cooper scooted quickly up the ladder. Severus stood at the bottom keeping an eye on him. Coupe stood next to him, and Severus looked over at him.

"Hello, Coupe," said Severus.

"Hello, kidnapping guy," replied Coupe without making eye contact. Severus ignored the insult.

"What you two can do, from what I can see, it's pretty special."

Coupe said nothing. Severus hesitated but then continued.

"Anyway, thank you for saving my life tonight."

"That wasn't me," replied Coupe. "That was all Cooper."

"Is that right? Then how come Cooper is climbing up this water tower to bring down the guy you put to sleep?"

Coupe didn't have an answer for that. Cooper had used him as a conduit, a conductor, to put Chase to sleep. But Coupe had to admit that he was the only one he could use in that way.

Coupe's thoughts were interrupted by Cooper appearing at the top of the ladder again. Now he had Chase draped over his shoulder like a sleeping child. Cooper had no trouble bringing Chase down the ladder and jumping to the ground. He turned to look at Severus. Coupe spoke for him.

"Where do you want him, kidnapping dude?" asked Coupe

"What? Cooper doesn't have a tongue?" asked Severus.

"Not for you. Don't forget about what you said about our parents. I don't see him opening up for you."

"You know I didn't mean that. I just had to motivate you."

"Maybe. Maybe not."

Severus realized he was not going to win them over, at least not right then and there. "Bring him down here to the van."

Cooper carried the sleeping Chase to the van, which was filled with the six gunmen who had fired on them. Their hands were now all bound behind their backs, and Chase's hands were likewise bound even though he continued to sleep. The six men were scary looking. Coupe wondered just how Chase had convinced them to attack Dr. Stein's remote compound. Their faces were grim. They were all dressed alike in dark camouflage. They had long beards and close-cropped hair. No doubt the questions in his mind and others would be asked, and soon. Cooper sensed that these men held equally hostile thoughts about him and Cooper. He did not understand why.

Severus closed the door to the van, and it drove off toward the security building.

"I'll walk you boys back down to the dormitory," said Severus.

"We don't need a babysitter." replied Coupe. "And you think we can just go to sleep after all this?"

"Yeah, you're right. On both counts. Though I'm thinking one of you would get to sleep. I'm just not sure which one of you."

Coupe took his meaning, but ignored it.

"We're going to the medical building to wait for word on Carrick," he said.

"I'll walk with you, if you don't mind," said Severus.

"Suit yourself," replied Coupe.

He's looking for information. Don't trust him, thought Cooper.

No shit, replied Coupe, silently.

After they walked for a bit, Severus began probing.

"So, uh, you two have really come to rely upon each other, haven't you?" asked Severus.

"Yep," replied Coupe quickly.

"What you two can do is pretty special," he persisted.

"Yep," Coupe replied again. Cooper had yet to speak to him.

"So, when did you learn you could do this stuff?"

"In school."

Severus now pressed for meaningful information. "Just what is it that you two can do?"

"Lots of stuff."

"Like what?"

Cooper and Coupe left Severus on the side of the main thoroughfare as they headed down to the medical building. For some reason Severus had decided it was momentously important to stop, bend down, and tie his shoes.

CHAPTER 37

Cassiopeia, Corwin, and Cotovatre were waiting in the medical building. Cooper and Coupe learned that even though Dr. Stein was by choice a geneticist, he was still a doctor and had spent part of his residency doing trauma surgery at a hospital in New York City. It turned out that was good news for Carrick. After about an hour of waiting, he came in to see them all.

"Carrick will be fine," he said with a satisfied smile. "He lost a lot of blood, but we are taking care of that, and his wounds have been surgically repaired. Would you like to see him?"

"Is he awake already?" asked Cotovatre, showing surprise.

"He was never put to sleep," replied Dr. Stein, looking squarely at Cooper. "Apparently whatever Cooper did for him meant that I was able to work on him without the need of an anesthetic.

Cooper said nothing. He just stared at the doctor innocently.

"Well, he is upstairs in the recovery area. You can go see him if you wish."

The group bounded down the hallway toward the elevators, hooting with glee. Dr. Stein could not help but smile as they scampered off to see their brother. He was satisfied that at least these remaining individuals would be successful, which brought his thoughts back to Chase. Dr. Stein pulled out his phone and quickly called Severus to get a status. Now his demeanor shifted to all business. After a short conversation, Dr. Stein put away his phone and left the building.

The group headed upstairs and found Carrick resting comfortably. He smiled as they all came in. He spied Cooper and gave him a thumbs-up.

"Thanks, Cooper. It was kind of weird having Dr. Stein fix me up being awake and all. But whatever you did worked."

"You didn't feel anything at all?" asked Cotovatre.

"It's not that I didn't feel anything; it's just that it didn't hurt," he replied and then turned back to Cooper. "How do you do it, Cooper?"

"I'm not really sure. The pain is still there. I just help you ignore it. It should stay just the way it is until you are able to ignore it all by yourself."

The teens settled down to discuss the early-morning events. They discussed seeing Chase and how he had changed since they last saw him. They wondered who the men were that had come back with him and how he had recruited them to help attack them. The teens stopped talking and looked over when Stanley entered. He gave his customary smile and looked at Cooper and Coupe.

"Dr. Stein has asked that I come collect you two," he said quietly. "He needs your assistance at the security building.

Cooper and Coupe looked at each other in their usual fashion. Then, Coupe just shrugged, and the two got up to go with Stanley.

"Did he ask for me?" asked Corwin.

"No, he didn't, Cory," replied Stanley. Corwin looked annoyed.

"Well, I'm coming anyway," he said tersely.

The four of them left together, leaving Cassiopeia and Cotovatre to attend to Carrick.

"Did he say what he wanted?" asked Corwin as they all got into the van to drive over to the security building.

"No, he didn't," replied Stanley. Cooper and Coupe already knew that. They did not have to ask.

....

Once at the security building, Stanley led them to an office where they found Dr. Stein talking with Severus.

"Boys! Thank you for coming over!" he said as they entered. When he saw Corwin enter behind them his smile slipped. "Corwin, I did not call for you for a reason. What we are about to undertake concerns Chase. I am well aware of your feelings toward him. That being said, I will allow you to stay if you assure me you will not try to cause him any harm."

"I won't."

"Very well," replied Dr. Stein. "Below us in a holding cell I have the six men that tried to kill us. I wish to find out more about them, but they are not talking. I am hoping that you two would be willing to put your unique skills to use and help me protect our small community."

"Yeah, we'll help," replied Coupe.

"Excellent!" replied Dr. Stein. "We will be behind a two-way mirror. They will not be able to see us, but we can see them. I have already tried to ask questions, but they won't answer. They quote Bible passages at me. I need to know more about them to determine if they still pose a threat. I do not expect them to answer my questions, but I believe this time when I ask them the questions you two will be able to sense the responses that they are unwilling to verbalize."

"Where's Chase?" asked Corwin.

"Safe and still sleeping," he replied.

They followed Dr. Stein to a stairwell that led them down two flights of stairs and into the basement. Once there, they went through a heavily secured door that Dr. Stein opened with his security card. There they found two more security personnel standing before the two-way mirror, watching over their new prisoners. The now heavily armed men nodded to Severus as he entered, and stepped back from the glass to allow Dr. Stein access with the three boys.

They looked through the glass. Inside they saw the six tall men who had attacked them. Some sat at a table, while others had climbed onto one of the six bunk beds.

To the side of the glass was a small control panel. It had a number of buttons as well as a speaker built into it. Dr. Stein walked over to this control panel. Before pressing any buttons, however, he looked back at the boys.

"Ready?" he asked. Coupe nodded for the both of them. Dr. Stein turned back to the control panel and pressed a button.

"Gentlemen," he said to get their attention. "It's Dr. Stein once again. I know you did not want to answer my questions previously, but I hope you have reconsidered. Where are you from?"

None of the men said a word.

"They are from Alabama," stated Coupe. "They are from a religious community that has a compound there. Out in the woods somewhere, like an old summer camp converted for their church."

Dr. Stein was quick to put this new information to good use. "Tell me about your religious community." Again, the men said nothing.

"They call themselves the Children of Caine," said Coupe. "They believe that the Bible is the true word of God. They follow it strictly, very strictly. Anyone who does not share in their belief shall be damned. Apparently, we are all damned and even worse than damned given how we were brought into the world. Our very existence is offensive to them. Not the kind of guys you want to have over for a cookout. The one staring at you from the top bunk is their leader. His name is Enoch."

"Thank you, boys," Dr. Stein said quietly and then pressed the button on the speaker once again. "Enoch, perhaps you could explain yourself. So far as I know we have never met, yet you came here to kill us all. Why?"

Enoch appeared surprised to hear his name called but quickly recovered his composure. He sat staring from the top bunk at the mirror which concealed them, his feet hanging over the edge. He slowly crossed his large arms across his chest. The room remained silent.

"Some of the others want him to explain to you why they are here, but they will not speak. He does not suffer disobedience lightly," said Coupe to Dr. Stein.

"Do you not wish to explain yourself, Enoch? Justify your actions? Perhaps some of your men wish to. Come tell me, Enoch. *'Of a truth, God will not do wickedly, and the Almighty will not pervert justice.'* Isn't that what the Bible teaches? *'Sanctify them in the truth; your word is the truth.'"*

Enoch looked furious and jumped down from the bunk. "That is not my word which is the truth; it is the Almighty's word that is the truth! And to hear it dribbling through your lips is like hearing it from the serpent himself! You desecrate those words when you utter them, Dr. *Stein.*"

"Well, that hit a nerve," said Dr. Stein. "And apparently he does not know where the Old Testament comes from."

Enoch strode over to the mirror and looked through it.

"You speak of perversions and wickedness? They are sins that God will not abide. I know of your work here. The one that escaped came to us and told us how you have perverted man from the original cast of Adam, the mold of Eve. You have taken them from God's likeness and turned them to your own.

"Your actions are an abomination! God will not allow you to tamper with his creation. He has tasked us with annihilating all that you have done. We will do as God bids! We will not be stopped. We will cast you all into the fires of hell, where you belong. We will be the willing hand of God removing the weeds from the crop of the righteous!"

Enoch turned, walked back to the bunk, and sat, eyes still blazing.

"He's optimistic, I'll give him that. Undaunted despite his present situation."

Coupe's brow furrowed, and he turned to look at Cooper, who was equally concerned. Cooper nodded slowly and said, "Tell him."

Dr. Stein turned, surprised to hear Cooper actually speak.

"Cooper senses that Enoch is waiting," said Coupe.

"Waiting for what?" asked Dr. Stein.

"To be . . ." Coupe paused, looking back at Cooper for confirmation, and then continued. "To be rescued."

"What?" Alarmed, Dr. Stein looked directly at Cooper. "Cooper, tell me what you mean. How are they going to be rescued?"

Cooper concentrated for a moment, staring at Enoch. Then he looked back at Dr. Stein. "He doesn't know how; he just knows that they will be rescued, and soon."

"Well, do any of them know how they are to be rescued?"

"No, none of the men in there."

"Then who does?"

"Chase does," said Cooper. "All Enoch knows is that Chase had a plan that included any situation where they got caught or killed."

Dr. Stein slowly shook his head. "What a great irony. I created the very thing that may well be our undoing. Come on, boys. Let's go see Chase."

CHAPTER 38

Chase was not far. He was across the hall in another secured room being watched by another man. He lay on a bed, still sleeping. Coupe found it singularly odd to look down upon himself sleeping, a quasi out-of-body experience.

"He should be tied up," said Corwin, entering the room.

"He's asleep," replied Cooper quietly.

Corwin glared at Cooper. "He tried to kill us. He tried to kill me twice!"

"Stop this, right now," said Dr. Stein quietly. "There are far more serious matters at hand than the petty squabbling between you two. Cooper, you put him to sleep. Can you wake him up?"

"Yes."

"Good. Once you have awoken him, will you please see if you can sense just what Enoch is expecting?'

Cooper hesitated. "I don't know if I can. I'm not trying to defy you, Dr. Stein. I know it is important. But last time I tried to get a sense of Chase, I couldn't. His mind was just too different, too mixed up. His thoughts were spinning around like a twister in his head. I couldn't latch on to anything useful. The only time I was able to get anything from him was when he was up on the water tower."

"Why was that?"

"Because he was focused. Well, sort of focused. I got the sense he was doing everything in his power to concentrate and keep himself there in the moment, but it was a struggle for him. It was only because of that struggle that I was able to kind of slip in. Well, that and Coupe. Chase was really too far away for me to do much of anything, I think."

"But you did," noted Dr. Stein.

Cooper shrugged. "Maybe," he replied.

"Wake him."

Cooper put his hand on Chase's chest. A moment later Chase awoke with a gasp. He looked around to see he was by no means alone.

"Where am I? What happened?"

Dr. Stein ignored the first question. "You were asleep, Chase, and now you are awake. I would like to ask you some questions."

"I haven't really slept for years. I forgot how it felt. It felt good." Chase rubbed his neck and then stretched his arms. He looked around the room and then yawned. "What time is it?" he asked.

Dr. Stein looked down at his watch. "It's a few minutes before six in the morning. Now pay attention to me, Chase. We know you have some sort of rescue planned. We do not need any more people killed or injured. Tell me what you have planned."

Chase stared back at him silently. Then his head snapped around and locked on to Cooper, whose face changed to one of shock and then fear. He stumbled backwards. Chase continued to glare at him. As his back hit the wall Cooper gasped, "Six! They are coming at 6 a.m.!" With that he let out a painful groan and slumped against the wall.

Dr. Stein darted over to him. "Cooper! Cooper! What's wrong?"

Cooper did not respond. Dr. Stein turned to Coupe for an explanation. Coupe was frozen in place, unresponsive too.

"What is going on!?" shouted Dr. Stein.

At that moment there was a tremendous boom from outside the stairwell. Someone had blown in the door. Severus was immediately on the radio calling in for assistance. The two men watching the prisoners from the hallway came over to Severus and darted into the room just as gunfire erupted down the hallway. Across the hall, they heard another loud noise. The men had picked up the table and were now trying to break through the window to escape. The glass was thick and reinforced, but it would not withstand that sort of assault indefinitely.

Corwin had once again dragged Dr. Stein to the ground when the bullets started flying. Chase sat on the bed staring intently at Cooper, but Coupe was still standing like he was caught in some sort of catatonic state.

"Coupe! Get down!" ordered Dr. Stein. But Coupe did not move. Dr. Stein tried to get up to pull Coupe down, but Corwin pushed him back down and jumped to pull Coupe to the ground. Coupe was placed next to Dr. Stein. He lay there apparently senseless. Dr. Stein slapped his face, but he got no response.

"Coupe!" he shouted again. "Get Cooper to make them tie their shoes!"

Coupe remained motionless, apparently senseless.

As Cooper tried to sense Chase's plan, Coupe had followed along, as he usually did. Chase's mind was a whirling mess, but the sleep must have done him some good because he was thinking coherently. Chase became aware of Cooper sensing him. But instead of shutting him out, Chase latched on to Cooper in his mind. Instead of pushing him away, he sucked him in and held him there in a choke hold of thoughts. Then they both began to spin around in the whirling madness that was Chase's mind. Chase was pulling Cooper down into his madness. He was going to drown him there.

Coupe was not going to let Chase have him so easily. He sensed Cooper slipping, and he grasped him with his own mind, pulling him away from Chase. He stopped him from being pulled away, but he was not strong enough to free Cooper. While the security doors were being blown and bullets began to fly, Chase and Coupe were stuck in a stalemate tug-of-war over Cooper. They were not oblivious to what was going on. Cooper and Coupe were very anxious about the attack; they simply could do nothing to help. Chase did not care one way or another. He expected that they would all be dead very soon and his mission complete. He would die content with that knowledge.

While Dr. Stein tried to rouse Coupe, Corwin looked over at Chase. He was still staring wide-eyed at Cooper, who had collapsed in the corner. Corwin knew his psychic abilities were limited compared to those of Cooper, but he tried to use them nonetheless. He reached out to Chase. As he did so, his eyes opened wide. He could sense the battle between Chase, Cooper and Coupe. At that moment he heard the glass from the cell across the hall finally break. The men were free. A moment later they were rushing at the door. The security staff shot two of them, but four others quickly overpowered the two men who had automatic weapons. Severus tried to keep them out with his pistol but was overwhelmed. The other men who had breached down the hall reached the doorway too.

Corwin knew there was only one way they were going to survive—Cooper. Corwin stood and walked to Chase. Picking him up, he threw his body against the concrete wall. Hard. Chase's head smacked against the concrete with a loud thud. He fell to the ground senseless.

Cooper awoke with a deep intake of breath. He saw the intruders shoot the man who had been watching Chase and push Severus to the ground. The Children of Caine piled into the room and lifted their weapons to shoot them all. He watched as they pointed their rifles at Dr. Stein, Corwin and Coupe. He felt Coupe's panic as fingers began to squeeze triggers. Cooper mustered all of his remaining mental energy and hurled a mental spike at the men, stronger than any he had mustered before.

In that moment, each one of the Children of Caine fell senseless to the floor. The room became eerily silent.

Dr. Stein was the first to speak.

"Severus, get us some help down here! Cooper, are they asleep?"

Cooper was still slumped against the wall. "I don't think they're asleep," he said quietly.

"What did you do?"

"I told them to stop, and they did."

Dr. Stein turned one of them over. He was awake in that his eyes were open, but he did not respond, even when Dr. Stein touched his eyeball. Drool poured from the corner of his mouth and puddled on the floor beneath him. Dr. Stein looked around; they were all that way.

Dr. Stein turned his attention to his own men. Three of them had been shot but miraculously were still alive. He began tending to their wounds and called over to Cooper.

"Cooper, please ensure that Chase stays asleep."

Cooper nodded and went over to help Coupe. As he stood him up, Coupe just leaned in and hugged him. "Thanks, Cooper."

"Don't thank me. Thank him," he said, pointing at Corwin, who was now staring at them.

The two boys walked over to him and pulled him in for a hug. "Thanks, brother," said Coupe. Corwin hesitated for a moment. Hugging was a new experience for him. But he just as quickly relented and put a hand on the backs of the other two boys.

"No problem," said Corwin. "I am glad I could help."

CHAPTER 39

Given the attack, Dr. Stein called the Consortium to report what happened and to seek additional help. It did not take long. Within an hour two unmarked Black Hawk helicopters arrived with heavily armed men in unmarked uniforms. A large cargo helicopter landed shortly after that, and several groups of men got out of that one too. One group had dogs. The Children of Caine were loaded by stretcher onto the cargo helicopter and taken away.

One of the groups from the cargo helicopter was a medical crew. They immediately went down to the medical building and assisted Dr. Stein with the injured security staff. He had ordered all of the Omicron Six to stay in the dormitory until told otherwise, and two of the heavily armed men came up and kept watch over them on the floor. They did not stop the teens from going into each other's rooms or hanging out in the hall, but they would not let them leave.

The group had their meals brought up to them by Stanley. They pestered him with questions, but he simply told them that Dr. Stein would come to see them but was very busy, so they would just have to wait. From their windows they could see activity going on around the campus. Men patrolled the entire fence line and appeared to stop and take great interest somewhere up behind the water tower. One of the campus's maintenance trucks was soon driving out there with a large roll of chain link fence in the bed. Later in the day Coupe spotted the dog team coming back up onto the main campus. They went into the main building, where Dr. Stein was located.

The past thirty-six hours had been hectic and, quite frankly, traumatic, so it was not really surprising that Coupe had one of his nightmares—the first in a long time. He awoke screaming, but Cooper was there for him and quickly put him back to sleep. What they did not expect was to have the two security officers kick in the door, thinking he was being attacked. That woke Coupe up all over again and sent both the boys screaming into the corner of the room. Once everything was explained, the two officers left, but that was the end of sleeping for those two. Coupe was very apologetic. Cooper thought it was kind of funny.

The second day of their confinement workers came up to replace the broken window in Carrick's room and the broken doors. Carrick had been forced to bunk with Corwin until it was fixed. Corwin complained loudly on account of Carrick sleeping naked. Eventually a compromise was reached. Carrick had to keep his pants on.

Perhaps the most significant change amongst the group was the absence of tension. Corwin no longer felt hostile toward Cooper or Coupe. He was now one of them in spirit. He understood Cooper and Coupe better. He knew what they had done. He had felt their battle with Chase. He accepted them. They even started to encourage his telepathic abilities, and they could tell that he was pleased that they had started including him in more of their silent conversations. It was like he was learning a new language and just starting to understand. When they did, it elicited a big grin, which in turn would cause Cooper and Coupe to grin.

At one point, Cotovatre became frustrated because she couldn't participate in their telepathic conversations.

"What? What are you three talking about? Is it my hair? Is it this shirt?"

When they awoke on the third morning their security was gone. Stanley came up and told them that Dr. Stein would like to talk to them all at ten, and he would be back to get them at that time. At the appointed time, the elevator opened and they all piled in with Stanley.

·················

Dr. Stein was waiting for them in the library. Once again he was up on the balcony, but today his demeanor was much more somber. His face looked drawn, and it appeared that he had not done much sleeping in the past three days.

"Come in, kids!" he said with feigned enthusiasm. "I have some treats for you on the table." They looked over to see donuts and pastries for them to enjoy. They helped themselves and then were seated.

"First of all, let me assure you that you are all safe," he said. "Chase has been safely secured, and the self-named Children of Caine are no longer a threat to anyone, both here on our campus or down in Alabama."

Dr. Stein spent about thirty minutes explaining what had been happening over the past three days—how the campus had been made more secure, how the Consortium had taken a very serious interest in the breach in their security and new measures were in place to prevent such a situation from happening again. The investigation had revealed that Chase and the Children of Caine had set up a camp in the woods about a mile from their campus. From that vantage they had conducted surveillance on the campus. It turned out that most of the members of the cult had military experience and were well trained.

"Who were they, and how did Chase find them?" asked Cotovatre.

"And why did they even believe him?" asked Cassiopeia.

Dr. Stein winced. "I am not sure how Chase found them, but Chase is very intelligent and he probably devised just whom he could most easily manipulate and then went out looking. He apparently found the Children of Caine. As to why they believed him, well, a team of specialists went down to Alabama to interview the remaining members of the cult. They did not initially believe Chase. That is why he abducted his victims. He would then take them down to the cult to prove what he said was true."

"My twin, Caroline," interrupted Cotovatre, "did he take her down there?"

Dr. Stein's face once again showed his pain. "Yes, he did, Cotovatre. I am so sorry. But neither he nor the Children of Caine will ever harm anyone else."

Cotovatre buried her face in her sleeves. Cooper put his arm around her in sympathy.

"What are you going to do with Chase?" asked Corwin. "I mean, he should be killed too."

"Chase is ill; he is not criminal. Your own observations should lead you to that conclusion."

"Either way, he is too dangerous."

"I suggest, Corwin, you leave those decisions to me. He has been taken to a place for safekeeping where he will be safe, and you will be safe. He will be held securely, much more securely than before. But I have no intention of killing him. He may not be beyond help. I will begin some medication regimens that may restore some of his faculties to their prior state. I am hopeful for him."

Corwin persisted. "But how will you know? He could just fake it again, just like he did with me."

"Well, with Cooper and Coupe here I expect he would not be able to fool us without giving himself away."

"Wait. What do you mean with Cooper and Coupe here, Doc?" asked Coupe. "Chase has been captured. The threat is over. Me and Coo—Cooper and I want to go home now."

Dr. Stein looked at them all. "I need to have a conversation with just Cooper and Coupe."

Once the others had left, Coupe wasted no time. "So, Doc, care to explain yourself? Just what do you mean that Cooper and I have to stay here?"

"Boys, I think it is best that, for now, you remained here. It will be safer for both of you and for everyone else."

"Now we are the threat? What did we ever do to harm anybody until we got here?" challenged Coupe, getting angry. "We've done nothing wrong! Either you let us go, or we will walk right out the front gates and walk home, even if it kills us."

Dr. Stein showed his frustration. It was obviously a subject that had been troubling him over the past few days. "Cooper, you mentally lobotomized ten men with a single thought! Don't get me wrong, I am not saying you were wrong to do that given the circumstances. But how can I justifiably let you go given the powers you seem to possess, the threat you could pose?"

"So what?" said Coupe, challenging Dr. Stein again. "He is less of a threat than any kid with a grudge and a gun. I don't see you rounding them all up. Cooper's not dangerous. I know his mind! I know how it works! I know how good he is, how pure his thoughts are. And even if he did become a threat, there is still me to act and stop him. He is already being observed, every friggin' day, every friggin' minute. He has to deal with me being in his head. A *threat*? Hell, you would not be standing here to question his actions if he had not done it. Come on, Cooper. Let's go pack our bags."

Cooper said nothing. He got up when Coupe called him and followed him out of the room, with a good deal of side-eye for Dr. Stein.

CHAPTER 40

They got back to the dormitory and went straight to their room, despite the inquiring glances they got from their siblings. Coupe immediately started packing a bag, and Cooper did the same.

"Maybe we can take one of the vans. If not, I say we hoof it on foot. We got plenty of warm clothes and I have a bunch of peanut butter. Trust me, it can keep you going for a long time."

"I just want to be home, Coupe."

"Me too."

As they were packing, their bedroom door opened. Severus stepped in. Once again, he was holding his dart gun.

"Dr. Stein would like to speak with you, Coupe. And just you."

"We are done talking," said Coupe.

"The easy way or the hard way, boys. You should know I am not alone."

"We *know* that you are not alone, dipshit," replied Coupe.

"Easy way or the hard way, boys."

"Again, allow me to speak for both of us, Severus. The easy way." Coupe turned to Cooper. "Wait for me here. I won't be long."

Severus led him out into the hallway where their four siblings were watching. So were six more security staff. Cooper followed them out of the room, smoldering with anger.

"Coupe, what am I to do with you two?" asked Dr. Stein, after Coupe had been returned to the library.

"How about you keep your word and let us go home?"

"Coupe, that was before I learned what Cooper could do. I should be angry with you two for withholding that information from me. It is crucial I understand your abilities."

"What do you think of us, Doc? That we knew he could brain-zap people before the attack? Before that all we had done was put people to sleep, make them walk away or tie their shoes. And Cooper didn't set out with the goal of making zombies. He just wanted them to stop and he was under extreme stress."

"That is precisely why I am concerned about letting him back out there, because he may be in another stressful situation and just want to make people *stop*. I must keep him safe, and everyone else safe too. He is simply too powerful. You should know I had to make a report of events to the Consortium. His abilities have, well, caused quite a stir. He needs further studying and he needs to be kept safe."

"If you force him to stay here, he will not cooperate with you. He'll just be a prisoner."

Dr. Stein was beginning to get angry, probably because he knew Coupe was right. "Well then, he will be a safe prisoner here, won't he!"

Coupe sat quietly staring back at Dr. Stein, trying to think of a way out of the situation. Deep Woods was not bad, but it was not their home. Coupe sensed daily how much Cooper was missing his home, missing his parents. For Coupe it had been easier. His life had been fairly transient until he landed with the Callisters, so he was used to a certain amount of chaos in his life. But for Cooper, he had only known one home and one family. Right now he was sorely missing that family and that quiet way of life. Coupe felt Cooper's desire to get home. It was like a hunger for Cooper, and each day it was denied, his starvation increased. He needed to go home, no matter what.

"He's not a threat when he is alone. Let him go and I will agree to stay."

"What do you mean he is not a threat?"

"His special powers, over other people, they only work when I am with him. So if I agree to stay here, he will not be a threat to the outside world, and you can let him go back to his parents."

"Why did you not tell me before?"

"We only just figured it out on the night of the attack! You gotta understand, Doc, we are working this stuff out for ourselves as we go along. You didn't send us out with an owner's manual. On the night of the attack Cooper was not capable of making those men tie their shoes until he was able to connect with me. Then it happened."

"Why is that?" asked the doctor.

"I'm really not sure. The power is all Cooper's. But I think he cannot focus it without me. He's the bright light. I'm just the lens."

"Fascinating." Dr. Stein's sat quietly considering what Coupe had just revealed. He stared at Coupe for a long time. "You are willing to sacrifice a great deal for Cooper. Your own freedom for his. If I am not mistaken, you will be severing yourself from the most important person in your life, simply so he can go home."

"It's not such a bad deal, Doc," Coupe lied. "I mean, I like it here. I like all the learning. I like knowing I will be fed and have a safe place to sleep. The other kids seem really happy here. I will miss him, but I will come around."

"I suspect you could, especially with Cassie's help. But what about Cooper? How do you expect he will react to your proposed plan?"

"I will just have to sell it to him."

"I still need to study him, study you both together."

"He will agree to return twice a year for a week so you can study him."

Dr. Stein paused to think, then said, "Very well, but he must come back here four times a year, for ten days each time. Now, let me see you *sell it* to Cooper."

Dr. Stein had Cooper summoned to the library, and a short while later he was ushered into the room. He came and sat next to Coupe. He sought out his thoughts, but Coupe blocked him out. Cooper gave him a suspicious look.

Uncharacteristically, it was Cooper who spoke first. "What's going on?"

"It's good news, Cooper. Well, sort of," said Coupe. "You are going home. You're leaving today."

"What about you?"

"I've been talking it over with Dr. Stein, and I think there are more opportunities for me here. I mean, the school here is top notch, way better than our high school. Dr. Stein has agreed to take me under his wing and personally manage my education. That is really important to me, something I did not consider before. The sky will be the limit for me, buddy! And you get to go home to your parents."

The last sentence really hit a nerve with Cooper. "They're *our* parents, Coupe." Then, "No! I am not leaving you here."

"Cooper, c'mon, buddy. Let's face it. They are *your* parents, not mine. You grew up with them, not me. I mean, I really liked it there. I will never forget what it was like to live with you and your parents, trust me on that. Best time of my life. But I bet over time your mom and even your dad would get sick of me.

"You know me. I'm damaged goods, and they still have not

experienced all the baggage I carry. It wouldn't be long before I stole something again, and then they would have to deal with that. I would prefer it if they didn't. And I like it here. I can read all I want and I'll get fed and have a place to sleep. It would be the best for both of us.

"And it's not like we wouldn't get to see each other again. If we do this, you will have to agree to come back four times a year. We can catch up then."

Coupe felt Cooper trying to get in his head. Cooper was shocked by what Coupe said, and he wanted to sense whether he was telling the truth or not. He was pretty sure he was not. Coupe continued to block him out. Cooper looked furious. He tried harder. Coupe pushed back even harder, refusing to let him see his thoughts. Cooper's face showed his increasing frustration.

"Boys? What's going on?" asked Dr. Stein.

"Stop that!" shouted Cooper.

Coupe said nothing.

"I know you're lying! I know this is not what you want! He has talked you into it. If you were telling me the truth, you would let me see for myself in your head!"

"Cooper, it was my suggestion. Read Dr. Stein. You'll see I'm telling you the truth."

Cooper quickly turned to Dr. Stein and learned that Cooper was telling the truth, he had suggested the plan, but he also read that Dr. Stein thought Coupe was doing it to protect him. Cooper turned to look back at Coupe, who felt Cooper trying to force his way into his mind. It was like he was hammering on the door to his brain. But Coupe held fast. Then he did something for which he was greatly ashamed but which he knew he had to do.

When Chase and Cooper had been fighting in each other's minds, Coupe had a ringside seat. He had sensed what Chase was doing to lock Cooper's powers up. And he knew he could do it too.

Once again Cooper started pounding his way into Coupe's

thoughts. This time even harder. Coupe could see Cooper breathing heavy.

"Boys? Is everything okay?" asked Dr. Stein.

Then Coupe did it. He grabbed hold of Cooper's mind with his own and he started squeezing it, pulling it in the same way that Chase did. He did not do it for long, just long enough to let Cooper know he could do it. Then he shoved his presence out of his head.

Cooper did not try to get back in. He stood in front of him now with his jaw hanging open. Cooper felt betrayed. Betrayed by someone he had come to consider part of his very being, betrayed by Coupe. To Cooper they had moved beyond friends, beyond considering each other as brothers. They had started to become two parts of one unified being. And Coupe had just torn it in two.

"It's better for me to stay here. You go home, Cooper. Tell everyone I will miss them."

Cooper backed away from Coupe, then turned and slowly walked out of the room.

"So, do we have a deal, Doc? You get me if you let him go home."

"So long as he returns so I can study your interactions more closely."

"He'll come back, but I think I just destroyed that from ever happening. Who knows, maybe Corwin and me can develop the same sort of thing."

"Doubtful."

"There's no harm in trying, if Corwin is willing. It might be a good idea for you to get Cooper out of here right away. I may not be in his head anymore, but I am pretty sure he is not pleased about what just happened."

"I will have Severus take him home right away."

"I'll steer clear of the dormitory until then."

"Perhaps a good idea."

CHAPTER 41

Coupe walked down to the lake. From there, he could keep his eyes on the dorm and see when Severus took Cooper home. Then it would be safe for him to return.

It was cold on the frozen beach. The winter sky had turned a dirty iron grey, and snow threatened. Coupe shivered against the biting wind coming across the lake. He hoped he would not have to wait for too much longer. His eyes watered from the chill. At least, that was what Coupe told himself.

Finally, Coupe saw one of the campus vans pull up in front of the dormitory. Severus and another man got out. Severus had his dart gun out and ready. The two went into the dormitory. A few minutes later they emerged with Cooper. He was carrying two bags. Before he got into the van he looked over and saw Coupe standing on the beach. Coupe offered a weak wave goodbye. Cooper just stared at him, then got in the van. Severus got in next to him, and the other man got behind the wheel.

Coupe stood on the cold, frozen beach and watched the van drive away. Now Coupe was sure that it was not the cold wind causing his eyes to water. His heart felt torn apart by what he had done. Cooper was going to miss him, that was certain. But Cooper really had no idea how much Coupe had let Cooper become a part of himself. Now that part of him was gone. And he had done it in a dirty way, using Chase's evil tricks to sever their contact. He was sure Cooper probably hated him right now. The only thought that gave Coupe any solace was that he had done it for Cooper, to get him home. While his method had been contemptible, the end result justified it.

Coupe walked back to the dorm and went to his room. Corwin, Cotovatre, Cassiopeia, and Carrick were out in the hallway talking when he came in. They tried to engage him, but he really was in no mood for company. He simply nodded and walked by.

Coupe's blankets were still on the floor next to the bunk beds, and his dresser was as he had left it, but Cooper's was empty, the drawers hanging open. Coupe just curled up in the blankets and tried to sleep, eventually able to nap lightly. He awoke late in the afternoon, just in time to get some dinner at the dining hall, but he sat alone, not tasting his food. When he was done, he did not want to get back to the dorm. It seemed empty to him now. Instead, he walked along the lake.

The wind was still strong and biting cold. Nevertheless, he put his head down and walked as far as he could. He had almost reached the far side of the lake when he finally turned around and looked back. By now it was twilight, and the lights of the campus gleamed through the darkness back at him, like somber Christmas lights.

It had started to snow. The wind whipped it almost sideways into his face. Coupe pulled up his collar and started back across the lake over the thick ice to the dorm.

He was still shivering from the cold when he walked past Corwin, who had stuck his head out his dorm room door.

"Are you okay?" he asked.

"Yeah, I'll be fine, just a little cold. I'm going to take a shower and go to bed."

"Well, let me know if you need anything," said Corwin.

The past few days had seen a bond building between the two. It had been the three of them, but now just the two.

The warm shower helped Coupe relax. He lay on the floor with his pillow and blankets, knowing he would be falling asleep the old-fashioned way tonight. He hoped more than anything his night terrors would not return, but he had a feeling that they would. His heart ached more than ever before in his short life.

It took a while, but eventually Coupe drifted off into a fitful sleep. A few hours later, he felt his sleep being invaded by his old enemies, the horrible thoughts that plagued him so many times in the past until Cooper had arrived and chased them away. Once again, they seemed real. Coupe started to thrash about on the floor and shout senselessly for help. He tried desperately to break free, but he could not. They had a firm grip on his mind, and he was suffering.

Then he felt pressure on his chest. His eyes flew open to see Corwin leaning over him with his fist planted firmly on him.

"Go back to sleep," he whispered. And he did. Twice more during that night, Corwin put his fist in Coupe's chest and willed him back to sleep, chasing the malignant thoughts away.

He awoke in the morning to a pleasant dream. This time it was not filled with all the horrible memories of his past. It was sunlit and full of hopeful promise. This time he was dreaming of Cooper and the way that they could share their thoughts. He was remembering how they would communicate in each other's heads, silently discuss any issue, any problems they faced. In this dream, Cooper was asking Coupe to help get them both out of Deep Woods together. Coupe explained they could not both leave, that only Cooper could leave.

But Cooper refused to go without him. Then Coupe realized he was not dreaming. Coupe's eyes shot open.

"Cooper, is that you?"

"You know it is," he replied from the bed next to him.

"How did you get back here?"

"I never left."

"What? But I saw you."

"You saw Corwin. We switched places so I could stay here and talk some sense into you. Right now Corwin is experiencing the end of his first night in the outside world with our parents."

"But you can't—"

Coupe didn't get to finish his sentence. Cooper launched himself off of the bed and stood over Coupe with his fists on his hips. The bright morning sun streaming in through the windows lit up one side of Cooper's body like electricity.

"I am really mad at you, Coupe. We don't get separated! You got that? By now you have to realize that the only way we really work alone is if we are together!"

"But, Cooper, I did it for you."

"Didn't we have this conversation a few months ago, after you got stabbed? Stop putting me in front of you! We are both going home. They are *our* parents and you know that. All that stuff you said yesterday to make me think you wanted to stay here and didn't want to go home to them—I know it's all bull crap. I waited for you to go to sleep so I could get a good look around inside your head while you were sleeping.

"Yesterday I watched you through that window walking around the lake like a stray that got kicked to the curb. Don't tell me you weren't hurting. I was even getting worried you wouldn't come back in. And don't you ever pull that twisted stuff that Chase did to me ever again!" Cooper's eyes flashed with renewed anger.

Coupe looked away, ashamed. "I'm sorry I did that, but I thought it was the only way I could stop you from trying to read me. And if I was to get you to leave, I had to make you think that I did not want to be with you and your—*our*—parents anymore. I feel really bad about that."

"Well, you should. It's like you kicked me right in the nuts. Don't ever do it again!"

"I won't. Do you forgive me?"

Cooper shook his head and sighed. Then he smiled down at Coupe.

"Of course I do, little brother. Just don't ever do it again or I'll put you in a headlock and give you a clownie." He sat back on his bed and shook his head again, smiling. "You are a bad liar."

"What?"

"All that stuff yesterday about it only being a matter of time until you started stealing stuff again. Don't forget I've been living in your head for as long as you have been in mine. I know why you stole in the past. I also know how honest you are. You wouldn't steal again, even if it meant going hungry. You are a good person, Coupe. You are not damaged."

"Thanks. Thanks for saying those things, but also thanks for not leaving without me. I think I could have made it here, but it would have been hard, really hard." He paused. "So, what are we going to do now? Dr. Stein isn't going to like what you did."

Cooper leaned back on the bed. "I have a plan," he said, smiling again. "When I came back to the dorm yesterday I told everyone else what was going to happen. I asked Corwin to switch places with me and he agreed. He even liked the idea of getting to go outside the gates. We did the switch so I could have enough time to get hold of you and talk some sense into you. Now it's time for stage two."

"What's that??"

"We go over to Dr. Stein—all of us—and announce that we are officially on strike until he lets us leave. We will not go to classes, we will not participate in any activities or experiments. Except for eating, we are going to stay in the dorm until Dr. Stein allows us to leave. If he won't let us into the dining hall, we'll stop eating. So, what do you think?"

"Better than my plan, I guess. No harm in trying, but don't forget, Cooper, he is a very powerful man."

"*He* better not forget that we are a couple of very powerful brothers."

"Yeah, he knows that for sure. That's what is making him so cautious, so the less talk about that, the better. And don't be making anyone tie their shoes or go to sleep as part of your plan. If the security staff want to start pushing us around, just let them, okay?"

"Got it."

They went out to rouse the rest of the gang, but they were already up and waiting. Cassie came over and gave Coupe a hug. "I think you are wonderful," she whispered in his ear as she let him go. Coupe blushed a little and Cooper laughed.

"Me too, Coupe," echoed Cotovatre.

"See, I told you that you're a likeable guy," said Cooper.

Once ready, they went to demand to see Dr. Stein.

"To what do I owe this pleasure?"

"We want to go home, and we would like for you to arrange for us to get there," said Coupe.

"Coupe, you are confusing me. As we agreed, Cooper has been taken home, but you agreed to stay here in return."

"Cooper did not agree to it."

"Yes he did, and he is at home right now enjoying his parents' company. Severus informed me that it was a very joyous homecoming. Cooper seemed quite overwhelmed by all the attention heaped upon him."

"That was not Cooper. That was Corwin. Cooper is sitting next to me right now."

"What do you mean?"

"Unbeknownst to me, Cooper went back to the dorm and told them what we were planning to do. He asked Corwin to switch places with him so he could convince me to go home with him. He has convinced me. I want to go home now. And until you agree to return us to our home, we are all on strike. We will do nothing but stay in our rooms, coming out only to eat."

Dr. Stein looked at all of them. "You're bluffing," he said.

"No, we are not. We will stay in there until you let us go home."

"No, I mean you are bluffing that Corwin is Cooper. He would never have left. This is just an attempt to change the terms of our agreement and, I expect, Corwin's attempt to get rid of you."

"Dr. Stein! I am just happy Corwin is not here to hear you say that," mocked Coupe. "He would have been very hurt. We have grown very close over the past few days."

"Stop this nonsense right now!"

"We are telling you the truth. Go ahead and think of something. Cooper will sense it and I will repeat it back to you."

Dr. Stein eyed them both suspiciously. "Very well," he said. Dr. Stein appeared to be searching his mind for something.

"Really, Dr. Stein? You need more imagination. *Red leather, yellow leather, red leather, yellow leather. I'm not the pheasant plucker, I'm the pheasant plucker's son, and I'm only plucking pheasants because the pheasant plucker's gone.* Dr. Stein, I didn't know you had a stutter as a child."

"Stop it at once! I believe you." He stood up and stared down at them. "Now what to do about it? I hope you recognize that you have exposed Corwin to considerable risk. Corwin has never been in the outside world, and usually there is a great deal of coaching done before we have allowed our subjects to go beyond those gates. It could be overwhelming for him."

"I am pretty certain that it is, but that is what made Cooper and me stronger. Corwin knew that risk, but he also wanted that opportunity. You are right to recognize the risk he took. He's been thrown in at the deep end, as the old saying goes. You can drop us off when you go to pick him up."

"Boys, we have already discussed this. I just cannot justify that risk."

"Then you will not get any cooperation from any of us. We will bring your grand experiment to an end right here and right now until you let us go."

"If you will not assist voluntarily, then I will be forced to conduct my research against your will!"

"You can't."

"And why not?"

"Dr. Stein, you most want to study how Cooper and I communicate, our special symbiosis, as you like to call it. In order for that to happen, you have to bring us together. Whenever you bring us together, I will ask Cooper to put me to sleep. We will frustrate every attempt you make to experiment on us."

"Your defiance is maddening!" shouted Dr. Stein, pacing back and forth in front of the assembled teens. "I never had these issues before you two arrived!"

"Defiance?" questioned Coupe. "You are the one who told us we would be able to return home, but then refused to honor those words. We are the ones who have been wronged. But how did we respond? You know that Cooper and I could have this entire campus tying their shoes until their fingers were bloody nubs.

"But we did not do that. Why? Because we would not do that. Instead, we came to you, not to force you to do what we want, but to make you listen to reason. You will get nothing from us unless we are allowed to go home. If you do, Cooper and I have discussed it, and we are willing to come back four times a year and cooperate with you and your research. That is the best that we can offer you. So, do we go back to the dorm, or are we going to collect Corwin? Poor kid is probably a mess by now, dribbling and wetting his pants and all. And wait until they try to send him to school. All those voices, Dr. Stein. You'll probably get him back nonverbal."

Dr. Stein continued to pace. He looked at the floor and then at the teens, then the floor again. Then he stopped and looked at them all.

"Very well, go pack your bags, Coupe. You are going home. Be ready in fifteen minutes."

The teens erupted in a great cheer of victory. Cotovatre ran over and hugged Dr. Stein, which initially surprised him, but then his face broke into a broad grin. "May we come with you to drop them off?"

Dr. Stein shrugged in defeat. "Why not? What's the point of a control group anymore? The Children of Caine destroyed that as well. Go get ready."

CHAPTER 42

It was that decision that led to a large black van, being driven by Severus—accompanied by Sammy, still wearing an orthopedic boot—pulling down the Callister's long driveway on a cold but sunny Sunday afternoon in March. Sitting behind them were Cooper and Coupe, Dr. Stein, Carrick, Cassiopeia, and Cotovatre.

The long ride had been a treat for Cooper and Coupe, and not only because they were going home; they also got to watch Cassiopeia, Carrick, and Cotovatre with their faces pressed against the windows of the van, seeing the outside world for the first time, asking a thousand questions and not waiting for answers before they asked more. At one point, Carrick tried to keep up with the passing shadows on the window, changing his camouflage as the shadows changed. At first it was difficult, but after a little practice he was able to do it. Everyone cheered. Dr. Stein took out his notebook and scribbled the protocol for a new experiment.

As the van rolled to a stop near the front porch, Cooper grabbed the van door, throwing it open. He jumped out, running into the house, Coupe on his heels. In a moment they were both through the front door.

"Mom! Dad!" shouted Cooper.

"What is it, Cooper? I thought you were upstairs lying down because you didn't feel well?" Evelyn's voice had come from the kitchen. A moment later her head popped around the doorway, and she saw both Cooper and Coupe standing in the hallway.

"Coupe!" she shouted with delight. "They said you didn't want to come back! I am so happy that you did!"

Evelyn ran straight past Cooper to give Coupe a hug. Cooper was momentarily confused but then remembered that his mom thought he came home yesterday. He just ran over and joined in their hug.

"Where's Dad?" asked Cooper.

"You know where he went, Cooper. He went to town to get something for your headache."

Cooper could sense Corwin. He was upstairs recovering from his first experience outside of Deep Woods Academy. Apparently, Evelyn had taken him shopping for a celebratory feast. The supermarket was his first experience with the maddening sounds of hundreds of other minds close to his. He had gotten pale and had to wait in the car. After that he barely spoke for the rest of the day. Today he had complained of a headache just to have some peace and quiet.

"Come on!" Cooper said, grabbing her hand, pulling her up the stairs.

"Cooper! What are you doing? Have you gone crazy? Should I call a doctor?"

Cooper pulled her to his side outside his bedroom door. It was closed.

"Ready?" he asked.

"Ready for what, Cooper?" She looked back and forth between Cooper and Coupe. Then Cooper threw open the door to his bedroom.

"Hey, Cory, how do you like my bed?"

Evelyn stared in shock as the figure lying on the bed took the pillow off his head and sat up.

"The outside world is harder than I expected," replied Corwin.

Evelyn looked back and forth between the two and fainted.

When she came to, she was on the living room couch. There was a man with a thin nose and iron-grey hair staring down at her.

"I apologize for that, Mrs. Callister. If I had known Cooper and Coupe were going to be merry tricksters, I would have stopped them. The shock was simply too much. They should have known better."

The two boys stood next to Dr. Stein looking guilty, but only a little guilty.

"Sorry, Mom," said Cooper.

"Yeah, sorry, Mom. I should have stopped him," said Coupe, who momentarily smiled at his brother, then quickly replaced it with a look of feigned gravity, just barely.

Evelyn then noticed the other three children seated in the living room and the two large men sitting with them. Corwin was also there and gave her a weak smile and a wave when she looked over at him.

"Can someone tell me what is going on?"

"Mom," said Cooper, "this is Dr. Stein. He is the doctor that . . . delivered me. He is also the one who chose you to be my mother. I think he did a great job with that."

"Please to meet you, Mrs. Callister," said Dr. Stein, holding out his hand. She shook it.

"Cooper has a twin?" she asked.

"Yes, Mrs. Callister, but there is more to it than that, and I think at this time you and your husband will need more information. A great deal more information. Information that must also remain confidential. Might I suggest that we wait for your husband to return and I will explain as best as I can and then answer your questions?"

She nodded, then looked again at Cooper and then back to Corwin. "I knew there was something different about you."

Evelyn got off the couch to make coffee and put out some fresh-made cookies. They were all once again sitting down and getting comfortable when Coupe heard Everett's truck coming down the drive.

"He's coming!" he shouted excitedly, jumping up.

"You are not to play that same trick on your father, Cooper," admonished Dr. Stein.

"I can go out and meet him though, right?" asked Coupe.

Dr. Stein thought for a moment and then nodded.

Coupe bolted out to the porch to wait. He pulled the hood of his hoodie up over his head and sat in Everett's rocker. Soon enough he could see his father's truck coming down the driveway. He pulled the hood further down to obscure his face and listened as the truck pulled to a stop in front of him and the engine grew quiet. Then he heard Everett opening his truck door. When he heard that he stood up and began to throw his hood back so he could shout "Hi, Dad!" Instead, he was struck in the chest by a 120-pound white flying beast.

Bryn hit him so hard she knocked him through the front door into the house. She then covered his face with kisses, grabbed his hood with her teeth, and pulled it off his face so she could lick him more. Roscoe joined in. Coupe screamed and shouted in joy at his reception. Then they noticed Cooper and came charging into the living room to love-attack him too. He fell to the floor so that he could hug them both at the same time, their tails wagging wildly. Dr. Stein, obviously not a dog person, looked horrified and stood behind his chair. He wondered if someone should call animal control or do something to help the children. Corwin came to his side.

"It's okay. They're dogs. They're friendly. We should get some."

"Wow, they're cool!" said Carrick.

"That one is Roscoe, and the big white one is Bryn!" replied Corwin.

Dr. Stein realized he had opened Pandora's box—the dog version, anyway.

Everett stood at the front door holding medicine in his hand, looking down in obvious happiness to see Coupe being devoured by the dogs.

"Coupe," he said quietly. "Glad you changed your mind and decided to give us another try. We'll do our best to make you feel at home here, rest assured."

"I do feel at home here. That is why I came back. Because it is my home."

Everett extended his hand and pulled Coupe up into a great big hug.

"Hugging is big here," said Corwin quietly to Carrick.

It was only then that Everett noticed all the other people in the living room and that Cooper had somehow doubled.

"Dad!" Cooper came flying into his dad's arms. "That's my brother, Corwin. He came home yesterday instead of me."

"That explains a lot," Everett said.

"And this is Dr. Stein. He's the doctor that gave me to Mom."

Everett held out his hand. "Thank you," he said. "And thank you for bringing Coupe back."

Dr. Stein took his hand and smiled in appreciation. He had not expected to get such a warm response.

"Don't get too warm and fuzzy," whispered Coupe in the doctor's ear. "Don't forget you have to tell him who you gave me to."

Once introductions were made, they settled down in the living room, and Dr. Stein gave a lengthy explanation about who he was in his typical bombastic style, and who each of the children were, along with their histories. Dr. Stein pulled no punches when providing Coupe's history, and it was clear to Dr. Stein that Evelyn and Everett were reassessing their opinion of him.

"What about the police? Are you sure there aren't any other people out there looking for these two?" asked Everett.

"Not anymore. As Severus explained to you yesterday, we have taken care of all that, on both local and national levels. Our organization has sufficient pull to ensure there will be no problems. Chief Dale will also be informed of the boys' return by our friends at the, um, federal level. I know he has been a good friend to the boys, but he will now be encouraged to let the matter rest. You should reinforce that with him when he comes out to talk to you about it, as I predict he will. But he has been encouraged not to look into it any further, and I am hopeful that everything will settle down and the boys will get back to their schooling, which I deem very important.

"There only remains the scheduling of their quarterly visits, but we can do that at another time."

Everett was looking at Dr. Stein keenly. It was a look Coupe had seen before. He remembered seeing it when he first met Everett down at his camp. He remembered seeing it while stacking wood after his fight. To Coupe it was a stare that patinated his father with wisdom.

"I'm presently not inclined to let them go with you," said Everett. "You are obviously very bright, Dr. Stein, but you have also acted recklessly with Coupe. He was a child. You experimented on a child."

"*My* child, one that I created! And for the good of all future children!" He bristled. It was DNA of his creation, after all.

Everett was not persuaded. "Life runs red in all of us, Dr. Stein. Strip everything away and a man still has the right to the space he occupies. No one else can own that space, just as you can't own air, or the sky above us. It don't transfer, even if you did create it.

"That you were able to do such a thing speaks to your intelligence. But I also have to say, how does it matter? The way he came into the world doesn't change his right to his space in it. Maybe you should come spend some time on the farm with us to remind you of that."

"Well, I chose you two, didn't I?"

"I suppose, but you didn't do that for Coupe."

"He needed a different environment," retorted Dr. Stein.

"How could you know that? How do you know that Coupe would not have turned out just as well as he did, even better perhaps, if you had provided for him the same type of home you provided for Cooper? Did you test that theory? You may have satisfied your scientific goals, Dr. Stein, but you fell short on your ethical ones."

The room was silent and tense. Dr. Stein thought about trying to explain further the need to put his test subjects through rigorous conditions to ensure that they had the genetic material to withstand such experiences, to be a viable and contributing addition to all of humankind, not just one individual, but he knew he would not convince Everett Callister. It did, however, confirm one thing for him. He had picked well for Cooper.

Coupe walked over to Everett, standing in the doorway. He put his arms around him. "Thanks, Dad," he said quietly. "Thanks for sticking up for me. I know you always will. That's why I feel safe here. That's why it is my home. Like I said, I wish I had met you long ago, but I didn't. As for Dr. Stein here, I am willing to go back and see him. What he is doing really is impressive. He did good raising Cassie, Coty, Carrick and Cory."

"Did *well*," said Dr. Stein quietly.

"See, he's always trying to educate us, that's for sure. And besides, I gave him my word, and that's important to me."

"Me too, Dad," said Cooper. "If Coupe goes, I go."

"You and your wife can come too, Mr. Callister. At least come up and take a look around to see for yourselves what we have to offer."

"And bring the dogs," interrupted Carrick, earning an elbow from Corwin and Cotovatre on either side of him.

"You can consider it sort of a quarterly vacation."

"I'm a farmer, Dr. Stein. We don't get quarterly vacations. This place will not run itself."

Dr. Stein regained some of his imperious nature and waved his hand dismissively.

"Don't worry about that. I'll send down a crew to run it in your absence. In fact, please let me know if there is anything you need to make your job easier. As I explained, I have some very powerful backers. If they can make my work easier by making your work easier, consider it done."

"You know how to run a farm?"

"Of course not. But I know people who will know how to run a farm. It is a matter of one phone call."

Everett was not sure whether to believe him.

"Well, my wife and I will discuss it with the boys and get back to you. But as I expect you know by now, they can be pretty persistent when they want something."

"That's all I can ask," replied Dr. Stein. "It's getting late and we have a long ride ahead of us. We should take our leave."

Severus and Sammy went out to start the van, and the group moved out onto the porch. As Cassiopeia approached Coupe, she grabbed him by the arm and pulled him into the kitchen. Coupe fixed her with an inquiring look and was about to ask her what was wrong when she quickly leaned in and kissed him gently on the lips. Light was streaming through the kitchen window, creating a glow around her as she stood in front of him.

"Remember, Coupe," she said, "you are not damaged goods. If I could talk Dr. Stein into filling the world with Coupes and only Coupes, I would do it." She leaned in and kissed him again, this time a little longer. "Now, don't forget to visit us."

With that, she was gone, heading out onto the porch, leaving Coupe in a world of happiness. He shook his head and followed after her.

Out on the porch he found Dr. Stein looking around. "Where is Cotovatre?" he asked.

Just then she came out the front door with Cooper behind her. He was grinning from ear to ear. Then, so was Coupe. "Here!" she shouted. "I was just saying goodbye to Cooper!"

Dr. Stein looked at her down his long nose. "Were you now? Very well. Time to get into the van."

"Hey, Doc, can they come visit us sometime?" asked Coupe.

"Who?"

"All of them!"

"Perhaps. Perhaps if you are willing to come visit me."

"Oh, we're coming," said Cooper and Coupe, as one.

Dr. Stein was the last one to get into the van. As he was closing the door Coupe asked one more question.

"Hey, Doc! Before you go, I've got one last question for you. Who is the oldest?" Coupe threw an elbow into Cooper's side.

Dr. Stein has heard this ongoing debate for weeks. "Oldest?" he replied. "That would be Corwin."

Corwin threw his arms up in a sign of victory from the back of the van.

"Okay, but after him?" asked Coupe.

"Cotovatre."

"And after her?"

"Carrick. Then Cassiopeia."

"Okay, but what about between me and Cooper?"

"Oh, between you two? That would be—" Dr. Stein closed the van door quickly without answering the question, and the van began to drive away.

"Quick, Cooper! Read him before he gets too far away!"

Cooper immediately reached out to Dr. Stein's mind, and Coupe quickly followed along to get the answer to their question. *Red leather, yellow leather, red leather, yellow leather. I'm not the pheasant plucker, I'm the pheasant plucker's son, and I'm only plucking pheasants because the pheasant plucker's gone.*

Dr. Stein continued to concentrate on that and only that until he was well beyond Cooper's range. He then sat back in his seat, smiling to himself for the long ride back to Deep Woods Academy.

THE SEQUEL

*T*he Omicron Six will return in the sequel *Blood for the Fisher King.* Visit *www.endywright.com* for more information. Below is an excerpt:

. . . .

The entire hayloft needed to be swept, and all the loose hay dropped down below to the manure pile. Several hay bales would have to be moved as well. It was a dirty job, so Coupe took off his shirt, tied a bandana around his face and picked up the broom.

After about three hours, Coupe was sweaty and caked with dust but nearly done. He stopped, though, when he heard two car doors being opened and closed. He could not sense Cooper, so he wondered who it could be.

Coupe walked over to the open hayloft door to look outside. He stopped frozen in place when he saw who it was. Standing below him next to the car was a man and a woman. He did not know who the man was, but he recognized the woman. It was Mary Daschelete, the woman who had pretended to be his mother for the first fourteen years of his life. Seeing her again and knowing what he now knew made her presence particularly painful.

The man reached through the car window and honked the horn a few times. He looked like the typical sort of guy his mother had always attracted, big and swaggering, usually accompanied by a bad attitude, a taste for liquor, and a quick backhand if anyone ever got out of line. He was a big muscle-bound brute wearing a T-shirt two sizes too small. He had a deep tan everywhere except around his eyes where his sunglasses protected him.

"Hello!" Mary shouted, still looking around.

Coupe said nothing, his eyes fixed on the woman who had been paid to be his mother, the woman who allowed Coupe, as a boy, to be physically and sexually abused by her boyfriends and a depraved priest.

He just stared at them. He wanted to quietly step back out of their sight, but he felt fixed to the hayloft floor, unable to move and unable to take his eyes off the woman who had abandoned him over a year ago. In reality, she had abandoned him long before that. She just made it official when she dumped him with her then boyfriend and did not come back.

Mary turned toward the barn and saw him standing up in the hayloft door. She quickly flashed her best bartender smile and waved to him, wiggling her fingers in her typical trying-to-be-nice attitude.

"Hi there!" she said. "I'm wondering if you could help me. I'm trying to find my son, Coupe Daschelete. Some people in town told me he has been staying out here."

Coupe said nothing; he just continued to stare. She had not even recognized him. The man that was with her stared back, clearly growing impatient.

"The lady asked you a question, buddy. Show some manners and answer her," he said.

Coupe looked at the man for a moment and then back toward his mother. He slowly reached up and pulled the bandana down. A look of recognition spread across Mary's face.

"Coupe! Look at you! You've grown so much, my boy! Come down so I can take a look at you!"

Coupe did not move, his heart aching with hurt. "What are you doing here?" he asked softly.

"I've come to get you!" she said. Then, looking at her boyfriend, she added, "*We've* come to get you! This is my new boyfriend, Kyle. I've been living with him down in Brattleboro. We saw you on the news last night, and I told Kyle we needed to come up here and get you right away. He's all for it!"

"Yeah, you're a heavy hitter there, kid," Kyle added. "Impressive. You're gonna get a bunch of press coverage. You might be able to score a few bucks off it, and I know a few people who could help you out with that. I got a friend who owns a gym too. Ever think of taking up fighting?"

Coupe saw it for what it was.

"You left me over a year ago. Now you're suddenly interested in getting me back?"

"I didn't know where to find you, honey. I only realized you was still here when I saw the news."

"Did you even come back and ask where to find me?"

His mother hesitated before she answered. "Yes. Of course. But nobody knew where you was."

A lie. Coupe did not need to be able to read her face to recognize the falsehood.

"Thanks for the offer, but I think I'll stay here instead."

"Coupe, family should be with family. Look at what these people got you doin'! They got you workin' as a stable boy in a dirty old barn!"

"These people are good to me! They are my family! They are kind to me, they care about me! I get food every day and new clothes and stuff when I need them. They do more than anything you ever did for me." Coupe quieted for a moment and then added softly, "They . . . they love me."

"And they got you workin' in the barn all covered in dirt! Where are they now?"

"They've gone over to the livestock auctions."

"So, they leave you to do all the work, and they get to go out and have fun? I don't think so. You need to come home with me."

"And live off government peanut butter? Maybe a ramen if you're being real nice? *I* don't think so!"

Coupe heard Kyle climbing the steps up into the hayloft and grew nervous. He knew the kind of men his mother liked. He knew what they could do. They had done it to him before. He looked down at the ground. Twenty feet was pretty high. His brother Cooper could do it easily, but him? Not so likely.

"Honey, that's all I could afford! I would have gotten more if I could have afforded it!"

"You always seemed to find money for the booze! Besides, I found out you used to get a check to take care of me. Funny how you never told me about that."

Her pleasant look disappeared. "That's because you wasn't supposed to know! How'd you find out?"

"I'm not sayin'!" Kyle had finished climbing the steps and was walking up behind him. "You guys gotta go now!"

Kyle's meaty hand clamped down around the back of his neck. Coupe tried to wriggle free, but Kyle grabbed hold of his arm and held him tightly.

"C'mon, kid, it's time to go. We'll have a good time. I've got some beer in the car. It'll make the trip just fly by."

"I'm not goin'! Let go of me!"

Coupe tried to struggle free, but Kyle was too strong. He started pulling him toward the stairs.

"Just drag him down here, Kyle!" his mother shouted. "We'll sort it all out on the ride back down to Brattleboro!"

"C'mon, kid, you heard your mother. Let's go!"

"She's not my mother! Now let go of me!"

Kyle switched his grip and put Coupe in a headlock. Then he squeezed down tight until Coupe squealed in pain.

"What's going on up there? Come on, hurry up! There's a car comin'!" Mary called out.

"You want to make this difficult, kid? I'll just choke you out and drag you down!" Kyle said.

The brute dragged Coupe toward the stairs. Coupe swung his fist as hard as he could right at Kyle's crotch. Kyle roared in pain and collapsed on top of Coupe.

"You wanna play it that way, kid? Fine by me, but you are in for a severe beating once we are clear of this place. I'll show you what pain is, you little shit!"

As they struggled, Coupe suddenly felt Cooper's presence in his head. He felt Cooper sensing his panic. He made a silent plea to his brother: *Help me! Help me!* . . .

This excerpt continues at www.endywright.com.

ACKNOWLEDGMENTS

For all kids or former kids that suffered at the hands of an abusive adult, this story is for you. You are all superheroes. You all have special powers. Make all your tomorrows better than your yesterdays.

CPSIA information can be obtained
at www.ICGtesting.com
Printed in the USA
LVHW030452301120
672994LV00006B/57